MADNESS IN THE RUINS

MADNESS IN THE RUINS

A MASON COLLINS CRIME THRILLER 1

JOHN A. CONNELL

NAILHEAD PUBLISHING

COPYRIGHT

To my wife Janine

Munich, Germany: The American Zone of Occupation
December 1945

Criminal Investigator Mason Collins felt as though he were being whisked through the landscape of a bad dream, the charred bones of what had once been Munich passing before him. His driver maneuvered the Jeep down the street as if in a road rally, swerving around piles of rubble, horse-drawn wagons and languid pedestrians. He honked the horn yet again when an elderly couple pushing a wooden cart stacked with their few belongings tried to cross the street at the wrong time.

"Corporal, you know the murder victim is already dead?" Mason said.

"Yes, sir."

"Then dial the speed down to somewhere below bat-out-of-hell."

The corporal slowed but purposefully veered narrowly by two German ex-soldiers still dressed in their shredded uniforms then sent up his middle finger, ""Dumb-ass krauts!"

"I'm only going to say it one more time, Corporal. You will can that crap, right now."

"Begging your pardon, sir, but you feel sorry for these people? First they're saluting Hitler and wanting to take over the world, and now look at them."

"Yeah, look at them."

Mason nodded at the pitiful scene before them. People huddled against the biting wind as they shuffled along a street lined with the blackened shells of buildings rising from a grave-yard of brick and stone. The heavy gauze of snowfall made them appear as lost souls wandering purgatory, custodians of the dead buried beneath the rubble. Except for the old and the very young, few men moved among them. Women, always women. A line of women extended for blocks, waiting hours in the cold for a Red Cross center to open, hoping to receive a loaf of bread and a few ounces of lard. Others scoured the rubble looking for wood not already burned to fend off the cold. They formed knotted daisy chains, salvaging brick and stone from the ruins, inspiring a new German word, *Trümmerfrauen*, meaning "rubble women."

The corporal was a boy of no more than twenty-one and fresh off the streets of New York City. His name was Sal Manganella, but everyone called him Salamander. A fitting nickname—all nose and chin. He noticed Mason looking at him and hunched his shoulders as if anticipating further rebuke. He relaxed when Mason looked away. "Word is, they offered you a discharge, but you turned them down."

Mason waited a moment before responding. "The army needs experienced cops, so I re-upped."

"Pardon my speaking freely, sir?"

"That doesn't seem to be a problem for you."

"Yes, sir... What kind of crackpot wants to stay in this hellhole when he could be a cop back in the States?"

Mason remained silent. There was no way he was going to get

2

into it with a snot-nosed kid whose only notion of the war was getting drunk and chasing fräuleins.

War-torn Germany *was* a hellhole. The nation had surrendered seven months before, but millions would continue to die. Disease, starvation, and winter's icy embrace had replaced the bullets and bombs. And murder flourished in the ruins. Retribution, greed, madness, jealousy, and desperation all fed a hungry beast. Murder happened every day, hundreds in a week, thousands in a month.

Mason had been a reluctant guest of the German army from December of 1944 until liberated in mid-April. After a two-month stint in a hospital with typhoid fever and dysentery, he'd been offered a discharge. Much to the surprise and delight of the army staff, Mason had volunteered to stay on. He'd worked an interminable six months at a desk job at U.S. Army headquarters in Frankfurt, before his request to be transferred to the Criminal Investigation Division had finally been accepted. And now, in less than two weeks after he arrived in Munich, he'd landed his first homicide. It felt good to be back in the saddle.

Maybe here, among these ruins, Mason could find a new beginning, regeneration in a festering wound.

Manganella made another sharp turn, nearly throwing Mason into his lap. Mason was about to chew him out when the corporal slammed on the brakes. Two U.S. Army military policemen held their hands high for them to stop. They stood in front of two Jeeps parked to block the road. Four other MPs and two officers formed a wall that blocked Mason's view of whatever was causing the screaming bedlam behind them.

"You're going to have to turn around, sir," one of the MPs said. "All hell's broken loose. We've got a bunch of locals fighting it out over a cellar full of wine bottles."

Mason stood up in the Jeep and peered over their heads. It was a madhouse. More than a hundred civilians were jammed in the narrow street acting as if possessed. Women screamed as they

3

fought each other, pulling hair or using wine bottles as clubs. Old men whacked anyone within striking range, while clutching bottles to their chests. In the midst of the pandemonium emaciated children darted between sparring adults, taking boxes dropped during the fighting then disappearing into the gaps of the collapsed buildings. People emerged from what looked like a simple hole in the rubble with wine bottles or whole cases tucked in their arms. Some men stood among the fighters, paying no heed to the swings of their alcohol-fueled competitors as they smashed the neck of a bottle and downed as much wine as they could before throwing away the empty, and breaking the neck of the next.

An MP sergeant stood on a Jeep with a bullhorn and was shouting in English, "Disperse. This is property of the US Army. You will be arrested. Disperse. That's an order."

Corporal Manganella laughed at the spectacle, while off to Mason's right a small group of journalists took notes or snapped pictures. One of the photographers caught Mason's eye, an unexpected beauty among the beasts. She had a broad face framing a thin, upturned nose and stunning blue eyes. Her black hair was pulled back in an up-do, victory-roll style, beneath a billed hat with the circular patch that identified her as a war correspondent sewn onto the crown. The journalist snapped another picture while sporting a mischievous smile. She, like the rest, was having a field day reporting on the day's version of chaos while the helpless MPs looked on.

Mason jumped out and stepped up to the master sergeant. "You better get this under control, Sergeant, or you're going to have a *real* riot on your hands."

The sergeant whirled around. "I'm goddamned trying—" He stopped when he saw Mason's CID bars. "We're trying the best we can, sir. The damned radios we've been issued are worthless. I had to send someone to headquarters for backup. They should be here in a few minutes."

Mason climbed up onto one of the MP Jeeps, which had a mounted thirty-caliber machine gun. He pulled back the charger and whirled it on the crowd.

The sergeant yelled, "Sir, that's against reg—"

Mason fired a long burst above the heads of the crowd. The blasts from the machine gun were deafening. The bullets shattered brick and stone.

The crowd stopped in unison, stupefied by the man with the machine gun. Some froze with fists or bottles still poised to strike. Mason shouted in German, "Stop this now. Get out of here. You do not want me lowering my aim."

There was no argument, no resuming the fight. Those who had been beating on their opponents a moment earlier were now helping them to their feet. They all began to disperse, women holding each other for support, drunken men staggering away, all leaving their once-prized booty on the ground or dropping it to the pavement with a crash. MP medics rushed in to take care of the injured sprawled on the wine-soaked pavement.

"Who the hell is the moron on that machine gun?" someone yelled at the far left side of the street. A bull-sized master sergeant came running up, red-faced with anger.

The sergeant pointed at Mason.

The master sergeant stopped in midstride, came to stiff attention and saluted. "A fine idea, sir. I'm not familiar with that method of crowd control. I'm wondering, sir, if you would have carried out your threat if they hadn't stopped."

"Have you been on the receiving end of machine-gun fire, Sergeant?"

"Can't say as I have, sir."

"I have. It's a great motivator."

"I'll remember that, sir. Anytime I want to make a point, I'll open fire on unarmed civilians."

The master sergeant stiffened and waited to be chewed out for his insubordination. Instead, Mason smiled and held out his hand. "Mason Collins."

The sergeant's shoulders relaxed and he gave Mason a hearty handshake. "Pleased to meet you, sir. I'm Vincent Wolski. Actually, Warrant Officer Wolski, now that I'm with the CID. Colonel Walton told me I was to partner with you—"

"I don't need any partners," Mason said and started walking back to the Jeep.

Wolski followed behind. "I'm just following orders, sir. What you do with that is up to you."

Mason pointed to Wolski's master-sergeant patch. "What are you doing with those stripes if you're CID?"

CID was the army's acronym for Criminal Investigation Division, the army's detective bureau.

"I was just transferred to the detachment this morning from the 508th C Company. Been here for two months as an MP until the orders came through to join you guys. Didn't have time to change out of my uniform. A driver was taking me to the crime scene when we ran into this mess."

The 508th Military Police Battalion was in charge of law enforcement for Munich and the surrounding areas.

Mason stopped and eyed him for a moment. The man was big enough to play tackle for the NFL, and Mason saw the keenness in his eyes. But Wolski's most endearing quality, Mason thought, would be his subversive sense of humor. "Tell your driver to go back to the station. You can ride with us."

"That was quite a display you put on back there," someone said behind him.

It was as much the velvety voice as the provocative statement that made Mason stop and turn around. The brunette reporter stood shoulder height and looked up at him with the same mischievous smile. She held out her hand. "Laura McKinnon with the Associated Press."

Mason shook her hand. "I don't talk to reporters."

"Why not? Are you afraid?"

"I saw you over there snapping pictures of a dangerous situation with a big smile on your face. That's when a little alarm bell went off in my head."

"It's not every day I see a soldier open fire on innocent civilians."

"Well, ma'am, I'm happy to report that the result was damage to a few ruined buildings. And if I hadn't done that, people could have been killed."

"A rather dire prediction. I think some soldiers miss the war and look for any excuse to discharge their weapon."

Even without Miss McKinnon's sly smile, Mason got the play on words.

"In June, while I was stationed in Frankfurt, three hundred recently released Russian POWs and displaced Poles rushed two tanker trucks full of industrial-grade alcohol. A drunken riot ensued that spilled over into the civilian population. It then grew to two thousand. In the thirty minutes it took for the MPs to arrive and the additional thirty minutes for them to decide to fire over their heads, over a hundred people had died from beatings or alcohol poisoning. Another three hundred and fifty were hospitalized. We'll never know how many would have been saved if they'd fired sooner. But you won't write about that. No, I can see it now"—Mason waved his hand in the air as if revealing a headline in bold letters —"'CID Chief Warrant Officer Opens Fire on Innocent Civilians.' That's why I don't like to talk to reporters. Good day, ma'am."

Mason turned and strode toward the Jeep before being trapped by her mesmerizing eyes. He jumped in the passenger's seat and signaled for Manganella to take off

"What the hell was that riot all about?" Manganella said as he reversed the Jeep and drove back the way they had come.

"Seems a group of civilians discovered a big wine cellar while recovering a couple of bodies from that collapsed building," Wolski said.

Once they were far enough away from the other MPs, Wolski pulled out a wine bottle from his overcoat and wagged it at Mason and Manganella. "A 1927 Chateau Lafitte. That cellar was full of the best French wines. Now half the stuff is soaking into the pavement. A damn shame. I doubt many of the bottles are going to make it back to the collection depot."

Mason took the bottle from Wolski and examined it.

Corporal Manganella said, "Some Nazi son of a bitch stole it from some poor French bastard. Spoils of war, sir."

"Maybe I could have done more to stop those people, but I felt sorry for them," Wolski said. "Can you imagine what a bottle of wine like this could get on the black market? At least a month's worth of food. Or better yet, a pile of blankets and a cartful of coal." He shook his head. "Mid-December and already as cold as my ex-girlfriend's heart."

When Manganella turned onto the main thoroughfare, Mason ordered him to stop next to an old woman leading two small children. He held out the bottle to the woman, urging her to take it. The woman reached out and accepted it as if he'd given her diamond tiara. Mason signaled for Manganella to proceed. Manganella giggled as he did so. Wolski remained silent.

Mason adjusted the side-view mirror to look at Wolski. He liked the fact that the man hadn't whined or complained. "You came from the 508th?"

Wolski nodded.

"Ever done any detective work?"

"Three years on the beat in Detroit, then three in vice squad before joining the army. My time on the force in Detroit is why they sent me over to you guys. That, and me driving my superior officer crazy."

"No homicide?" Mason asked.

"Vice isn't just about busting hookers and smut dealers. I collected evidence, ran interviews."

"Well, that's better than some of the jokers they've put in CID."

They entered another street of burned-out apartment buildings with boarded-up storefronts on the ground floor.

Wolski leaned forward. "So, about your machine gun remark... you must have seen some action."

"Enough."

"I didn't think you CID boys saw much fighting."

"I was an intelligence agent for G2 intelligence attached to the 422nd Regiment."

"I heard they got chewed up pretty bad in the Bulge."

"Overrun and surrounded. I was out on a patrol and wound up behind enemy lines. They roughed me up pretty bad."

"You were a POW?"

Mason tended to avoid discussing it with anyone who hadn't been in combat, but Wolski was growing on him. "A subcamp of Buchenwald for two weeks then transferred to a couple of POW stalags."

Wolski sat back in his seat. "Buchenwald? Damn. No wonder..."

"No wonder what?" Mason said and turned to Wolski.

"No offense, sir. You got the right, is all I was going to say."

Corporal Manganella parked in front of a four-square-block, seven-story factory. The structure still stood, but it had been clearly gutted by fire, its brick scorched black by intense heat and smoke. Thick wooden beams propped diagonally against the wall kept it from collapsing. A handful of Jeeps and army-green sedans were parked in front of the building. Four MPs held back a small crowd of curious civilians.

Mason instructed Corporal Manganella to stay with the Jeep. As he and Wolski made their way through the crowd of German onlookers, Mason said, "All I ask is you don't stumble over your own two feet. Watch, listen, and do what I say."

Wolski gave him an exaggerated salute. "Yes, sir."

At the factory entrance, Mason showed his CID badge to one of the MPs. The guard told them to go straight through and across the courtyard to the loading docks. A sergeant would direct them from there.

Mason and Wolski entered an enclosed driveway just wide enough for small trucks. On their left, they passed a former shipping office with its windows crisscrossed by slats of wood. Somewhere inside the dark room a baby cried. Through the gaps Mason could see crumpled blankets and a tiny field stove like the German soldiers used to carry. People now lived in these ruins, having no other place to go. With estimates of up to 70 percent of the city damaged or destroyed, virtually any hovel that sheltered against the cold and the rain and snow had been occupied by the homeless.

Thirty feet of driveway opened up to a courtyard. High stacks of debris were piled everywhere. Tents and lean-tos dotted the grounds, all empty for the moment, since the "residents" had been herded outside during the investigation.

"What misery," Wolski said.

Mason grunted an acknowledgment. He'd seen enough misery in the last two years that words no longer seemed sufficient.

They crossed the courtyard, where an MP sergeant waited below a loading platform.

"This way, sir," the sergeant said.

Mason and Wolski clambered after him up a pile of rubble and into the building's shipping department, where rolling platforms and conveyor belts sat in twisted heaps or crushed under the debris of the collapsed floor above. Guiding with his flashlight, the sergeant led them through the dark maze. The sound of drops of melted snow echoed in the open space. Snowflakes somehow found an opening that the fading afternoon light could not.

"What have we got, Sergeant?" Mason said.

"A couple of women found the body. They'd been searching for firewood and came out screaming. Nearly started a panic with the rest of the people using this place as a shelter."

"Most of these people have seen plenty of dead bodies," Mason said. "What made them panic?"

"You'll have to see for yourself, sir. I've seen a lot of corpses, but nothing like this."

They entered a short hallway then a stairwell. Metal stairs led upward. Snowflakes and streams of water tumbled down from a large hole in the roof, seven stories above. Wolski hesitated at the bottom step. The sergeant said, "It'll hold a big fella like you. We only got two flights."

The weakened stairs groaned as they climbed. Even ten months after the bombing raid that had devastated this area, the building still reeked of the acrid smell of spent explosives, smoke, and now decay.

On the third floor they entered another open space. Burned army blankets, uniforms, and canvas tents were fused together in long blackened rows. The stench grew pungent, like that of burned hair.

"You should see about getting a team with a genny and work lights," Mason said. "We're going to be here awhile."

"Already ordered, sir," the sergeant said. "Should be here any minute. The photographer just got here, and the scene techs are on their way."

At the far end of the room, Mason saw flashlight beams

beyond a set of collapsed doors. He quickened his pace, with Wolski and the sergeant close behind. Mason's foot inadvertently kicked a piece of metal, sending it across the floor. The clanging brought someone from the room to investigate. Mason was hit in the face by a blinding flashlight beam.

"Who's there?" the man holding the light said with an underlying tone of fear in his voice.

Mason shielded his eyes from the light but could see the man only in silhouette. "Get that light out of my face."

The beam swept away, and Mason recognized the egg-shaped frame of Havers, another CID investigator. It hadn't taken more than an hour on the first day for Mason to figure out Havers: a reasonably competent investigator who did as little as possible to accomplish a task, and as much as possible to lick his superiors' boots.

"As if we didn't have enough people around here already." Havers half-blocked the door and glared at Mason. "This is my investigation. I was first on the scene."

"Talk to the colonel if you have a problem," Mason said as he pushed past Havers.

Almost pitch-black beyond the group's pool of flashlights, only the echoes of shuffling feet and low murmurs hinted at the immensity of the room. Mason lit his flashlight, as did Wolski. A wall of men stood in front of them, six MPs Mason didn't immediately recognize, and Havers's CID partner, who always looked pained to be associated with Havers. They all wore grim expressions, and a few looked as though they might run to a dark corner at any moment to empty the contents of their stomachs.

"Someone want to fill me in?" Mason asked.

Havers stepped in the middle of the group as if to claim his territory. In the harsh light from the flashlights Mason could see by Havers's taut, blanched face that he was profoundly shaken by whatever waited in the darkness behind him. Without looking, he pointed to the dark center of the room. "Up there on the column."

None of the others seemed anxious to look again. Mason and Wolski moved forward and trained their flashlights toward the center of the vast room. A huge portion of the upper two floors above them had collapsed, taking their floor with it and crashing to a stop thirty feet below. Mason and Wolski now stood at the edge of a gap twenty feet across. With their flashlight beams, they found the thick support column of concrete and steel. Their eyes followed the beams up the column then stopped.

Wolski gasped and took a quick step back. "Tell me that wasn't a man."

M ason remembered to breathe after his stomach finished doing a Saint Vitus dance. Lashed to the column, halfway up from their level, hung an armless and legless corpse. Only the head remained attached to the eviscerated torso, which had been split down the middle. A Y-shaped cut started at each shoulder and met at the sternum, then a single slash descended to just above the man's groin. His ribs had been pulled back, exposing his organs, his face frozen in agony and terror. In Mason's two years in combat zones, he'd seen torn and mangled corpses; he'd seen the atrocities at Buchenwald. But this man had been ritualistically butchered.

A flashbulb went off, startling Mason. More flashes went off, making the bloodless torso appear stark white against the black space.

"Jesus almighty," Wolski said.

Mason let out a sigh to ease his outrage. "Welcome to homicide." He waved the beam around the torso. "Whoever killed this person put some kind of mesh across the body to keep the organs from falling out." He looked at Wolski, who'd turned pale. "You notice what's missing, though?" Mason asked Wolski the question to help Wolski concentrate and not lose himself in the gruesome scene.

"You mean, other than his arms and legs?"

Mason trained his beam on the spot. "He's missing his small intestines." Then, without looking at the group, he spoke loud enough for the rest to hear. "I hope this area was searched for clues before any of you tromped on it."

Havers charged up to Mason, while averting his eyes from the corpse. "Look, Collins, I know what I'm doing. So far we haven't found anything except the footprints of the two women who discovered the body. What we haven't been able to figure out is how anyone could get that body up there."

"The right question is why," Mason said. He searched the rubble around the base of the column with his flashlight beam then the area above the torso. "Get up on the fourth floor and look around," Mason said to Wolski. He turned to the MPs. "I want four of you downstairs now. Start interviewing the people who live in this building and the surrounding neighborhood. The other two of you go down to the base of the column and search for clues. And don't wipe out any footprints."

Havers got in Mason's face. "We've all heard about your snitching on fellow police officers in Chicago. No one wants to work with you. You can't give these men orders. I'm in charge here."

"Then why haven't you searched above and below? Or figured out a way to get that body down?"

"I don't answer to you. The victim's probably a kraut who ripped off someone on the black market and this is a revenge killing. Dead krauts are on every street corner. They don't interest me, and this won't interest the colonel. So get off my case."

"How can you tell? For all we know he's an American or Brit."

Havers could only puff out his cheeks in response.

"It shouldn't matter. No one should have to suffer that kind of cruelty." Mason took a breath, then tried a more conciliatory tone. "Look, Frank, Colonel Walton told me to come over here and take charge, and I could use your expertise. How about if you help Mr. Wolski look around on the next floor?"

"Go to hell," Havers said, and stormed off.

Someone came up behind Mason and muttered, "Jesus H. Christ." Mason turned to see Major John Treborn, the chief medical examiner. Mason had met him briefly, but introduced himself again.

"You're the criminal investigator who came in about two weeks ago."

Mason nodded.

"Well, welcome to the zoo," Treborn said and stepped up to the edge of the gap. Mason joined him. Treborn examined the corpse with the beam of his flashlight. "I can tell you one thing from here," Treborn said. "He was killed, dismembered, and bled dry somewhere else before being hung up there like a slaughtered animal. And look at the shoulder joints and the hips. Clean, surgical cuts." He looked at Mason. "What do you think? Revenge killing, sending others a message?"

"If this were a revenge killing they wouldn't have been so meticulous with the butchering then strung him up like a trophy."

"I can see this case getting really ugly," Treborn said. "Maybe you should have let Havers take it."

Wolski called down from the edge of the fourth floor. "Sir, you need to see what's up here."

As Mason headed for the stairwell, he met four men bringing in the generator and lights. He told them to set up the lights in the next room and see about getting the body down without contaminating the scene. "Major Treborn will supervise."

Once Mason was alone climbing the stairs, images of the

corpse projected themselves onto the dark surroundings as if burned onto his eyes. On the fourth floor, he entered a room full of scorched sewing machines and looms. Up ahead, Wolski stood near the edge of the collapsed flooring with his flashlight trained on something hidden from Mason's view.

"Seems our friend left us some kind of crazy message," said Wolski. "No blood on the floor. Looks like he drained them like the torso."

The sight was one of the strangest Mason had ever seen. On the floor, five feet from the broken edge, lay the victim's arms and legs. The killer had arranged the limbs in the shape of an X, the stumps joining in the middle. Four additional stakes formed a crude wooden cross between them.

"I'll be damned if I know what it's supposed to mean," Wolski said.

"I don't think he left this message for us."

They both walked to the edge of the drop-off and looked down at the column, then up to the floor above.

"One thing's for sure," said Wolski, "he either had help or he's a hell of an engineer."

"That, or maybe a mountain climber."

"Mountain climbers know how to hang dead bodies, do they?"

"You're going to have a wiseass remark for everything, aren't you?"

Wolski smiled and shrugged.

"How's your German?" Mason asked.

"I was born in Pomerania, but the family moved to Wisconsin when I was five—"

"That's really fascinating, but I just want to know how your German is."

"Now he pulls out the sarcasm."

Mason started to say something, but Wolski beat him to the

punch. "Fluent. My German's fluent. Sorry, I just used to get a lot of flak because I could speak it."

"Go tell the photographer and the doc to get up here. Then I want you to go help with the interviews. Planting that body on that column and making an art show out of the body parts took time and had to make noise. Somebody's got to have heard or seen something."

Wolski left, and Mason searched for any signs the killer had been there. A broad survey of the area turned up nothing, no shoe prints, no evidence of any activity that might explain how the killer managed to suspend the body or attach it to the column. Everything seemed to be as it had been since a fire caused by incendiary bombs had ravaged the building. He scanned the exposed edge of the concrete around the collapsed portion of the floor with his flashlight, slowly and carefully. A quarter of the way, light glinted off the hammered surface of what he'd thought was exposed rebar embedded in the concrete floor. He got on his knees and studied it closely. It was a spike. A sweep of his flashlight revealed three more. The killer had driven spikes at intervals of ninety degrees, like the four points on a compass, around the hole. The man must have engineered some kind of pulley system to lower himself and mount the body.

Why go to that much trouble?

Mason noticed something else: From his kneeling position, he could see the faint relief of imprints in the ash. They weren't from shoes or bare feet. But what? Cloth? Like ghostly disturbances, they didn't follow a definite form from one print to the next. Now that he knew what to look for, he saw they continued around the hole's edge. He followed them with is flashlight, and on the opposite side the trail led to and from the hole, extending outward into the darkness. As he followed the prints, he noticed another set of markings. The killer had been dragging something heavy, like a sack... or dismembered torso. *Odd*, Mason thought, *the killer had been so meticulous covering up his tracks, and now this? Maybe he's fallible after all.*

Mason passed a series of partitioned office spaces filled with charcoal replicas of what had once been office furniture. The trail wove around piles of debris and fallen light fixtures. Finally, at the far end of the room, the trail stopped at a steel-reinforced door. On the floor, ash and scattered fragments had been scraped away in an arc, proof that the door had been opened recently. The soot on the door handle had been rubbed off as well. He reached for a handkerchief in his back pocket and, in doing so, turned the flashlight away from the door. That was when he noticed a very faint light leaking from under the door.

He froze and listened. He pulled out his M1911 .45 automatic and slowly pushed the door lever to make as little noise as possible.

The rusted lever screeched. Mason shoved the lever and jerked open the door.

Though daylight had turned to the gray gloom of dusk, the light was still a shock to his eyes. At the same moment he heard a creak and clank of metal. A black shadow flew at his face. He dived sideways. Something sliced through the arm of his coat as he fell. He shot up to an elbow and aimed the pistol, ready to fire. But it wasn't a man charging him with a knife. The moving object was a thick metal pipe with a scalpel strapped on the end. It had been rigged above the door frame to swing in when the door was opened.

Mason got to his feet, stopped the pipe from swinging, and stepped out the door onto the fire escape. Metal stairs descended to an alley. He examined the rig—a clever bit of engineering. The killer had knowingly left the footprints to lead someone into the trap. It wasn't designed to kill, unless by chance the short blade entered the neck or the heart. In all likelihood, he was sending a message: Whoever follows does so at his peril.

And Mason had willingly walked right into it.

He turned to go back inside and stopped. On the exterior face of the door, crude letters in red paint spelled out a message in German:

THOSE WHO I HAVE MADE SUFFER WILL BECOME SAINTS AND THEY SHALL LIFT ME UP FROM HELL.

3

"Sweet dreams, ladies," Corporal Manganella said as Mason and Wolski climbed out of the Jeep.

Mason grunted. Wolski gave him the middle finger. Manganella gunned the engine and raced away, leaving them in the dark. Much of the city's electrical grid still waited to be restored, and even the buildings requisitioned by the military suffered intermittent electrical service. Mason peered down the street. Vague skeletal shapes of the buildings were visible by the light of the moon. He thought of the killer out there somewhere, stalking prey in this ruined city, a city in chaos with legions of easy prey.

The 13th CID detachment satellite station on Sophienstrasse was once the financial headquarters for the Nazi regime. The building's unremarkable blockhouse architecture was rendered even bleaker by the blackened granite from the raging fires. The first wave of U.S. occupying forces had blasted off the ubiquitous Nazi swastika but left the Third Reich eagle for some reason, then proceeded to scratch graffiti into the smoke-stained stone.

Mason and Wolski passed through the multi-arched portico

and approached the entrance. Two sentries, stationed on either side, saluted them.

"Poor bastards freezing their asses off," Wolski said.

"At least no one is shooting at them."

"Coming from someone else, I'd say they were looking on the bright side. But with you, I see a problem with compassion for your fellow human beings."

"My compassion's not going to make them feel any warmer."

When they entered, Mason felt relieved to be immersed in light and heat after so many hours in the dark and cold of the damaged factory. A row of desks, then a line of offices, filled the open-floor lobby. A couple of typewriters clacked; a telephone rang. Except for everyone wearing army-green instead of blue, the place reminded Mason of any large police station, and it always gave him a pang of nostalgia.

As they headed for a staircase at the far side of the lobby, the lead watch sergeant looked up from his paperwork. "Mr. Collins. Colonel Walton wants to see you right away."

"It's almost nine," Mason said to Wolski as they mounted the stairs. "What's Walton doing here this late?"

"Can only mean trouble."

The next floor sported the same arrangement of desks and offices, the same faded beige walls and black-and-white tile floor. Most of the investigators were on this floor, with a few privates and corporals doing administrative work at a front pool of desks. Wolski split off to an area in the center of the room dedicated to the lower-ranked investigators. Mason continued on to the colonel's outer office, where a staff sergeant typed away, looking up only long enough to wave Mason on through.

On a bench opposite the sergeant's desk sat an elderly man dressed in black with a salt-and-pepper goatee and reading glasses perched on the end of his nose. He had a gaunt face with deeply etched lines and piercing hazel eyes. Mason didn't have time to wonder who the peculiar man might be. He had bigger concerns, one of which waited behind the next door. He knocked.

A powerful voice boomed through the door, "Enter."

What had been some high-ranking Nazi financial official's office now served at Colonel Walton's pleasure. The large room dwarfed the desk, which sat front and center. On the wall behind the colonel hung several maps: the city of Munich; postwar Germany divided into its four zones of occupation—American, British, French and Russian; and one of the American zone, which included Bavaria. To the left of the desk stood an over-stuffed sofa and high-back leather chairs. Not for the first time, images flashed through Mason's mind of some Nazi official sitting behind the same desk planning the financing required for the annihilation of one ethnic group or another.

Havers stood to one side of the colonel's desk, hat in hand, and somehow managed to shoot Mason a hateful gaze while maintaining a smarmy smile for the colonel. Given another time and place, Havers would have made an excellent candidate for Nazidom.

Mason stopped in front of the desk and saluted. "You wanted to see me, sir?"

"I wanted your damned report. Havers has been here for more than an hour."

"Yes, sir. I waited until the medical examiner, Major Treborn, could give me his initial findings, and take the body... parts off to the lab."

"That just happened?" the colonel asked, glancing in Havers's direction. "The victim—Allied or German?"

"That's to be determined. We found no clothing or documents saying one way or the other. His head and body were shaved. No physical traits to speak of, except he was uncircumcised. I'm having Mr. Wolski make calls to the various division and battalion headquarters to see if any servicemen are reported missing."

"Havers believes the victim is German."

"So far, there's no evidence to confirm one way or the other. Mr. Havers jumped to that conclusion on his own."

Havers butted in, "I've already had my deputy investigators already check all bulletins about missing army or American civilian personnel, and none of them match the victim."

"Mr. Havers should be aware that it takes a couple of days for someone to be filed as missing. Then a couple of days for the bulletins to make the rounds. Plus, it doesn't take into account personnel on leave or those sent out on travel or extended duties." He addressed Havers directly, "And if you'd waited for Major Treborn's report, you'd know that he puts the time of death at no more than a day and a half, tops."

"You arrogant son of a bitch," Havers said.

The colonel banged his desk. "That's enough." He pointed his index finger at Mason. "I won't have any disrespect of your fellow investigators. We work together or not at all. Now, get on with your report."

"I assume Mr. Havers filled you in on the state of the body."

"Yes, but I want your version."

Mason told the colonel about the torso being lashed to the column, the mesh around the organs, and the display of limbs on the floor above. Colonel Walton showed no reaction, though Mason's stomach contracted in retelling the details. "We couldn't find any recent fingerprints. Any imprints they found of fingers or hands indicate the killer was probably wearing nonfibrous gloves. Footprints indicate that the killer also wore some kind of cloth over his shoes or boots. We estimate his shoe size at between ten and eleven. I'd like to go back to the scene tomorrow, but my guess is we won't find anything more. This guy was meticulous and only left traces he wanted us to find."

Colonel Walton nodded.

"The canvassing turned up nothing. No one claims to have

seen or heard anything. We'll continue canvassing in a wider circle tomorrow."

"I heard about your close call with his booby trap," Colonel Walton said.

Mason nodded and fingered the slice in the left arm of his coat, then pulled out his notepad and read the message the killer had left on the fire-escape door.

"So not the work of rival gangs?" Colonel Walton asked.

Mason shook his head. "This is a psychopathic killer. I believe this isn't his first and it won't be his last."

Colonel Walton's desk sergeant came in with a large manila envelope. "This was just delivered from the photo lab, sir, for Mr. Collins." He handed Mason the envelope and left.

"The crime scene photos," Mason said.

"Not right now. I have a late dinner engagement, and I don't want to ruin my appetite."

No doubt Colonel Walton had a beautiful young fräulein waiting for him as well. Mason had heard about the colonel's revolving door of lovely girls. From the time U.S. forces had entered Germany, an edict had been issued that all Allied personnel were forbidden to fraternize—"fratting," as the men called it—with the enemy civilian population. It didn't take long for the non-fraternization rules to be ignored, especially where young ladies were concerned. By the end of July, the army had pretty much given up on the unpopular edict. A couple of packs of cigarettes could buy you an evening. And if there was one thing the army had plenty of, it was cigarettes.

A flush of red popped onto the colonel's cheeks under Mason's knowing gaze. "That will be all, gentlemen."

Collins and Havers started to leave when the Colonel said, "Mr. Collins, just a few more questions." Mason turned, as did Havers, but the colonel waved a dismissive hand at Havers. "You can go."

Colonel Walton leaned back in his chair and studied Mason. "Havers is a good investigator, but he's had little homicide experience. Few of my investigators do. That's why I sent you out there to investigate that murder. It's why I accepted your transfer request—with some reluctance, I might add." He plucked a file off his desk and opened it. "You've been here, what? Twelve days?"

Mason offered only a slight nod; he knew what was coming.

"We should have had this talk when you first arrived," Colonel Walton said into the open file. "I know about you being fired from the Chicago PD for kickbacks and shakedowns—"

"Colonel, those were trumped-up charges—"

The colonel jerked up his head and glared at Mason. "You will let me finish. I have your statements on the affair. I'm aware of the controversy surrounding you." He paused and turned his attention back to the open file. "I only bring this up because of tension concerning you and the other intelligence agents while you worked human intelligence at G2. I don't need it, and I'm expecting you to defuse it. You got exemplary marks for your investigative work, but there are criticisms of being too independent, less than stellar regard for authority, et cetera, et cetera. You keep that kind of thinking out of this outfit, or I'll see to it you go back to pushing papers in Frankfurt. You think joining the CID is a new start for you. Well, I say it's the end of the line. You've been blackballed back home. No city police department will hire you. You screw up here, and that's it. Am I understood?"

Mason acknowledged. Colonel Walton rose from his chair and went to a file cabinet. The colonel, a good-looking man with chiseled features, stood a head taller than Mason, and Mason measured six feet. As deputy provost marshal of Munich, he could have assigned a CID warrant officer to supervise the detachment; some would say a hands-on kind of guy while others considered him an overbearing, power-hungry pain in the ass. He opened a drawer and took out a bottle of cognac along with two glasses. Mason welcomed a drink—maybe two or three after what he'd witnessed in the warehouse. But this gesture wasn't a peace offering or sharing a drink among comrades in arms; more a pacifier for what was about to come.

The colonel offered Mason one of the glasses. "A VSOP distilled in 1870. About six months' worth of your salary would buy this in the States. Here, I traded it for a smoked ham and five pounds of coffee from some wealthy hausfrau." He held up his glass. "Cheers."

They both took a sip of their drinks, then Colonel Walton asked, as if in casual conversation, "How's the train robbery case going?"

"Sir, you have my latest report, so I'm not sure what your point is in asking." Though he had a pretty good idea.

"I'm not required to have a point. Answer the question."

"After the gang robbed a trainload of army supplies and PX goods, I was able to trace them to Augsburg. I alerted the 385th MP train security battalion. They laid a trap for the gang at the Augsburg train station, but the gang started shooting their way out —sub-machine guns, grenades, the whole bit—and escaped."

"That's right. And that gang of about twenty U.S. deserters, with another forty or so DPs, are out there plundering the countryside."

DP stood for "displaced person." When Germany surrendered there were more than ten million displaced persons in Germany: ex-prisoners of war, ex-concentration camp internees, and people from every Nazi-occupied country brought in as slave labor. For years the slave laborers had been forced to work in the factories, on the farms, or as domestic servants. Now released from bondage, a majority of the ten million had already made their way home, but hundreds of thousands remained in Germany, and some of them had decided to take advantage of the chaos of a war-torn country and formed gangs that roamed the countryside, raping, stealing, and murdering.

Colonel Walton continued, "Two MPs and two civilians were seriously wounded. That case deserves some serious attention, don't you think?"

"Because of their widespread activity, it has turned into a zone-wide investigation. I'm coordinating with three MP battalions and their CID detachments in Frankfurt, Stuttgart, and Mannheim. I'm working the Munich end, but for the moment it appears the gang has moved west into other areas of command."

Colonel Walton downed his cognac and offered Mason another pour, but Mason declined. He needed a clear head for what was coming.

The colonel shrugged and poured another for himself. "You know the situation we're facing. There are over six hundred thousand soldiers and support personnel in the American zone, most of them homesick and resentful for not being sent home. Mix in low morale, boredom, and an unlimited supply of food, booze, and cigarettes, which millions of starving and desperate locals will give them anything in trade—and I mean anything—and it's a potent mix for graft, drunkenness, narcotics, rape, and murder. It's a goddamned madhouse. The MP battalions and the CID detachments are overloaded with cases. More than half our men have never done police work. And as fast as we can train them, the army's sending them home."

Colonel Walton let out a tired sigh. Mason listened to the distant clacking of a typewriter and hum of the electric space heater while waiting for the colonel to get revved up again. He didn't have to wait long.

"The point I'm trying to make in all this is: I can't have you stuck on this homicide case with no leads, no evidence, and—I have to be honest with you here—in all likelihood one German murdered by another. Now, you can continue to pursue the case in a supervisory capacity. See what the ME says after his autopsy, but then I want you to give other cases your full attention. It may sound callous, but there are too many other cases that concern the army more than what goes on between Germans."

"We don't know if the victim is German. And even if he is, what if the killer is an American? And, sir… killers like this? They don't necessarily stop on their own. This guy even referred to 'those' he makes suffer. What about his next victim?"

The colonel slammed his hand on the desk. "May I remind you, Mr. Collins, that the CID's primary job—your job—is to investigate crimes committed by and on U.S. military personnel."

A few seconds passed while neither spoke. Mason knew the colonel was sizing him up, remembering the complaints about Mason's pushing the boundaries of authority. Remarks from fellow officers and the command ranks would no doubt claim that Mason was not a team player, which left the colonel mulling whether it was worth putting up with such battles to benefit from Mason's investigative experience.

Finally, the colonel said, "I'm going to bargain with you. As long as you work other cases to my satisfaction, including this train robbery fiasco, I'll let you and Wolski follow up any leads that arise in this case. I guarantee you that if we find out that the victim or the killer is American, or any other member of Allied forces, you will have my full support in pursuing the murderer." He rose from his desk. "Stay here."

Colonel Walton went to the door, poked his head out, and said something Mason couldn't hear. He then stepped to one side to let someone enter. The craggy-faced man who'd been waiting outside stepped in. He eyed Mason with a solemn expression. The colonel gestured with his hand for the man to follow him.

"Chief Warrant Officer Collins," the colonel said, "this is Herr Oberinspektor Becker of the Munich Kriminalpolizei." The Kriminalpolizei was the German police detective bureau.

With a slight chill, Mason realized why the man had caught his eye earlier: He reminded Mason of his own German-born grandfather. They wore the same goatee and had the same steely eyes. His grandfather had been a devout Lutheran and the family tyrant. As a child, Mason had shied away from the man, avoiding him whenever he could. Fear transformed into acrimony as he grew older. Now he faced what appeared to be a living, breathing incarnation of the old buzzard. And a German cop, to boot.

Becker made a slight bow with no more of a smile than what was required. "I'm very happy to make your acquaintance," he said in a thick German accent and deep baritone voice.

Mason stepped forward and they shook hands. Becker's hand was warm and dry, and he had a surprisingly firm grip for someone who looked to be in his mid-sixties. Like Mason's grandfather, Becker comported himself with a grim visage and a stiff spine.

Colonel Walton maneuvered between them to break their mutual stare. "Gentlemen, over here, please," he said, and led them back to the desk. "Have a seat." He took his place behind the desk, while Mason and Becker sat in the chairs facing him. "Inspector Becker is our chief liaison officer for the Munich police."

From his time working as an assistant on the general staff in Frankfurt, Mason had witnessed firsthand the backroom politics that established how the occupying Allies, from a standpoint of sheer manpower, could police the entire country's population with only military police. To have any hope of maintaining order, they had to turn to the existing indigenous police forces. The problem was, the German police forces had been absorbed into the SS by Heinrich Himmler, and most policemen were required to be card-carrying members of the Nazi Party. Each day the Allies dismantled more and more of the Nazi-era system, but it had been impractical, even hazardous, to dismiss every German policeman.

To make sure they weren't putting fanatics or brutal members of the Gestapo back into positions of authority, the intelligence services continually combed through the Nazi-era police force files. Nonetheless, Mason suspected that a lot of the bad apples were slipping back into the police stations and halls of justice.

Becker cleared his throat and said to Mason, "Colonel Walton and Criminal Investigator Havers gave me information regarding what you discovered at the Mannstein Fabrikswerk factory. I can assure you that my colleagues and I will do our utmost to continue the investigation."

Mason turned to the colonel. "You're handing the case over to the Kriminalpolizei?"

"The Kriminalpolizei will augment the investigation. You know that we always coordinate with them when cases involve German civilians. We do the main investigation, but hand over German perpetrators to the German authorities."

"No one said the perpetrator is German."

"I concur with Investigator Collins," Becker said. "Is it not America which seems particularly fertile in producing psychotics who commit multiple homicides?"

"No one said anything about multiple homicides," the colonel said.

"And it seems, Inspector," Mason said, imitating Becker's phrasing, "that Germany is fertile in producing mass murderers."

The colonel stiffened in his chair like he was going to have a heart attack. "Now, wait a minute, Collins!"

Mason continued to glare at Becker, but Becker bowed his head slightly and smiled. "Touché."

Mason turned to Colonel Walton. "Sir, we can do this without the inspector's help. If the killer turns out to be German, we'll hand him over to German authorities."

Becker spoke before Walton could respond. "I and many of my fellow officers are natives of Munich. We know the city and its people better than you. And while your experienced investigators keep leaving for the United States, we gain qualified officers every day. Perhaps we should lead the investigation. We can be much more persuasive in convincing witnesses to come forward—"

"Yeah, we've all heard about how persuasive the Gestapo could be," Mason said.

The colonel shot up from his chair. "That's enough! I've warned you about your attitude. That war's been fought. We won't be fighting it again, here. Is that clear?"

Mason nodded.

"That goes for you, too, Inspector."

Becker bowed his head. "My apologies, Colonel. My officers and I are happy to cooperate."

"Fine. Now both of you get out of here."

Mason blew past the pool of desks and entered his office. He flicked on the ceiling light then slapped the file folders onto his desk. Before he could sit, Becker knocked on his open door.

Mason sighed. "Yeah, come in."

Few Germans made Mason uneasy these days. When they had been shooting at him and taken him prisoner, yes, but not after their devastating defeat. But Becker not only personified his later tyrannical grandfather, he also stirred his memories of the brutal German military police and the terror of the camp guards, and he resented the man for it.

Becker took two steps into the room. "I would like to apologize for my part in our dispute."

"Forget it," Mason said, but Becker had the look of a parent waiting for the right response. "Okay, me too. We're both cops. But I hope I don't find out you were a Gestapo goon arresting political dissidents or hunting down escaped American POWs."

"I remained in Kripo during the war. I only investigated serious crimes and had nothing to do with security enforcement.

Your colonel thinks very highly of you. I hope we can work together in harmony."

Mason sat at his desk and started leafing through the files. "Whatever works to solve the case, right?"

Becker tilted his head in agreement. "I respect your fervor. A man never fully forgets the victims. Especially the brutal ones."

Mason stopped fussing with the files and looked up. Becker had been a cop for decades before him, and he probably had a lot more skeletons stuffed in his closet. "This one does have me pretty rattled. I've never seen anything like it." Mason looked at his watch. "It's after eleven now, and it's going to take me an hour to type up my report. I'll have someone make up a file in the morning and send it over to you."

Becker removed a business card from his pocket and placed it on Mason's desk. "I will have my colleagues begin a search for witnesses tomorrow morning. It will be difficult to identify the victim. There are hundreds of thousands of German refugees, deserters from every army…"

Mason fed a sheet into his typewriter. "Not to mention all the freed concentration camp prisoners and slave laborers your comrades didn't manage to eliminate." Mason turned to Becker. "Look—"

"No need to apologize." A smile formed in the corner of Becker's mouth, but his nostrils flared; he was obviously struggling to maintain his composure. "I understand you have reasons for your animosity. And old enemies do not become friends overnight. We will have a pleasant working relationship."

By way of conciliation, Mason said, "Once I have the medical examiner's report, I'll send that to you. And as soon as I have a sketch artist draw up the victim's portrait, I'll send over copies of that as well."

"Good. We'll post them on the usual missing-persons boards

and see that all the surrounding community police departments receive a copy."

"Then we'll have all our little crumbs in a box, congratulate ourselves for our fine efforts, while we wait for the bastard to butcher another victim." Mason turned his attention back to his typewriter.

Becker lingered for a moment. "It never becomes any easier. I can attest to that. But beware of the bitterness." He shifted his winter coat to his left arm and donned his hat. "Good night."

Mason returned the farewell as he typed. He didn't think about what he was writing. He'd done enough reports that his brain went into autopilot. But Becker's parting words continued to repeat in his head. He'd thought himself beyond bitterness, having exchanged it for the anesthesia of spartan indifference.

Guess it's not working.

An hour later, another knock came at the door. It was Wolski. "What's with Boris Karloff?"

Mason chuckled. "He does look like Karloff at that." He pulled a cigarette out of the pack lying on the desk. He offered Wolski one. Wolski declined. "He's our German police liaison," Mason said. "Did you get anywhere with the calls about missing personnel?"

Wolski referred to a piece of paper in his hand. "During the last thirty-six hours there remain four hundred sixty-five personnel unaccounted for. That's just in Munich and the surrounding area." He pointed at Mason's report. "You finished with that thing?"

Mason nodded. He pulled the final page of the report out of the typewriter.

"How about a nightcap? I know a nice, quiet bar…."

"No, thanks. They've finally got me out of that hotel and found something more permanent. I want to get settled in."

"Corporal Manganella was to show you to your new quarters,

but he went off duty a half hour ago. He asked if I'd take you over there."

Mason put out his cigarette then stood and stretched. "Yeah, why not?"

~

MASON AND WOLSKI HAD TO STOP THE JEEP BEHIND A LINE OF waiting army vehicles. At the intersection, an MP conducted traffic and held up their street so a column of tanks and armored cars could cross.

"Did they start the war again and not tell us?" Wolski said.

They had stopped in front of an upscale hotel and nightclub miraculously unscathed by the war. It now served as the officers' mess and officers' club. Near the curb and positioned on either side of the entrance, Mason noticed two boys no older than ten. They were filthy, rail-thin and dressed in rags. Then he saw why they were there. The place was always busy with army and military government personnel coming and going, and each time one of them dropped a cigarette butt on the sidewalk, the boys dashed to the spot and picked it up. A small girl of five collected the butts from the boys and held them in a bundled rag. They didn't smoke them. They collected them. Cigarettes had become the de facto form of currency on the black market for Germans, and the only reliable way to procure food and clothing. Any area frequented by U.S. soldiers and government personnel offered an ideal location to collect the butts, which were then exchanged for food at collection centers where the unburned tobacco was used to make new cigarettes.

The Jeep started to move just as an MP rushed out of the officers' mess and chased the kids away. The kids ran across the street and dived into a hole in the wall of a destroyed building.

Mason felt a twinge of sadness for the kids. As the Jeep

passed, he kept an eye on the hole. Somewhere in the rubble those kids tried to survive.

Wolski finally parked in front of a brick town house. "Not bad. They've put me in the McGraw Kaserne. Like living on a prison block."

Mason climbed out and retrieved his gear from the back.

"Oh," Wolski said and reached into his pocket. "Almost forgot to give you a key to the house." He handed it to Mason. "I'll pick you up at oh-seven-hundred." Wolski made a cursory salute and drove away.

The Army Corps of Engineers had yet to restore power to this block, so Mason was left in the dark, but the moon reflecting off the snow gave enough light to show that the townhouse stood in a row of similar town houses untouched by bombs. Like a series of capricious tornados, bombs had devastated entire neighborhoods and bypassed others, reducing one house to a pile of dust while leaving its neighbor remained completely unscathed.

Standing there, Mason could almost imagine being in some corner of the world where the war had existed only in headlines or radio broadcasts. The warm light of candles emanated from a room on the ground floor. Behind the lace curtain, silhouettes of people communed around a dining table. Like coming home to family... not his, someone else's.

He heaved his duffel bag onto his shoulder and walked up the stone steps to the front door. Before he could insert the key into the lock, someone opened the door. A round-faced captain with red cheeks and equally red hair stepped aside to let him in.

"You must be the new guy," the red-cheeked captain said. "Come in out of the damp cold and into the dry cold."

Mason stepped in and they shook hands.

"Mike Shaw."

Mason introduced himself then followed Shaw down a short hallway. The place reeked of cigarette smoke and spilled beer.

Shaw stopped at the entrance to the dining room, where three other officers sat around the dining table playing poker. Shaw introduced them, but Mason paid only enough attention to learn that they were all quartermaster officers.

"Care to join us?" Shaw said. "We got beer and whiskey to keep us warm. There's a heating-oil furnace, but the oil's in short supply. Hopefully, we'll have some by the end of the week."

"Thanks, but I'm going to hit the sack."

Shaw shouted toward the back of the house, "Hey, Johann." He turned back to Mason. "We got servants. An old couple and their fourteen-year-old granddaughter." Shaw said the last part with a lascivious glint in his eyes. "A piece of jailbait. The only thing keeping me out of her panties is a couple of years." He laughed, his red cheeks jiggling. The others chuckled, but Mason gave him a cold stare.

Shaw noticed Mason's expression and stopped laughing. He cleared his throat. "They're okay people. Used to be the owners of this house until we moved in. I'm sure they were loyal little krauts, but no official Nazi Party affiliation."

From behind, Mason heard a raspy voice say, "*Guten Abend.*" He turned to see Johann standing in the hallway. He looked to be in his seventies with a thin, haggard face. Fine wisps of his silver hair were tousled from having to rise from sleep in answer to Shaw's summons. He wore what had been an expensive tailored suit coat that was now fraying at the edges.

Shaw made the introductions. Only Johann's glassy eyes moved in response; he'd probably overheard Shaw's comments. Mason joined Johann without another word to Shaw. Johann raised the candlestick he was holding and moved toward the stairs. At the base of the stairs, Johann offered to take Mason's duffel bag.

"*Nein, danke. Ich kann es tragen,*" Mason said, indicating that he could carry it himself.

Johann's eyes widened in happy surprise. In German, he said, "You speak German. Good. I am too old to learn English." He mounted the stairs with surprising agility. Mason followed.

"Are you, your wife, and granddaughter staying in the house, too, Johann?"

The old man stopped and turned to Mason. "Herr Steiger, please. I will call you Herr Collins, and you call me Herr Steiger. I can tell you are a man of respect, and I request only that one courtesy from one civilized man to another."

Mason nodded for Steiger to continue. They climbed the remaining stairs and moved down a wide hallway. From what Mason could see by the flickering candlelight, the hallway was decorated with fine antiques and wallpaper depicting a bucolic eighteenth-century hunting scene.

"You have some very nice things, Herr Steiger."

"We receive a small stipend for housing soldiers from your army, so fortunately we have not been obliged to sell much for food. At least, not yet." He gave Mason a melancholy smile. "To answer your question, sir, we live in the kitchen and cellar. A pitiful arrangement, but we know many families forced out of their homes to accommodate you soldiers, and they now live in squalor. We are grateful. Especially for my granddaughter. Only God almighty knows what would have happened to her if we'd been forced to live on the streets."

They stopped at the last door on the right, where Steiger unlocked the door and handed the key to Mason. He then stepped aside so Mason could enter the cold room.

"They continue to promise us electricity and heating oil, but it has yet to happen." Steiger lit an oil lamp on the nightstand. The light revealed a masculine room: framed representations of heraldic crests above a heavy oak bed, a knight's shield and crossed swords above a dresser laden with family photos.

"This was my son's room before he married and joined the

Wehrmacht." He eyed Mason as if watching for a reaction. "He was not SS, Herr Collins."

"I know the distinction." Mason saw the sadness in Steiger's eyes, his hunched shoulders, as the man surveyed his son's room. He felt sorry for the old man's loss. If only they had thought of that before allowing the Nazis to bring war to the world.

"I hope you will forgive us leaving the room as it was when he was a boy. He was killed in Russia in '42."

"It's fine. I'll leave everything the way it is. I'll just need to clear away the desk for my work."

"Of course." Steiger turned to go then added, "There's wood in the fireplace, if you wish. My wife and I will have coffee and breakfast ready at six-thirty. Dinner is at seven."

"I'll take breakfast, but I doubt I'll be back in time for dinner in the evenings."

As Steiger started to leave, Mason said, "Herr Steiger, I'm sorry about your son. Too many fathers lost too many sons."

Steiger tipped his head and left, closing the door behind him.

In a few moments Mason had the fire going. As he stood next to the fireplace for warmth, he surveyed the framed pictures competing for space on the mantel. Most were photographs of Steiger's son as a youth: a freckled-face boy, bespectacled, and thin like his father. There was a portrait of the son as a man, dressed in an academic gown of a university, capturing the same boyish grin that pushed up on his glasses. Then the obligatory picture of the son in his Wehrmacht uniform—this time with a forced smile. The last group was mostly snapshots of the son arm in arm with an attractive woman holding a baby. None of these had the son in uniform. The parents had probably added those long after the son had left home, married, and died.

What a waste.

Mason had very few photos from his childhood. His family never took pictures. No one had created a shrine to his youth.

Whatever photos they'd had, his mother had burned during one of her alcohol-induced fits of rage. That was shortly after his sister's untimely death... as his grandmother preferred to call it.

Mason was born in Germany, but at the age of 5, and three years after his father was killed in World War One, his mother, along with her parents, had immigrated to Ohio. A year later his mother had married a manipulative and cruel man named Robert Collins. But just two years into the marriage, his mother had become a devotee to the god of alcohol, and his stepfather, whether because of his mother's alcoholism or his long-time mistress, skipped town, never to be seen again. It took six years, but finally his mother's liver gave out. It was his grandparents who'd raised him from the age of twelve. Stern and cold, his grandfather had little to do with him, but what his grandmother had lacked in affection, she'd made up for it with gentleness and patience, tolerating and eventually mollifying his rebellious teen years. His grandfather died when Mason was in high school, so she'd become the only family member left in his life. He tried to keep in touch with her, writing letters from time to time. As much as he feared being heartless like his grandfather, he feared most becoming self-destructive like his mother. He felt the pull of both dark familial traits running like venom in his veins.

All in all, home didn't exist for him. Maybe home had become anywhere he'd stopped for more than a few nights and laid his hat —even this charred ruin of a city.

5

DECEMBER 10, 1945

I *t is 765 days since the end of our being, since the descent, since the beginning of the black days, whereupon we sold our soul to the demons that haunt us now.*

We have so many sins to atone for, and that cry out to be released. We must act or the heavy burden of our sins will drag us down into the deepest pit where exists nothing but eternal pain and horror. We must act or we will be strapped upon a table and cut upon in eternal agony.

It is so hard to carry on.

The man set his pen down. His prayers and the entry in the diary had calmed him. Now he could concentrate once again.

In the weak light of a gas lantern, he turned his chair, picked up a small metal file, and began to make the finishing adjustments on a delicate brass ring. The edge of the ring had an irregular pattern and was spanned by thin spokes. He held the ring up at eye level and examined his work. A smile signaled his satisfaction. He then turned to a two-foot-tall mechanical rabbit. It stood on its hind legs and held a violin to its chin, bow at the ready. The glassy eyes stared at a sheet of music poised on a music stand. A music box of polished mahogany served as the podium.

He inserted the brass ring onto a brass shaft that held a series of similar rings. With a jeweler's screwdriver, he fixed the shaft to a complex mechanism exposed in the rabbit's back. It required an exacting hand, but he possessed both a craftsman's touch and the deft fingers of a surgeon.

What a great joy it had been to find this marvel in the burned ruins of a townhouse. It was no children's toy, but a valuable automaton made by a French watchmaker in 1850, with the watchmaker's stamp still visible on the brass plate. Most of the surviving contents of the house had already been "salvaged" by neighbors, the elderly owners having made the unfortunate decision to remain during a particularly devastating bombing raid. And when he'd entered the house he could still detect a faint odor of burned flesh.

He always enjoyed exploring the ruins. Where most people regarded them as symbols of tragedy, he saw them as symbols of rebirth. The fate of the occupants meant nothing to him. They were all wretched vessels of sin and depravity—as his mother had always reminded him.

He closed the backing of rabbit fur, which had been damaged by fire but he'd repaired, then turned the key clockwise three times. With a flick of the switch, a Strauss waltz resonated in the room. The rabbit bowed the strings and fingered the fingerboard in time with the music. It swayed and swiveled its head and blinked as if concentrating on the music.

He noticed the bowing arm still made erratic movements, meaning there were still adjustments to be made. Still, the repairs were almost complete, and for a moment he relaxed and enjoyed the performance. It reminded him of his childhood, and the music box his father had given him, a more humble version with a motionless rabbit playing a trumpet on a base that turned with the music. The memory brought up images of his boyhood bedroom, but with that there always came another vision—a flash of his mother's face as she shrieked at him about sin and the impurity of the flesh. And the worst, telling him that men were the origin of all impurity, the penis a vile instrument...

The rabbit grinned at him. The man's back stiffened. It wasn't supposed to do that. He blinked. The rabbit had returned to playing.

The lantern flame fluttered, exaggerating and distorting the shadows. He felt the air shift as if disturbed by a great presence. His pulse pounded in his temples, and his bowels cramped.

Oh, God, not so soon.

The music stopped. The rabbit became lifeless, with its head turned in his direction.

They were coming. The voices would whisper and hiss at first, then rise until the screaming overwhelmed him. He had very little time.

He took up his pen again and entered a final sentence:

As we write this, we feel the stirrings, the pleading for further action, more glorious beatifications...

Another wave of wretched memories swept over him.

The other *He* who dwelled within him crawled up from his bowels like a cancerous cloud, bringing with it the memories of the inception of the black days: the gates of the prison and a descent into a hell so abhorrent that he'd bargained away his soul for a pitiful life among the damned; losing control of his bowels as he peered at a door opened just enough to let out a blinding light, as an unseen force propelled him slowly to the operating room where he dared not go, consuming him again and again until he could no longer look upon the world in cleanliness: visions and voices haunting a weak man until he breaks.

He shot up from his chair, his hands gripping the edge of the table for support. He was completely naked. The frigid air cramped his muscles and stung his skin.

Discomfort is not enough.

He took the lantern and descended a set of rickety stairs. He came to a floor-standing mirror. He could gaze upon only his naked torso, the upper third of the mirror painted black so he could not see his face and—most importantly—*his eyes*. From a table he picked up a short leather strap he had fashioned. Short nails protruded through the leather with a rawhide string attached on either end.

He placed the lantern on the table and wrapped the strap around the base of his penis and scrotum. He turned with reverence to a man-sized representation of the cross his mother had worn around her neck, the cross that had dangled near her breasts as she bent low and prayed for his condemned soul. With a rawhide string in either hand, he took one deep breath and yanked. He bit his lip to stifle a scream. He fell to his knees, doubled over in agony. Even as he did so, his penis became erect. There was no sexual gratification. His penis responded to pain. Just as it stood erect with the ecstasy of each Chosen One's beatification. Just as it had, the previous morning on the street, when he'd passed his next Chosen One. The excitement of knowing rushed hot blood to his groin. When he had caught a glimpse of the Chosen One's face, he knew the voices had brought him someone in the likeness of a suffering innocent he had once known, his first encounter, his first initiation into an abominable existence.

The excruciating pain forced the other *He* back into his bowels. *He* was gone, for now. The unrelenting visions, the screams of the innocents, the memory of his sins quieted, if for only a few hours. But the strap would stay on for a few more minutes. Then sleep would come.

We must rest, for we have glorious plans for the next Chosen One.

6

M ason entered the narrow alley that ran along the rear of the factory where the victim had been found. The morning sun hid behind a heavy veil of fog that froze to anything it touched. He shivered once from the cold, and his feet ached from the close call with frostbite during the previous year's horrible winter. *I should have asked for a post on the damned equator.*

He stopped next to the fire escape and looked up to the fourth-floor landing where the killer had rigged the booby trap and left his grim message.

Wolski came around the corner, stifling a yawn. "You got here early."

"Couldn't sleep."

Wolski lifted a Thermos. "Coffee?"

Mason accepted, and Wolski poured some into the Thermos cap. "Colonel Walton thinks you're out investigating the train robbery. Corporal Manganella told me where you really were."

Mason looked at Wolski, who turned an imaginary key to lock his lips. Mason took a sip of coffee. "I've been out here trying to imagine how someone could kill and dismember a body in one place then transport it here. All the surrounding buildings have been searched for blocks around. No sign of the killing taking place there, so he had some distance to travel."

"He sure as hell couldn't have carried it, so that leaves transporting by car, wagon, or cart."

Mason pointed to the center of the alley. "There's a mix of tire and wagon-wheel tracks."

"I just can't see the killer coming by wagon with a cut-up body in the back, in the middle of the night through MP patrols and checkpoints."

Mason shrugged. "It's still possible. This is a big city, and he could know enough back streets to pull it off. Could be he has an after-curfew pass or permit. If he came by car, it means he'd have to be with the army or the military government."

"And you think he came down this alley and went up the fire escape?"

"He couldn't have gone in the front. Too many witnesses." Mason pointed to a hole in the base of the factory wall thirty feet from where they were standing. "Then there's that hole."

As if on cue, an MP emerged from the hole and said, "Mr. Collins, the engineer would like to see you. If you'll follow me."

Mason and Wolski ducked low to enter the hole in the wall, then climbed down the rubble to reach the basement level. They followed the MP through several corridors before coming to an open area with a series of boilers. The engineer stood at the base of the same column to which the killer had lashed his victim. They had to negotiate heaps of concrete slabs fallen from the floors above to join Lieutenant Edwards, the engineer.

The daylight made little difference in the dark factory; the place still felt gloomy and oppressive. Work lights had been distributed throughout the crime scene, but Edwards still had to use his flashlight to scan the floors above them.

"Begging your pardon, Chief," Edwards said with a Tennessee

drawl, "but I don't think the killer used the fire escape to carry the body up there. It'd have been easier to lift the corpse from down here." He pointed his flashlight at the spikes driven into the exposed flooring of the fourth floor. "He probably hooked pulleys on those spikes up there, then attached the body to ropes down here and hoisted it up to a spot on the column and tied off the lines."

Mason nodded. Much as he'd guessed. "How do you think he got up there to secure the body to the column?"

"Well, it's easier to drop down from above than to lift your own weight. I'd say he rappelled down to the spot, either from the fourth floor or the next one up, and grabbed on with his legs. That way he'd have free hands to lash the body to the column."

"It took some know-how to rig that all up," Wolski said.

"Not really," Edwards said. "It's pretty simple even if you have some basic mechanical or engineering skills. Welders and maintenance workers use these kinds of rigs all the time for hard-to-reach areas."

Mason nodded. "All right. Thanks, Edwards."

"Don't mention it," Edwards said and left.

"Well, that goes a long way to explain *how* he did it, just not why," Wolski said.

Manganella called down to Mason from the second floor. "Chief, word came in that Major Treborn has a preliminary report for you on the autopsy."

As Mason headed for the stairs he said to Wolski, "You stay here and coordinate the canvassing by our boys and the German police."

"I'd like to go along." Mason started to object, but Wolski added, "Like you said, I've got a lot to learn about homicide. Watch and learn, remember?"

"You might change your mind after your first time at an autopsy."

Wolski jumped down off the pile of rubble and followed Mason down a maintenance corridor. "The message he left on the door talks about saints and hell. Must be a religious guy."

"Could be," Mason said. "But I think the message refers to his own personal hell. One he's desperately trying to escape. He doesn't kill out of perverted lust or thrills. He doesn't torture for pleasure or power over his victims."

"Maybe he'll move on. Hit a different city for each killing. It'd be easier to stay under the radar that way."

Mason had already thought about that, and wouldn't admit it to anyone, but he hoped that wasn't the case. He wanted to be the cop to take this guy down. He wanted him badly. "It's possible, but Germans have travel restrictions, and these types of killers are as likely to stay in one place as they are to move around."

As they climbed the stairs, Mason said, "Let's look at this murder another way. What can the killer's methods tell us about him that he may not have intended to communicate?"

"Well, he has medical knowledge. Some engineering skills since he's good at rigging up the dead weight of a corpse. You say he's probably working alone, so, lugging a heavy corpse around in the dark, he's got to be fit and agile. With the curfew and night patrols all over the city, you said yourself he might have a pass. He might have a car. Hell, he might even be disguised as a U.S. soldier."

Mason picked up Wolski's train of thought. "Or could be he's in the U.S. Medical Corps."

That stopped them both, as they considered this possibility. Mason could tell by Wolski's look that he didn't want to go there.

"We've got to consider every angle," Mason said.

They emerged from the dark factory, squinting against the daylight, and headed for Manganella and the Jeep.

"You want to start looking at Medical Corps personnel?"

Wolski said. "We can't have access to those files or start questioning personnel without a damn good reason."

"We start by scanning MP and CID files for any arrest reports involving medical personnel."

"Then if we come up with a list of suspects on vague information and have to get permission to interrogate them? What kind of shit's going to hit the fan if the army brass finds out we suspect one of our own?"

"We tread carefully," Mason said.

"Like hell," Wolski said as they climbed in the Jeep. "That's treading into a minefield."

THE U.S. ARMY MEDICAL CORPS HAD TAKEN OVER A MUNICH police forensics lab and morgue, a nondescript blockhouse in the Maxvorstadt district. The front-desk receptionist gave them directions to Major Treborn's office. They followed the hallway, passing desks and small offices of the major's staff of doctors, technicians, and secretarial workers. At the end of the hallway they came upon Major Treborn's office. Mason and Wolski waited outside the open door while the major lambasted someone on the phone.

"And tell the captain that if I don't get those replacements and supplies soon, I'm going to personally embalm him in his sleep." He listened a moment, then said, "I don't give a damn. No more excuses. Get it done." He hung up. "Get in here, you two."

Mason and Wolski removed their caps and entered. Major Treborn was still clearly worked up about the phone call. "We've got five cases pending. A private who expired under mysterious circumstances, a Negro sergeant knifed to death, two vehicular manslaughters, and a major's wife, who the major claims fell down some stairs. The Judge Advocate's office is chewing out my ass for things to go faster, and army lawyers are breathing down my neck. Understaffed, undersupplied and working in an outdated facility. There's partial structural damage to the building, water leaks, intermittent electricity, and no clean room to keep contamination of evidence down to a minimum."

Major Treborn sat back in his chair and rubbed his eyes with the palms of his hands. "You've got a hell of a case, Collins. I've never seen anything like this. I've heard of them but never been involved in one personally. I've had the occasional mutilation, but yours…" Treborn shook his head, and his attention went somewhere for a moment. "I haven't written up the final report, but I knew you were anxious, and this case is exceptional." He looked at both of them in turn. "You ready for the trip down horror lane?"

As they followed Treborn down two flights of steps, he began filling them in: "The victim's a male. Mid-sixties. No semen on the body or in the anus, and his genitals are intact, so we can rule out the sexual angle."

"You have a better estimate of the time of death?" Mason asked.

"The last few days the temperatures haven't gone above freezing, so that makes it harder to pinpoint by body temperature. He was virtually bled out, so lividity is minimal."

They reached the subbasement floor and proceeded down a long corridor. Treborn continued, "The same goes for putrefaction. Cold temperatures screw that all up." He turned to Wolski when they stopped in front of a wide steel door. "You been to one of these before?"

Wolski shook his head. He managed to maintain a neutral expression, but Mason could see his neck and jaw muscles bulge from tension.

Treborn said, "If you have to vomit, make sure you do it in the sink." He pulled a metal lever and opened the door.

Despite the cold, the pungent odors of formaldehyde and

disinfectant assaulted their nostrils. The large, rectangular room had white concrete walls, though the white was now tinged in shades ranging from ocher to tobacco-stain brown. They passed rows of shelves containing various boxes of laboratory supplies and bottles of chemicals, followed by two overloaded desks and two long workbenches laden with lab glassware, microscopes, and X-ray photographs. Then, beyond these chaotic trappings of any research lab, came the defining objects of a morgue: four porcelain autopsy tables flanked by large sinks on one side and three rows of six refrigerated storage lockers for the deceased.

Mason and Wolski followed Treborn to the first autopsy table. Mason and Treborn took opposite sides, while Wolski chose the foot of the table as if thinking a little more distance might lessen the shock.

After one quick glance at Wolski, Treborn pulled away the white covering, the disturbance of air bringing up the scent of decaying meat like a butcher's shop on a hot day. Beneath lay the head and torso of the victim. Wolski stepped back as if pushed by an invisible force. Mason remained where he was, though icy fingers squeezed his stomach. Dead bodies he was used to—the clouded eyes, the marbled flesh—but this man had died in midscream, his eyes and mouth wide in agony and terror. The "Y" cut from the shoulders down to the pelvis was now sewn closed with coarse thread. There was a sewn incision from ear to ear around the top of the head, where Treborn had removed, examined, and measured the brain.

"I'd put the time of death at between eighteen and thirty-six hours before the time the engineers were able to bring the body down, and approximately four hours before being hung up on the column."

Mason looked up at Treborn. "It would have taken him a good hour or two to rig the body."

"Assuming he was working alone," Wolski said.

"Oh, this guy is working alone," Mason said. "These kinds of killers rarely share, and definitely not one who makes such a spectacle of his handiwork."

"He could have rigged the whole thing beforehand; then it'd be a matter of an hour or so to tie it up there."

"It's possible. Even with that, to rig the body to the column, place the limbs on the floor above, cover his tracks, then set the booby trap. That's two to three hours. That means the place where he killed was a maximum of an hour or two from the factory."

Treborn said, "Before you get too carried away, remember the four hours is just an estimate." He turned the victim's head slightly and pointed to the back of its neck. "I did find a contusion on the basal ganglion from a blunt instrument. This occurred hours before death. A blow like this could have rendered the victim unconscious or semiconscious."

"What are those purple bands across the shoulders, hips, and forehead?" Mason asked.

"They're also on the arms and legs," Treborn said. He motioned for them to follow him to the next table. Once there, he pulled aside a covering sheet. No less shocking than the torso were the severed arms and legs. "See the two purple bands on the arms?" He pointed to the wrist and upper arm; the skin within the bands looked jagged and ripped as if someone had taken coarse sandpaper and shredded the skin down to the muscle and tendon. "Here we have them on the thigh, calf, and ankle. These abrasions are where the killer tied the victim down with restraints. It's the most solid evidence that this victim was strapped down and tortured." He pointed to the Y incision in the torso. "Plus, look at those cuts. They're jagged, like the victim had struggled. Then there's the fluid in the lungs, around the heart. The throat is swollen with lacerations from screaming. Rigor mortis set in very quickly, judging from the tension in his muscles. Especially around the jaw."

Mason scanned the skin of the torso, arms, and legs. "Aside from the obvious, I don't see any other outward signs of torture."

"I didn't find any," Treborn said. "No lacerations, puncture wounds, or burns."

Mason had a sickening feeling he knew the answer to his next question. "Then how was he tortured?"

Treborn pulled the sheet up to cover the limbs. "My guess, he was cut open while he was still alive and without anesthesia."

They all turned slowly to look at the silently screaming corpse.

Treborn continued, "He was sliced open, his ribs cut from his sternum with heavy shears, then extended out with retractors. The same procedure you'd perform for an autopsy, but on a living man. His intestines were surgically removed. The killer left the heart and lungs intact so as not to kill him, though I venture to guess the victim was half-dead, unconscious, or out of his mind by that time. The arms and legs were removed, each one with surgical precision. That's how he finally died. Exsanguination—he was allowed to bleed out. The killer fixed the cloth mesh to prevent the rest of the organs from falling out, so he could hang the torso by the head to drain the rest of the blood. He did that carefully, but there is a slight abrasion on the victim's neck."

"Any clues to his identity?" Wolski asked.

"He was uncircumcised, so we can rule out Jewish or Muslim, and since a higher percentage of American males tend to be circumcised, the odds are he was European. He was at least middle class, from the dental work. Plus he had an appendectomy. He wasn't a laborer, by the condition of his hands, though he has some pronounced arthritis in his lower back and hips. Also, he does show the onset of malnutrition."

Mason cursed under his breath.

"That's good, isn't it?" Wolski said. "That he's not American?

I for one am glad this crazy son of a bitch isn't hunting Americans."

Mason shook his head. "It also means that Colonel Walton is going to put this case on the low-priority pile." He turned to Treborn. "So, with the malnutrition he's probably a middle- or upper-class German who wasn't a combat soldier or laborer."

"Or a displaced person or ex-concentration camp inmate, though then he would have shown signs of long-term malnutrition or abuse. And you can't rule out other Europeans. There were plenty of experts in various fields brought in from Nazi-occupied France, Holland, Belgium, Sweden...."

"We can dangle that idea in front of the colonel to keep him from burying this case," Wolski said.

"Regarding your suspect," Treborn said, "I can tell you that he knows human anatomy and surgical and autopsy techniques. He is not your man off the street. You might be looking at a doctor, nurse—anyone with specific medical expertise. I'll write up a full report and send it to Colonel Walton tomorrow. I sent samples to the toxicology lab in Frankfurt, but I doubt there will be anything relevant to your investigation."

"If there ever is an investigation," Mason said.

"I hope there is. You need to find this killer before he does something like this again."

7

M ason turned heads when he and Wolski entered the squad room, the amused looks following him as he crossed the room. Mason figured he must have firmly planted his feet into some kind of horse manure, but damned if he could figure out what.

Wolski apparently noticed it too. "Maybe you should check your fly."

Mason nodded toward Colonel Walton, who madly waved for Mason to come to his office. "Looks like I'm about to find out." He passed through the outer office, where Walton's secretary shook his head like a disappointed parent. Mason ignored the man as he knocked on Colonel Walton's open door and entered. "You wanted to see me, sir?"

Colonel Walton retreated behind his desk and thrust the newspaper in Mason's direction. "That doe-eyed look of yours means you haven't seen today's *Stars and Stripes*."

Mason took the paper and looked at the special guest column Colonel Walton had featured in the top fold. A knot formed in his stomach when he saw a photograph of himself during the riot, standing on the Jeep and firing the machine gun. In bold typeface it declared, "CID Investigator Demonstrates New Method of U.S. Occupational Diplomacy." The byline read, "Laura McKinnon, Special Reporter," with a thumbnail sketch of her smiling face.

Anger and embarrassment both fueled the flush in Mason's cheeks. "Colonel, the riot was getting out of control—"

Colonel Walton held up his hand for Mason to stop. "I've talked to the MPs handling the riot. General Jenkins, the Provost Marshal, wanted to bust you down to private. I had to eat crow and defend you because I need you. But you do something like this again, and I won't lift a finger to help you. Do you understand?" When Mason nodded, he turned his attention to the folders in Mason's hand. "That the ME's report on the slasher case?"

Mason handed the files to the colonel. "Major Treborn's formal report will be here tomorrow. Those are copies of the autopsy photos, dental prints, X-rays, and my notes."

The colonel leafed through the files. He winced at the autopsy photos. "Sweet Jesus." He looked up at Mason. "Tell me what you found."

Mason told him about the ME's estimate of the time of death before being hung on the column, the victim being strung up to be bled out, probably after hours of excruciating torture. The colonel fell back in his chair with a look of repulsion when Mason told him the ME's opinion that the killer had made autopsy-style incisions and dissected the victim while he was still alive. "The surgical methods and the dismemberment show the killer has medical expertise. I'm still convinced this was a ritual performed by a psychopath. This is not going to be his only killing."

"Yeah, you've said that already. Any luck on the victim's identity?"

Mason had known that question was coming, and he hesitated

while trying to formulate an answer. "Statistically, the man is likely to be European, but we can't definitively rule out that he was American."

"Statistically?"

"A combination of factors. The fact that he was uncircumcised. Signs of malnutrition…"

"I don't know of one U.S. soldier in this entire occupational zone who could claim starvation. The victim has to be German."

"Or a DP or former concentration camp inmate. Major Treborn also pointed out that there were a lot of foreign national experts the Nazis brought in from their occupied territories, so the victim could have been one of our allies. Sir, I request we pursue this case with urgency. We have to do anything we can to stop this killer from doing this to anyone else."

"My order stands. The army works like a big-city police department: quantity not quality. Keep this case in the fire but continue with your other ones."

Mason hesitated. He knew what was coming but he had to ask. "Sir, I also request permission to access the army's Medical Corps personnel files—"

"You what?"

"Major Treborn confirms that in all likelihood the killer has medical expertise. And the fact that the killer can mover around after dark, transporting a dismembered corpse without being noticed, points to someone with permits or in uniform."

"For me to grant access to confidential personnel records, you're going to have to come up with something better than that. What about a German physician or a DP with medical training?"

"We'll pursue those avenues with Inspector Becker's help. But we can't rule out U.S. personnel."

"If you come up with evidence, anything that would convince me and the Provost Marshall's Office, then there'll be no question. But for now, you're shooting in the dark here. No. Permission denied. Get to work on those other cases. I want to see progress on that train robbery. Now, get out of here."

MASON LEFT HEADQUARTERS FEELING EXASPERATED AND DRAINED. He'd spent the afternoon and early evening reviewing the train robbery case, including conducting more pointless interviews. It was all an exercise in futility, but the colonel kept looking over his shoulder or making surprise visits to the interview room. And all the while, Mason couldn't get the slasher murder out of his mind: the victim's unbearable suffering, the horrors of the autopsy, and the vexing lack of leads.

Before heading home, he needed to do something worthwhile, some little gesture of comfort. He went by the PX and caught the staff just as they were closing. With a little persuasion they allowed him to buy a bundle of chocolate bars and some cans of ham, peas, and fruit cocktail.

Fifteen minutes later he stood across the street from the hole in the destroyed building where he'd seen the orphans flee after being chased away by the hotel MP. The two boys he'd seen gathering cigarette butts sat just outside the hole. When Mason crossed the street they scurried inside. He heard whispered voices and scuffling of feet in the darkness beyond the hole. He placed the box containing the chocolate and food on the ground just far enough away from the opening that at least one of the children would have to come out.

"I'm not here to hurt you," Mason said in German. "I have food."

No response, no sound of movement from within.

"Is no one hungry?" He waited a moment. "Okay, then I'll

have to throw it away." The older of the two boys who had been sitting outside the hole peeked out. Mason backed away a few steps. "There's chocolate, ham, peas, and fruit."

The boy looked to be around twelve, with a dirty face and dressed in an adult-sized overcoat. He made one tentative step onto the sidewalk. A few murmured voices behind urged him on. He approached the box, keeping his eyes fixed on Mason.

Mason squatted. The sudden movement startled the boy. "What's your name?"

"Kurt."

"My name is Mason. Are you the oldest?"

"The oldest boy."

Some of the other children vied for space at the hole to peek out. Kurt pointed to his younger cigarette-collecting companion. "That's Dieter." He then pointed to a freckle-faced girl of around six. "And that's Ilsa." The introduction seemed to give Ilsa the courage to jump out of the hole and peer into the box. She grabbed a chocolate bar and dashed back inside.

"Everyone has to share, okay?" Mason said. He tossed Kurt a can opener. "Be sure the little ones get enough to eat."

Kurt nodded, and Mason backed away. Once he'd walked far enough down the street, he heard shuffling and excited voices. He looked back and saw fifteen or more children attacking the contents of the box. Kurt was trying to dole out the food equitably, but the children were too hungry to listen. He looked at Mason, clearly afraid that Mason would be angry if he failed to maintain order. Mason waved and Kurt waved back.

As he walked away, pulling his coat tight against the cold, he silently wished them well and vowed to try to do more. He had relieved their hunger for a few days, but the worst of winter was yet to come. How many would survive?

It was a humbling feeling for Mason to consider that no

matter how many lives he could save from the hands of a crazed killer, it paled in comparison to those facing death at the hands of a cruel winter.

8

"Queen takes rook," Mason said.

Another eruption of cheers and groans. Mason could tell by the chants of the GIs surrounding their table that his opponent, a major in the Third Army's Signal Corps, was downing another shot of whiskey.

Lose a chess piece, down a shot.

Mason heard his opponent slam the empty shot glass down on the table then slap the timer.

"Knight to queen's knight five," someone said for Mason's benefit. The actual chessboard was invisible to Mason. He wore a blindfold, though the major did not. But he had a perfectly clear image of the board and the positions of the pieces in his mind, as if he could have reached out and touched them.

Despite all the grief his grandfather visited upon Mason as a child, he had taught Mason the skill and art of chess—even if it involved cracking Mason's fingers with a ruler if he made a bad move. And as Mason improved, his grandfather had forced him to play blindfolded. It had served Mason well. He became so good over the years that by the time he reached his senior year in high school he had turned his skills into a small money-making enterprise, becoming a sort of pool shark for chess. He could triple-down the bets by donning a blindfold and challenging his unwitting opponent to one more game.

Mason figured his exceptional memory, particularly conjuring up images in sharp detail, had come about from being forced, time and again, to track the state of the chessboard in his mind or suffer pain inflicted by his grandfather. Like exercising some normally neglected muscle, the process had developed a part of his brain so that he could bring up certain images in crystal clarity. But normally, unlike with chess, he had limited control over which images stuck; usually they were confined to ones with strong emotional ties. He could instantly recall his grandmother's face: As if looking at a photograph, he could describe the angle of her lips when she smiled or frowned, and give an exact count of her wrinkles and blemishes. Or recall his ex-wife in that first week of bliss before their love had turned sour: the contour of her breasts and the intricate folds in her opal irises. But the ability had its downside. He could conjure a precise image of the mangled body of his murdered partner or, like a movie projected on his eyelids, the horrifying weeks he'd spent behind the gates of Buchenwald. Any detective would wish for this skill, but Mason's never manifested without the accompanying emotional bonds of love or horror.

The timer ticked down the seconds....

"Knight to king's bishop six," Mason said and slapped the timer.

The crowd murmured and exchanged bets.

"Bishop captures knight," the major said.

Another roar. Mason felt for a shot glass lined up next to him and downed the whiskey. Mason had already lost eight pieces and consumed an equal number of shots. The major played well, but perhaps not well enough. "Queen captures bishop," Mason said. "Checkmate."

With a final roar from the crowd, Mason removed his blindfold. Money exchanged hands. The pile of dollar bills grew next to Mason, but he hardly noticed. Among the GIs, and just behind the hapless major, stood the brunette reporter, Laura, her blue eyes fixed on him. A flush of warmth coursed through his chest even while he gave her a disapproving glare.

The crowd broke into small groups, heading for the poker tables or the bar. Mason began to collect his dollars, while the winning GIs shook his hand or slapped him on the back. A shadow fell onto the stack of money, then the scent of honey and lavender arrived a moment later.

"That's quite a trick," Laura said.

"It's not magic," Mason said without looking up. "Just skill and a lot of practice."

Laura took the chair next to him and sat.

"I don't have anything to say to you," Mason said.

"That's right; you're afraid of me."

"Like Will Rogers used to say: 'Never miss a good chance to shut up.'"

"You're just full of folksy wisdom," Laura said and drank one of the untouched shots of whiskey. "Didn't you like my article?"

"It nearly got me busted down to private."

"Did you read the whole thing?"

"The headline was enough."

"Well, if you'd read it, you'd know I ultimately defended your actions. If you hadn't done what you did a lot more people would have gotten hurt. And just so you know, the picture and the headline were my editor's idea."

"If you say so."

Laura leaned on her elbows. "I came over to apologize. The article shouldn't have come out that way. I never figured *Stars and Stripes* would do that to a soldier who was just trying to do his duty, but my editor saw an opportunity to make a splash.

He's looking to get onto a private newspaper as soon as he can."

Mason stuffed his earnings into his pocket. "All right. Apology accepted."

Those eyes captured him again, and he and she looked at each other without a word for a moment.

Finally, Laura said, "A girl sits down at your table, and you don't offer to buy her a drink?"

Mason waved for the waiter, a German man, to come over. Laura's eyes never left him as she ordered a gin fizz. When the waiter left, Mason asked, "What are you really here for?"

"I can't come over to a handsome man and say hi?"

"Normally I'd be all right with that, but somehow I get the feeling you're the spider and I'm the fly."

Laura smiled, acknowledging his point. "I'll level with you: I'm writing an extended piece about the American occupation, mostly the personal side. I'll leave politics and policy to others. I'm more interested in the single soldier and citizen. The military cop and the black marketers. I've already made a contact in the black market, but you're my first cop. When I saw you at the riot I got curious about you, so I did a little digging around. I know some of the staff at CID headquarters in Frankfurt pretty well…" She shrugged. "General Jenkins, for instance."

"How well?" Mason was surprised at his sudden spark of jealousy.

"That's not the point. What I'm getting at is that your story interests me—"

"No way. You're not going to write about me."

"I'm not writing your biography. There will be a lot of different people all folded into a long narrative. Come on, just a few questions. I'll keep it anonymous."

Mason didn't know if the attraction was mutual or if she was playing him for a sucker. Maybe it was the whiskey, but he decided to hang around and find out. "I tell you what: You ask a few questions, then it's my turn. Tit for tat."

Laura smiled. "No questions below the belt."

"Deal."

The waiter returned with the drink, and Laura started playing with her cocktail swizzle stick. Her eyes flitted between her drink and Mason as if she were deciding which questions to start off with first. "I heard you had a pretty tough time as a prisoner of war. You could have shipped home, but you decided to stay in the army and Germany. Why?"

"I hear the real estate's cheap."

"Seriously. After what you've been through, you have to admit: It's an intriguing choice."

Mason studied her for a moment. "I'd bet the bank that you did more during the war than write human interest stories about WACs and nurses."

"Wait a minute. We had a deal. You haven't answered my question."

"I'll get to it. Bear with me for a minute."

"Yes, I covered more than WACs and nurses. But usually when I talk about it to a guy I'd like to get to know a little better, it intimidates him. His eyes start searching for the closest exit."

"I'm not most men."

"I'll be the judge of that." She took a sip of her drink, and Mason wondered if it was to fortify herself before bringing back the memories. "I covered the 93rd Bomb Group flying missions out of England. I rode in a bombing raid over Germany. Flak exploding all around; German fighter planes shooting holes in the fuselage. It was terrifying. I was with the 12th Army Group fighting around the Falaise Pocket. The Eighth Infantry Division in the Hürtgen Forest. I went into Dachau a week after it was liberated. I saw... terrible things."

"And you're still here, aren't you?" Mason said. "Just like me."

"There are a thousand postwar stories to tell. I wouldn't be much of a reporter if I didn't want to tell at least some of them, and what better place to find them in than war-torn Germany?"

"I rest my case. They try to beat you down, you get back up again. I'm a detective. I've always wanted to be a detective. That's why I joined the Chicago PD. That's why I took this job. What difference does it make whether I'm a cop here or there? What difference does it make if I'm CPD or CID? And why not in a place that needs it more?"

Laura sipped her drink then shrugged again. Mason was learning her "tells"—her shrugs and sudden interest in the table were signs she was about to say something he wouldn't necessarily want to hear.

"I heard about Chicago," Laura said.

"That was below the belt."

"Don't clam up now. We're finally getting somewhere. I don't know you, but I can read people pretty well. You look relaxed but you're all tight inside like you're going to burst the seams of that perfectly ironed uniform. Soft eyes but a proud jaw. I'd bet the bank that you were given a raw deal."

"If you've heard about it, then there's no reason to repeat it."

"I haven't heard it all." She shrugged again. "I know you were sacked."

That hit a raw nerve, and Mason blurted out, "I was framed because I went to the chief with evidence of drug dealing by fellow police officers."

"And now no big-city police department would hire you, but why not be a small-town detective or county sheriff? You'd still be doing what you like."

"I wouldn't be happy handing out parking citations or busting up domestic disputes. Plus, I don't see myself in a little house with a picket fence on a suburban street, waving good-bye to the wife, and little Bobby and Suzy, as I get in my Packard with my badge and gun and pretend I'm doing some good...." He stopped himself from going any further.

She studied him for a moment. "Behind your noble cause lies something else." She squinted her eyes as if peering into Mason's mind. "I would guess you probably come from a broken home, hence your disdain for picket fences and normal families. And the very institution you swore loyalty to turned out to be corrupt and betrayed you. Now you compensate for it by trying to fix everything broken in the world. Superman disguised as a humble cop who will single-handedly bring criminals to their knees and save the world from pain and suffering. A hero with a chip on his shoulder."

"Ouch," Mason said and rubbed his jaw as if someone had just given him a right hook.

Laura was about to speak, but Mason held up his hand. "Uh-uh-uh. Now it's my turn."

"Shoot. If you dare."

"What I'm wondering is why you chose to put your life on the line just to write articles for newspapers."

"Oh, here we go. You think that kind of work should be exclusive to men?"

"I believe a woman can do whatever she puts her mind to. It's just I suspect that behind your noble cause lies something as well." Mason imitated Laura's mind-reading squint. "My guess, you come from a privileged family, wealthy and then some, with overachieving parents who constantly pushed you to become who they thought you should be. Maybe a doctor or a lawyer, or just married to a New England aristocrat. By your accent, I'd say Boston?"

"Providence."

"And going on dangerous assignments has been your way of

thumbing your nose at your parents, while at the same time you push yourself to the extreme to prove to them that you can achieve great things, even if it means getting killed or injured in the process."

"I'm proud of what I do. And I think telling the world about the sacrifices of our soldiers is a good thing."

"I think it's great, too."

Laura's scowl unfurled into a look of surprise. "Excuse me?"

"Not many people would have the courage to put themselves in the line of fire when they didn't have to, man or woman. And I bet you've had to put up with a million men who wanted to get into your panties rather than give you a story, or who refused to let you tag along because they saw you as weak and vulnerable. That takes guts and determination. But what you're playing is a rich-girl's game: satisfying that rebellious streak only the privileged get to indulge in. You mingle with the lowly GI and get him to talk using your college-educated wit and debutante charm. But when it comes to really spending some quality time with a soldier, you can't climb down the social ladder lower than a general—"

"Now wait a minute."

"Don't get me wrong. I find you very attractive, but you're too rich for my blood, and I'm too lowborn for you."

"You don't know anything about what I like or don't." Laura gathered her things and stood.

"You're not going to ask me any more questions?"

"Yes, when hell freezes over." Laura turned and walked out the door.

9

F rau Eva Hieber shuffled through the slush on Karlsplatz. The damp cold had crept through her wool overcoat hours before. Last winter, she had her ermine fur coat to keep her warm, the one that Friedrich, her husband, had bought for her in 1938. But she had exchanged that, along with her grandmother's set of china dinnerware, the antique grandfather clock, and much of her jewelry, on the black market for food and clothing for her nine-year-old son and eleven-year-old daughter.

She had no deep attachment to those things, not like her wedding ring or the very last gift Friedrich had given her for her birthday, the upright piano. Those things she refused to sell. She and Friedrich would play duets together on many nights before the war, before Friedrich was killed in Italy.

Most of the food she'd bartered for a few weeks earlier was already gone. She tried hard to ration the amounts and had relinquished her share for the children. The worst of winter was yet to come, and she knew she would eventually have to give up the piano.

Today was the second time she'd walked all over the city posting notices and scanning through the untold thousands of others. Trees, lampposts, and boards erected in the large intersections and community centers were covered with little squares of paper, some with photos: "The Frieder family of Goethestrasse is searching for Lily Frieder—16 years old." "Manfried Jung, if you read this, please come to 22 Denissstrasse. Your wife, Margo." "Ilse and Werner are looking for their mother, Frieda Hoffmann. We live on 16 Briennerstrasse. Please help us."

Eva shook her head at all the sad messages. She hoped her brother-in-law had left one for her. He'd been missing for five days. On a community board next to Karlstor she unpinned a message rendered unreadable from time and weather and stuck up her own in its place.

She barely had the pin sunk into the board when she saw it. On a board on the opposite side of the street was a large black-and-white notice with a sketch of a man. Even from that distance, she could tell it was her brother-in-law. Even though the sketch showed a man who was completely bald, she could never mistake the face.

Dread made her legs leaden as she approached the notice. It looked official, which always meant bad news. Halfway across the street she could read the block letters: IF YOU KNOW THIS MAN PLEASE CONTACT OBERINSPEKTOR BECKER AT POLIZEIPRASIDIUM, 2-4 ETTSTRASSE."

She started to cry, the warm tears burning her icy cheeks. She couldn't catch her breath. Her legs buckled, and she fell to her knees.

Oh, Richard. Please, not Richard.

He had been the only stabilizing person in her war-torn existence, and the last remaining member of her husband's family.

People gathered around her, inquiring if she was all right. She didn't hear them. She simply didn't know how she could go on.

∾

Mason sat at his desk, rubbing his forehead while listening to the other end of the phone line. Wolski entered with his coffee cup and leaned against the file cabinet.

"What was that, sir?" Mason said. He looked up at Wolski and rolled his eyes. "Could you spell that for me? V-i-t-r-u-v-i-a-n. Da Vinci and Cosmology." He finished noting the conversation. "Right. Thank you, sir." He hung up the phone.

"What was that all about?" Wolski asked.

"I've been getting a bunch of calls about the sketch we sent out showing the killer's arrangement of the victim's limbs. That was a major over at OMGB, a professor of art history and philosophy. He said the arrangement is a copy of a Da Vinci drawing"— Mason checked his notes—"the Vitruvian Man. And some nonsense about cosmology and man's body proportions in relation to the universe."

OMGB stood for Office of Military Government for Bavaria.

"Now there's a stretch. You hear back from the division chaplain's office?"

"He said the limbs and stakes symbolize…" Mason had to look at his notes again. "Chi-Rho, a Christian cross from Roman times made with the first two letters, X and P—our *ch* and *r*—, of the Greek word for Christ."

"That makes a little more sense."

"Wait, I'm not done yet. I also received calls saying it's an ancient Egyptian symbol, a Celtic Taranis wheel, and a Buddhist dharma wheel."

The phone rang, and Mason said, "This'll probably be the Chinese interpretation." He answered the phone, listened a few moments, then hung up. "Better finish your coffee. We're going out. Becker's got something for us." He stood and walked over to the coat rack and put on his overcoat. "What did you dig up?"

"Have you been to the CID records room? It's cold, damp,

and dark. And whoever set up the system should go back to filing school."

"Why do you think I sent you?"

"I've gone through most of the arrest records involving U.S. and Allied doctors and medical staff, but most of them only go back to June of this year. Everything else is at the main records archives in Frankfurt."

"Anything promising?"

"Not much. There's a major accused of bondage murders of prostitutes, but his file has been sealed—at least to someone of my pay grade. The story is he managed to elude arrest and is rumored to be back in the States. A couple of other homicides, but nothing that comes close to our killer's methods. I couldn't get anywhere near Medical Corps personnel files."

"I'm working on that one."

Mason and Wolski walked out of his office and headed for the stairs.

Colonel Walton leaned out of his office door and called after them, "I assume you're following up on a lead about that train robbery."

Mason turned to face Colonel Walton as he walked. "Yes, sir."

Colonel Walton eyed him with skepticism, but Mason quickened his pace and shot down the stairs before Walton could ask any more questions.

OBERINSPEKTOR BECKER WAITED FOR MASON AND WOLSKI BY AN open manhole in the middle of a wide plaza bisecting Ludwigstrasse. A phalanx of German policemen surrounded Becker and the manhole, while another squad of German police had spread out to the nearby buildings to canvass the occupants or to control the gathering crowd of onlookers.

Wolski parked the Jeep under the shadow of the ragged remains of the Siegestor, Munich's version of the Arc de Triomphe. Mason had been around small groups of German police, but this was his first experience with so many gathered in one place. He couldn't help a feeling of unease. The green police uniforms were mostly cannibalized Wehrmacht uniforms, and seeing these men barking orders or standing at attention in perfect lines in the plaza made the hairs on the back of his neck stand up.

"Gives me the creeps walking around a place with so many Germans in uniform," Wolski said.

"You read my mind," Mason said.

The feeling dissipated, however, when several of the policemen nodded respectfully, and Becker smiled as they shook hands.

"What have you got?" Mason asked.

"I'll let you see for yourself."

"In the sewers?" Wolski said.

Becker began to climb down the metal ladder. "We don't have to go too far."

"Ah, the glamour of police work," Mason said.

"My uncle had a pig farm. Nothing could smell worse than that," Wolski said.

They followed Becker down the ladder and met him in a man-sized tunnel of timeworn brick. Mason detected a pungent-sweet odor just below the sulfurous miasma of sewage. A small stream of brackish water trickled along the bottom of the tunnel.

"This way," Becker said.

Mason and Wolski turned on their flashlights and followed Becker.

"There has been another development in the last hour aside from what you are about to see," Becker said. "A woman by the name of Frau Hieber came into our precinct this morning and said she recognized the victim from the sketch we posted throughout the city. She identified him as Richard Hieber, her brother-in-law. She said he has been missing for five days. He was a doctor with a small private practice. He also worked at a clinic on Rhein-strasse. I telephoned the clinic. Several nurses confirmed that he hasn't been seen at the clinic since Monday."

"A doctor killing a doctor," Wolski said.

"There could be any number of reasons why the killer chose him," Mason said, "but it's something to keep in mind. Did Frau Hieber know of any rivalries with another doctor, or him receiving threats of any kind?"

"Both Frau Hieber and the clinic staff said he was a kind man. Everyone respected and had great affection for him. He had no enemies that anyone knew of, and he was rather reserved, spending most of his time at the clinic or helping his sister-in-law with her children. He studied at Berlin University. He was a surgeon in the Luftwaffe with a rank of major, serving mostly on the eastern front. We are trying to obtain his records, but we have to request Luftwaffe records through the American army. The amount of red tape...."

"We'll take care of that," Mason said. "What about a wife or immediate family?"

"His parents died before the war. His wife and daughters were killed in the Battle of Berlin."

.   A moment of awkward silence passed between them—the tragedy of it all, the loss of so many families.

"I have Frau Hieber's address," Becker said. "She has consented to another interview if you have additional questions."

Mason shook his head. "Sounds like you covered everything."

"She drew out his usual path to the clinic and listed the places he visited on a regular basis. I'll give you everything once we're done here."

"Good. I'd like to talk to the clinic staff."

"Of course."

The tunnel ended, and the three detectives climbed down a short ladder that descended into a large square chamber of concrete and brick. Two sets of stairs led to platforms at various levels. Pipes and electrical conduits covered much of the ceiling and snaked into smaller tunnels. Twelve feet below, dark water rushed through an open trench. A group of German police stood in the corner of a platform, while others searched the area with their flashlights.

Mason identified the odor he'd detected in the tunnel: the unmistakable stench of putrefaction.

"This is a maintenance area accessing several sewer branches," Becker said over the sound of the rushing water. "A couple of workmen made the discovery this morning. The last time anyone came down here was a month ago."

Mason and Wolski followed Becker to the corner where the policemen were gathered. There, next to an intricate metal grid, lay a limbless corpse. The skin had turned greenish-yellow and black. Much of the torso had gouges or chunks missing. The eyes and nose were gone. The mouth gaped wide.

Mason felt his stomach contract. Wolski turned away for a moment. Mason tapped him on the shoulder and eyed the ladder behind them, but Wolski indicated that he was okay.

"Unfortunately, the rats have feasted on the corpse for some time now," Becker said.

"Looks like the body's been there two or three weeks," Mason said.

Becker nodded. "You see the Y incision is the same."

"He cut open the rib cage but didn't distend it like in the other victim. Since the organs are in pretty bad shape, we'll have to wait for an autopsy to see if he removed any of them."

Wolski took a step back, suppressing a gag.

"I need you to contact headquarters and the ME's office. Get them down here right away."

Wolski gave Mason a weak but grateful smile and left.

"What about the arms and legs?" Mason asked.

Becker led him to an upper platform on the other side of the chamber. Two legs and an arm lay on the platform in a haphazard fashion. Rats had consumed much of the flesh and muscle.

"If the killer arranged them in a similar pattern, we'll never know," Becker said.

"Did he leave a note?"

Becker shook his head. "And, fortunately for the sewer workers, neither did he engineer a booby trap."

"His method is cruder, and he didn't display the corpse like before. But it's him. It looks like he's refining his techniques. The torture and butchering aren't enough. He wants his killings to be a spectacle."

Becker turned to look at Mason. "Then what are we to expect from his next one?"

10

His excitement filled him with a surge of energy and strength, the cold having no effect whatsoever. He fought to maintain a somber appearance, emulating those around him, their heads held low by the burdens of subjugation. It had been his punishment to wander among the masses of oppressed and oppressors, among the ruins, amid the suffering, step past the rubble still hiding the dead, tramp upon the ashes of the incinerated.

Today was the day, and he was ready, the sap in his left coat pocket and the bottle of his mixture of diethyl ether and chloroform in his right.

He kept pace with the Chosen One, ten meters behind, with his hat pulled down on his lowered head. His left hand clutched his coat tightly under his chin, with the collar high across his cheeks and mouth, as if protecting himself from the wind and blowing snow. But he was not cold. An electrical heat radiated deep inside, and his groin was engorged with hot blood.

Dusk still illuminated the sky. The place where he would strike lay another kilometer away. He knew the path the Chosen

One traveled at this hour of the day, and in ten minutes he would quicken his pace. She would stay on Schlellingstrasse, a large street cutting across the Maxvorstadt district, then turn on a narrow street of ruined buildings.

The crowds of pedestrians grew thicker as they approached an intersection. Women carried children bundled in their arms. An elderly man pushed a cart with sacks of weeds to make a thin soup. A group of ex-Wehrmacht soldiers huddled around a barrel fire.

U.S. Army Jeeps and olive drab sedans roared by. On the corner, American MPs randomly checked identity papers. German police stood alongside them or patrolled the streets in pairs. The voices placed many obstacles before him, trying to prevent him from attaining his salvation. But he had spent months learning Munich's damaged landscape. He had memorized every street, the areas where he could trap his prey, the routes for taking the bodies back to the place of sacrifice. And now he knew the places where he would make altars of the sacrificed for beatification, each one would be more glorious than the last, pleasing the dark spirits that held him on this odious sphere. It must work. He longed for an ending to it all, an ultimate sacrifice that would culminate in his resurrection.

This time *They* had led him to a Chosen One in female form, frail but tall, with a broad nose and eyes black as soot that matched her full, wavy hair. But most of all, *They* had sent him One with one leg slightly shorter than the other. He judged that the defect had not been present at birth but rather had resulted from a fracture, an injury that had shattered bone and, once healed, left her to limp the rest of her life. He knew well the type of injury; he knew the source. After all, he was a doctor. He had treated enough shattered and abused bones to know. Her face and her limp—how perfect. How magnificent for him to discover One so like those he had sinned upon in the past.

She left her companions on the final segment of her journey home, turning onto this forgotten street. It was supposed to take her home the quickest way. He knew she shared the apartment with two other women, only two blocks from the end of this narrow and dark street, a mere hundred meters of burned and crumbling structures. He imagined her being warned not to use this street. A warning unheeded—another sign she had been chosen for him.

The woman glanced behind as she entered the street, but he had already slipped into a shell of a building where he had previously cut a path through the ruins. He moved quickly, knowing he had only a few seconds to reach the spot. She always quickened her pace as she walked along the broken buildings. He knew the path by heart and moved in almost total darkness. At one moment he got a quick glimpse of her as she passed a hole in a building's outer wall. Fifteen meters to the doorless entrance. There the street took a sharp angle.

At last, he slipped out onto the street and waited behind a recess in the wall. A pile of rubble shielded him from view by anyone arriving from the opposite direction. If his timing were precise, no one would see. The woman would simply vanish.

Four seconds later, she passed him. He allowed her to take two more steps. With silent motion, he swept his right hand from his left coat pocket. He knew exactly where to strike with the sap. She barely had time to react to the noise, the zip of fabric on fabric, before the elongated sack full of ball bearings struck her at the base of the skull. A faint cry of pain escaped her lips before she fell dazed to the cobblestones.

He had to be quick. He lifted her by her armpits before she completely settled on the ground. It took only five seconds to drag her back into the depths of the ruined building, then another five to pour the chloroform-ether mixture and smother her face with the soaked cloth. Just the right amount would put her in a deep sleep. He needed her quiet for two hours.

After that, it wouldn't matter how much she screamed.

11

M ason stood on the sidewalk and flicked his still-burning cigarette into the street. He watched it take flight in a high arc, the red crown glowing bright against the night sky. Thursday evening and still no progress on the slasher case. He and Wolski had spent the morning canvassing in a wider circle around the factory then hitting a brick wall trying to gain access to U.S. medical corps personnel files. The rest of the day, they had to spin their wheels tracking down dead leads on the train robbery case—per Colonel Walton's orders. A couple, laughing, arm in arm, already a few hours into the drinking part of the evening, staggered past him and entered the officers' club. The warm light, the odor of food, and the sounds of Benny Olsen's Big Band came out onto the street for a moment, contrasting with the scene of ruins all around. The door closed, and Mason was in the calm darkness again. He looked to his right and across the street at the dark opening of the orphans' shelter, the hole in the wall where he had left food two nights before. Kurt sat just outside the hole. Mason waved and Kurt waved back.

Mason was about to cross over when he heard an army sedan's horn honk as it rushed up to the club. The car skidded to a halt directly across the street. Wolski jumped out of the driver's seat, ran around the front of the car, and opened the passenger's door. He then bowed like a chauffeur. A young woman emerged and took his arm. Wolski beamed as he led the woman toward the club's entrance. That made Mason smile; Wolski was smitten.

They met Mason at the top of the stairs. Wolski introduced his girlfriend, Anna. Anna smiled sweetly. No more than nineteen, she had a soft, round face. Not beautiful but pretty, the kind of *Mädchen* face *Life* magazine would put on its cover to portray the rosy-cheeked future of Germany. After all she must have been through, all the horrors of a dictatorship and war, she'd managed to hold on to her aura of youth and innocent charm.

"Didn't you bring a date?" Wolski asked.

"I'm fresh out," Mason said.

"I can't believe you came to a dance without a girl. A couple of packs of cigarettes will get you a willing fräulein."

Anna playfully slapped Wolski on the shoulder, though Mason could tell she was embarrassed by the remark.

"I don't believe in buying a young lady with cigarettes," Mason said.

"Maybe the girl of your dreams is waiting inside."

"Let's go in and find out."

They all entered the club. Light, warmth, and the band playing "Drum Boogie" greeted them. The officers' club had taken over what had been a German dance club. It was of open design with several descending levels leading down to the large dance floor full of uniformed men and ladies in gowns, then a stage accommodating the thirty-piece band. Many of the high-ranking officers and military government officials had brought their families over for the holidays. And because the club was hosting a pre-Christmas bash, anyone above the rank of master sergeant had been invited. The place was packed. The couples on the dance floor looked like a school of sardines trapped in a fishing net, hopping to the beat, shoulder to shoulder, back to back.

Then, like a glint off that roiling sea, Laura McKinnon caught Mason's eye. The reporter and her partner danced near the center of the crowd. She had exchanged her green uniform for a black lace-back, floor-length evening gown and looked stunning. Then he noticed that she was struggling to keep her dance partner, a gray-haired colonel, at arm's length, but either he or the crowd kept pushing them together.

"Go ahead and get a table," Mason said to Wolski. He descended the three shallow steps, penetrated the wall of dancers, and excuse-me'd his way toward the center. As he got closer, he could see Laura getting more agitated by the colonel's aggressive hands. Her face lit up when she saw him breaking through the final layer of dancers.

Mason positioned himself behind the colonel and tapped on the man's shoulder. "Mind if I cut in?"

"Beat it, mac," the colonel said with an icy glare.

"Sir, I would appreciate if you could be a gentleman and allow me to cut in."

"She's with me, so go take a hike."

"I was trying to avoid this...." Mason pulled out his CID badge and held it up for the colonel. "Colonel, this lady is under investigation. I suggest you step away before I'm forced to charge you with impeding an officer of the law."

The colonel released Laura like she'd given him an electrical shock. He glanced at them both with a skeptical eye then retreated into the crowd. Mason turned to a surprised Laura, took her hand and waist, and began to dance.

"Thanks, but I can take care of myself," Laura said.

"I'm sure you can."

"Then why the Tarzan routine?"

"I wanted to apologize for the other night. I went too far, and I'm sorry."

Laura smiled. "You hit pretty close to the bone."

"You did, too."

"I have half a mind to walk away."

"What's the other half say?"

"To put up with you long enough to get your story. That, and the murder at the factory."

"How did you know about... Oh, that's right, your general boyfriend, Jenkins. Where is he? Won't he be jealous of us dancing?"

"He had other obligations."

"His wife is in town?"

"Don't be nasty. What about your date? Won't she be jealous?"

"I didn't come with one."

"I guess I'm not surprised. Big in muscle, low on charm."

Mason chuckled. The music stopped and everyone applauded. The bandleader announced that they would be taking a short break. Laura pointed toward the top of the steps. "That guy is smiling at you like a proud father."

Mason saw Wolski standing near a group of tables with his arms crossed and a big grin. "That's my partner."

"Are you going to introduce us?"

Mason offered his arm and Laura took it. He led Laura up to Wolski and introduced them.

"A reporter?" Wolski said. "Isn't that like fraternizing with the enemy?"

"Not you, too," Laura said.

"Ah, I was only kidding."

"I think she got that," Mason said. "Your smile's so big we can see your tonsils."

"Come over and join us," Wolski said and nudged Mason to say something.

"Yeah, join us," Mason said and thrust his thumb Wolski's way. "This guy's a pushover. Put on a little charm and he'll tell you anything."

"In that case, lead the way," Laura said

They had to squeeze past tables full of raucous diners, and after helping Laura to her chair it took some acrobatics for Mason to get seated.

Once Wolski settled in, he studied Laura for a moment, then snapped his fingers. "I didn't recognize you out of your reporter's outfit. You were at that riot. I got a big kick out of that article about our chief." He laughed then stopped abruptly when he saw the expression on Mason's face.

The waiter came by with the menus, and they ordered cocktails. Anna nearly bounced in her seat when a waiter passed with a tray full of food. She opened the menu and grinned like a kid in a candy store.

"Anna, are you getting enough to eat?" Laura asked.

"Thanks to Vincent." Anna smiled at Wolski. "The American authorities issued my mother and me the number five ration card. Only fifteen hundred calories per day. The other Germans call the five card the 'death card' because one cannot live long on only that much food. And people usually can't even get that much."

"I hope that's not the only reason she hangs out with me," Wolski said.

"No!" Anna said. "I like you very much, but sometimes I don't understand you."

"So, Laura," Wolski said, leaning into the table, "I've never met a woman war correspondent before."

"There are more of us than you think. You name a theater of the war, and there was a woman correspondent covering it."

"How did you get in that line of work?"

"I thought *I* was supposed to ask the questions," Laura said. She looked from face to attentive face. "Okay, fine.... I was doing fashion photography in Paris when Germany invaded France. I had a French boyfriend at the time. Actually, we were engaged to be married. He was killed at Dunkirk. I guess instead of falling apart, I decided to cover the German advance and their march into Paris. I managed to get out in the nick of time and make my way to London. Then I got assignments covering the London Blitz, and it took off from there." She caught Mason staring at her. "What?"

Laura so beguiled Mason that he hadn't realized he was staring at her. "Nothing," he said as nonchalantly as he could.

"All right, boys, that's enough about me. I want to find out how the murder investigation in going."

"You know we can't divulge anything about that," Mason said.

"Off the record, then," Laura said and held up her right hand. "I promise."

"Go ahead, Chief, tell her," Wolski said. "Maybe she can see an angle we haven't thought about."

Mason still hesitated.

Laura continued to hold her hand up as if swearing a solemn oath. "Off the record is off the record. Honestly. I wouldn't be able to do my job very well if I betrayed that."

Mason signaled Wolski with his eyes that Anna shouldn't hear what he was about to say. Laura picked it up right away. "Anna," she said, "why don't you wait a few minutes in the ladies lounge. I'll come and get you when we're finished."

Anna glanced at Wolski, who nodded. She looked disappointed, but she left the table and headed for the ladies' lounge.

"Okay," Mason said, "off the record is one thing, but before I go on, I have to ask you not to share this with anyone else. No one. Something like this could create a panic."

When Laura agreed, Mason described what they'd found in the factory, how the body was mutilated and displayed on the column, the precision cuts, the severed limbs displayed in the bizarre fashion, the hours of torture the victim had likely endured. He told her about the body in the sewer, and that in all probability it was a victim of the same killer. "I've seen and heard about butchering murderers before, but nothing like what this killer does. I think this is just the beginning."

"Like Jack the Ripper?" Laura asked.

"I don't get how anyone could kill like that," Wolski said. "And this one being a doctor, for chrissake. Doctors are supposed to save lives."

"You think he's a doctor?" Laura asked.

Mason said, "According to the medical examiner, every cut the killer made was surgically precise. The guy didn't just cut off the arms and legs, he surgically removed them."

"Some people think Jack the Ripper was a doctor," Laura said. "Then there's the doctor everyone's talking about in France; they're saying he could have killed up to seventy men, women, and children. It's all over the French press."

"His surgical skills and the fact that he can move around at night after curfew points to someone in an army uniform. In all probability, someone in the U.S. Army Medical Corps. We've checked MP and CID arrest records and looked for any open murder cases suggesting a killer with surgical skill, but nothing turned up. This killer has been able to elude detection and probably has no previous record. We need to get into medical personnel files and search for criminal background checks, psychological profiles, reprimands, disciplinary actions, anything that might hint at someone liable to commit this kind of murder."

"Only we can't get clearance to access medical personnel files," Wolski said. "Our commander has put that strictly off-limits. They're okay with us searching for a suspect as long as he's not American."

"Hm," Laura said, tapping her fingernails on the tabletop, a faraway look in her eyes.

"What is it?" Mason asked.

"I have an idea... if you're open to it."

"Shoot," Wolski said eagerly.

Laura looked to Mason, who nodded for her to go on.

"Let's make a deal," she said. "I get you access to the medical personnel files, and you give me exclusive access to your investigation. I get to know what you know, but I don't publish anything until you've caught your man. What do you say?"

"And how are you going to get us that kind of access?" Mason asked.

Laura gave them a sly smile. "I know the chief medical officer for the Third Army's medical battalion, Brigadier General Morehouse." She furrowed her brow at Mason. "And don't get the wrong idea. He's a good friend, and that's it. I caught him in a rather compromising position—to say the least—and I promised to keep it quiet. He promised me a favor. Maybe it's time to cash it in."

Mason looked at Wolski as he considered Laura's proposal. Wolski raised his eyebrows, clearly prompting Mason to accept the deal.

"Exclusive access to our investigation doesn't mean tagging along. We'll share information and lines of investigation, but you don't publish anything that the other newspapers don't already have until we're done."

"It's a deal."

As they all shook hands, Mason wondered if he'd just grabbed a bobcat by the tail. If so, he was enjoying every minute of it.

Mason exited the officers' club after the party carrying a box of leftover food collected from the club's kitchen. The master sergeant overseeing the kitchen had agreed to prepare two dozen bags containing full dinners. Wolski, Laura, and Anna were waiting for him on the sidewalk.

"Didn't get enough to eat?" Wolski asked.

"I've got a delivery to make."

Instead of accompanying them to the car, Mason crossed the street and placed the carton of food a little bit away from the hole of the orphans' shelter. Kurt came out to investigate.

"I brought you all…" Mason didn't have to finish. The scent of hot food had reached their noses. All the children climbed out, and this time Mason didn't have to back away. He smiled and said, "*Guten Abend*," to all of them.

They returned the greeting, but then stopped and looked with suspicion at something behind Mason. Mason turned to see Laura come up to his side. She took his arm and stood very close. Her broad smile made the children relax.

A girl of eleven or twelve poked her head out and tried to pull herself onto the sidewalk. Two younger boys had to help her the rest of the way. Mason felt his heart constrict. Laura squeezed his arm.

The girl's left leg was missing from the knee down. She reached back into the hole and brought out a pair of battered crutches, then raised herself up and stood back from the rest. She wore a discarded Wehrmacht overcoat cut off to her ankles, but the bulky coat couldn't hide her skeletal frame. Her pale skin seemed to be stretched across bone. She had all the features of a beautiful girl hidden under a layer of dirt.

Mason couldn't help staring at her.

Laura asked the girl in German, "And what is your name?"

"Her name is Angela," Kurt said. "She doesn't talk much."

Kurt's younger companion, Dieter, added, "She doesn't have her leg."

"Yes, we see that," Mason said. "But you should be kind to her about that."

Dieter nodded earnestly, and the youngest children began grabbing for the bags of food. Kurt barked at them to thank the nice man. Then as each one took a bag he or she bowed slightly and said, "*Danke*." Kurt took his and Angela's bags last.

Laura asked the children if any of them were sick, and Mason added, "We could bring a doctor."

Kurt shook his head. "Just food. And, if you please, cigarettes. We can buy stuff with cigarettes."

Mason pulled out his almost full pack and handed it to Kurt. Kurt's eyes brightened as if he'd been given a brand-new bicycle.

Mason looked at Wolski and whistled. "Got any cigarettes?"

Wolski came over, Anna following him, and tossed a couple of packs to Mason.

"There's another two packs," Mason said to Kurt. "But I don't want to see you smoking them."

"No, sir."

And Angela added in a soft voice, "Thank you, sir."

Mason bowed. "You're welcome, my lady. Now go inside before you get too cold." He waited until Kurt helped Angela return to their shelter, and then turned for the car.

Anna left Wolski's side, rushed up to Mason, and kissed him on the cheek.

Wolski smiled slyly at Mason, as if an impostor's true identity had suddenly been revealed.

"What?" Mason asked.

"Nothing at all." That smile again. "Hey, I know a great club we could go to. It's got a nice mix of regular army and locals. How about you guys come with us? I stole a bottle of the colonel's scotch just for this occasion."

Laura glanced at Mason, then said, "Thanks, but I've got to get back to my hotel and finish an article that's due tomorrow. I also need to put in that call to General Morehouse."

"I'll pass, too," Mason said. "I'll walk Laura back to her hotel, and then I'm going to hit the sack. If Morehouse gives us access to those files, we're going to have a long day tomorrow."

"Suit yourselves," Wolski said. He climbed into the car with Anna and drove away.

Mason and Laura turned a corner, leaving the lights of the club behind. The light of the moon took over, washing the ruins in a ghostly glow. They walked in silence and entered the big plaza, Marienplatz. On their right was the neo-Gothic Neues Rathaus, intact but gutted by fire. The intricate facade, the arches, turrets, statues, and gargoyles, all reminiscent of a Gothic cathedral, stood out in stark relief from the hard light of the moon.

"So, you don't have a current girlfriend?"

"I've been here barely two weeks, plus I've been a little busy. I had a girlfriend when I worked as a paper pusher in Frankfurt. A nurse. But that didn't work out."

"No girl back home?"

"An ex-wife."

"That didn't work out, either?"

"'Ex' would be the giveaway. Six weeks of bliss, then a year of pain. She sent me a Dear John letter right after I landed in France."

"Poor boy."

"It was mutual, though it was pretty rotten of her to do it just when I was about to go into combat."

"What about family?"

"Just a grandmother. She and my grandfather raised me when my mother died. I was twelve. My stepdad took off long before then. I have no idea where he is, and I don't want to know."

A group of inebriated soldiers passed them on the other side of the street. They went in and out of the light from a couple of bars and restaurants that served late for the soldiers.

"You were right about my parents," Laura said. "They're both overachievers. My father is a biochemist and a U.S. congressman, and my mother is a writer and teaches medieval and Renaissance literature at Brown University. They both pushed me so hard to follow in their footsteps that they suffocated me."

"How did they react to you becoming a fashion photographer and a war correspondent?"

"What do you think? My mother cried and my father yelled. Then my father cried and my mother yelled. It got a little better when they saw my articles being published. My father and I barely have two words to rub together, but my mom told me he keeps a scrapbook of every article of mine he can find in print. But it wasn't just me who had them pulling their hair out. My older brother became a cop for the Boston PD. You see? I know a little about cops."

Mason stopped and looked at Laura. "Then you know they can be a lot of trouble."

"So can reporters."

A quiet moment was broken between them when two army Jeeps drove by on patrol. A couple of GIs whistled at Laura.

"I'd better get back," Laura said.

Mason held out his arm and they walked in silence for a while.

"So, what happened in Chicago?" Laura asked.

Mason stopped. "There you go again."

"Come on, we all have ghosts in our closets."

"I thought it was skeletons."

"Don't change the subject."

Mason tried to look angry, but her eyes, her smile, melted away his aggravation. He extended his arm again, and Laura took it and they resumed their stroll.

"I was partnered with one of the best men I've ever known. He'd been a detective going on eighteen years. I really looked up to him. Detective Sergeant Dave Lupin. About three years after I became a detective, Dave and I were investigating a series of drug-related murders. But every time we tried to make a bust, someone tipped them off. Each time we found an eyewitness, the witness disappeared. Dave started suspecting an inside job. I refused to believe it. Back then I never imagined sworn police officers would murder, torture, and steal to take over the drug trade."

"But that's just what some of them did."

Mason nodded.

"Did your partner—"

"Dave."

"Dave. Did he take it to your commander?"

"You have to understand one thing. In every police department there's what's called 'the blue code of silence.' No one rats on a fellow officer. It's not written anywhere, it's not taught at the academy, but it might as well be chiseled in stone and mounted on every precinct entrance, like Moses had delivered an eleventh commandment."

"But did Dave go to someone?"

"Not before he had enough concrete evidence. He worked on it for six months. The commander started sniffing around and gave us a stern warning. *I* kept warning him—"

"Didn't you want to stop these crooked cops?"

"I knew something was going on, but I still couldn't believe it was fellow detectives. If there's one thing to this day that still hurts, it's how stupid and naive I was."

"Dave didn't share the evidence with you?"

"No. He said it was to protect me. Then, Dave met me one night and handed over everything he'd found out. I didn't understand why he was giving it to me. He said it was my turn to step up to the plate. He walked away and two hours later he was shot in the back. They collared a junkie for it, but I knew better."

"What did you do with the evidence?"

"I was scared. So, I went to a motel outside of town and read everything. It was incredible. It was horrible what these guys had done and were doing. The next morning I stashed the evidence in a bus station locker. And you want to know how stupid and naive I was? I went to the commander."

"Oh, no. What did he say?"

"Nothing. Absolutely nothing. I waited for two days, expecting to get a bullet in the back. Then out of the blue, I got transferred to a precinct on the other side of town and reduced down to patrolling a beat. That really steamed me, so I went to the assistant DA and told him about the evidence. The guy patted me on the back and shook my hand and said he would take care of it."

"And nothing was done about it."

"That's right."

"You should have gone to the press."

"I did. I made an appointment with a reporter, but that same day I was busted for kickbacks and extortion. They'd planted evidence and bribed some lowlifes to testify against me. They claimed Dave had falsified all the evidence because of a vendetta Dave and I had against these guys. They fired me but didn't prosecute me. Everyone went along, from the mayor on down. Sharing the wealth and crushing the story."

"I'm sorry you had to go through all that."

"It sticks me in the ribs once in a while, but I don't let it get me down."

"You're a better man for it."

"There you go."

"Well, this is me," Laura said, and they stopped in front of the Hotel Vier Jahreszeiten, a high-class hotel reserved mostly for army brass and military government officials.

Mason smiled. "You know, the only other person I've told the whole story to is my grandmother."

Laura went up on her toes and kissed him. Mason kissed back. They slowly broke the embrace.

"I'd better go in," Laura said.

They said good night. Laura entered the arched entrance, then turned and waved before going inside. On the twenty-minute walk back to his billet, Mason couldn't help his silly grin. His reverie came to an abrupt end, however, when he saw the figure waiting outside his house.

"You're needed, sir," Corporal Manganella said, standing next to a parked Jeep. "There's been another one of those murders."

13

Corporal Manganella drove the Jeep through a district where the train tracks converged from the countryside and cut a wide swath through the west side of the city. During the Allied bombing raids, the bombardiers had used the web of tracks to line up their targets, and this area had been hit many times. For blocks on end, they passed nothing but the ruins of warehouses and working-class housing. In some sections closer to the tracks only dust and craters remained.

The corporal pulled the Jeep up to a small church flanked by empty hulks of apartment buildings. The church's steeple, the stained glassed windows, half the roof, and the front portico were all gone. The exterior stone had been scorched black from the fires.

Outside the church, a group of German police stood on one side of the entrance, while four U.S. Army MPs stood on the other. Because of the curfew, there were no spectators, except for those who peeked out from glassless windows or behind half-open doors.

"This is it, sir," Manganella said.

"Damn, not in a church."

"Not much of a church left."

Mason climbed out and told Corporal Manganella to stay with the Jeep. Inside, every available candle illuminated the interior. Two MPs and a German police officer talked to a priest in a corner near the confessional. Another MP stood with Inspector Becker in the center of the church facing the altar. The remaining intact pews had been stacked against the wall to make room for the primitive wooden scaffolding that supported the remaining church roof.

Becker turned as Mason approached and greeted him with a grim face. Then Mason noticed what the two had been craning their necks to look at—the last intact chandelier. It hung from the pinnacle of the roof some twenty-five feet above the floor. The chandelier spanned five feet across, with eight spokes that extended to its thick brass outer ring. Upon the chandelier lay a naked woman's torso. As he'd done to the previous victim, the killer had shaved her head, and he'd arranged the severed arms and legs upon four branches of the chandelier to form the same X pattern, overlaying the remaining four branches that formed a cross. Bodily fluid, tinged red, dripped slowly from the wounds and puddled on the floor.

"My God," Mason said, "a woman this time."

"The priest discovered her," Becker said. "He had come into the church several times this evening but never noticed her until he saw the puddle."

The sound of several vehicles rushing up to the entrance reverberated through the church. The crime scene techs and the ME came in a moment later.

"The priest alerted the local police and they called me," Becker said. "I have three officers searching for anyone who might have seen something." He pointed to the scaffolding. "The killer must have used that to mount the body."

"Footprints? Traces of blood?"

"Aside from the priest's prints, nothing."

"I'm sure we're not going to find anything he didn't want to."

"I arrived only twenty minutes ago, so I have not had time to do a thorough search."

The three crime techs came up to Mason and stared at the horror on the chandelier. Mason instructed them to set some lights up and directed the photographer to commence taking pictures. It took his loud voice to break their stares and get them moving. He asked one of the tech sergeants, "Where's the ME?"

"He was right behind us, sir."

Another Jeep pulled to a stop long enough to deposit a passenger, then drove away again. Wolski entered a moment later. He looked rather unhappy. "Pulled away from the loving arms of a beautiful woman just to freeze my tail off. Not to mention having to look at your ugly mugs…"

Mason pointed up at the chandelier.

Wolski turned his head upward. "Damn."

"Is this church still in use?" Mason asked Becker

"The priest and some parishioners are trying to save it, but it has been condemned."

Mason looked from the chandelier to the scaffolding. "Looks like about a six or seven-foot gap. This guy's quite an acrobat." He went over to the scaffolding and pulled on a support beam. "Give me your flashlight," he said to the MP. The MP gave it to him, and Mason trained the light on the scaffolding and followed the beam up to the ceiling.

Mason climbed the scaffolding and stopped when he was just above the level of the chandelier. He tried to concentrate on the rigging, but his eyes were pulled to the tragic sight of the young woman. She looked to be no more than her mid-twenties. Like the others, her mouth hung open in a last scream. He found himself squeezing the scaffolding boards until his knuckles turned white. Summoning all his willpower, he turned his gaze away and examined the cable. "The killer must have rigged a pulley system using the exposed ceiling joists. I'm sure the cable holding the chandelier wasn't meant to support the weight of a body."

Becker called over to the priest, asking him if the chandelier could be lowered. The priest told him yes, that one could lower it by the crank mechanism against the north wall. Wolski walked over to investigate.

Mason scanned the support cable with his flashlight beam. The cable looked new. He followed the cable up toward the ceiling and found the pulley attached to the ceiling beam. The cable should have angled off the pulley to the north wall, but instead it angled off to the scaffolding.

The killer had rigged a whole new cable. The crank didn't control the chandelier.

Mason jerked the flashlight beam up to the pulley again. In the shadows of the inverted V-shaped ceiling, Mason could just make out the original cable. Something was wrong. It didn't angle down as it should, and it appeared taut, as if bearing a great weight.

He heard Wolski releasing the cable lock to lower the chandelier. "Vincent, stop!"

Too late. Wolski turned the crank a quarter of a revolution. A loud metallic clank reverberated from high above. With the groan of straining wood, out from the shadows rushed a thick wooden beam. It swung downward from the center of the ceiling with the speed of a swinging hammer, straight toward Wolski.

Wolski froze.

Mason yelled like a drill sergeant to a soldier, "Wolski, hit the dirt!"

At the last moment, Wolski dived. The tree-trunk-sized ceiling beam slammed into the wall. The entire church shuddered, mortar and stone tumbling to the floor. Mason felt the scaffolding shake then sway. Becker and two MPs raced over to Wolski.

"Is he all right?" Mason shouted.

The answer became obvious when Wolski jumped up from the floor, cursing as he turned in circles. "Goddamnit! Son of a bitch!" He shook his fist at the ceiling. "You asshole. Isn't it enough butchering people? You've got to booby-trap the place too?" He bent over with his hands on his knees and took in deep breaths. An MP medic tried to check him for injuries, but Wolski waved him off.

Mason climbed down from the scaffolding and went up to Wolski. "Why don't you get with a couple of people and find the right way to lower the chandelier. It's attached to the scaffolding. Get the victim down and we'll finish up. Then I want to share that bottle of scotch with you."

Wolski gave Mason a fleeting smile, took one last deep breath and went into action.

"Let's go talk to the priest," Mason said to Becker.

The two detectives walked to where the priest stood with the German officer. The officer introduced the priest as Father Vogel and stepped away.

Father Vogel's eyes were moist and his hands shook. "Who would do such a thing? What kind of creature...?" He stopped to regain his composure.

"When is the last time you entered the church before discovering the body?" Mason asked.

"I come in almost every night at the same hour to pray for the revival of this church. But now I fear God has sent a sign that this place is no longer sacred."

"Yes, I understand," Mason said. "So, for example, last night you didn't see or hear anything unusual?"

The priest shook his head as he focused on something invisible.

"Can you think if one of your parishioners might have exhibited strange behaviors, anything suspicious in the last few weeks?"

"I haven't had parishioners since bombs destroyed this church and the neighborhood. I am at a loss as to how many parishioners of mine have actually survived."

"You didn't see anyone loitering around the church in a suspicious manner?"

Father Vogel shook his head, but it was apparent that he had entered some internal world. Mason looked at Becker to see if the inspector had anything to add. Becker shook his head, and they both thanked the priest, then Mason asked an MP to see that Father Vogel got home okay.

The MP started to lead Father Vogel away, but Father Vogel turned back to Mason. "Inspector Collins, you have no idea who could have murdered a woman so brutally and desecrated God's sanctuary?"

"We're trying, Father."

"I am a practical man. I believe in the holy scriptures and never imagined that demons really exist. But to cut up that poor woman in such a way then use her corpse to make a Christian symbol is the work of true evil."

Mason glanced back at the chandelier. "Do you mean the Chi-Rho cross?"

Father Vogel shook his head and pointed to the chandelier. "The Chi-Rho should have the *P* shape at the head. Here, there is none. The four limbs and the four remaining spokes of the wheel create an eight-pointed baptismal cross."

"Can you think of any reason why the killer would form a baptismal cross?"

"It is a sign of regeneration and resurrection. Eight is an important number: the eight days from birth to baptism, and the eight days between Christ's entry into Jerusalem and his resurrection."

Mason turned to Becker. "That make any sense to you?"

"Perhaps he evokes this symbol to aid in the victim's transformation into sainthood, or out of his own desire for redemption."

"What a horrible thought," Father Vogel said. "This demonic murderer mocks our holy church. An abominable desecration. You find him, sir. You find him."

"Yes, Father. Thank you," Mason said.

Father Vogel allowed the MP to lead him away.

"To add to your burden," Becker said. "Now God holds you personally responsible for finding this murderer."

Mason looked at Becker and saw he was serious. "You're not joking, are you?"

"I find it vaguely humorous that he chose you for the task."

"You're a religious man?"

"I am a devout Catholic, so, yes, I am religious. You find that difficult to imagine?"

"And how did you reconcile that with collaborating with the godless Nazis?"

Becker raised his eyebrows. "Every soldier believes that God is on his side. Do you not feel the same way?"

"The way I always understood it, he's not a big fan of war. But if I had to bet which side he chose, all I'd have to do is look around and lay pretty good odds it wasn't yours."

"God does not abandon the vanquished any more than he rewards the victors."

"If you say so."

They both noticed that Wolski and four MPs had figured out how to lower the chandelier and went over to observe. As Wolski and the others strained to lower the chandelier, Wolski said, "I'd like to know how one man accomplished all this."

The assistant medical examiner, Captain Sykes, arrived. He was the leading night shift ME, and a man who looked more like a bookkeeper than a soldier: portly figure, wispy gray hair, and thick black glasses. He came up and stood next to Mason and Becker. They all watched as Wolski and a couple of the MPs lowered the chandelier onto two pews that had been placed underneath to support it.

All eyes were drawn to the terrible sight. No one spoke. As with the victim in the factory, her eyes and mouth were frozen in a last moment of horror, her torso cut open, and ribs pulled back exposing her organs. The difference was, this time, the lungs were gone.

"My God," Sykes muttered.

The three of them stepped up to get a closer look. Somewhere near the front of the church a generator roared to life, and a few in the silent group jumped at the sound. The work lights flickered then came up to full power.

"The incisions are exactly the same...." Becker paused. "She is so young. What a hideous tragedy."

"Looks like the same surgical precision removing the limbs," Mason said. "She has the same abrasion marks where she was strapped down...." Mason, too, had to stop. He tried to remain objective, pretend the body was an inanimate object, but he couldn't block from his mind the images of her screaming in agony, her absolute terror at being helpless while someone cut into her.

"Are you okay?" Becker whispered.

The question brought Mason out of his visions. "All right, everyone, let the ME and the techs get in here and do their jobs."

Mason and the others stepped away, and they all breathed easier with a little distance from the victim. One of Becker's officers came up to them, though his eyes were fixed on the victim. Becker shifted over to block his view. "What is it, *Wachtmeister*?"

"There's a man outside who says he saw someone going in the church last night."

"Take us to him."

A few moments later Mason and Becker stood in front of a thin man with sunken eyes. He was dirty and unshaven, as there was little running water or means to heat it in this part of the city.

"I live in the building across the street," the man said, pointing to a battered apartment building diagonally across from the church. "I couldn't sleep last night and heard a noise about one o'clock in the morning. When I looked outside, I saw a man pushing a cart through the street. I thought it odd, a man in civilian clothes out past curfew."

"Did you see his face?" Mason asked.

"No. The man wore a long dark coat, though I could not tell the color. And a hat very low on his head. Homburg, I believe."

"Can you give us any physical description?" Becker asked.

"I think he was tall... but from across the street and from the third floor it was hard to tell. Plus, it was very dark."

"Did you see what was in the cart?" Mason asked.

"He took a large bundle wrapped in dark cloth from it, then carried it into the church."

"Do you think you might have seen this man before? Maybe someone from this neighborhood?"

The man gave them an embarrassed smile and swept his hands across his tattered clothes. "Not from this neighborhood, sir. Even from my window I could tell it was a very fine coat. I'm a tailor, you see? Beautifully tailored, the coat was. And in very good condition."

Mason sighed in frustration. This man could describe the coat in detail but not the man himself.

"Oh, and besides the bundle, he also carried a large cloth bag... canvas, I believe."

"He took all this into the church?" Becker asked. The man nodded. "Did you see him come out again?"

The man shook his head. "I heard noises, like something hammering and moving things about. I thought he was repairing the church, or perhaps making a shelter for himself. Another homeless man."

"At one o'clock in the morning?" Mason said. The man shrugged and gave another sheepish smile. "How long did you watch from your window?"

"Maybe thirty minutes. It was very cold, you see."

Mason and Becker thanked the man and were about to return to the church when another German policeman came up to Becker. "So far, no other witnesses, sir," the policeman said. "However, several people reported hearing a wagon in the early hours of the morning."

"Where was this?"

"Around the corner and up the street a block."

"No one saw the wagon?"

"No, sir. But several people informed us that the street can get quite busy with wagon traffic because of the salvage and demolition work. Rarely at night, but sometimes."

Becker thanked him and turned to Mason. "Should we assume that the killer arrived by wagon, and then came the rest of the way with the cart?"

"I've thought about this before. A wagon points to a civilian, but I don't see how he could get around in a wagon without being noticed. He'd have to possess an after-curfew pass or permit." Mason paused to reflect on this. "It's time to look closer into that possibility."

Mason and Becker reentered the church just as an ambulance pulled up. Two medics got out and retrieved a stretcher from the back. Captain Sykes met Mason and Becker in the vestibule. He looked rattled.

"He took her lungs," Sykes said as if still trying to believe the words.

"To help you with time of death," Mason said, "a witness saw a man, who we believe is the killer, carry into the church what we think was the body, about twenty-four hours ago. And from what we know of the last victim, he kills within twelve hours before that."

"That'll give me something to go on," Sykes said. "We'll obviously have more after the autopsy. Needless to say, she was killed and drained of blood before being transported here. The small puddle on the floor is simply leaking bodily fluids mixed with traces of blood."

"Also consistent with the other ones."

"Are you the lead investigator on this case?" On Mason's nod, Sykes handed him a small square of parchment. "I found this pinned to her back."

On it was scribed another note from the killer:

That saints enjoy their beatitude and the grace of god more abundantly they are permitted to see the punishment of the damned in hell.

"It's a quote from Thomas Aquinas," Becker said.

Mason let out a heavy sigh. No killer was more unpredictable and dangerous than one who believed that murder and torture empowered him to open the gates of heaven and survey the depths of hell.

14

M ason and Wolski stopped just inside the double doors of
the main structure in the McGraw Kaserne complex, an
immense grouping of buildings originally built for the Nazi
bureaucracy and now taken over by the Third Army. A long,
austere hallway lay before them, and at the other end a master
sergeant occupied a desk. Like Cerberus, he guarded the entrance
to the underground vaults containing the U.S. Army personnel
files.

"Now we'll see how much juice your girlfriend has," Wolski
said.

"I keep telling you, one moonlit walk back to her hotel does
not a girlfriend make."

"She should be. She's gorgeous, smart, brave. I can't believe
you let her go last night."

"Come on, Cupid. We've got a long day ahead of us."

They began the long walk down the hallway. It was eleven
a.m. Friday morning. Mason had received Laura's message at
CID headquarters an hour before, saying that Brigadier-General
Morehouse had cleared the way for them. He and Wolski had
stopped by the church crime scene and met with Inspector Becker

again. Becker's team had widened the canvass and examined the lone wagon tracks left in the snow the night before, but nothing relevant had turned up and the trail had petered out. The autopsy would be performed tomorrow, and the sketch of the female victim would be distributed that afternoon. Little else could be done immediately, so the message from Laura had come at an opportune time.

As their footsteps echoed loudly in the empty hallway, the master sergeant looked up from his newspaper with vigilant eyes. His intense stare and clamped jaw said he took his gatekeeping job very seriously.

Mason spoke out of the corner of his mouth. "I imagine we're about to violate any number of army regulations."

"Even if we get in there, Colonel Walton's gonna have our hides when he finds out."

"Who said anything about telling Colonel Walton?"

"Yes?" the master sergeant said when Mason and Wolski stopped by the desk.

"I'm Chief Warrant Officer Collins from the CID, and this is Warrant Officer Wolski—"

"Yes, sir," the master sergeant said and shot to his feet. "I was expecting you." He retrieved a ring of keys from the desk drawer and turned to a heavy wooden door.

"She definitely has the juice," Wolski said under his breath.

The master sergeant unlocked the door and led them down a set of stairs to the basement level. "There are a couple of privates, file clerks, at your disposal if you need them. You shouldn't be disturbed. Things are pretty quiet down here." He unlocked another door at the end of the hallway and entered.

Mason and Wolski followed close behind then stopped in their tracks. The dimly lit room held fifteen long rows of file cabinets. Wolski whistled at the size of it.

"We've got most of the army personnel records for the

southern and western U.S.-occupational districts. The only one bigger is in Frankfurt. Well, I guess D.C.'s got the biggest. You'll find medical personnel files on rows four, five, and six." As the master sergeant walked back to the door, he said, "If you need anything just holler."

"A bottle of aspirin and a gallon of coffee," Wolski said.

"Excuse me?"

"We'll be fine for now," Mason said. "Thank you, Sergeant."

They both surveyed the room. Mason felt sure that Wolski, like he, was trying to steel his will for the coming task.

"Well, let's get to it," Mason said.

They spent the next eight hours poring through the files, and after three hours they enlisted the two privates for help shuffling files back and forth. The day's search brought more frustration than suspects. They found a few doctors described as deviant. Some had been accused of physical or sexual abuse of patients, but few were still posted in Germany by the time the murders began. As it turned out, only five files provided any kind of vague suspects, and without crime scene fingerprints or other clues, they couldn't justify digging any deeper without alerting Colonel Walton that Mason had "sidestepped" direct orders. And by the end, it turned out Wolski's request to the master sergeant had proved prescient: they both came away with a great need for aspirin.

MASON STEPPED INTO HIS OFFICE AND DROPPED HIS BRIEFCASE ON the desk. The clatter of typewriters and the nagging phones made the spikes in his head dig deeper into his temples. The pain, plus the frustration of a full day spent without concrete results, made his foul mood boil over. He stared a moment at the stack of files covering his desk and was tempted to shove everything off and grind them into the floor.

A knock on the open door stopped him.

"Don't do it," Wolski said.

"I'd just have to turn around and pick them up anyway." Mason sat at his desk and rubbed his forehead. "Five files and nothing earthshattering. We'll check out the suspects, but it's looking like we should start thinking in terms of Germans or DPs. Becker's team is checking all the civilian doctors and surgeons, so let's take a more serious look into U.S. issued night passes and permits, then cross-check them with identification and denazification papers. Maybe something will turn up."

"Assuming the killer didn't get a counterfeit, there could easily be ten thousand legitimate ones. That could take weeks if it's just the two of us. We need more manpower."

"I'll see what I can do."

"I can imagine Colonel Walton's face when you ask him about that."

Through the pebbled glass on Mason's office door, they could see the silhouette of a private hesitating just outside. Wolski opened the door. The private snapped to attention. "What is it, Private?"

"Sir, the colonel wants to see Mr. Collins right away. He's at OMGB headquarters, General West's office."

"Friday evening at the general's?" Wolski said. "That can't be good."

Mason gathered his coat and hat, and said to Wolski, "Contact public affairs at OMGB about those night passes."

"Oh, sirs," the private interjected, "the colonel told me to ask everyone if they know the whereabouts of the colonel's cognac and several bottles of scotch."

Mason and Wolski exchanged looks, and Mason said, "No, we sure don't."

"The colonel's been in a killing mood since he found his bottles gone."

"Well, good luck with that investigation," Wolski said.

MASON ENTERED A LARGE CONFERENCE ROOM WITH FULL-WALL wood paneling, marble flooring, and a sedan-sized fireplace. A long table of mahogany dominated the room. At the far end sat Colonel Walton; General West, the Third Army's provost marshal; and a major whom Mason did not know. They were in the middle of a heated discussion when Mason stopped at the head of the table and saluted. Colonel Walton waved him to come forward.

"You know the general, don't you?" Colonel Walton said.

Mason acknowledged the general. "Yes, of course. How are you, sirs?"

General West finished a sip of coffee. "That remains to be seen."

General Jenkins eyed him with what seemed to be contempt. Perhaps he'd already heard about him and Laura.

"And this is Major Bolton, of OMGB civil affairs," Colonel Walton said.

Major Bolton was a small man with a wiry mustache. With quick, birdlike motions, he stood and leaned across the table to shake Mason's hand. Colonel Walton invited Mason to sit. Mason pulled out a chair and angled it to face the three inquisitors. He immediately felt the warmth of the fire, knowing it wasn't the only heat he was going to feel in the next few moments.

"Where are you with this investigation after last night's discovery?" General West asked.

Mason filled him in, though there was little new since his last report. He mentioned the eyewitness, the reports of a wagon, and the priest's idea that the victim's arrangement on the chandelier symbol was of a Christian baptismal cross.

"This latest murder, of the young woman, is an act of cruelty and savagery," General West said. "The first two victims, from the factory and sewer, we were able to keep pretty well under wraps, but accounts of the young woman last night are spreading around this city like wildfire. It's upsetting the civilian population. I've got the Munich city council pressuring me to solve this, and they insist on giving the German police a more active role in the investigation. They claim we're not doing enough because the victims are German."

Mason glanced at Colonel Walton, but Walton didn't bat an eye.

"Frankly," General West went on, "I don't care what the Munich city council thinks, but we've got enough problems on our hands without half the city's population too afraid to come out of their homes, and the other half clamoring for justice."

Mason wondered where in all this was the desire to solve this for the victims. "Sir, we need to double the MP patrols, especially in the backstreets. We need double or triple the checkpoints—"

Colonel Walton tried to object. "Mr. Collins—"

Mason cut him off. "General, I need more manpower if I'm to carry out a proper investigation. I need more MPs and investigators at my disposal, with a dedicated operations center. We need enough men to interview the female victim's family and associates, we need periodic monitoring of the crime scenes and the victim's paths and frequented places, and we need to check U.S.-issued civilian night passes. Now that we've almost exhausted our search through U.S. Medical Corps personnel files—"

"You what?" Colonel Walton blurted out.

Mason realized he'd just blown his undisclosed investigation into the army's medical personnel files. "Right now, the German police are trying to cover all the doctors and hospitals, but I'd like to have at least two teams of ours cover them as well. And that doesn't include DPs with surgical knowledge—"

"Mr. Collins, that's enough!" Colonel Walton said. "This grandstanding of yours has gone too far. The very idea that you investigated U.S. Medical Corps personnel without my permission, that you think you can make demands or dictate terms to the general… You are one breath away from disciplinary action."

General West raised his hand, and Colonel Walton stopped. There was a moment of silence in the large room while the general lit his cigar. Jenkins avoided any eye contact with Mason. A log in the fire snapped. Another broke apart at its burned-out center, sending sparks up into the chimney. Mason waited for the hammer to come down.

Instead, General West nodded and said, "If more manpower will get the job done, then I'm prepared to put at Mr. Collins's disposal all the investigative resources we can spare. Pull out all the stops and get this case solved." He turned to Colonel Walton, whose face had turned crimson with anger. "Frank, I know you have your hands full out there. But this kind of case unnerves everyone. What this killer does to his victims riles up a population already weary of murder and death. The idea that a Jack the Ripper type psychopath is roaming the streets could seriously disturb a population that's already at wit's end."

Major Bolton cleared his throat for attention. "I've already recommended that we keep these stories out of the press. The *Stars and Stripes* has agreed not to publish any articles relating to this case, and since we control the German newspapers, there won't be any printed in those, either."

Mason glanced around the room hoping that no one noticed the look of guilt on his face. If anyone found out that he'd leaked information about the case to Laura, it would surely be the end of the line for him as a CID criminal investigator.

General West puffed on his cigar. Everyone waited for his final word. "You laid out a pretty big shopping list. We're undermanned as it is, but I don't see that we have any choice. Frank, see that Mr. Collins gets his wish for more investigators. I'll notify the MP company commanders to beef up patrols and checkpoints." He pointed his finger at Mason. "But I better have results. And fast. If I see you can't handle this case with alacrity and efficiency, then I'll find someone who will."

A t ten a.m. the next morning, Manganella dropped Mason off in front of the morgue. Wolski was waiting for him.

"I see you finally got my message," Wolski said.

"What's up?"

"The ME has his autopsy report, and Becker is bringing in the victim's two roommates to identify the body. Where've you been?"

"Over at the JAG office talking to a lawyer about a major, a surgeon, who went nuts in Bad Tölz and killed two civilians."

"Anything promising?"

Mason shook his head. "He made regular trips to Munich, but not the days around the killings."

They entered the front offices of the morgue and proceeded down the hallway.

"How did the meeting with the brass go last night?" Wolski asked.

"The good news is we're going to get a contingent of investigators to work with us and an operations room."

"And the bad news?"

"We have to solve it fast or we're off the case. Plus, I let slip that we've been snooping around Medical Corps personnel files."

"You were an agent in military intelligence and couldn't keep that under your hat?"

Mason shot him a dirty look, but Wolski ignored it. He seemed quite content with the artful jab to Mason's ribs.

Mason and Wolski descended the stairs and found Major Treborn in the morgue.

Major Treborn greeted them. "Inspector Becker should be here any moment with the girls. I'll give you a rundown of what I've found while we wait."

"Do we have to look at the body?" Wolski asked.

"Nothing you haven't seen already," Treborn said with a sly smile. "Doesn't matter. I fixed up the remains for the girls."

Treborn retrieved a file off a table. "The time of death, best as I can figure it, was about twenty-four to thirty-six hours before discovery. I found the same contusion on the back of the neck. The victim suffered the exact same wounds—tortured, dismembered. The only difference is, as you know, her lungs were surgically removed. The rest of her organs are intact. She has the same abrasions from being strapped down...."

"Any sign of sexual assault?" Mason asked.

"None. However, there is one thing I noticed. One of her legs is shorter than the other. Sometime in her not-so-distant past, her left leg was severely fractured. The surgeon didn't do a very careful job. Looked rushed. I don't know if that has any significance."

"Meaning she had a limp," Mason said.

"With her leg like that, there's no doubt."

Mason thought a moment. "Dr. Hieber, the victim from the factory, you said he had arthritis in his lower back and hips, right?"

"Let me check," Treborn said and went over to the shelves full of files. "I've seen so many bodies come through here, it's hard to keep them straight." He found the file he was looking for and opened it. "Yes, advanced arthritis, especially in the hip joints. There was wear on the knee joints from trying to compensate."

"Then in all likelihood, he limped, too?"

Treborn looked up at Mason over his reading glasses. "Yeah, he probably would have. What are you thinking?"

"The killer chooses his victims for a reason. Could be a coincidence, but maybe something about the limping touches off the killer."

Mason was about to say something when the door to the autopsy room opened. Becker led in the two women and introduced them. They both looked to be in their midtwenties. Gisela was tall and thin with an angular face and black hair. Though she held tightly to the other woman, she gave the Americans a defiant expression. The other's name was Irma, a pale, frail-looking woman, with softer features, who stood only to Gisela's shoulders. They wore what were probably their best clothes, which showed signs of wear and were stiff from the crude detergents they were forced to use.

Mason greeted them in German and introduced Wolski and Major Treborn. "Major Treborn is the chief pathologist. He and Herr Oberinspektor Becker will accompany you to view the body."

Becker placed his hands on their shoulders. "Are you ready?"

They both nodded. Irma shuddered. Gisela maintained her steely expression, though Mason could tell she was as frightened as her companion. Major Treborn led the way. They proceeded slowly past the desks and shelves and into the autopsy area. Mason and Wolski stayed behind and watched as the group approached the middle examination table. Becker stopped the pair six feet from the table. Major Treborn waited for Becker's signal, then pulled back the sheet just enough to uncover the victim's face. It was steely Gisela who cried out and turned away. Irma became the strong one and tried to comfort Gisela.

Becker asked them if they knew the victim. Through their tears, they both said yes, and again yes, when Becker asked if they were sure. Major Treborn covered the victim and asked if they would mind going to his office so that the detectives could ask them a few questions.

As Becker passed Mason and Wolski, Mason said, "We'll give them a few minutes."

Back up on the ground floor, Mason, Wolski, and Treborn waited in Treborn's office. Treborn kept looking at his watch.

"I've got three days' worth of work to do between now and eight o'clock."

"You fixed up the victim's face nicely," Mason said.

"I couldn't have those poor girls see their friend looking like she did when she came in. What that young victim went through... I have a daughter about her age."

Becker opened the door and brought in the women. Gisela and Irma sat in chairs facing Treborn's desk. Treborn took his place behind the desk, while Becker sat on the desk facing the girls to give them moral support. Mason and Wolski stood off to one side near the wall.

In a soft voice, Becker said, "Would you please tell these detectives what you told me?"

Gisela stared straight ahead and said nothing. Irma took Gisela's lead and did the same thing.

Becker urged, "Gisela, Irma, please."

"We don't talk to Americans," Gisela said.

"They are trying to find the killer. The more they know, the better chance of finding him."

"I told *you* what we know. Now you can tell them."

Becker said to Mason, "The victim's name is Agneth

Lehmann. She was a roommate of these women. They live in the Maxvorstadt district and have been together for two years."

"Did Agneth say anything about someone following her? Someone who may have threatened her or wanted to harm her?"

Again, a wall of silence. Mason tried to check his temper. He sensed Wolski tensing up as well. Irma was about to say something, but Gisela put her hand on Irma's arm. Irma stopped.

"I'm sure you have your reasons for not liking Americans," Mason said, "but we're here to stop these killings."

Gisela snorted. "Why don't you arrest the Ami soldiers who raped me? Then we'll talk about helping you."

Mason noticed Wolski bristle even more at the word "Ami," a term used to express contempt or animosity for Americans. He gave Wolski a shake of his head then said to Gisela, "If you can give me their names or identify them, I promise you they will be arrested."

Gisela snorted again. "The same answer I received from the other American police. They promised but did nothing. Why don't you Americans leave us alone? Go! Haven't you done enough? My mother and father are dead. My brother is rotting in one of your prisons. And then I am raped."

"We'll do what we can," Wolski said with anger in his voice, "but right now, we're here to talk about Agneth," Wolski said. "This is about finding whoever did the horrible things to her and punish the killer. It's about stopping him from doing the same thing to another innocent victim."

Mason stepped up to the desk. "If you withhold information that could help us find the killer, and the killer murders another young woman, you will regret it and feel partly responsible."

Irma looked down at her lap. "Agneth said she thought—" Gisela squeezed Irma's arm, but Irma yanked it away. "No." She looked at Mason. "The last week or so she complained that she felt a man was following her."

"Did she describe him?" Mason asked.

"The man always wore a long, dark blue coat and hat, so she never saw his face. She said he was tall with broad shoulders. She kept getting glimpses of him in reflections of windows and the like. After that, she started walking to work or home with a group. She only walked one short street alone before reaching the apartment building. It was just a short street—two, maybe three minutes after leaving the group. I warned her to take the long way around, but it has been so cold the last week."

"Where did she work?"

"At the Ludwig-Maximilians-University hospital. She was a nurse."

Mason felt a blush of excitement. Maybe they had a pattern. "Did she know or ever work with a Dr. Richard Hieber?"

Gisela looked up at Mason with alarm. "She didn't, but I met him a few times. Do you think he is the killer?"

Mason shook his head. "He was another victim of the same killer, like Agneth." Mason wanted to avoid fueling rumors about a chain killer loose in Munich, but it seemed the surest way to get Gisela to talk.

"Another victim like Agneth?" Gisela said. "What do you mean?"

"Agneth and Dr. Hieber were tortured and dismembered in exactly the same way. One man killed them both."

Both women stifled cries of alarm and held each other's hands.

"Do you understand now why it's so important to find Agneth's killer?" Mason said. "We don't want him to do the same horrible things to anyone else."

"Dr. Hieber... he came to the hospital a couple of times every month," Gisela said. "He would come to consult and help with particularly difficult cases. He was a very good epidemiologist."

"You work at the hospital, too?"

"We all do. We are all nurses. Irma and I, and the group that Agneth walked with to the hospital and back home."

"We'd like to talk with the rest of the group. Maybe they noticed something."

Mason looked back at Wolski, but he saw that Wolski already had his notepad out. Between Gisela and Irma, they named four other nurses.

While notating the information, Wolski asked, "Can either of you think of any doctor or other staff at the hospital who you think might fit Agneth's description?"

They both thought a minute. "There's a male nurse, Siegfried … I don't remember his last name," Gisela said.

"He's not tall," Irma said.

"But he's very strong."

"He is rather odd. Very sad, I think."

"Can you blame him for that?" Gisela said.

"What do you mean?" Mason asked.

"He was a soldier on the Russian front. He was badly burned on the face and arms. He had wanted to be a surgeon before the war, but he lost three fingers on his right hand."

"He is bitter, but quite gentle, I've found," Irma said. She brightened at remembering something. "What about Dr. Scholz?" She looked at Gisela, who nodded in agreement. Irma said, "He's a surgeon at the hospital. He's tall, maybe forty years old.…"

Mason snapped his head to look at Wolski, who nodded back. It was time to move.

16

The Ludwig-Maximilians University complex had taken numerous direct hits from the bombing raids, and the LMU hospital was no exception. Composed of a series of wings, the university's building branched out in every direction, and the majority of the three-story structures of granite blacks and arched windows were blackened from incendiary bombs. Here and there along the front, other bombs had taken large bites out of the facades, and Mason wondered how they could still run a hospital amid so much damage.

Mason had come over in the Jeep with Manganella. Wolski and an MP pulled up next to him. Mason instructed Manganella and the MP to keep watch on the doors.

"You see a tall, forty-year-old surgeon high-tailing it out of here, and you tackle him," Mason said.

"How are we supposed to know he's a surgeon?" Manganella asked.

"He'll be the only tall guy in a white lab coat trying out for the hundred-yard dash."

Mason and Wolski entered a large lobby of wood and marble. The smell of disinfectant hit them immediately. To their right, a large area had been allocated for the enormous number of people seeking care. With the exception of the Schwabing hospital taken over by the U.S. Army, most of the other Munich hospitals had suffered almost total damage, leaving the university's hospital to serve the majority of the local population. Women with frail children, the elderly, and those suffering from severe malnutrition, the cold, and limited sanitation had taken every available bench, even the surrounding floor. There were a few ill or injured men, most among them ex-soldiers with missing limbs or mangled bodies. Babies crying, moans of pain, and sounds of chronic coughs echoed in the great hall.

Mason and Wolski hesitated and looked over the crowd. Mason knew the worst was yet to come, when deep winter set in and long-term malnutrition took its toll. Even in mid-December there were the sporadic sights of the dead, those who had collapsed on the sidewalk or died in a hovel, only to be laid on the sidewalk for collection by burial details.

They walked up to the receptionist's counter. A nurse stood behind the counter and talked on the phone. She kept her back to them as she spoke. Mason cleared his throat to get her attention, but she shot up her index finger for him to wait without turning around. The area around her desk was decorated with photographs and postcards depicting bucolic scenes of the Bavarian countryside: a deer in the trees, a rugged cabin on a hill overlooking a sapphire blue lake. Probably her way of coping with the ruins she had to face every day. She finally hung up and turned to Mason. A flash of fear passed across her face when she saw two US soldiers.

"Where can we find Dr. Scholz, please?" Mason asked.

"He is seeing patients at the moment. If you would like to wait, he should be finished in an hour."

"I'm afraid that won't be possible. We would like to see him right away. If you could please direct us."

"He is very adamant about not being disturbed while making his rounds."

Mason held up his CID badge. "We are United States military police. We must insist on disturbing him."

The receptionist turned to a nurse standing behind her and whispered something in her ear. The nurse nodded and rushed off. "His office is on the fifth floor, east wing, room five-two-four. That nurse will notify the doctor that you are coming to his office."

At the far end of the lobby two elevator cages sat next to a broad marble staircase. Mason and Wolski stopped at the elevators, but both had signs announcing they were out of order.

"How the heck do people who can barely walk get to the upper floors?" Wolski said.

"The old-fashioned way."

On the fifth floor, they followed a series of corridors that led to the east wing and found room 524. Mason knocked and entered without waiting for a response.

Dr. Scholz sat behind his desk and, even sitting, he seemed to tower over it. Though colossal in frame, he possessed a disproportionately small head and a weak chin under a thin-lipped mouth. Mason and Wolski's aggressive entrance startled him, but he recovered quickly, reverting to a stony expression as he stood to greet them. "Gentlemen, I would invite you in, but I see you don't require it. How can I help you?"

Mason introduced himself and Wolski, informing the doctor that they were CID criminal investigators. He watched the doctor's reactions carefully, but the doctor only returned a smug smile and flared nostrils. Before taking a seat Mason signaled Wolski with his eyes and nodded toward the coat rack in the corner of the room. On it hung a long, dark blue overcoat. Wolski arched an eyebrow then leaned against the wall and stared hard at Scholz.

"I'll come right to the point, Herr Doktor," Mason said as he took the chair facing Scholz's desk. "We're investigating multiple homicides, and we'd like to ask you a few questions regarding the case."

The doctor drew his head back as if puzzled by the statement. "Ask me? What have I—"

"A nurse, by the name of Agneth Lehmann was murdered three nights ago. She worked at this hospital. Did you know her?"

"No. But I am sorry to hear this. There have been so many deaths—"

Mason interrupted again. "According to one of her roommates, Agneth had complained of being stalked by a very tall man with broad shoulders before being murdered."

"I don't know what this has to do with me," Dr. Scholz said. "I am certainly not the only tall man in all of Munich."

"Another victim of the same killer came to this hospital on a consulting basis. Dr. Hieber. Did you know him?"

"Not personally, but I do know who he was. If I understand correctly, you suspect me, because both victims were associated with this hospital and murdered by someone described as a tall man?"

"What is your area of medical expertise?"

"I am a thoracic surgeon."

"The reason I ask is that the victims were both surgically mutilated. Our medical examiner and chief forensics expert determined that the killer was medically skilled. A surgeon perhaps, like yourself."

"Nor am I the only tall man with surgical skills living in Munich."

"You have to admit, the list of suspects gets pretty small when you put them all together, Herr Doktor."

Scholz sat back and grabbed the arms of his chair. "You are questioning the wrong man."

"Can you tell us what you were doing on the evenings of December ninth and twelfth?"

"This is preposterous. I have done nothing wrong."

"Maybe you don't understand how serious we are. Refusing to cooperate makes us suspect you even more."

"You are no better than the Gestapo," Scholz said. "You are harassing an innocent man. You have no evidence, no proof, yet you assume me guilty."

Mason returned the doctor's conceit with a smug smile of his own. "You know how many criminals I've busted who claimed they were innocent or said I was questioning the wrong man? We have enough circumstantial evidence to question you, and we will be forced to bring you into headquarters if you won't account for those evenings. We will search your home. Your family and the entire hospital will know what you are suspected of doing. Prove us wrong."

The doctor's gaze wandered the room. Mason could see a growing panic in his eyes. Time for a strong nudge. "Mr. Wolski, we're taking this man to headquarters."

Wolski came off the wall, withdrew his handcuffs, and approached the doctor.

"No, wait. Please. I remember now," Scholz said. "The twelfth, my wife and I went to a concert at the university."

"Wife?" Mason said.

"Yes. Is that illegal for Germans now?" Scholz tried to regain his superiority even as he desperately patted the pockets of his pants. "I believe I still have the ticket stub in my coat."

Scholz stood, and Mason backed off a step. Scholz pointed to his overcoat hanging on the coat rack. He tried to say something, but he was too flustered to get it out.

"Go ahead," Mason said. Out of the corner of his eye he saw Wolski's hand close to his holstered pistol. The doctor reached behind his chair for something. Mason was ready for any attempt at escape. Scholz towered over them. It would take both investigators to bring down a desperate man his size. But, to Mason's surprise, the doctor brought a cane around in front of him and leaned on it heavily as he stepped around the desk toward the coat rack.

"What happened to you?" Wolski asked. "You injure yourself recently lifting something heavy?"

Scholz stopped and gave them an indignant look. "I've had chronic back problems for two years. A heavy beam fell on me during a bombing raid. It shattered my ninth and tenth thoracic vertebrae. It's a miracle I can stand at an operating table, but it troubles me to walk and lifting anything heavier than a book is out of the question." Upon noticing Mason's and Wolski's looks of skepticism, he said, "Must I produce the operating physician and hospital records? Or shall I strip and show you my scars?" He limped over to the coat rack and fished around in his overcoat pocket. He removed the two ticket stubs and showed them to Mason. "For the evening of the twelfth. An outdoor concert on the university's campus."

Mason's disappointment made him speechless for a moment. "You understand that we will have to verify all of this. We'd like to talk to your wife."

"Of course," Dr. Scholz said. He hobbled over to his desk and wrote something down. He turned back to Mason and handed him a piece of paper. "My address. She will confirm everything I've said."

Mason took the paper. "We'll be in touch." He then signaled for Wolski to exit. Mason stopped at the door and turned back to Dr. Scholz. "Herr Doktor, if we'd been the Gestapo, you'd have been arrested without proof, tortured for a confession, sentenced in a mock trial, and executed. I would advise you to keep that in mind."

Mason was about to close the door, when Scholz said, "I apologize for the remark."

That made Mason stop. "Forget it," he said and shut the door.

Mason and Wolski walked down the hallway in silence for a few moments. Mason had to digest his disappointment, and he figured Wolski had to do the same.

"You should have made him show you his scar," Wolski said. "He still could have injured himself lifting the body or rigging that damned booby trap."

"I watched how he favored the cane to the left and his right foot. The rubber foot on the cane and his right shoe are worn down the same way. He's had that injury a long time."

"At least you could have kicked the cane out from under him for that Gestapo crack."

At first, Mason tuned out the persistent paging over the speaker system. That background noise came with every hospital. But by the time they reached the staircase the pager's voice sounded more insistent: "*Paging Dr. Scholz. Please respond. You have an emergency in operating room four.*"

Mason and Wolski exchanged a look of alarm and burst into a run back toward Dr. Scholz's office. They rushed into the office, but the doctor was gone. Back out in the hallway, Mason intercepted a nurse. "Have you seen Dr. Scholz?"

"No," the nurse said. "We've been looking for him everywhere. It's not like him to disappear like this."

"Is there another way down to the ground floor besides the main stairs?"

"There are fire exits at both ends of this wing. The closest is that way, behind you and to your right."

Mason said to Wolski, "Take the main stairs and see if you can cut him off on the ground floor. I'll take the fire exit stairs."

They split up. Mason found the fire stairs, a narrow, winding staircase. His heart sank when he couldn't hear any footsteps on the metal stairs. He flew down to the first floor and came out of the staircase by the emergency room entrance. Wolski ran up a moment later.

"Check the front. See if Manganella saw him exit that way. I'll check the back."

Mason dodged doctors and nurses as he ran through the emergency room. He blew out the back entrance and searched the small parking lot meant for ambulances and delivery trucks. An alleyway at the far end branched off in both directions. Then Mason saw two army-uniformed legs writhing between the ambulances. He ran up and discovered the MP, Private Wagner, gagging as he held his neck. Mason called out for a waiting ambulance driver to get some help.

Wagner sputtered, "Asshole got me with his cane. He took off that way." He pointed to the alleyway off the left side of the lot.

Mason ran out into the alleyway and followed it until it emptied out onto the main street. He looked frantically left and right. Dr. Scholz had disappeared.

17

The chief administrator, Dr. Sauber, tried to keep up with Mason as the two moved down the main hallway of the hospital's administrative offices. "Herr Collins, I have a hospital to run."

"No one is stopping you," Mason said.

"Your insistence to interviewing everyone in my hospital interrupts the smooth operations of—"

Mason ducked into an office where one of the surgical nurses was working with an MP sketch artist on a portrait of Dr. Scholz. "Are you about done with that? We've got to get that sketch out there."

The sketch artist looked up from his work. "Yes, sir. Putting the final touches on it now."

Mason looked at the sketch. "Yeah, that's him. Go ahead and get it down to the printing offices. Then see a Corporal Hitchins on the CID floor. He'll see it gets distributed."

Mason continued his walk down the hallway with Dr. Sauber in tow.

"Sir, your policemen guarding every entrance and checking

everyone coming and going is creating confusion and anxiety, even frightening some patients from seeking care."

"I'm sure those MPs are treating everyone with patience and respect."

"But, Herr Collins—"

"Dr. Sauber, a surgeon at your hospital is a cold-blooded murderer. I would expect that you would want to do anything in your power to help us track him down."

"Not at the expense of my patients—"

He was interrupted again when Wolski fell in step with Mason and said, "The address Scholz gave us turned out to be bogus—just a pile of rubble. The 508th has beefed up patrols and everyone has a verbal description of Scholz. They've got MPs at the train stations and tripled their checkpoints. We've also got the description out to the outlying MP stations."

"You are turning my hospital into a three-ring circus," Sauber said. "There are patients' lives at stake. I can't have you taking my staff out willy-nilly and interrogating them to serve what I see as a futile process."

"Dr. Sauber, I'm willing to bet that your staff is more concerned about having worked alongside a murderer, and that this hospital allowed patients to go under the knife by a surgeon who dismembered people in his spare time. That is why I want you to wait in your office until I find a moment to ask you some questions."

Sauber's eyes popped wide in alarm. He stopped and watched Mason for a moment before retreating in the opposite direction.

Mason and Wolski entered the main lobby and hovered near the area for waiting patients until Inspector Becker concluded his interview with a hospital orderly. Two of Becker's men circulated among a small group of staff who worked on the surgical wing getting their statements. Becker dismissed the orderly and walked up to them.

"Dr. Scholz maintained his anonymity quite well," Becker said. "No one, so far, can offer anything beyond his professional life here at the hospital."

"Nothing about his past? Where he lives? Where he goes?" Mason asked.

Becker shook his head. "Other than complaints of him being arrogant and aloof, he seems to have been widely respected as a surgeon and considerate of his patients. What about the search of his office? Did you find anything that could help?"

"We both got the impression that he'd arranged everything for a quick getaway. No agenda, no pictures, notes, letters, not even a matchbook. Nothing personal at all. A lower drawer in desk was open and things disturbed like he'd kept something there in case he had to make a quick exit."

"He did leave a Bible, a rosary, and his crucifix," Wolski said. "I guess psychopathic killer can dispense with the religious stuff if he's on the run from the law."

"How are your guys doing with the door-to-door searches and canvassing?" Mason asked Becker.

"We have as many men doing this as we can spare. As you know, we are still woefully understaffed. The process is slow, but it will be done. We did send out the bulletins to suburban and rural police stations."

"We still have most of the surgeons to interview about Scholz," Mason said. "I plan to go at the administrator now."

"We have a list of all surgeons and surgical staff," Becker said. "My second is organizing an interview schedule. Some will have to wait until tomorrow when they come on shift"

Mason nodded. "Why don't you get started with those who are here now, and we'll join you as soon as we can."

Mason and Wolski left Becker and headed for the administrative offices. Mason said, "I want you to go talk to the chief of surgeons"—he checked his notes—"a Dr. Tritten. He's waiting for you in his office on the fifth floor."

Wolski started to peel off, but Mason told him to wait. He pointed in the direction of the main entrance. Colonel Walton, trailed by four CID investigators, had just entered the lobby. "The cavalry has arrived," Mason said with a tone of sarcasm.

Mason and Wolski met Colonel Walton and his entourage near the reception area.

Colonel Walton stopped and put his hands on his hips. "Before I get to the fact that you let the suspect escape—"

"Colonel, we had nothing on him," Mason said. "He had an alibi for the night of the factory victim's murder, which we were going to verify—"

"You disobeyed my direct order to stay away from U.S. Medical Corps personnel files."

"Sir, we concentrated on MP and CID arrest records involving medical personnel. If we had questions, we consulted with the personnel records office." Mostly true, though "consulted" meant Wolski and he rummaging through the records office themselves.

"I warned you about disregarding my authority," Colonel Walton said. "If this case didn't have General West breathing down my neck, I'd throw your ass out of here. And now that your prime suspect turns out to be a German surgeon, you went over my head for nothing."

Wolski butt in. "That we *have* a prime suspect should account for something."

Colonel Walton turned his glare to Wolski. "When I want comments from the rookie I'll ask for it." He pointed to the four men behind him and said to Mason, "I brought you four additional investigators. They're yours for the duration of this investigation, as per your request to General West, which I might add you also saw fit to go over my head about. You'll have two more by the end of the day. They're coming over from Company C's detachment."

Mason knew Timmers and McMillan. Colonel Walton introduced the other two as investigators Pike and Cole. "We're setting up an operations room at headquarters, as we speak," Colonel Walton said. "Something you'll definitely need now in order to track down the suspect you let escape. Now, tell me what you have so far."

Mason told him about what had led them to Dr. Scholz, the interview, the subsequent escape, and where they stood in tracking Scholz down.

Colonel Walton nodded and let out a tired sigh. "I've got to get back and explain this mess to his holiness, General West. You find this doctor and fast."

When Colonel Walton left, Mason turned to the new investigators. "Any of you speak German?"

Timmers halfheartedly raised his hand. "I do, sorta."

Mason said to Wolski, "See if you can scrounge up a couple of interpreters and get them interviewing surgical staff. Maybe Becker can help you out. Then see the chief surgeon. I'm going to find out what Dr. Sauber has to say for himself."

DR. SAUBER WAS TALKING EXCITEDLY ON THE PHONE WHEN HIS secretary let Mason enter the administrator's office. Sauber echoed the same complaints he'd voiced to Mason, but in a woeful tone. Mason caught "*Liebchen*," or "darling," before Sauber cupped the mouthpiece and lowered his voice. Apparently Sauber had called his wife to share in his distress—though she was not entirely sympathetic, because Sauber hissed something unintelligible into the phone before slamming down the receiver.

He turned to Mason with a politician's smile and gestured for Mason to sit.

Unlike the German stereotype of fanatic order, Sauber's office exuded chaos. Stacks of file folders, books, and newspapers cluttered every space. Mason had to move a stack of folders from the high-back chair before he could take a seat.

"Just put that anywhere," Sauber said. He swept his hands wide to include the entire room. "You see what I have to put up with? I am severely understaffed and bursting at the seams with patients."

Mason searched for an open spot. "I hope you don't smoke in here, Doctor." He finally plopped them on the floor and sat. "I apologize for the disturbance. We won't be here any longer than we have to. But you do understand the seriousness of the situation."

"Of course, sir. Anything I can do to help."

"Good. You can start by supplying me with any documents relating to Dr. Scholz: his personnel file—address, family, place of birth, et cetera. Where he practiced before coming to this hospital, where he studied medicine."

"You will be pleased to know that I have already ordered that those documents be compiled and sent to my office. They should be here anytime now. If it helps, Doctor Scholz speaks with a light Swabian dialect."

Mason noted that on his notepad. "When did Dr. Scholz start working for this hospital?"

"This past June. Around the middle of the month."

"Did you know him from before? Or did he just walk in and ask for a position?"

"He came to us."

"What kind of evaluation process did you perform before hiring Dr. Scholz?"

"I don't understand."

"How deep did you check into his background? Did he have a criminal record? Was he wanted by the American or Allied authorities for war crimes?"

Sauber's face turned red, and his hands moved in tempo with his words. "His... his papers were in order, I assure you. He had a denazification certificate. He had his Kriegsmarine discharge papers."

"Did you verify their authenticity?"

"You must understand...." He took a moment to wipe his brow with a handkerchief. "At war's end we were in desperate need of qualified surgeons."

"Then, no."

Sauber shook his head. "The system for such verifications was extremely difficult, what with the damage to the infrastructure, the chaos, people and records spread hither and yon. They still are. Such a thing would have taken too long, and we needed him immediately. I might add, he proved himself spectacularly in the operating room. I was delighted to have him. When such a gift is presented to you, you don't ask questions."

"Where was he during the war?"

"He was a surgeon in the Kriegsmarine. Though I must admit, there were some discrepancies concerning his service records."

"Such as?"

"They had a Friedrich Scholz, but not a Heinrich Scholz."

"And what did Dr. Scholz say about this?"

Sauber leaned into the desk. "Well, he was rather vague about it," he said in a muted voice as if he'd suspected something odd all along. "When I first heard about Dr. Scholz's... hasty departure this morning, I reflected upon my evaluation process for hiring him. As a matter of fact, I put in a call to the University of Heidelberg, but they have no record of a Heinrich Scholz obtaining a degree at their university."

Mason had expected something like this. The man had expertly covered his tracks up to now, and probably used a false name. And it was not uncommon for those escaping justice in the postwar chaos to obtain the identity of someone recently deceased or killed.

The office door swung open after a quick knock. A gray-haired man with chiseled features swaggered into the room. He thrust out his hand toward Mason. "Ah, you must be Criminal Investigator Collins. Dr. Tritten, chief of surgeons."

Mason stood and shook his hand while looking at Sauber, prompting another solicitous smile from Sauber. "I took the liberty of inviting Dr. Tritten to this interview. I hope you don't mind."

Tritten didn't wait for a response. One moment he was heartily shaking Mason's hand, and the next he was planting himself on Sauber's desk. "Now, how can I help you in this matter?"

Mason shot Sauber another glance before retaking his seat. He figured Sauber had asked for reinforcements to deflect some of the pressure off the interview, and they looked like two coconspirators seated together, facing Mason. "Dr. Tritten," Mason began, "I'm sure you're aware that we suspect Dr. Scholz is responsible for a series of murders—"

"I was shocked, to say the least," Tritten interjected. "I can't imagine Heinrich would be capable of such a thing." He exchanged a look with Sauber, who nodded in affirmation.

"As chief of surgeons, you're probably the most familiar with Dr. Scholz at this hospital."

"That is most likely true, but Dr. Scholz was not an easy man to get to know. I'm sure you want to ask me what I know about his personal life, but I haven't much to give you."

Another complicitous nod from Sauber.

"Did he ever mention family or friends?"

"No, not friends, but he occasionally talked about his wife and son."

"He has a son?"

"I've never met them. Usually a proud parent likes to show pictures of his family, but he never showed them to me or anyone else that I know of. He did speak of them in reverential tones. Nothing specific, really. Simply in terms of how they had changed his life and helped him through the dark years of war. Gertie and Max are their names."

"I assume they live with him?"

Tritten looked at Sauber, who shrugged and said, "We would assume so."

Mason looked at his watch. "Are those files coming anytime soon?"

"Any minute, sir."

"Did Dr. Scholz really suffer from a previous back injury?"

"To my knowledge, yes," Tritten said.

"For a man who seemed to need the use of a cane, he made a pretty fast getaway. Not to mention committing those murders."

Tritten and Sauber exchanged glances, then Tritten produced a roughish smile. "Now that you mention it, I observed him several times without it. In my opinion, he used it more as a psychological crutch than as an aid for walking."

Mason was losing his patience. The two doctors were obviously telling him things they thought he wanted to hear to get him off their backs.

"Was Dr. Scholz a religious man?"

"I noticed he wore a crucifix," Tritten said. "Plus, I heard that he prayed and made the sign of the cross if a patient died on his operating table."

"Did you notice or hear of any odd behavior: anxiety, nervous tics, fits of temper, things like that?"

"No, nothing."

"Did he express anger or a desire for revenge? Hatred or prejudice toward people or group of people—persons in the medical profession, for instance?"

Sauber shook his head emphatically and looked to Tritten for help.

"No," Tritten said, "though once in passing he mentioned a preference for nature and solitude over the company of people. But nothing that would lead either Dr. Sauber or myself to imagine that Dr. Scholz could do such a thing. To be frank, I'd like to think that he's innocent of the charges."

"The classic question is, if he were innocent then why did he run?"

"Everyone has something to hide, Herr Collins. Something to be ashamed of."

Tritten had inadvertently opened a crack in his confident facade. He knew more than he was telling. They both were. Tritten covered it with a big grin, but Sauber suddenly found his desktop extremely fascinating.

"What is it that you're not telling me, Doctors?"

"I meant nothing by that statement," Tritten said. "I only proffered speculation as to why he decided to run from the authorities."

"You know what it could mean for the hospital if we discover that one or both of you is withholding vital information about a murderer."

Silence from both of them.

"Do either of you have any idea where he might have gone? Any idea where he might be hiding?"

"How could we possibly know that?" Tritten said at the same instant that Sauber again shook his head.

Sauber's secretary poked her head in the room after knocking. "The files you requested, Dr. Sauber."

Mason stood. "I'll take those, please."

The secretary looked to Dr. Sauber, who nodded for her to comply. She handed the files to Mason and left. Mason remained by the door as he scanned the documents. Dr. Scholz's personal information listed his home address—naturally a completely different address from the one Scholz had given them at the end of the interview. It might not be his real address, either, and Mason doubted that Scholz would be there waiting to be arrested, but it would still be Mason's next stop.

18

"Might have known he was up to no good," Frau Wruck, the landlady, said.

"Why do you say that, ma'am?" Mason asked. "Did he exhibit any strange behavior? Frighten you?"

"Frighten me? After all I've been through? No, he's just a pompous ass. Acts like he's the king of the world. People like that are always up to something."

Frau Wruck led the way, mounting the stairs to Dr. Scholz's apartment. For a seventy-plus-year-old, she handled the three flights of stairs with the vigor of a woman thirty years younger. She spoke in Bavarian slang, which Mason struggled to understand.

"When did Dr. Scholz rent the apartment?"

"I'd say, the first of June." She stopped and thought. "Yeah, the first of June," she said and continued up the stairs.

Wolski and Timmers followed behind Mason. Two MPs kept watch below in case Scholz was foolish enough to show up.

"Do you see him very much?" Mason asked.

"Hardly ever. He comes and goes at odd hours. Creepy, if you ask me."

"What about his wife and son?"

Frau Wruck stopped again and turned as if she hadn't heard the question. "What's that? He has a wife and son?" She shook her head and continued the climb. "Never seen a boy, though I have seen the doctor with a woman a few times. If he has family living up there then I need to charge him more rent. As a matter of fact, I should be charging him a *lot* more. When he first came here, I felt like I'd finally got a prestigious—and finally a *paying* —tenant. I gave him a break on the rent because of that, but now I've got some hotshot banker living here with his wife. This once-rich man had no other place to go. So, I charge him a bundle. And you know what? He pays it, and he's happy to do it. I'm learning. You know, I was just the guardian before the owner took off. He put me in charge until he gets back. Haven't seen him since."

"You said Dr. Scholz came and went at odd hours. Did he ever leave the premises after curfew?"

Frau Wruck stopped at a door, bringing the group to a halt. She chuckled as she fished for her keys. "It's not *that* hard to get around the curfew. If you've got the gumption there's a way." She finally found the right key and inserted it into the lock.

Mason put his hand on hers to get her attention and put his finger to his mouth, telling her to be quiet. When she saw Wolski and Timmers with their guns drawn, she retreated to the opposite wall. Mason unlocked the door, pushed it open, and let Wolski and Timmers enter with their guns held high. Mason slipped in behind them.

The three investigators split up, Mason silently instructing Timmers to take the kitchen, and Wolski to search the bedroom. A quick room-to-room search of the apartment confirmed what Mason had expected, that Dr. Scholz was not there. He then returned to the living room, and found Frau Wruck standing just inside the front door.

"He ain't here, is he?" Frau Wruck said.

"No, ma'am."

"At least he's paid-up 'til the end of the month."

"Do you talk to him much? Maybe talk to him about him having a second residence? Or a place he likes to go when he's not staying here?"

"Hell, most folks don't have a primary residence, let alone a second. Is he rich, or something?"

"I wouldn't know. But thank you for your time. We'll take it from here."

"Don't you boys do any damage to the apartment. I want to rent it out again, and I don't have the money to fix it up."

Mason reassured her and asked her to wait downstairs. When she left, Mason took a moment to survey the room. The absence of photographs or artwork on the walls struck him first. Either the doctor was obsessed with neatness or he didn't spend much time actually living there. Mason checked the coal-burning fireplace, but it looked like it hadn't been used in a while. A search through the books and cushions turned up nothing. He moved on to the small bathroom, which contained a handful of toiletry items all neatly arranged.

It turned out that all the surprises waited for him in the smaller, second bedroom. Though the room had a simple iron-frame bed, area rug, and dresser, it appeared that the room served more as a showplace for Scholz's family. All along the top of the triple dresser sat close to thirty framed photographs of two people who Mason assumed were his wife and son, mostly formal portraits, some tinted, all depicting two smiling faces. Several were wedding pictures. In a couple his wife, Gertie, wore a nurse's uniform. The boy, Max, looked to be twelve or so, wearing either a suit and tie or his school uniform. A rocking chair had been placed so that the chair's occupant could behold the photographic collection. A spindly end table accompanied the chair, where

Scholz had placed a half-full bottle of schnapps and a drinking glass.

Mason tried to imagine the doctor sitting there, what had driven him to kill and butcher, what had prompted him to set up these pictures and rock in front of them, drinking schnapps, raise his glass to toast his family before getting on with his butchering. How could he be so evil while still functioning perfectly in society? Mason could see and understand the dark side of the man. He'd experienced enough of the evil that men could do in the camps to know it very well, but he couldn't understand how someone could live in both worlds. That didn't make any sense to him.

He bent low and noticed a steamer trunk under the bed. He knelt and pulled it out, disturbing the layer of dust coating the floor. The trunk slid easily, and he brought it to rest by the rocking chair. The lid opened with a creak of protest.

Wolski poked his head in the room. "The guy can't have more than a day's worth of clothes in the bedroom. What's all that?"

"Kid's toys," Mason said as he proceeded to pull out cast-iron soldiers, stuffed animals, a spinning top with a carousel design, a jack-in-the-box, and finally a music box shaped like a grand piano.

Wolski stepped into the room to get a better look. "This must be the boy's room."

"I don't know what this room is. Like the rest of the apartment, there's nothing that says anyone lives here."

After emptying out all the toys, Mason noticed a tray insert at the bottom. He lifted it out, then removed a folded woman's dress wrapped in tissue paper. "This stuff must be his wife's: dresses, shoes, hairbrushes...." He stopped. Beneath the woman's things he found a creased and water-stained envelope devoid of writing. It contained a folded letter. Mason took out the letter and read it. "It's from a woman in Stuttgart, 1942. A Heidi Mendel."

. . .

DEAR HEINRICH,

I have the sad task of informing you that Gertie and Max have been missing since the last bombing raid. It took me a week to compose myself before I could face writing you with this unhappy news. Mother says we should continue to hope....'

MASON STOPPED READING AND PUT THE LETTER BACK IN THE envelope.

"Who are Gertie and Max?" Wolski asked.

"Scholz's wife and son. That explains the photographs and the schnapps."

"Scholz's sister or sister-in-law, sounds like," Wolski said. "This is getting stranger by the hour. Next thing you know, we're going to find Scholz's wife's and son's preserved bodies are in the icebox."

Mason started to put the items back in the trunk. "Let's finish up and get out of this mausoleum."

MASON ENTERED THE WIRTSCHAFT ALTER HOF AND SPOTTED Laura waving at him from a corner booth. He crossed the room and slipped onto the booth across from her. She wore her correspondent's outfit, a conservative brown wool suit coat and skirt, but still looked as amazing as she had in her evening gown.

"May I say that your perfume is almost as seductive as the smell of beer and bratwurst?" Mason said.

"Are you trying to upset my bourgeois sensibilities with that blue-collar remark?"

"It means I'm starving."

"But a simple declaration isn't good enough for you. And speaking of good enough, I thought for a first date you'd have asked me to somewhere a little more romantic."

"Who said anything about a date? I asked you to meet me here to get you up-to-date on the investigation. I promised I would, so here we are."

"That's just an excuse. You're really just too shy to come out and say it. That's sweet."

"And you giving me sass is a way to hide that you're head over heels for me."

"I hardly know you."

"Not to know me is to love me." Mason waved for the waiter. "Thanks for arranging access to the Medical Corps personnel files. That was pretty impressive."

"Find anything?"

"Not much. There are a few possibles we might look into, but now that we have a prime suspect, we probably won't need to."

"I've noticed there hasn't been one article about the murders in any of the newspapers. Not even a blip. No editor will touch it. Even if I wanted to publish something, no one will print it."

"Then our exclusive arrangement is working out good for you."

"I don't like it when the press is censored. It sets a bad precedent, even for an occupational force."

"In this case, I think it's justified."

"It's never justified. People have a right to know."

"To know what? That there's a mad killer on the loose and the police appear powerless to stop him? Normally I'd agree with you, but legitimizing the rumors might incite people to resort to vigilante justice. They could turn to the underground networks that want to form a Fourth Reich and pine for the good old days of the iron-fisted Gestapo to bring back order."

"Rumors can be more dangerous than the truth, you know."

"This is where we differ, reporter and cop."

"Is that a problem?"

"Not for me."

The waiter arrived, and they both ordered bratwurst and beer.

"I can't stay long," Mason said. "I've got to get back to head-quarters."

"I heard about your snafu at the hospital." Mason was about to respond, but Laura laughed and held up her hands. "Truce. Okay? Tell me what happened today."

Mason quickly summed up what had led them to Scholz; the interview and escape; then the manhunt, the hospital staff interviews, and the bizarre findings at Scholz's apartment. "The CID detachment in Stuttgart is trying to track down the woman who wrote the letter about his wife and son, a Heidi Mendel. The MPs and German police are distributing the sketch of Scholz. I imagine calls will be coming in any time now from people with mostly well-intentioned but erroneous sightings."

"Let me get this straight: Scholz had two tickets to a concert, says it was his wife, but she's been missing for three years?"

Mason nodded. "I had someone check with the concert hall manager. It was a single-night performance and every seat was taken. One of the ushers said she seated a tall man with a thirty-something blond woman that evening in those seats."

"And he had some kind of shrine to his wife and his son in a place he rarely stays?"

The beers came. Mason sipped his while Laura thought a moment.

"It sounds like to me like he feels guilty," Laura said. "He still loves them, but he's created a shrine to their memory in an out-of-the-way place. He goes there when the guilt becomes too much, drinks his schnapps in front of the photos, asks for forgiveness, then leaves. He's got a lover, and he feels guilty about it."

"Interesting theory. But based on what?"

Laura shrugged and started fidgeting with her beer mug. "I've known a few married men and widowers. None of them could stand to be alone, but they always felt guilty about stepping out on the little woman. Most of them, anyway."

Mason felt a pang of jealousy, and though he thought he hid it well...

"I see that look in your eyes," Laura said.

"What?"

"That look of condemnation."

"I'm just wondering if I can keep up with you."

"I've had a few wild years in my past. So what?"

"Laura, I'm not judging you. Let's get back to the subject."

"Fine," she said. "Let's start with that woman at the concert. If the doctor has a lover, she could be hiding him. Find the lover, and you just might find your killer."

"That's not bad. Ever thought about being a detective?"

"Being a reporter is a little like being a detective. Sometimes to get at the truth, you have to dig for it."

Their dinners arrived, and they fell silent a few moments.

"So, how about a real date next time?" Mason asked. "That is, if you're not committed to a certain CID general."

"That smacks of jealousy. You're not the jealous type, are you?"

"My grandma used to say that the only useful thing about jealousy is it makes you recognize what you want; then all you have to do is go after it."

"Smart woman, your grandmother."

"So? What about it?"

"About what?"

"A date. A reporter and cop. A modern-day Capulet and Montague."

"Haven't you got enough on your plate right now?"

"Meaning, you do."

Laura shrugged. "Maybe there's something I can do about that. Something I should do before we ever think about becoming star-crossed lovers."

"Fair enough," Mason said. He downed one last bite of food and rose from the table. "I have to get back." He stopped next to her, leaned in, and kissed her.

"Too bad you have to rush off," Laura said.

"We both have some business to take care of first. Then watch out."

Mason gave her a peck on the forehead and left.

19

Corporal Manganella intercepted Mason as soon as he walked in the front entrance of the station.

"What is it, Sal? Can it wait until I've had my morning coffee?"

"Sorry, sir, but there's a woman waiting for you in the auxiliary room near the cages." He motioned for Mason to follow him through the downstairs lobby. He looked at his notes and strained to pronounce the name, "A Beata Walczak. She's Polish."

"Thank you, Private, I figured that out by the name."

"A German cop brought her in. She doesn't speak English, and I guess her German ain't so good, either. The German cop said she has information about Scholz but refused to say anything to them. She insisted on talking to the American detective in charge." They stopped at the closed door of the room used to search arrestees before putting them in the overnight cells. "She was pretty upset, so we put her in here."

Mason saw Wolski breach the front entrance and signaled for his partner to join him. Wolski met him by the door, eyes sunken and bloodshot.

"Did you get any sleep last night?" Mason asked.

"A couple hours. I spent most of the night shuttling between the 508th headquarters, the OMGB public safety office, and the CIC records division. So far nothing on a Dr. Heinrich Scholz. There was a Heinrich Scholz, but he was an aviator killed in North Africa. A Helmut Scholz, a low-level bureaucrat in the propaganda offices in Berlin. But so far, a Dr. Heinrich Scholz doesn't exist."

"It figures he's using an alias. Did you also try the name Mendel in your search?"

Wolski moaned.

"I'll take that as a no."

Wolski nodded toward the closed door. "Who's in there?"

"We're going to find out."

They entered the room together. A thin, brown-haired woman sat at the small table. Her shoulders were drawn deep into her chest, her head bowed low, her eyes fixed on some unseen vision. Mason and Wolski sat at the table across from her.

"I understand you wanted to talk to me, Frau Walczak," Mason said in German.

Frau Walczak looked up at Mason, and he had to suppress a shiver. He'd seen eyes like hers many times before, in the faces of the inmates at Buchenwald. Wolski cleared his throat and shifted in his chair, alerting Mason that he had been staring at her in silence.

Mason introduced them and asked, "I understand you have information on a Dr. Scholz?"

Frau Walczak removed a folded and crumpled piece of paper from her pocket and laid it on the table. She opened it with shaking hands and flattened it. It was the sketch of Scholz they had distributed. "This man sterilized me," she said in German with a thick Polish accent.

"What do you mean, ma'am?"

She jabbed the photo with her forefinger. "He... sterilized me. In the camp."

"This man? Dr. Scholz?"

"I do not know his name. But he was at Ravensbrück. I will never forget his face."

"Ravensbrück concentration camp?"

She nodded. "I was resistance fighter in Poland. They arrested me and put me in Ravensbrück. This man was SS doctor at the camp, and he selected me. They forced me to hospital barrack. He..." She fought for a breath as she wiped a tear with a trembling hand.

"If you need a moment..."

She shook her head and choked back her tears. "He injected something into my uterus. The pain, you cannot imagine. Then two days later he took out my uterus. I will never have children. He ruined my life. He did this to many women. Some children, too. Little girls...."

Mason pulled out a photo reproduction of Scholz's portrait from his personnel file. He placed the photo in front of Frau Walczak. "This man? Are you sure?"

Frau Walczak nodded. "I am sure."

"And you're sure you can't remember his name?"

"No one ever spoke his name. Only the nurses talked to me."

Mason glanced at Wolski, who understood the silent command. Wolski shot out of his chair and left the room.

"When did this happen?" Mason asked.

"Winter of 1942."

"Were you liberated at Ravensbrück? And was this doctor still there?"

"In late 1944 I was sent to two other camps. I was at Dachau when the Americans liberated us." She looked into Mason's eyes. "You find this man. You hang him for what he did."

Mason took her hand and held it while she wept.

～

MASON MOUNTED THE STAIRS TO THE CID FLOOR. HE COULD SEE Wolski sitting at his desk and on the telephone spreading the new information to all departments. Colonel Walton and Havers were in the middle of a heated discussion in the colonel's office, so Mason waited outside the door. He didn't have long to wait; Colonel Walton ordered Havers to quit sniveling and get back to work.

Havers stomped out of the office and blocked Mason's way. "Colonel Walton gave me your train robbery case. And while you guys have been floundering around trying to find that Ripper, the same gang knocked over a payroll train. If we don't get paid, we'll know who to come for."

"They actually pay you for what you do?" Mason asked, then turned and walked into Colonel Walton's office.

Colonel Walton angrily shoved papers around on his desk. "I suppose you're here to ruin my perfectly crappy morning."

"I just talked to a witness who says that Scholz was an SS doctor at Ravensbrück, but she never heard his name."

"You're sure she's positively identified the guy?" Colonel Walton said.

"The look in her eyes when she pointed him out didn't leave much doubt in my mind. I would like to request access to files pertaining to Ravensbrück concentration camp. Maybe that way we can discover his real name. Then see if we can find someone who was there to give us more information about him. Maybe where he lived, where he went on leave, his habits, if he was transferred to other camps."

"I'll have to mark this day on my calendar, the day you decided to request this from me instead of going over my head." He gave Mason a stern glare before acquiescing with a nod. "I'll put in a call to General West."

Mason left Colonel Walton's office and headed for the operations room located on the next floor. Wolski caught up with him on the stairs.

"I called 508th headquarters and OMGB and gave them the Ravensbrück lead," Wolski said. "Becker was out, but I left him a message."

"Yeah, good," Mason said as they entered the new operations room—really a conference room with a dozen chairs, a blackboard and corkboard, and a table with two telephones. Timmers and McMillan answered the constantly ringing phones. As Mason had predicted, tips and sightings had been coming in since the sketch of "Dr. Scholz" had been distributed. Aside from Timmers and MacMillan, Mason had already met Pike and Coles. The other two had come over from Company C: Mancini and Curtis.

"I hope you all enjoyed your five hours of sleep," Mason said. He walked up to the corkboard, where he'd pinned up photographs from the three crime scenes and one of Scholz. "I'm sure everyone here is running into the same problem, that there are no records for a Dr. Heinrich Scholz. He was using an alias, which knocks us back a step. You'll see from your copy of the letter found in his apartment that his sister-in-law went by Heidi Mendel, so be sure to include that name in any of your searches. However, we have one new development. I just finished talking to a woman who identified Scholz as an SS doctor at a concentration camp called Ravensbrück."

The phones fell quiet for the moment, so Timmers and MacMillan joined the group. Mason then reviewed the rest of Frau Walczak's statement. He spelled out the names on the chalkboard, and the investigators notated the information. "Wolski and I will coordinate with the different departments to track down any documents pertaining to this man. I'll also have Inspector Becker see what he can do on his end. The rest of you continue with your assigned tasks. Timmers and MacMillan still have the three

remaining surgeons and about twelve surgery staff left to interview at the hospital this morning." He turned to Cole and Pike.
"What about the canvass around the doctor's apartment?"

"Not much more than the landlady said," Cole said. "He was
rarely seen, once or twice with a blond-haired woman in her thirties—that's the best we could get for a description. No one knew
or talked with him."

"I checked in with our German police liaison, Inspector
Becker, earlier this morning. Nothing new from the canvass
around the hospital. Our man seems to have disappeared."

Mancini raised his hand. "A few tips have come in that might
be worth looking at."

"You and Curtis check them out. Wolski and I are going to
have another go at the chief of surgeons and the chief hospital
administrator. Remember, this is our prime suspect, but I don't
want to drop our other lines of investigation. Also, Scholz—or
whatever his real name is—may strike again, and we know he
transports the bodies by night, so when we've exhausted the
canvasses and interviews, Mr. Wolski will assign a team to go
through U.S.-issued night passes or related permits to civilians.
I've asked our German liaison, Oberinspektor Becker to check out
all liveries to see if one of them rented a wagon and horses to
someone fitting his description. Maybe we can pin down the area
he usually operates in."

The phone rang and Wolski answered it.

Investigator Cole raised his hand. "I used to deal with civilian
passes and permits over at 508th headquarters. We're talking
about doctors, ambulance services, city administrators, police,
fire, utility and maintenance workers...."

"It's a lot of ground to cover, I know—"

"Chief," Wolski said when he hung up the phone. He
motioned for Mason to come over. "That was Colonel Walton. He
talked to General West about getting the files on the Nazi doctors.

It's going to be close to two weeks before all formal requests and orders are moved through channels."

"Then we forget about channels."

"You're not planning to go over General West's head, too, are you?"

Mason moved for the door. "You can take it from here. Get these teams moving."

Wolski called after him. "Where are you going?"

"To see a friend at the CIC."

20

M ike Forester, a major in the army's Counter Intelligence Command, or CIC, had a small corner office on the third floor of the McGraw Kaserne's main building. When Mason knocked, a raspy voice told him to enter. Forester, a heavy smoker, was lighting one cigarette from the hot crown of another as Mason walked in.

"Mason. Good to see you. I heard you were in Munich working for the rival team."

The office had large windows, upon which Major Forester had hung venetian blinds that were tightly closed. Mason took a seat. "As much as I hate Nazis, I didn't want to spend my days hunting them down."

"CIC's not all Nazi chasing." Forester lowered his voice, as if someone might be eavesdropping. "Now that we've beaten the Nazis, there's a new threat, and it could be bigger and bloodier. I see another war, God help us, brewing with the Commies. We need good intelligence men to find out what the Russians plan to do with the sixty divisions they've got planted on the borders. If war comes, we'll be slugging it out in Germany. They've already got a battalion of spies snooping around on our side. You could be a great asset for our team."

"I'm a detective, not a spy. Thanks, though, for the offer."

Forester shrugged as he puffed on his cigarette.

"What's with the closed blinds?"

"I'm handling some highly classified stuff, and in the army's peerless wisdom they gave me an office with wall-to-wall windows." He offered Mason a cigarette, but Mason declined. "What can I do for you?"

"I'm following a lead on a case of multiple homicides—"

"I heard about those butcher jobs," Forester interrupted. He had a hyperactive personality and rarely let someone finish a sentence if he could hurry the conversation along. "You've got a Jack the Ripper on your hands."

"How did you know about the murders? We've been trying to keep that under wraps."

"Mason, this is the CIC."

"We have reason to believe our prime suspect is a doctor—"

"And you're here because he's probably ex-Nazi who worked at one of the camps."

Mason smiled. "The only name we have for the suspect is an alias, but a Polish woman identified him as an SS doctor. She says he sterilized her at Ravensbrück. I need access to the concentration camp records to see if we can positively ID the man and track down anyone who knew him. I tried through regular channels, but no dice."

Forester turned serious. "What makes you think this guy is your suspect?"

Mason gave him to rundown about the killer's methods and surgical skills, as well as his messages about being in a personal hell, the events leading to the interview with Scholz, his escape, and the subsequent manhunt. "So far, an ID photo is all we have to track him down—" Mason stopped. "What do you find so amusing?"

"Let's just say that investigating the wrong Nazi doctors right now might be a political hot potato."

"What are you talking about? They're war criminals. If they're not dead, they're in prison camps, or on the run. All I'm asking for is access to information on the people at Ravensbrück performing experiments, their whereabouts—"

"I know what you're after. But right now that all falls under the purview of American and British intelligence. Some intelligence higher-ups might not like you perusing classified files."

"Classified? I...." Mason stopped and speculated on Forester's meaning. He'd known the man for two years. They'd worked together in intelligence, and Forester had missed suffering the same fate as Mason in the Battle of the Bulge only because Forester had been on a forty-eight-hour leave to Paris. Mason could tell by Forester's eyes and his cock-eyed grin that he was trying to encourage Mason to continue speculating.

"It comes back to this future war with Russia, doesn't it?" Mason said. "Intelligence wants to know anything the Nazi doctors learned by experimenting on innocent people before the Russians get to them first. But this guy sterilized women. What can they learn from that?"

"Are you sure he wasn't involved in other experiments?"

"Like what? Are you talking about chemical weapons?"

Forester gestured for him to keep going—an irksome game of charades.

"Other weapons?"

Forester waited expectantly.

"Biological?"

Forester's eyes signaled that he was close to the truth. "Now, if you worked for us at CIC, I'd see to it you had the clearance to see any file you want."

"You're talking to a cop, Mike. For me, anyone who committed a crime like that should suffer the worst kind of punishment, and not be given immunity for what he knows."

"Sometimes you have to look the other way for the greater good."

"I'll make you a deal: I only look at the people involved in sterilization at Ravensbrück. You have your people review the files first and pass on any that don't threaten American intelligence interests."

"It's my duty to inform you that until Intelligence deems any file irrelevant, for as long as that takes, then you will not be permitted access." Forester made another sly smile. "It is also my duty to urge you *not* to go to Frankfurt and see a Colonel Donaldson at the Judge Advocate General's office and request those files from him."

Mason returned the smile. "JAG and the war crimes tribunal have subpoenaed all files for the Nazi war crimes trials."

"I'm not at liberty to discuss it. I can say that, politically, the trials take precedence over intelligence concerns, though there are certain dossiers that are still considered classified and deemed superfluous to the evidentiary process."

Mason stood and they shook hands. "I won't take up any more of your time."

"Nonsense. You'll have to come by when you've got a free evening, and we'll have dinner, get drunk, and reminisce about old times."

"And see who can make up the biggest lies."

Forester held on to Mason's hand just a moment longer. "You sure I can't persuade you to come over to the other side?"

"I tell you what: If it looks like the Russians aren't going to stay on their side of the fence, I'll be the first to sign up."

Mason turned to leave, but Forester stopped him again.

"Be sure to say hello to that beautiful reporter friend of yours."

"How did you…? Forget it. I don't want to know."

THE DOCTOR BUTTONED HIS VEST AND PULLED AT THE BOTTOM hem so that it lay properly across his broad shoulders. He slipped on a green suit coat and brushed lint from his lapel. All must be perfect to create the illusion. His hand passed through a ray of sunlight that pierced the gap in the shutters. Only supreme control kept him from flinching, from imagining his skin burning at a mere brush of sunlight.

The sun mocked him, and he cursed it, as if it were a heavenly spotlight shining down upon him: *There he is, the sinner!* The hated rays, insistent, piercing, violated his room.

He took a long, calming breath, and he shifted to the left to avoid the light. Lately, he found it had become more difficult to cope with the burdens placed upon him. The exultation after each beatification diminished more quickly; the rapacious hunger surfaced more frequently. It would start deep in his groin and surge upward, over-whelming him until nothing else mattered but finding his next Chosen One, like Sisyphus triumphantly reaching the summit with the stone only to have it roll downhill so that he must begin again.

How long? How many beatifications must he perform? How long could he continue to elude the authorities? They might even be close on his trail at this very moment.

He stepped up to a mirror by the door, but before looking at his reflection, he adjusted it to be sure it showed only the bottom half of his face. He shifted to his right and the mirror reflected back a plain yet kindly face, one that people wanted to trust. He checked his teeth and his nostrils, the knot of his bow tie. His round, dark brown eyes were the only feature he could never look at.

They terrified him. Once in the last year, he'd caught a glimpse of those eyes. And when he had looked into the mirror that day and his eyes caught him staring, they showed him all the hideous things he had done. The eyes had taken him on a journey, passing images of the screaming innocents, the terror in their faces.

So many. God forgive and deliver me.

He took a deep breath, relegating the memories to a sequestered place in his mind. After one last check of his tie, he pulled on his white lab coat. With his back straight and chin high, he crossed the short hallway and entered a small office. Then, through another door, he entered an examining room.

Twice a week for the past five months, each Sunday and Thursday, he'd ministered to sick children, and he offered this charitable service in hopes of some redemption in the eyes of God. Especially the children, the children being closer to the divine. And he was determined to make the most of today's session, as it would be his last. It had become too dangerous to continue.

On the examining table sat a boy of eight years. He was recovering from dysentery, but between the illness and malnutrition the boy was more bone than flesh. The muscles had already atrophied. His eyes lacked the spark of life. The boy's mother stood next to him and held his bony hand.

He had seen so many children come to his office in similar or worse conditions. Malnutrition weakened them, but the disease from poor sanitation and contaminated water ravaged them. Newborns and the youngest infants didn't stand a chance.

He leaned in to check the boy's ears and eyes. His face not inches away, he could hear the boy's shallow breathing, feel the heat from his body. His hand quivered... just once, but he looked at the mother out of the corner of his eye. She hadn't noticed.

He pressed the stethoscope to the boy's chest and heard the steady thump of his heart. He could almost hear the rush of blood in the boy's veins. The hunger flared, starting in his groin and flaring in his gut. Whispers seemed to come from inside the boy's chest. A cacophony of voices like water rushing through a pipe. The sounds rose from the boy's lungs and into the stethoscope until he could no longer hear the boy's heartbeat.

Please, not now!

"Herr Doktor? Are you all right?"

The mother's voice snapped him back. His own heart pounded, and he could feel beads of sweat on his forehead.

"Yes, thank you," he muttered. He turned his back on the child and dabbed at the perspiration with his handkerchief, buying time to clear his head. They were like hunger pangs, like a suspended moment before orgasm, when nothing else mattered, when all his energy, his mind, focused on the next hunt and beatification.

He felt the mother's and boy's eyes on him. A shrill voice from within warned him that they knew. They could see through his facade, see the demons ravaging his soul.

Please, not a child. I will do anything, but don't demand a child.

"Herr Doktor?"

He turned and forced a smile. His hand twitched. He had an erection. *They must leave.*

"Franz is getting better," he said in his most assuring voice, "but you must make sure he has enough to eat. And boil your water."

"But how? We have the number five ration card. I have three other children…."

He no longer heard the mother. She continued, almost in tears, now, but the rush of urges flooded his mind. As if invisible hands pushed him forward, he approached the boy, his eyes focusing on the boy's bare chest where he would make the incisions....

With a shaking hand, he reached into his pocket and pulled out a wad of Reichsmarks. He counted off a thousand and shoved them into her hand. She mouthed words, but he couldn't hear.

"Please, you must leave. Dress your boy and leave."

The mother released a flood of tears. She was thanking him, he was sure.

Panic, revulsion and craving engulfed him. *Take them. Take them both. Imagine the ecstasy. No more hunger. A double beatification. Mother and child, together....*

His entire body convulsed in one great shudder. "I demand that you go at once!"

As they rushed to leave, he fled for his connecting office and slammed the door behind him. He fell to his knees and said to the heavens, "Please, not a child."

21

It was just shy of noon on Monday morning when Mason exited the military train at the Frankfurt central train station and stepped into a bone-chilling fog. Another train had pulled in just before Mason's, returning from the countryside. Every day, city dwellers would take their jewelry, cameras, furs, brandy, anything left of their valuables and trade with the farmers for food. The train cars bulged with desperate and hungry Germans. So full, in fact, that many had to cling to the outside using the handrails, and the warmer passengers had to help pry their near-frozen fingers from the ice-cold metal.

The worst scene was of another train that had arrived thirty minutes earlier from Czechoslovakia. The Czechs were expelling all ethnic Germans from the Sudetenland, close to two million of them. Ethnic Germans had lived there for generations, but after Hitler and the war, they were no longer welcome. Entire families were forced from their homes with only what they could carry and were loaded onto open freight cars to make the days-long journey into the heart of Germany.

Most of the passengers still wandered the platform with no place to go. Others helped officials remove those who had died from cold after the long trip, many of them children or the elderly. Mothers wailed over their dead children; children wailed from hunger and the freezing temperatures. The expulsions from Czechoslovakia and Poland had just begun, and millions more would follow.

Mason caught a taxi waiting in front of the station. He gave the man directions and watched the crumbled cityscape pass by. Frankfurt had suffered more damage than Munich. In Munich there were rows upon rows of burned-out shells of buildings, but in Frankfurt entire blocks contained only piles of brick and stone, little to indicate that a great city had stood there. There were few landmarks left, whole streets no longer existed, and while Mason was stationed there, he had gotten lost many times. Fortunately, the taxi driver knew how to navigate this wasteland and bring him to USFET headquarters.

USFET stood for United States Forces, European Theater, the designation for supreme headquarters of all American forces in Europe. This was General Eisenhower's home away from home. The building that housed USFET was reportedly the most massive building in all of Europe, and, in Mason's mind, one of the most notorious—the headquarters of IG Farben, the company responsible for developing the chemical, Zyklon B, used to gas millions in the death camps.

The building sprawled for most of four city blocks, with six nine-story buildings connected by a central lobby. After three security checks, Mason entered the gargantuan lobby. It was originally built as a temple to the corporate gods: marble, marble everywhere, with two identical ascending staircases in aluminum, and a back wall of glass looking out onto a reflection pool circled by statuary. Now it was a general's temple to the gods of war. Rumor had it that it had been spared Allied bombs on Eisenhower's orders so he could adopt it for his headquarters.

On one side of the lobby, two immaculately dressed soldiers

stood at attention behind a reception desk. Mason approached the desk and both soldiers snapped a salute. Mason wondered how many times a day the poor guys had to do that.

"I should have orders from Colonel Donaldson's office waiting for me," Mason said.

Mason had contacted Colonel Donaldson in JAG, the Judge Advocate General's office, as his CIC buddy Forester had recommended. Mason suspected that Forester had paved the way for him, because Colonel Donaldson's office had responded immediately to his request, instructing him to see a Colonel Marsden.

The guard handed Mason his clearance orders and directed him to wing F, first floor. It took a good fifteen minutes of elevators and hallways to find the door labeled, COLONEL HUGH MARSDEN, DIRECTOR, WAR CRIMES COMMISSION DOCUMENT REPOSITORY. Mason entered a large rectangular office. On one side was a long reading table; on the other, a desk cluttered with files, picture frames, and a cluster of replicas of ancient Egyptian statuettes—at least, Mason assumed they were replicas. Behind the desk and above a row of file cabinets hung portraits of Field Marshal Montgomery and King George VI.

A moment later, Colonel Marsden exited a reinforced door opposite the reading table. He was tall and thin with graying temples and a salt-and-pepper mustache. He wore a crisply pressed British officer's uniform sporting a fistful of campaign ribbons and medals. His gait was parade-ground straight, never bending at the waist, and swiveling on his heels.

They exchanged salutes. Marsden found his place behind the desk. He had an air of formality but with a hint of a smile, as if something privately amused him.

Mason offered Marsden the letter from Colonel Donaldson, but Marsden waved it away. "No need for that, Mr. Collins, and do, please, sit." Marsden leaned back in his swivel chair and folded his arms in his lap. "I'm all attention."

Mason could see immediately that Colonel Marsden enjoyed his role as gatekeeper to the vaults of knowledge, and he knew he would have to do a little tap dancing to gain access to the keys of the colonel's realm. "Well, sir, as Colonel Donaldson's letter states, I have—"

"Yes, I know what the letter contains. Colonel Donaldson explained that you requested access to documents in our repository. I know you're a criminal investigator with the CID. All of these things are known to me. I am more interested in your purpose and selected goals."

"The purpose, sir, is to identify the perpetrator of a series of murders," Mason said flatly.

"The room behind that door is full of documents on tens of thousands of perpetrators of murder. Perhaps you could narrow it down for me."

Mason took a deep breath to keep from saying something he'd regret later. "I have reason to believe that our prime suspect in a series of particularly brutal murders was once an SS doctor at Ravensbrück." He pulled out the photograph of Scholz and laid it in front of Marsden. "He's about six-four with a small head, glasses, weak chin, and thin lips. He went under an alias of Heinrich Scholz. A witness accuses him of sterilizing her and other women in the winter of 1942. Do you recall having any information on this man?"

Marsden shook his head. "But you don't understand—"

"If I could have access to files pertaining to this doctor, his experiments, who he worked with and where the surviving ones are now—"

Marsden shot up from his chair. "Come with me."

Mason followed him to a reinforced door.

"I am not here to impede you," Marsden said. "I am your first step, your first source of information if you will. As a matter of fact, I have taken a keen interest in the Nazis' medical atrocities.

The very idea that an entire group of self-proclaimed healers could turn into cold-blooded, sadistic killers is so egregious and aberrant that it fascinates me."

Marsden opened it and stepped aside for Mason to enter. What had been one of IG Farben's immense research labs now housed floor-to-ceiling shelves loaded with boxes. The room seemed to go on for the length of a football field and just as wide. A bustle of men and women in uniform or civilian clothes searched or filed documents throughout the room.

"There are four more rooms like this one," Marsden said. "There is no card catalog you can browse through. *I* am the card catalog."

"You made your point, Colonel."

Marsden started walking along the wall to his left. After four endless rows of shelves, he said, "Ah, here we are," and turned to enter the row. "The next five rows deal with human experimentation." He continued down the row, looking up and down at labeled boxes. "Believe it or not, you are looking at a very incomplete collection. If you were hoping to discover information on every doctor or experiment, then you'll be disappointed. At Ravensbrück, in particular, the SS guards destroyed their files before fleeing the advancing armies. The Russians overtook some of the biggest death camps, Auschwitz for example, and any captured documents are in their hands. We get them only when deemed necessary."

Marsden found a box he was looking for and rifled through the contents. "There are photostatic copies of documents from camps the British Army captured, and we're still in the process of compiling documents or copies of documents from all the various document repositories hoping to one day create a central repository in Berlin. Witnesses are still coming forward and being interviewed, which leads us to new information, new doctor suspects."

"How many camps had doctors doing medical experiments?" Mason asked.

"We know of ten, so far."

"And the number of Nazi doctors?"

"Woefully imprecise," Marsden said as he pulled out a file folder. "Plus, it depends on how you count. There were many camp doctors, though some were there to evaluate arriving prisoners, separating the healthy ones for slave labor, while sending the rest to the gas chambers. Some were assigned to stem the spread of camp diseases, like typhus and tuberculosis. There were staff administrative doctors whose job was to oversee medical operations; they'd supervise or delegate requested experiments by the military or the scientific community."

"How many Nazi doctors performed or assisted in the human experiments at the camps?"

"I would guess fifty or so. But that's only a guess. Some are just now coming to light. And that doesn't count the prisoner doctors."

Mason stopped. "*Prisoner* doctors?"

Marsden found another file and was distracted by what it contained. "Hm? Oh... yes, many inmates who had worked as doctors or other medical professionals were forced to work as medical staff under command of the Nazi doctors." Marsden tucked the file under his arm and turned down another aisle.

Mason remained where he was, his mind digesting the idea. The murderer had left messages at the crime scenes intimating, Mason believed, the killer's desire to escape his own personal hell. And what could have driven a man more to believe he's in hell than being forced to participate in vile human experimentation?

"Mr. Collins?" Marsden said from the next aisle over.

Mason caught up to Marsden. "Do you have any idea how many prisoner doctors there were?"

Marsden thought a moment. "Potentially, I would say several hundred, particularly if you included dentists, pharmacists, radiologists, pathologists…. The prisoner doctors took on a variety of duties: treating ill or dying inmates, disease control, and hygiene, especially in the labor camps."

"How many do you have information on?"

"At the present time, I would say a little over a hundred."

"And they came from…?"

"Everywhere," Marsden said. "Jews, Poles, Czechs, Frenchmen, even Germans."

"Germans?"

"We know of a few, though there were at least three million imprisoned German civilians. And that's not counting the quarter of a million German Jews. So statistically speaking, there had to be a large number of German inmates who were doctors. I imagine at least a handful of them were forced or, for survival, volunteered to partake in experiments." He pulled out another file, then continued to lead Mason down the aisle. Suddenly he stopped, pulled out a box and leafed through the folders. "It seems a bit of a stretch to speculate that because your killer was involved in human experiments it drove him to murder."

"I never said that was the cause."

"But you have considered it a possibility."

"Not until you told me about the prisoner doctors."

Marsden continued down the aisle, plucking out files as he went. "You said the killer has been committing particularly brutal murders. May I ask in what sense?"

"He's been performing the equivalent of autopsies, but on live victims. He's removed a different organ each time, then dismembered all four limbs and arranged them in a bizarre way. And everything he's done, as crazy as it may be, has been done with surgical precision. Literally."

Marsden furrowed his brow as he thought. "There are other

experiments that follow more closely to your killer's methods. Including another series of experiments at Ravensbrück."

"I'll see those too."

Marsden held up a handful of files and waved them in front of Mason. "Right here." He then moved around to the next row. "Also, you must keep in mind that many of the doctors were transferred around to different camps, so your killer doctor could have been at other camps besides Ravensbrück. Especially toward the end of the war when the Nazis evacuated the eastern camps ahead of the Russian army." He found another box, grabbed a series of files, and held them up for Mason to see. "Contained in these are some of the most dastardly of them all. These are reports about performing operations, even vivisection, on inmates with no anesthesia."

"What exactly is vivisection?" Mason asked.

"Well, pretty much what you just described your killer is doing. Dissecting a body while it's still alive."

Mason's mind raced as he digested this information. "Maybe our killer participated in those experiments as well. What about the doctors involved? Do you know who they are?"

Marsden allowed himself a brief smile of pride and patted his armful of folders. "Follow me."

Mason followed Marsden out of the room and into another with shelves, researchers' desks, and a row of reading tables. The room buzzed with clerks and researchers. Marsden stopped at a clerk's desk. "Could you have some tea brought over to reading table twelve, please?"

Marsden then led Mason to the last reading table, which sat away from the commotion. Marsden dropped the stack of files on the table and sat. Mason pulled over a chair to sit beside him.

"As to your question," Marsden said, "I can speculate that several doctors operated on victims without anesthesia. Most of the information we have about these acts so far is from inmate testimony. Many of these procedures were intentionally not recorded, and most of the victims of these kinds of horrendous operations were killed then cremated or put in mass graves. We're still searching for live inmates who can give us more details."

"Where did the operations take place?"

"We know of Auschwitz, Mauthausen, Sachsenhausen and Buchenwald. But bear in mind, the doctors who performed these kinds of atrocities were rotated around to different camps—two years at one camp, six months at another."

Mason felt a chill when Marsden mentioned Buchenwald, the place where he stayed for two weeks. Somewhere in the camp, not far from the barracks where he slept, Nazi doctors had been doing unspeakable things.

"There are enough accounts to corroborate the existence of at least five doctors. We haven't been able to establish their identities definitively yet, though. The two most talked about were known by nicknames to the inmates: the Angel of Death and Dr. Death. The Angel of Death was a doctor working at Auschwitz. Among the many other horrendous experiments he performed, we have accounts of him vivisecting pregnant women, removing the uterus without anesthesia. We believe his name is Josef Mengele, but details are sketchy. The doctor referred to as Dr. Death, possibly Aribert Heim. We know he was at Mauthausen concentration camp in Austria. He injected toxic substances directly into the hearts of his victims and timed how long it took for them to die. But worst are the stories that he cut people open, removed an organ, and observed how long the victim would survive on the operating table. He studied thresholds of pain while, for example, removing the victim's stomach."

"That's very close to what we're dealing with," Mason said.

Marsden pulled out a small photograph from a folder. "This is an ID photo taken from the personnel files at Mauthausen and believed to be Aribert Heim, a.k.a. Dr. Death. He's still missing, by the way."

The photograph showed a blond man around thirty, with a handsome, almost boyish face, a high forehead, and pronounced chin. Mason felt his excitement wane and fell back in his chair. "That's not our guy."

Marsden said, "Looking at that chap's face makes it hard to imagine him performing such hideous acts. A demon with a choirboy's face. And don't forget that if there are two doctors of this nature, then there are certainly more. Either they are yet to be unmasked or they have melted into the chaos and escaped."

A corporal arrived with a tray with a teapot, two cups, milk and sugar. He poured out the tea into the cups and left. Marsden added sugar and milk, then passed a cup over to Mason. After Marsden took a sip, he slid another set of files across the table.

"These are the experiments conducted at Ravensbrück. I believe they are the closest in similarity to your killer's penchant for dismemberment. One of the most heinous was a study for regenerating or transplanting bone and tissue to wounded German soldiers. Their insane idea was that they remove bone, muscle, or nerves from camp prisoners and transplant them onto battle-maimed soldier patients."

Marsden opened one of the files in front of Mason and leafed through the documents until he found what he was looking for. It was a black-and-white photograph of a large vat filled with a clear liquid. Floating in this liquid were scores of legs cut off at the hip, arms with shoulders, even a few complete lower torsos.

"They amputated entire legs and arms that included the shoulder blade from one victim then tried to transplant it onto another victim," Marsden said.

Mason stared at the photograph, a devil's butcher shop, a hideous and cruel display. His mind conjured images of the severed arms and legs of the killer's victims. Was the killer's dismemberment a coincidence, or was he performing a ritual to purge his sins for performing or assisting in these savage procedures?

"Obviously," Marsden said, "all of the amputee victims died or were killed. Can you imagine being put to sleep on an operating table, only to wake up with someone else's limb attached to your body? Then, if you recover your senses, your body rejects the foreign limb, sepsis sets in, then gangrene, and finally a painful death."

Marsden handed Mason a set of papers stapled together. "Finally, this is my list of each camp's known Nazi medical staff and the prisoner doctors. It is certainly not complete and is constantly being updated. Some are dead; some are still missing. A number of the names have to be confirmed. Therefore, it's quite possible that your killer will not appear on the list. He's likely managed, like many others, to elude detection."

"Do you have photos of the doctors?"

"Only about half, I'm afraid to say." Marsden gestured with his hands to include everything laid out on the table. "All these files contain duplicates of documents and photographs that you may take with you. There's enough here to get you started. What I propose is having copies made of the camp records where the experiments we've discussed were performed. I will include all prisoner testimonials given when the camps were liberated, and those produced for the upcoming war crimes trials, and send everything to your headquarters. It's a considerable amount of material, but in them you may discover witnesses or clues that may lead you to your killer."

As Mason glanced at the typewritten pages of Marsden's list, he said in a muted voice, "That will be great, Colonel." He was too distracted to say more. The pages contained column after column of the atrocities. Even after all Mason had seen in his career as a cop, it couldn't dull the emotions, the empathy for so many innocent victims. "I'm beginning to see why the killer believes he descended into hell. No one performing these procedures could be sane."

"There are a few Nazi doctors who committed suicide at the end, though one will never know if that was out of unbearable guilt or fear of retribution. The frightening thing is, most of the Nazi doctors who have been discovered and interviewed appear as sane as you or I. They aren't wide-eyed insane asylum escapees. They're cold, calculating family men who all feel they were justified by the furthering medical science or they maintain they were unwilling puppets of the Nazi state. And while the majority of the SS guards and doctors emerged in relative health, it was the inmates who suffered from a great many psychological problems. Unfortunately, aside from accounts recorded by the liberating armies, there has been little official documentation on the mental health of inmates immediately after liberation. The priorities at the time were bringing the inmates back from the brink of death."

"I don't see how anyone could emerge from that kind of hell and remain sane."

"Apparently, your killer didn't."

22

M ason stood at the chalkboard in the operations room finishing up on a diagram. A web of lines linked columns of the known Nazi doctors with the medical experiments at the Ravensbrück, Mauthausen, and Buchenwald concentration camps, and the doctors' movements between the camps. Next to him on the corkboard, Mason had pinned up the crime scene photographs, plus the photographs of doctors and experiments Marsden had given him.

Wolski sat at the desk talking on the phone trying to out-argue a lawyer at JAG's war crimes division, though it appeared the verbal battle was not going Wolski's way. Mason and he had spent the morning poring over the documents Marsden had supplied, and now they were in the process of trying to set up interviews with Nazi camp doctors who'd worked with "Scholz" at Ravensbrück and Mauthausen.

Mason felt a presence behind him and turned to see Colonel Walton staring at the two boards with a furrowed brow.

"What a grim display," Colonel Walton said. "You got all this from Marsden at the repository?"

"Yes, sir. Believe it or not, what you see here is just the tip of the iceberg. These are only the experiments that correspond to the killer's mutilations. Also, since the killer could have been transferred, we have the other camps where the human experiments mirror the killer's methods."

Wolski hung up the phone and walked over to Mason and Colonel Walton. "No go on Hans Eisele. His lawyer refuses to let him talk to us."

"Did the JAG lawyer remind Eisele's lawyer that his cooperation might help him avoid the death penalty?"

Colonel Walton scowled at Mason. "I assume *you* concocted this phony offer."

"We passed the offer through JAG. They were okay with it as long as we let the doctor's lawyers know it was nonbinding."

"You went directly to JAG with this? Mr. Collins, I will not tolerate you going over my head. Run things through proper channels or I will shut you down."

"I apologize, sir. I wanted to move on it first thing this morning…" Mason decided to stop before he made it worse.

"In any case," Wolski said to defuse the situation, "the deal's not going to work with Eisele. The Dachau war crimes tribunal already sentenced him to be hanged. It came down just a few days ago. And JAG won't even think of offering him an appeal or reduced sentence."

"Sir, I do have another request to run past you," Mason said, ignoring the colonel's deepening scowl. "The doctors who performed human experiments at Ravensbrück are being held at Dachau." He walked over to the corkboard and pointed to photographs of the doctors. "Among other things, these three amputated countless inmates' arms and legs to study the viability of transplanting them onto injured soldiers." He pointed to the photo of the vat filled with human limbs. "Since the witness puts the killer at Ravensbrück, I think the best next step is to talk to them."

"The witness put him in the camp in 1942," Colonel Walton said. "Even if one of these assholes talks to you, you're probably not going to get enough information to find Scholz."

Mason continued, "The canvasses, the interviews have come up dry. The CID in Stuttgart isn't having any luck tracking down Heidi Mendel. So, while the other investigators track down night passes and permits, and Inspector Becker checks liveries and wagon owners, Wolski and I can go at these doctors. They are to be tried at the international war crimes trials at Nuremberg, but that won't take place until late next year. That means they'll have a long time to think about their possible death sentences. If we can get the JAG lawyers to agree, I want to offer them the same nonbinding deal."

"Plus, we have a trump card," Wolski said. "At the Dachau trial thirty-six of the forty defendants were sentenced to death. We can hold that over them like the carrot and the stick."

"What about former inmates who worked as medical staff?" Colonel Walton said. "Why not go after them?"

"They're spread all over the place. We're tracking down the ones we have names for, but they've either gone back to their native countries or are in Russian-occupied zones. It's gong to take some time to find any willing or able to do an interview. These doctors, however, are thirty minutes away." Mason paused. "We need a name for our suspect, sir. A real name. Can we do this?"

Colonel Walton nodded. "I'll handle it." He walked up to the chalkboard. "You've listed vivisection and surgery without anesthesia. What about talking to those doctors?"

"That's why we were trying to talk to Eisele," Wolski said. "He allegedly conducted vivisections and unnecessary amputations at Buchenwald. We're trying to track down some of his staff. There were also two doctors doing the same kinds of things at Mauthausen, a Hermann Richter and Aribert Heim, but their whereabouts are unknown."

"There are still two of those maniacs still out there?" Colonel Walton said.

"Probably more than that," Wolski said.

"Jesus." Colonel Walton felt for his cigarettes in his front pocket but came up empty.

Mason offered him one and lit it for him. Colonel Walton made it to the door before turning back to them. "Oh, and you two have nothing to do with my missing cognac and scotch?" He eyed them with suspicion. They both shook their heads. "I'm going to get to the bottom of this. I assure you."

"Maybe get Havers on it for you, sir," Wolski said.

"Bah," Colonel Walton said with a wave of his hand and left the room.

Mason looked at Wolski. "Do you still have some of his scotch?"

"Sure. Hidden in your office."

Mason feigned a scowl before turning back to the chalkboard.

Wolski whistled. "We have our work cut out for us. I wonder how many Nazi doctors are going to be willing to talk to us."

"And I wonder how I'm going to restrain myself from beating them to a pulp."

23

"The last place I want to be caught in, dead or alive," Mason said.

"This time the bad guys are the inmates and the good guys are running the camp," Wolski said.

That gave Mason little comfort. He was back in the kind of place he'd sworn never to come near again, a concentration camp. Passing through Dachau's stone-arched gate made the hairs on his arms stand up. Wolski was right, though: instead of the Jews and political prisoners from Germany and every country Nazi Germany had occupied, the prisoner barracks now housed Nazi war criminals, SS officers, and high-ranking Nazi officials.

Still, the transition did nothing to dispel the haunting images of the walking skeletons, the overflowing mass graves, the heavy pall of disease and rotting corpses.

"Maybe this wasn't a good idea," Mason said.

"What, you coming here, or interrogating Nazi doctors?"

"Both."

Wolski stopped the Jeep in front of the main administration building. They climbed out, but Mason paused at the base of the steps to stretch his neck.

Wolski could clearly see the tension building in Mason. "Just try to take it easy in there, or we'll never get anything out of the bastards."

They entered the building and showed their IDs and Colonel Walton's written orders. They handed over their weapons and were escorted by two MPs to a small interview room with a single high, barred window. A small square table bolted to the floor sat in the middle with three chairs arranged around it. No one was there yet, so Mason and Wolski sat in the chairs. One of the guards remained and stood inside the room next to the door.

Wolski read off the file in front of him: "Dr. Fritz Fischer, a major in the Waffen-SS and assistant to Ravensbrück's chief doctor, General Karl Gebhardt. This guy's a real charmer. He partook in the experiments removing muscle and bone from inmates and transplanting them onto other patients. He also participated in the sulfanilamide experiments where they made cuts on a patient then inserted infectious bacteria, or wood shavings, glass, or the like, into the wound and let it fester. Both procedures resulted in agonizing death or injury."

Mason shot up from his chair. His lungs yearned for more air, and he moved to the small window and took deep breaths. Outside the high window he could see the top third of a guard tower, and he knew that just beyond these walls around him lay row after row of prisoner barracks and the high barbed-wire fences. Visions of Buchenwald....

"Chief, are you okay?" Wolski asked.

Mason forced a smile and turned to face the room. They heard heavy footsteps approaching the door. Wolski took a spot near the window, and Mason moved to stand near the table. Two MPs entered escorting a man of six feet tall and in his early thirties. He looked more soldier than doctor, with his broad chest and the nose of a boxer who'd lost too many bouts. He marched in stiffly, his jaw clenched and nostrils flared. Mason was struck by the eyes:

his eyes showed a bit too much white, the kind of eyes that made people purposely cross the street to avoid getting too close to the one who possessed them.

The first MP removed Fischer's handcuffs, while the other stepped outside and returned with a chair, placing it in a corner. Fischer's German lawyer entered, a pudgy, gray-haired man. The lawyer had insisted on being present during the interrogation, and Mason had agreed. He looked at them with tired blue eyes and sat without a word.

"We'll be right outside," one of the guards said, and they closed the door behind them, leaving the lone MP to stand guard inside the door.

"Have a seat," Mason said to Fischer in German.

"I prefer to stand," Fischer said.

Mason stepped into his line of sight. "That wasn't a request."

Finally, those wide eyes made contact with Mason's. He stepped around Mason and sat with his back straight and arms in his lap. Mason came around the table to face Fischer but remained standing.

"What do you want?" Fischer said. "I have already been interrogated many times. I have nothing more to add."

"We're army criminal investigators and not here to interrogate you about your activities at the camp. You give us any information that could help us, and we make sure a letter commending your cooperation in a military matter is put in your file. Might even be enough to sway the judges to spare you the death sentence. Did you understand our offer, Herr Fischer?"

Fischer said nothing.

"I'll take your silence and the fact that you're here as a yes."

"I will not incriminate anyone," Fischer said while maintaining his gaze at the opposite wall. "You are wasting your time."

"How about we decide what's a waste of our time?" Mason said and sat across from Fischer. He placed the photograph of

"Dr. Scholz" in front of Fischer. "We believe that this man, a surgeon, was involved in experiments at Ravensbrück, including the sterilization of female inmates."

"I told you, I will not incriminate anyone, and certainly not my fellow doctors."

"Even if it means stopping him from killing your own people?"

Mason signaled for Wolski to give him a file folder from his satchel. Wolski stepped over to the table and handed Mason the files. He remained at the table, while Mason laid out crime scene photographs of the three victims in front of Fischer.

"These victims were your own people." He pointed to each one. "These two were doctors, and she was a nurse. They were all Nazi Party members and ex-medical staff at Mauthausen." The last part was a lie, but Mason hoped it might inspire him to talk if the victims happened to be fellow Nazis and fellow murderers in the guise of science.

It seemed to work. Fischer finally glanced at the photographs. He blinked, swallowed hard, and looked away. That was the most Mason felt he could expect from the cold-blooded butcher.

"He's going after former concentration camp medical personnel," Mason said, continuing with the lie. "And, believe it or not, we're assigned to stop him. Now, I'll ask you once again, do you know this man? Can you identify him for us?"

Fischer returned his gaze to the wall.

"We're not involved in prosecuting anyone for what was done in the camps. All I ask is his name, so we can bring him to justice."

"If you truly believed in justice," Fischer said, "neither I, nor anyone loyal to one's country, pledged to perform one's duty, would be put on trial for war crimes. We all believed in acting for the greater good of the Fatherland and pledged to carry out all orders without question. You are army. You understand that orders must be obeyed. That loyalty is a sacred duty of all soldiers."

Mason leaned in toward Fischer's face. "My army never ordered the mass slaughter of millions of people. My superiors never ordered me to maim, mutilate, and execute innocent prisoners."

Fischer's lawyer stood. "Herr Collins, you will not harass my client."

Wolski cleared his throat as a signal for Mason to calm down. Mason held up his hands to the lawyer. "My apologies."

The lawyer sat, satisfied that he had scored a small victory.

"Dr. Fischer," Mason began again, "the point is, there is no more war. There is no more Nazi Party. There are no more orders to obey. It's peacetime, yet a fellow doctor you worked with is torturing and killing German citizens. He isn't doing it because of orders. He's not doing it for science, to better the Aryan race or that kind of thing. He's out there committing horrible crimes on the German people. A German butchering victims for his own designs."

"No German would do such a thing. And this man is innocent of any charge you bring against him."

"Just then, you talked as if you know him."

Fischer blinked again.

"You do, don't you? Come on Dr. Fischer, just his name."

"I will not give you his name. I won't betray a solemn trust. I knew him. I knew his wife. I am telling you, this man would not, could not, ever do such a thing."

"Did you know that his wife died in Stuttgart? His son as well? So it's possible that the grief was too much for him. It pushed him over the edge. We want to bring him in, not kill him. Help us, Doctor."

Fischer shook his head and muttered to himself. "It's not possible. He was a good husband and father. A solid man who believed in our cause, believed in his science, a thoracic surgeon with a first-rate reputation. He was an avid hunter; he cultivated roses. A gentleman. He lived life to the fullest. I have too much respect for him. Therefore, I will not betray him. That is final."

Wolski walked over to the table. "What about giving us names of those who may have assisted him? You won't have to betray him by giving us those names: staff, nurses, any prisoner doctors...."

Fischer's eyes narrowed. "You want me to name prisoner doctors so you can find witnesses to testify against me."

"Christ almighty," Wolski said. "Can't you get it through that thick Nazi skull? We have nothing to do with prosecuting you. We're trying to find a killer."

"Herr Collins," Fischer's lawyer said.

Mason held up his hands again to acknowledge the objection.

"I understand your reluctance to talk about former colleagues," Mason said. "That's why we offered this deal. If you help us, we'll help you. You know how many of your German comrades were sentenced to death in the Dachau war crimes trial, the first of many trials. And you will be tried by an international tribunal—not just Americans, but by French, English, and Russian prosecutors. They have even more reasons to seek vengeance than we do. I want you to think hard about what we're offering you. I can't guarantee anything, but it can certainly help."

Mason paused to let that sink in. He pointed to the photographs. "The killer who did this is right here in front of you." He moved to the opposite side of the table from Fischer and leaned in to get into his line of sight. "Come on. Give us a name. Anything."

"As you said," Fischer said, "the war is over. There is no National Socialist German Workers' Party. All we have left as a people is our bonds to our fellow Germans."

"This man is a mad butcher of men, Doctor. If you won't help us"—Mason jabbed the photographs of the victims—"then their blood is on your hands."

Fischer grabbed the edges of the table. "He was none of those things. I have told you enough. To name him or give you any more information would confirm my association with any experimental procedures. To say more would be an admission of guilt."

Fischer folded his arms and let out an impatient sigh. He turned to his lawyer and nodded. The lawyer stood as a sign that they were done.

"I'll give you one more chance to put something positive in your file. The rest of it is pretty damaging."

Fischer remained stony. Mason looked at Wolski, who shrugged. He nodded to the guard. The guard went up next to Fischer. "Let's go."

When they left, Mason gathered up the photographs. "Who's next?"

"Two more today. Gebhardt before lunch and Herta Oberheuser after."

Wolski opened a file folder. "Gebhardt's a major general—" He grunted with surprise. "Get this, he was the president of the German Red Cross. How's that for irony?"

One of the MP guards knocked and entered. "Gebhardt's changed his mind. He refuses to talk to you guys. I know you were supposed to interview Herta Oberheuser after lunch, but she's available now, if it's okay with you."

"Show her in."

24

The same two MPs who had brought in Fischer now led in a slight woman with short brown hair. Her high cheekbones emphasized her haunted eyes and sullen frown. Dr. Herta Oberheuser was one of the few female doctors—perhaps the only one, as far as Mason knew—to be accused of performing grisly and agonizing experiments on concentration camp inmates.

Oberheuser's lawyer came in just behind her. He nodded then sat in the corner chair. Mason gestured for her to sit. She pulled her long black coat tight around her and sat. Wolski took his place by the window. Mason stopped by her chair and offered her a cigarette. She took it with a curt, "*Danke.*" Mason lit her cigarette and sat opposite of her. She avoided Mason's gaze, while taking hungry puffs off the cigarette.

Mason introduced them and ran through the offer, repeating that they were detectives and not there to prosecute her. He laid out the photograph of "Scholz" as before, and told her about his methods and the state of the victims. "We know he worked as a surgeon at Ravensbrück, and he sterilized female inmates. We're hoping you might help us identify this man."

Dr. Oberheuser exhaled a cloud of smoke and stared at Mason for a moment. "There were many doctors who worked at Ravensbrück. Many only a short time. I never paid attention to their names."

"Let me tell you about this particular man—"

"I am not interested."

Mason remained silent a moment and watched for anything in her expression that might indicate a desire for redemption. "As I've said, we will put in a good word for you if you cooperate. It may even save your life."

Oberheuser stole a glance at Mason, then puffed on her cigarette to mask her moment of doubt. Mason signaled Wolski for the photographs. He laid them out in front of her. She glanced at them with a remote expression.

"Those aren't concentration camp inmates," Mason said. "One of these people was killed within the last month, and the other two within the last two days. The killer tortured and butchered these innocent German citizens. And you know what else? They were all doctors."

He paused. Oberheuser said nothing as she crushed the cigarette into the ashtray. Wolski stepped over and offered her another, then returned to his place under the window.

Mason waited until she had her second cigarette lit. "I'm guessing you believe what you did was to further medical science and was meant to help wounded soldiers. And you did that work under direct orders."

"I did the best I could as a woman in a difficult position."

"Yes," Mason said, "though not so difficult as the ex-inmates."

Oberheuser stopped in middrag and glared at Mason. "You have a very strange way of persuading someone to help you."

"The persuasion should come from those photographs. Those innocent people suffered untold agony. Maybe all the agony and death at the camps drove away your humanity, but I'm willing to guess you managed to hold onto it."

Oberheuser shifted in her chair. "You cannot imagine what living in that camp could do to a person."

"I want you to consider for a moment that you and I are just two people. We are not adversaries. We are not American and German, but two people. A detective trying to stop a killer from murdering innocent people and a doctor who is concerned enough to help stop these horrible crimes."

Oberheuser flashed a menacing smile at Mason through the cigarette smoke swirling around her face. "You cannot play this childish psychological game with me. We will always be adversaries as long as I remain a prisoner."

Mason shoved the two most gruesome photographs against her hands. "These people had nothing to do with your imprisonment. They were doctors and nurses, healers, trying to help your countrymen survive in the ruins of Munich. They were grabbed off the street, strapped to an operating table, cut open, and dissected without anesthesia. Their limbs were hacked off while they were still alive, and they were allowed to bleed to death. All the while they were wondering, why me? Who will help me? Who will stop this beast from doing this to other Germans?" He stabbed the photo of the dead nurse with his forefinger. "This could have been you or one of your colleagues." He pointed to the other photos. "An uncle or a brother or cousin or friend. Right now the killer is still out there stalking his next victim, and he'll keep doing it until he's stopped. These were not camp inmates already condemned to death by the Third Reich. There is no National Socialist policy behind these slayings. This is not science! All I'm asking you to do is give me the identity of this killer."

It was her snide expression more than her silence that got to Mason. He wanted to wrap his hands around her throat... He suddenly became aware of Wolski approaching the table, probably guessing Mason's flaring temper.

Oberheuser crushed out the cigarette with a shaking hand. Her eyes were glassy, not from tears but from some internal conflict.

Wolski tossed his pack of cigarettes on the table in front of her. "Keep the pack." The doctor clutched it in her hand. Wolski slipped into the third chair as if joining friends for a drink. He lit a cigarette for himself, took a puff, then slumped in his chair and sported a boyish grin.

A quiet moment passed between them. While Mason and Wolski let Oberheuser absorb everything Mason had said, Mason studied the woman sitting across from him. For some reason, he felt more unsettled by the idea of a woman doing such horrible things. Perhaps it was his notion that women were more nurturing; to spurn the instincts of motherhood required an even darker soul, a deeper commitment to evil. He'd read witness testimony in her dossier that she'd injected children with oil or evipan, watched them slowly die, then cut off their limbs and removed internal organs.

When Mason was a young boy, his mother had routinely bordered on a nervous breakdown from the alcohol, but she still held sway over him. She was his world. He rarely saw his stepfather before he left for good, so his mother was the sole person with the power to make his spirits soar, or, with a simple look, devastate him. And on occasion, as she slipped deeper into her alcohol-induced depression, she would try to drag him with her into that dark place in her mind.

But in this small interrogation room he looked upon a frail woman, her shoulders hunched and arms tucked close to her sides. Yet when she'd had absolute power over her "patients," Mason felt sure she had wielded it with great zeal.

Whether Mason's persuasion or Wolski's boyish charm had softened Oberheuser, she began to speak....

"His name is Dr. Gunther Albrecht. He was at Ravensbrück for about a year starting in the spring of 1942."

Wolski wrote this down.

"Did he ever work with you?" Mason asked.

"No. I was aware of his experiments in sterilization, but we never shared information. He was answerable to Dr. Gebhardt only. Most of his... experiments, if you want to call them that, were done in another part of the camp from mine."

"Did you ever socialize? Did he talk about family or friends?"

"I didn't care for him. He didn't think much of women except how to exploit them. I do know that his parents both died sometime before the war. I met his wife once, a mousy thing. Not very interesting."

"Is there anything you can tell us that might help us find him? For example, did he mention any favorite getaways? Maybe a vacation home, hunting lodge?"

"Hunting lodge?"

"Dr. Fischer said he was an avid hunter," Wolski said.

"I wouldn't know anything about that. The only hunting I saw him do was for anything with a vagina. He thought he was a real ladies' man, but the only women he could bed were the inmates I suspect he raped. He acted very dignified around the other doctors, but behind closed doors..."

"Can you give us names of any of the nurses assisting him? Any staff?"

"There were two other prisoner doctors that I recall, one a Jew who was later sent to Auschwitz, and a Polish woman who, I heard, was executed last spring before the Red Army overran the camp."

"No one else you remember besides the ones who are dead?"

"I did not decide their fates." She took a long drag on her cigarette. "You might want to look up a German prisoner doctor. I never knew his name, but I heard some of the inmates called him the Healing Angel. He assisted Albrecht sometimes." She leaned forward on her elbows and lowered her voice. "It was rumored that Albrecht experimented with amputees, switching limbs from one subject to another. This German prisoner doctor supposedly assisted him."

"And you can't remember his name?"

"No, and I would be surprised if he's still alive. I have no direct knowledge of this, but many of the prisoner doctors who were thought to know too much or who could not efficiently perform their assigned tasks were usually executed or sent back to labor details."

"Do you know where Dr. Albrecht was before Ravensbrück, or where he went afterward?"

"He was transferred to another camp. Auschwitz or Mauthausen, I believe."

"Frau Oberheuser—" Mason began, but Oberheuser interrupted him.

"Frau Doktor."

"Right. Do you know who he may have worked for at Auschwitz or Mauthausen?"

"I can only speculate. Dr. Clauberg visited our camp in the winter of '42. Clauberg was interested in Albrecht's work on mass sterilization. Albrecht also assisted Dr. Kiesewetter quite often, and the two seemed to spend time together. Clauberg went to Auschwitz, and Kiesewetter went to Mauthausen at about the same time. Shortly after they left... Oh." She suddenly paused, staring into the cigarette smoke between her and Mason. "I almost remembered the prisoner doctor's name... Dr. Ram... Ramstein, Ramsdorf. Something like that. Anyway, he followed one or the other of them."

Mason looked at Wolski and saw Wolski was already writing it down.

"Frau Doktor," Wolski said, "we'd like a list of the other

nurses, staff and prisoner doctors who assisted Dr. Albrecht, you and Drs. Gebhardt and Fischer."

"I've told you enough," Oberheuser said. "I will not supply names of witnesses who could testify against me or my colleagues." She stood and nodded to her lawyer, who stood as well.

Mason and Wolski shot up from their chairs. "Frau Doktor," Mason said, "it's very important that we have those names. We need to talk to them to see if we can get more information, anything that might help us track Dr. Albrecht down."

"I told you what I can. I will give you no more," Oberheuser said and joined her lawyer by the door.

Wolski nodded to the MP guard, who knocked on the door. The two escorting guards came in, but Mason held up his hand for them to wait.

"Withholding information negates the agreement," Mason said. "Those names, Frau Doktor."

Oberheuser's lawyer whispered in her ear. She recoiled in anger and yelled, "*Nein!*" She shoved her hands toward the guards, who handcuffed her and led her out of the room.

Mason gathered up the photographs and said, "Let's get out of this snake pit."

"How about we have a notice circulated to the rest of the prisoners to let us know if they can supply any information?"

"Okay, write it up real quick."

"Already done." Wolski pulled out a piece of typewritten paper from his satchel. "Might I also suggest that the very next thing we do is find the nearest bar?"

"So ordered."

25

Mason stood at the chalkboard in the operations room when Wolski shuffled in the room, squinting against the bright overhead lights.

"Morning, sunshine," Mason said.

"You got in early."

"I didn't pound 'em back like you did."

"I've got a good excuse. I kept thinking about those goddamn Nazi doctors. Felt like I brought the stink home with me but couldn't wash it off."

"That's why I got in so early. Couldn't sleep."

The rest of Mason's team started arriving in twos and threes. The six investigators and four MP squad leaders gathered chairs and set them to face Mason and the boards.

"Good morning. We'll see how everyone stands with their assignments, but first I want to go over what Mr. Wolski and I learned from the Nazi doctor interviews." He stepped over to the chalkboard and wrote as he spoke. "Scholz's real name is Dr. Gunther Albrecht. He was definitely at Ravensbrück for most of 1942, doing mass-sterilization experiments and probably other human experiments. We believe he was transferred to either

Mauthausen or Auschwitz, maybe working alongside a Dr. Kiesewetter or Dr. Clauberg. I have an incomplete list of known doctors, nurses, and medical staff who worked at Ravensbrück at that time. The list is short, but we're going to try to track as many of them down as we can." He turned to Timmers and said, "Now that we have his real name, I want you and MacMillan to search for any documents relating to Albrecht's past. Anything you can find, right down to what he preferred for breakfast."

Mason pointed to Investigator Pike. "Anything new from the LMU hospital staff interviews?"

"They gave us nothing we haven't heard. No one knew him outside of work. Pretty much a dead end."

"What else have we got?" Mason asked.

Cole raised his hand. "Mancini and I have been plowing through the civilian night passes. Nothing so far under Scholz or Mendel."

Mason nodded and turned to one of the MP squad leaders. "Sergeant Hague?"

"We're still patrolling the areas around a ten-block radius of the hospital, the crime scenes and the place where the nurse was abducted," Sergeant Hague said. "Got zip, so far. I'm betting this guy is too careful to frequent the same areas where he committed his crimes."

"The guy's no superhuman, and he could make a mistake. I'd hate to miss an opportunity if he does decide to return to the scenes of his crimes or use the same hunting grounds."

A knock at the door stopped Mason. A staff corporal opened the door and gestured for someone to enter. Inspector Becker stepped in with another, younger man dressed in a green overcoat. All eyes turned to them.

Becker removed his homburg hat and said, "Gentlemen." The other man murmured, "*Guten Tag.*"

"Come in, Inspector," Mason said. To the room: "Gentlemen,

for those of you who haven't met our German police liaison, this is Oberinspektor Hans Becker. He's leading the German side of the investigation."

Becker introduced the other man as his assistant, Inspektor Mannheim. A couple of Americans mumbled a greeting, while others offered cold stares.

Wolski jumped up and headed for the door. "I'll get a couple of chairs for you from the outer office."

"Thank you, Mr. Wolski, but that won't be necessary," Becker said.

Wolski shrugged and returned to his seat.

"Actually, Herr Oberinspektor," Mason said, "could you come up front and give us your progress report?"

Mason knew most of the team still felt uneasy about Germans in positions of policing authority, but since they would have to work together, he figured they'd better get used to the idea. Admittedly, he was still getting used to it himself.

Becker cleared his throat and strode up to the front. Before turning to face the men, he glanced at the chalkboard with the listings of concentration camps and the Nazi doctors. He looked at Mason with a pained expression, obviously putting together what it all implied.

"I'll fill you in after the meeting," Mason said.

Becker nodded, clearly uncomfortable standing by the many damning names and places on display. He cleared his throat and said in English, "First, I would congratulate all of you on your fine police work and your dedication to solving these horrible crimes against German citizens. The German police hold you all in high regard and look forward to our continuing cooperation. The people of Munich are very grateful, and you are all a great example of the principles of the American democratic system."

Becker paused as he looked around the room. The little speech worked. Most of the men appeared more relaxed and ready to listen. "First of all, we have just identified the first victim," Becker said.

"The one found in the sewer?" Mason asked.

Becker nodded and referred to his notepad. "A Dr. Adolphus Reinhardt. He was practicing family medicine in the suburb of Milbertshofen."

As Mason wrote the new information out on the chalkboard and the men made notations, Becker continued. "We have officers —I believe your word is canvassing?" A few nods. "Canvassing door-to-door all around the hospital and his apartment. We're also checking every livery and possible wagon owner in the city. This, of course, will all take time as we have a limited number of trained officers available to us, and they have numerous other duties to perform. Unfortunately, we have not obtained any substantial leads up to this time."

Mason pointed to Sergeant Hague and said, "Inspector, if you can provide a list of where you've been and places left to visit, we can have some of Sergeant Hague's team help out."

"Sir," Sergeant Hague said, "we don't have that many MPs who can speak good German."

"Perhaps we can form teams," Becker said. "One American and one German, to go out together. It would greatly improve our ability to cover such a large area in the shortest amount of time."

"Oh, yeah," Sergeant Hague said, "that's going to go over big with my boys. I can't ask them to team up with kr—" Hague stopped and glanced at Becker from the corner of his eye.

"We'll discuss that later, Sergeant." Mason turned to Becker. "Anything you would like to add, Inspector?"

At that moment, Becker looked old and tired. He bowed his head and walked to the back of the room to join Mannheim.

The door opened, this time without a knock. Two privates carried in a large trunk labeled, *Restricted. CID eyes only. Attention Chief Warrant Officer Collins.*

One of the privates said, "This came in from Colonel Marsden at the repository, sir."

Mason directed them to set the trunk down next to him. Wolski broke the seals and opened it. Mason and he began removing file folders.

"These are copies of documents, photos, ex-inmate affidavits, eyewitness accounts," Mason said. "This is what most of you will be going through in the next few days. I want you to split up into groups and divvy up the folders." He had to speak up over the groans. "I want you to find and separate out any information on Dr. Albrecht. One of the camp doctors we interviewed mentioned some prisoner doctors who worked with Albrecht." In brief, Mason explained the role of the prisoner doctors in the camps. "Other inmates referred to one of Albrecht's prisoner doctors in particular as the Healing Angel. If you can get the identity for that man, or for anyone else who assisted Albrecht, then find out if they're still alive and where we might be able to reach them." A thought came to him as he was speaking, "Also, cross-check any names that match employees at the Ludwig-Maximilians-University hospital. If Albrecht managed to evade detection and got work there, then there may be more. Pay attention to detail. The slightest reference might be a clue. There are also transcripts from the first Dachau war crimes trial and the Belsen trial, both of which just wrapped up, plus JAG and War Crimes Commission lists of potential witnesses for upcoming proceedings. Remember, many of the medical staff, including the prisoner doctors, were transferred around over the years, especially as the Allied forces began to overrun the camps. This is probably only the first trunk. Others will likely be coming over the next few days."

This elicited another round of groans.

"Okay, gentlemen, start divvying up the material and get to work."

As Wolski started organizing the folders into piles on a long folding table and guiding the work of the various teams, Mason walked over to Becker.

"That was a nice speech you made," Mason said.

"I am learning how to talk to you Americans. I just think like a coach at an American football game. You always seem to need your egos boosted."

"The term is 'sucking up.' I bet you guys had lots of practice at that before we came along."

They both smiled, their initial animosity having turned into a game.

"Mr. Wolski and I are going to go back for another run at the hospital administrator and chief of surgeons. Care to come along?"

Becker shook his head. "We must check a few reported sightings. Besides, you and Investigator Wolski will scare them more than I will."

"I'm counting on it."

26

M ason roamed Dr. Sauber's office, fingering books on the shelves, opening cabinet drawers, and leafing through things on Sauber's desk; not usually Mason's style, but it unnerved Sauber to no end. Wolski's imposing stance next to Sauber's desk certainly added to the administrator's fluster.

"Herr Collins, please, I've already told you all I know."

"That's hard for us to believe," Wolski said, "since you concealed and lied about Albrecht's identity and his activities at Ravensbrück."

Mason opened one of the file folders stacked on a chair. "You've already violated a number of regulations by aiding and abetting a war criminal. If you want to stay out of prison, I suggest you tell us everything."

Sauber dabbed his brow. "As I said before, we were desperate for surgeons. I was the one with reservations. But Dr. Tritten pressured me into hiring him."

"That's odd. Dr. Tritten said the opposite." In fact, Tritten had offered nothing, but Sauber didn't know that. "He said you'd threatened him with exposure of his Nazi past if he didn't agree."

"That's a lie!"

"It's his word against yours. If you two can't agree on the truth, then we'll be forced to have you arrested for the cover-up. However, if you cooperate, nothing of this incident needs to leave this hospital. Tell me what you know about Albrecht. His friends, anyone else at this hospital who may have concealed his true identity. That person may be harboring him."

Sauber suddenly became very still.

Mason stopped his travels around the office and stared Sauber down. "There is someone else, isn't there?"

Sauber shook his head as he held his breath.

"Someone at this hospital also knows."

"I don't know... I mean, no."

"Who are you protecting, Doctor?" Wolski barked.

Nothing from Sauber. Mason could see the guilt in his face. "It's because he's concealed the true identities of other staff at this hospital."

Wolski leaned on the desk, prompting Sauber to lean away. "Why Doctor, shame on you. That could be very bad for you. Very bad."

Mason stepped up to the desk as he spoke. "Who else are you conspiring to conceal? Which one of them is hiding Dr. Albrecht?"

"I don't know what you're talking about."

Wolski dropped his handcuffs on the desk in front of Sauber. Sauber nearly jumped out of his chair, then jutted out his index finger in the general direction of Tritten's office. "He's the one. He talked me into hiring those people. I protested but he insisted. I'm trying to run a hospital. You've seen what we're up against. You can't arrest me for looking the other way. He's the one you should arrest."

Mason softened his tone; he didn't want Sauber to have a

heart attack. "Provide us with a list of names. We are not here to persecute you. We are here for information. But we will be forced to arrest both of you if you do not cooperate."

Wolski took the lead from Mason and lowered his voice to a soothing tone. "Giving us the list will convince us that your only concern is caring for your patients. We respect that, and we want to help you." He placed his notepad and pen in front of Sauber, then lifted away his handcuffs.

Sauber stared at the blank page as he wiped more perspiration from his brow.

"Someone at this hospital is harboring a murderer," Mason said. "Write down the names, Doctor."

Sauber picked up the pen with a shaking hand, but his hand hovered over the page.

The idea of other staff at the hospital having hidden Nazi pasts had not occurred to Mason until that morning. Someone had covered Albrecht's tracks, protected him from detection. Someone at the hospital who had helped him escape. Warned him of their arrival the day of the interview....

He remembered Laura's words: Albrecht had a lover. Find the lover and find Albrecht. It was a woman employed at this hospital. Then he recalled the eyewitness testimony of neighbors around Albrecht's apartment and from the concert hall: They had all stated having seen Albrecht with a blond woman in her middle thirties....

"The receptionist," Mason said aloud.

Sauber slowly looked up from the notepad. He didn't need to say anything. Mason knew by the look on his face. Wolski spotted it, too. Sauber had just confirmed it.

Seconds later, Mason and Wolski took long strides down the corridor and into the lobby. The receptionist stood behind the counter talking to a young woman with a baby. When Mason and

Wolski were halfway across, the receptionist noticed them. Her eyes widened with fear, and she burst into a run.

Mason and Wolski dashed after her. Heads turned; people jumped out of the way. Just before the receptionist made it through the front door, Wolski grabbed her. She screamed and cried out for help.

Mason held up his badge. No one made a move to interfere with the two American military police officers. Mason joined Wolski and helped wrestle the receptionist to a vacant corner.

"Where is Dr. Albrecht?" Mason said.

"Let me go!"

"You're hiding him. Where is he?"

"I am not hiding him."

"You're harboring a murderer. Do you want to go to prison?"

"He's not a murderer."

"Then why did he run away?"

"He ran because he didn't want to be arrested. He knew you Amis would put him on trial for war crimes and hang him. Just like you did to the people at Dachau. He didn't murder anyone."

"You're lying. Where is he?"

"I don't know!"

Mason spun around to face the reception counter. "I'll be right back," he said to Wolski. He marched over to the counter. An image had been growing in his mind since the interview with Fischer. A picture behind the counter, one of several bucolic images of rural Germany. Dr. Fischer's remark about Albrecht being an avid hunter had seemed innocuous at the time, but Mason hadn't realized why it stuck with him until now. He plucked the receptionist's photograph of a chalet-style cabin from where it had been taped to the inside wall of the counter next to her desk. He turned it over. Someone had written on the back: *Your father and I are having a wonderful month here. Do come down, darling. Mother.*

Mason returned to the corner and held up the photograph. "Albrecht is hiding in your family's cabin, isn't he? Where is this?"

The receptionist turned her head into Wolski's arms.

"Where is this cabin?" Mason yelled.

The receptionist collapsed and began to weep.

THE LARGE CHALET-STYLE CABIN STOOD ON THE LOW RISE OF A hill and overlooked a lake. A hundred yards of field separated the cabin from the forest that circled the hill. Mason knelt in a thicket a few yards into the forest and peered through the snow-laden trees with his binoculars. Becker knelt next to him and did the same thing. Wolski and the other investigators observed from strategic points around the perimeter of the hill. Becker also had a twenty-man contingent of officers waiting for orders to charge the cabin.

"No smoke in the chimney," Mason said. "He's either being very careful or he isn't there."

"It is possible he saw us coming," Becker said. "Or he could be out in search of food."

"Or his next victim."

The cabin door opened, and they crouched lower in the thicket. A figure hesitated in the dark doorway, then glanced around before disappearing again into the cabin.

Mason spoke into his Handie-Talkie. "Go, go."

Mason and Becker stood and walked out of the forest with a group of Becker's men. The others surrounding the hill emerged from their posts. Then all started a cautious climb up the hill with their guns drawn.

Albrecht breached the doorway, emerging backward this time as he led a horse out of the cabin. Unaware of the approaching circle of police, he mounted the horse. He froze in the saddle and watched the men climb the slope.

Mason called out, "Stay where you are, Albrecht. You're under arrest."

They were still two hundred feet away when Albrecht dismounted the horse and tapped the horse's flank. The horse trotted away. Albrecht stood still and stared at them. Mason quickened his pace, as did the others, and the circle tightened. Albrecht came to attention, head back, chest out. Mason suddenly had a bad feeling....

In a swift, fluid motion, Albrecht pulled out his Luger, jammed the barrel in his mouth, and fired. He slumped to the ground just as Mason and the others reached him. Everyone stared at the crumpled body as Mason checked for a pulse. Albrecht was dead.

Mason felt nothing resembling relief or satisfaction, none of the emotions he would have expected at finding the killer. While the others talked excitedly or congratulated Mason, the only feeling that persisted for Mason was that of perplexity.

APPLAUSE ERUPTED WHEN MASON, WOLSKI, AND BECKER entered the building, and it continued when they entered the CID squad room. Most of the other investigators and staff stood and applauded, though Havers refused to join in. Colonel Walton stepped out of his office and leaned against the door frame. He offered a weak smile but refrained from clapping.

Mason allowed a few men to shake his hand as he made a beeline for his office. Wolski and Becker entered a moment later and the applause died down.

"What's wrong with you guys?" Wolski asked. "We got the killer."

Becker looked at Mason with an expression that said he knew what Mason was thinking. "He didn't seem to be the type to commit suicide," Becker said.

Mason nodded in agreement.

"What difference does it make?" Wolski said.

"The notes at the crime scenes... the symbols, the references to rising up from hell," Becker said.

"Yeah, what of it?"

"If he really was as religious as he indicated, if he was truly a Catholic, then he knew that suicide was a sin that would send him to hell."

"He could have used all that religious mumbo-jumbo to throw us off the track. Look, not only did he torture and butcher here, in Munich, but he did the same thing in the concentration camps. I don't get you guys. Acting glum when you should be happy and proud." He looked at both of them. "You two are like a couple of old hunters. Once you've bagged the game, the fun is over."

Becker and Mason exchanged knowing looks.

"Now you two are just giving me the creeps," Wolski said. He pointed toward the squad room. "Colonel Walton is still standing by his door, waiting for us to give him a rundown. Unless you're looking for a battle, we better go over there and talk to him."

Mason gestured for Becker to go first.

"After you," Becker said.

As soon as they exited Mason's office, Becker's second in command intercepted Becker and pulled him aside.

Mason and Wolski turned to watch them but continued on their way to Colonel Walton, who had remained at the doorway to his office and looked unwilling to wait.

"Glad you two finally remembered how to find my office," Colonel Walton said.

Before Mason could respond, Inspector Becker called his name loudly.

All heads turned to Becker.

"What is it?" Mason asked.

Becker, white-faced, rushed up to them.

"There has been another murder."

Like an immense stone ribcage, the remnants of Munich's great Frauenkirche cathedral walls arched upward to nothing, a result of the vaulted ceiling collapsing under the pounding of Allied bombs. The damaged cathedral reminded Mason of some ancient Roman temple that had slowly crumbled, leaving only a vague impression of its proud past.

Mason had paused a moment next to the small convoy of Jeeps and army sedans that had brought him, Wolski, and two other CID investigators to the scene. He continued to stare at the hallowed ruins, dreading what he would find. His team gathered around him, waiting silently as if unsure of what to do without Mason's leadership to get them rolling. Mason hissed a curse and headed for the cathedral, feeling like he'd been kicked in the teeth.

Wolski trailed him and tried to talk him down from his anger. "Maybe Albrecht slipped into town and murdered this victim, then slipped back out again."

"He got on his horse and galloped thirty-plus miles into town, found a victim, cut him up, placed him in this church, then galloped back just in time for us to find him? Or, I know—he killed a victim near the lake, then strapped the bloodied corpse on the back of his horse and rode into town to hang it here. Yeah, that's what he did."

"It's possible."

"Face the truth. We hunted the wrong man."

Becker and Mannheim met them, and together they climbed the broad, shallow steps. A group of women stood to one side, some crying and one hysterical. It was apparent by their overalls and hair wrapped in scarves that they had been toiling to clear the tons of rubble. Other women stood around two small mining cars that sat on short rails leading from the church to a dumping site on the cathedral plaza.

An MP intercepted Mason. "Sir, we found some fresh wagon-wheel tracks just on the other side of these mine-car rails." He led them to the spot, and there, in the mud, were deep ruts left by a set of wagon wheels.

"Aren't these from the wagons that haul off the rubble?" Wolski asked.

"I checked on that. The wagons that haul off the rubble are twice as big. The tracks they leave are much wider and they stop on the opposite side."

Mason nodded and said to the MP, "All right. Get the word out. We're back to looking for a civilian with a wagon."

Becker instructed Mannheim to lead the interviews of the women who'd discovered the body, while Mason, Wolski, and he proceeded through the collapsed south wall. Large chunks of stone still littered the floor, interring the wooden pews. On the remaining columns of the nave, stone carvings of saints looked down upon them... except the fifth and final one. Instead of a saint, a mutilated corpse hung in its place.

The crime scene photographer was already at work. MPs and their German counterparts set up a line to hold back the growing crowd of spectators, while others searched for possible witnesses.

Becker muttered a prayer. A German policeman rushed into the shadows and vomited. Some of Mason's investigators had thus far witnessed the crime scenes only through photographs. Now face-to-face with the real thing, some turned away with blanched faces.

The victim was another woman. Her arms and legs were gone. She had been strapped to the column, her head cinched back so her lifeless eyes and frozen scream faced the gray clouds and heaven. From neck to pubis, every organ had been removed. The rib cage, split apart as before, was wired back to reveal an empty torso.

"Son of a bitch," Wolski murmured. "Wasn't it sick enough the last time?"

"First the sewers, then a factory, then a church," Mason said. "Now a cathedral. He keeps looking for bigger and bigger stages."

"Well, what's goddamned next? After a cathedral, how much higher can he go? The gates of heaven?"

Becker said, "One of my men reports that they have yet to find the victim's limbs."

Mannheim approached them. "None of the women saw anything. They had been working in a corner section for about twenty minutes before the one who is hysterical discovered the victim."

The engineers leaned two ladders against the column. The crime scene techs were about to climb up, when Mason said, "Wait. I need to have a closer look before you go up there. Plus, the killer could have rigged a booby trap." He turned to Becker. "Care to join me?"

Mason hesitated at the bottom rung of one ladder and took a few deep breaths before climbing. Becker's expression remained neutral, but he too took slow steps up the other ladder. They both watched for any signs of a booby trap, but as they reached the top it became clear that nothing but the woman's corpse waited for them.

At the top, the angle of his ladder brought Mason's nose close to the torso and the victim's face. In spite of the cold air, he could detect a sickly sweet odor of old blood and the beginnings of decay. He glanced around the cathedral from this high angle. There were cops everywhere combing the area. "If he rigged a trap we would have come across it by now."

"Perhaps he ran out of time," Becker said and put on his reading glasses to get a closer look at the corpse. "The same fashion of amputation."

Mason had to admire Becker's composure. "Everything is the same, right down to the wire holding the body. Except he keeps trying to outdo the last one's setting. Each place is more and more public. Each time he's taking a greater risk. And each victim is more mutilated than the last."

"Though his displays are not for us."

"For God or the angels?"

Becker looked at him over his reading glasses. "It seems likely."

Mason noticed a square piece of paper pinned to the back of the woman's neck. "I found something." He pulled out a pair of tweezers from his shirt pocket and gently unpinned the paper. The killer had left a note written in crude lettering. "Looks like your theory that he'd run out of time is correct." He showed Becker the hastily written message then read it aloud. "This saint suffered, as did Christ, and she shall clear for me a path to heaven."

Becker turned his gaze back to the woman. "This poor creature."

"I've seen enough," Mason growled, and they climbed down.

Major Treborn met them at the bottom of the ladder.

"My God, the butcher didn't leave me much," Treborn said. "Where are the organs?"

"Don't know," Mason said. "Haven't found the limbs, either."

"I remember the good old days when I had an entire cadaver to examine."

"See what you can do to pin down the time of death. If the victim was killed more than a few days ago."

"I heard about what happened at the cabin. I've been doing this a long time. These things happen in an investigation."

Mason said nothing. He and Becker stepped away and let Treborn and the technicians do their jobs.

Mason looked up to the jagged remnants of the ceiling. "Feels more like a tomb than a church."

Wolski intercepted them from the left. "We found the arms and legs."

Mason and Becker followed Wolski across the nave toward the altar. They had to negotiate scaffolding and piles of collected rubble until they came to a wooden cross mounted where the high altar used to stand. Timmers and two German police were there, standing in a semi-circle and staring down at the base of the cross. Timmers pointed to the arms and legs lying on the floor and arranged in the same X and cross pattern.

"The baptismal cross again," Mason said, then squatted to get a closer look. He pointed to the woman's right leg. "There's a large patch of bruising around the knee, and it looks swollen. Maybe the killer got careless this time." He turned to Wolski. "Get the ME over here."

Wolski returned with Major Treborn a moment later. Mason pointed out the bruised area around the knee, and Treborn examined it in the light of Wolski's flashlight.

Treborn shook his head. "This bruising is at least a couple of weeks old." He stood. "Probably a bad sprain."

Mason thanked Treborn, who returned to the area near the column to resume examining the body.

Becker looked up at the ribs of the church. "Investigator Wolski is correct in asking where he will go next."

"What other principal churches are in the city center?" Mason asked.

"Saint Peter's, Saint Michael's...." Becker stopped. "I should have thought about this before. Saint Michael's Church."

"What about it?"

"The church claims to have the skulls of two saints, Cosmas and Damian. They are patron saints of surgeons. One of their miracles was cutting off a man's diseased leg and attaching a healthy one so the man could walk again. The saints are often depicted standing over a patient with a severed leg at the foot of the operating table."

"Those saints' skulls are here in Munich?"

"Yes. It may have nothing to do with our killer, but it's possible. And Saint Michael is the archangel who battles evil spirits and ascends the deceased to heaven."

"That's where we're headed," Mason said. He called out to Timmers, "Sam, I want you to take command here. Make sure the ME gets everything he needs, continue the canvassing, and make sure the techs get over here to process this area."

From across the cathedral and echoing off the stone walls came a man's cry. "Emily! No! My God, Emily!"

Mason and the others rushed over to where Major Treborn was examining the body. Three MPs were pulling another MP away from the area. Tears flowed as he continued to scream her name. Mason turned to another MP, who looked shaken by his friend's grief.

"What happened?"

The MP didn't respond and continued to stare at his friend.

"Soldier, I'm talking to you."

The MP snapped out of it. "The dead girl, sir. She was his girlfriend. A nurse, sir."

Mason looked at Becker, acknowledging the inspector's accurate guess.

"Emily O'Brien. She worked at the 98th General Hospital," the MP said.

Mason whirled around. "What? She was American?"

"Yes, sir."

Mason stood silent for a moment. The tragedy was the same. The woman's nationality didn't change the horror of it. But it was going to change everything else. He already had a measure of army brass support for the investigation, but now higher brass, politicians, and the press would come down on him with a vengeance, let alone the idea that he'd let them get sidetracked on a bogus lead.

"Help your buddy calm down, but don't let him leave," Mason said. "We need to talk to him."

The MP left to help the others. They led the grief-stricken MP to a pew set against the wall and sat him down as they talked to him.

"The guy's in shock," Wolski said. "You're not going to get much out of him."

Treborn stepped up to them. "I covered up the body, and the ambulance team is coming in." He looked at the MP. "A hell of a thing to see your girlfriend like that. I give it twenty-four hours and then all hell's going to break loose."

"Believe me, I've thought of that. The brass will be second-guessing when I should take a crap." Mason signaled for Wolski to follow him. They walked over to the MP, who was now quiet, staring into the distance and heaving with every breath. Mason squatted next to him. He asked one of the MPs the man's name.

"Bill Shankton."

"Bill, I'm the principal investigator of these murders. I'm sorry for your loss. I know it's hard, but I need to ask you a few questions."

Shankton took a deep breath and gritted his teeth, then nodded. "When did you see Emily last?"

Another MP said, "Sir, can't this wait?"

"If he knows something that can help find this killer, then I need to know it now. Not when Bill feels better."

Shankton looked up at Mason. He wasn't much more than twenty-five; still a boy, as far as Mason was concerned, and he would wear this scar for a very long time. "I saw her three nights ago. We had an argument. Then I had a couple of twenty-hour shifts, and I wanted to calm down." He looked away. "It wasn't a big thing. How was I supposed to know...?" He took another deep breath.

"Do you know if she talked about anyone stalking her or bothering her in any way?"

Shankton shook his head. "Not that she told me."

"We believe the suspect is a tall, broad-shouldered man, usually wearing a hat and a long, dark blue coat. You notice anyone like that when you were with her?"

Shankton trembled at the thought. His eyes began to glaze over as his control waned. "I don't know. I don't know."

"Where was she living?"

"In the barracks at the hospital."

"All right. You take it easy for a while, but I want you to think about anything you might remember that might help us. Remember, the more we know, the faster we can track this guy down."

Shankton snapped his head around to face Mason. "Track him down, my ass. You chased the wrong guy. You guys don't have squat. You all got your thumbs so far up your asses you don't know whether to shit or swallow."

A couple of the MPs put their hands on Shankton's shoulders to quiet him.

Mason stood. "When you're ready to talk like a policeman and a soldier, let me know if anything comes to mind."

Most of the MPs looked anywhere but at Mason, but a few gave him hard stares. They didn't have the killer to rip apart, so they steered their wrath his way, to the one powerless to stop the killings. And Mason knew the army brass and populace of Munich would soon be doing the same thing.

Mason stepped away with Wolski in tow. He could feel their stares on his back. His steps were slow and uneven; the guilt weighed heavily on his shoulders.

"I know Shankton," Wolski said. "A stand-up guy. You're not going to report—"

Mason got in Wolski's face. "When did you start thinking I was some chickenshit, that I'd give a rat's ass what he just said?" Mason marched over to Timmers, who was still standing next to Treborn. "Mr. Timmers, take Mancini and Cole and talk to Emily O'Brien's coworkers and friends. Find out what places she frequented, and see if the girl said anything to them about being followed."

Mason said it with so much force that it left Timmers glued to the spot. "Go!" Mason yelled, and Timmers hurried off.

"Don't let what that MP said get to you," Treborn said. "You've got to keep a clear head."

Mason walked off without a response. He headed for the exit and called out, "Herr Oberinspektor Becker, if you'd come with me, please." Then, "Wolski!"

Mason stopped on the cathedral steps. A large crowd had gathered and was still growing. The word had spread. MPs and German police kept them back fifty feet from the steps, but they didn't need to see inside to know what had happened. He was sure the group of women who'd discovered the body had told anyone who'd listen about what they'd found lashed to the column.

Just as Becker and Wolski joined Mason, a woman yelled out, "The Amis care nothing for dead Germans! We are not safe in our streets!" Another cried out, "The German police are American puppets. We want justice!"

"We want justice!" A man repeated the shout.

In no time, the crowd took up the chant, the cries combining in a unified roar.

"They now have reality to add to the rumors," Becker said. "I cannot blame them for their fears."

Mason descended the steps, and Wolski and Becker followed him into the crowd. The spectators moved away to let them pass, while some deep in the crowd continued to yell:

"The murderer is an Ami soldier."

"The Amis care nothing about us."

A woman grabbed Becker's arm. "Please, Herr Oberinspektor, we walk the streets in terror."

Becker patted her hand as he continued walking. "We are doing everything we can."

The three finally emerged from the crowd and walked in silence the two long blocks past piles of rubble and the skeletal shapes of buildings to Saint Michael's Church. Remarkably, the church's high, sturdy walls remained standing despite direct bomb hits on the roof. Inside, the immense barrel-vaulted ceiling was completely gone. An intricate web of scaffolding kept the walls from collapsing, though the ornate Baroque altar still stood at the far end. A priest led a handful of worshippers in an afternoon service.

"Many of the statues and artwork, and the pulpit, were removed once they realized that Munich would inevitably be bombed," Becker said.

"And the two saints' skulls?"

"The reliquary and its contents are also in safekeeping. They were displayed in one of the side chapels. The first one on the right."

"You seem to know this place," Mason said.

"I should. I come here for mass every Sunday. This is my church, you see."

Mason moved forward along the west wall to get a better look at the worshippers. Workmen stopped briefly to look at them before going back to the task of shoring up the walls.

"I don't see much of a reason for the killer to come here," Wolski said. "It's not higher up the scale than a cathedral." He looked around. "Plus, it's too open. Too public."

"The killer has managed to get around that problem so far," Mason said. "This is as likely a place as any for his next display."

The three reached a point where they could survey the twenty-plus worshippers. Except for a scattering of elderly men, they were all women.

"We'll set up rotating teams to keep an eye on this place," Mason said. "Maybe have routine checks at the other main Catholic churches, at least in the center of town."

"And what are they going to be looking for?" Wolski said. "All we have is the vague description."

"It'll have to do for now."

"So, we're back to square one," Wolski said.

Mason suddenly felt the weight of the case bearing down on him. He squatted and shifted chunks of stucco as he thought. "Albrecht seemed so perfect: the description, his concentration-camp history, a thoracic surgeon, to boot."

"Yeah, except that he only ran from us because he didn't want to be arrested as a war criminal."

"Okay. But we're not back to square one. We've learned a lot about the killer, and we've developed lines of investigation we can still pursue." Mason juggled a piece of stucco as he thought. "What do we know about the killer?"

"He's tall and broad-shouldered, strong, smart, and a religious fanatic," Wolski said.

"He's surgically skilled," Becker said. "He's able to move

around at night and more than likely uses a wagon to transport the bodies."

"And he chooses doctors or nurses," Mason said, then paused. "There must be thousands of doctors and nurses in this city, German and American. Why those four victims? What made him pick them?"

Wolski sighed to express his frustration. "There's nothing physically that links them: hair color, eyes, ages, sex were all different. Could be that each one just happened to be in the wrong place at the wrong time."

Becker shook his head. "I concur with Investigator Collins. There is some attribute that we are overlooking."

Mason stood and surveyed the church. Near the worshippers, an elderly woman helped a much older man approach the pews. The man struggled to walk, his body bent with age, and he leaned heavily on his cane. "We didn't overlook one element; we just shelved it when we went after Albrecht: Doctor Hieber and the German nurse, Agneth, both limped." He turned to Becker.

"Yes, of course," Becker said. "Dr. Reinhardt's widow—"

"The victim we found in the sewer?" Wolski asked.

Becker nodded. "She said that he limped due to a gunshot wound he'd received during the war."

"Do you really think that's it?" Wolski asked.

Mason dropped the piece of stucco and brushed the dust from his hands. "I've got an idea." He headed for the exit. "Let's finish up at the cathedral, and then we're going back to headquarters."

28

M ason, Wolski, and Becker entered the main entrance to headquarters. The entire department seemed to be on high alert. A watch commander yelled out assignments to a squad of MPs. Multiple phones rang.

"That pack of brass by the stairs is here for my hide," Mason said, pointing to a group of frowning high-ranking Third Army officers and military government officials who stood at the base of the stairs.

They watched a corporal descend the stairs and summon the officers to come up to one of the upper floors.

Mason, Wolski, and Becker waded through the MPs and headed for the stairs. Opposite the stairs, on a wooden bench, Laura sat talking to a flirtatious corporal. She saw Mason and stood as he approached.

Mason said to the corporal, "I bet you have something more important to do."

The corporal saluted and scurried off. Wolski waved hello to Laura before heading up the stairs. Mason led Becker over and introduced him to Laura. Becker tipped his homburg hat and gave her a slight bow. He then followed Wolski up the stairs, leaving Mason and Laura alone.

"Sniffing for a scoop?" Mason said.

"I don't need to sniff. The news about the cathedral killing is already buzzing around town. I don't see how anyone can keep this out of the press."

Mason led her to a corner away from the commotion. "What are you doing here?" he asked.

"I'm glad to see you, too."

"Things went from bad to worse in the last few hours, and there's a bunch of brass upstairs waiting to rake me over the coals."

"I heard about Albrecht. I'm really sorry. That must have been a blow. I came by to offer you a shoulder to cry on, but then news about the cathedral came in."

"Laura, I haven't got time."

"I know, but these latest developments *do* deserve a sit-down, don't you think? Come to the hotel tonight. I'll have a drink waiting for you."

"I have no idea when I'll be able to get out of here."

"I'll wait up." Laura started to leave then turned. "Do I need to remind you about our deal? Be there."

Mason felt a warm flush as he watched her go, while a number of the MPs craned their necks at her passing. He mounted the stairs and discovered Wolski and Becker waiting for him at the top.

"It was business," Mason said.

Wolski gave him a knowing smile. "Sure… okay."

The two investigators followed Mason up to the third floor. When they entered the operations room, Wolski asked, "So, what was the rush getting back here?"

"Give me a moment to check it out, then I want to bounce an idea off you two and see if I'm not out in left field on this." He turned to Wolski. "In the meantime, I want you to get on the horn and see if you can reach one of Emily O'Brien's nursing friends. We'll talk to them at length later, but right now I want to know if Emily had some kind of limp."

Wolski headed for the bank of phones. Mason immediately went to one particular pile of documents and leafed through them. It took a few minutes for him to find the affidavits and photographs he sought. He then laid them out on the table.

By that time, Wolski had returned from his phone call. "Emily O'Brien was in a skiing accident about two weeks ago and sprained a ligament in her left knee. Her friend said she'd just gotten off the crutches and still had a pretty pronounced limp."

Mason nodded and referred to the documents laid out on the table. "These are affidavits and photographs from Ravensbrück. They mostly have to do with the experiments with bone transplants and testing sulfanilamide on intentional wounds. Close to a hundred inmates were used in those experiments, and the ones who survived were permanently disabled. Most all of the surgically caused injuries involved the victim's leg."

Becker turned to Mason with a look of realization. "The survivors had pronounced limps. So, you're saying that, though Albrecht is not our killer, it's possible another doctor at Ravensbrück could be?"

"Or a prisoner doctor. When I talked to Marsden at the war crimes depository he mentioned that the camp experience could have driven the killer mad—"

"But Albrecht wasn't insane," Wolski said.

"Exactly. Marsden also said that the Nazi doctors were found to be sane, even ordinary. On the other hand, a large portion of the *inmates* displayed a whole variety of psychological problems. Maybe our killer was a prisoner doctor. I know it's not much to go on."

Wolski shrugged. "It's worth looking into."

"We jump-start the other lines of investigation, while looking into concentration-camp prisoner doctors. We concentrate on Ravensbrück, but also look at Mauthausen and Buchenwald. That German prisoner Doctor Oberheuser mentioned the Healing Angel, who assisted Albrecht. Let's step up inquiries on him."

"Maybe we should go back at Oberheuser," Wolski said.

Mason nodded. "You're the devious one. Figure out a way to convince her to talk to us again."

"In the meantime, we can look again at the few files we have for U.S. Medical Corps personnel and continue to check on citizen permits and night passes."

"My men will resume a full search of the hospitals, doctors' offices, and surgeons in the area, plus the liveries and stables," Becker said. "Albrecht is probably not the only surgeon who hid his past."

Wolski retrieved a sheet of paper from another stack of documents and laid it on the table for Mason and Becker to peruse. "While we were still investigating Albrecht, I was running down this list of prisoner doctors and nurses we obtained from the Mauthausen and Ravensbrück camp documents. I was able to track down one lady doctor in Berlin."

"Then set up an interview."

"She's in the Russian zone. The red tape to petition her for an interview is a mile long. The others are scattered everywhere, so it's going to take more than a few days to arrange interviews. Some are too traumatized to talk, some are still too ill... but, we were able to contact a Czech prisoner doctor. He was an inmate at Mauthausen. A Dr. Blazek. The problem is, he's in poor health, and the Czech authorities are balking. Unless it's for the war crimes trials, they're not interested in cooperating."

"I'll get Colonel Walton on it and see if he can convince JAG to come up with a story to get him up here."

A corporal knocked on the door. "Sir, you're to report to conference room six on the fourth floor."

"The brass are done sharpening their knives," Mason said.

Wolski and Becker wished him luck.

While Mason dreaded the lambasting he was sure to receive at the meeting, he still felt the flush of renewed energy. "Okay, let's get back at it."

THE WINDOWLESS CONFERENCE ROOM CONTAINED A LONG TABLE, a handful of folding chairs, and a chalkboard. The ten high-ranking brass formed a horseshoe around one end of the table.

No chair waited for Mason. He snapped to attention, saluted, and took his place at the opposite end of the table. He knew some of the ten men from Third Army and OMGB sitting around the table: General West and Major Bolton of OMGB civil affairs from the last meeting, Major Blaine, the commander of the 508th Military Police Battalion, and Laura's "boyfriend," General Jenkins, the commanding officer of all CID detachments in the American zone. Then, of course, Colonel Walton standing just behind the others.

Colonel Walton growled out introductions, then got to the point. "In light of the new developments, we're here to decide whether to pull you off this case and bring in someone with more competence and experience. Someone who can get this case solved."

"Yes, sir."

"Is that all you have to say?"

"Permission to speak freely, Colonel?"

Walton's face reddened. "That's why we brought you in here!"

"Bringing in someone new is your gentlemen's prerogative,

but it would take time to get him up to speed. We've already spent hundreds of hours on this investigation. Someone new could slow things down, making it take longer to apprehend the killer."

"You requested more manpower, and we gave it to you," General West said. "You wanted liberty to access military personnel files, and we gave you that, too. We've given you what you asked for, and in return we expected results. Do you have any results, Mr. Collins, other than pursuing the wrong suspect?"

"Though it turned out that Dr. Albrecht was not the killer, our investigation has brought to light several promising lines of investigation." Mason summarized their latest theories, lines of investigation, and findings in short order. "Any of those could lead to more information on the killer's name and a more complete physical description. With that information in hand, we can orchestrate an all-out manhunt."

"A full-blown manhunt could chase him out of town," General Jenkins said. "There are also a half million people, with every bombed-out building providing a hole to crawl into. I wonder if you've thought all this out well enough to lead to success."

"Sir, we're hunting a meticulous killer who leaves no evidence, kills seemingly at random, and is cunning enough to avoid any eyewitnesses. That would challenge the biggest city police department or the FBI. I believe we are conducting as competent an investigation as any skilled police department. Plus, we have the advantage of military control, curfews, random identity checks, travel restrictions for all German citizens, and, in this instance, a cooperative and vigilant population. There is no doubt in my mind that we will find him."

Mason did have plenty of doubts, but he wanted more than anything to stay on the case, and if it meant lying like the best politician, he was going to do it. He'd worry later about why. A voice within urged him to tell them to find some other poor sap to put up with the heartburn of frustration and crushing self-doubt with each new victim. He knew some chain killers were never caught; he knew some just stopped after the body count reached twenty or thirty. That sometimes the failed hunt resulted, for the detectives, in ruined careers or black marks on their records, not to mention the risk of living with remorse and guilt the rest of their lives.

"A convincing speech, Mr. Collins," General West said. "The main problem is—when? I'm starting to get questions from Eisenhower's general staff, even the muckety-mucks in Washington, for chrissake. I can keep them at bay in the short term, but meanwhile the locals are already in a frenzy, and it's about to get worse. This whole situation is going to make governing difficult. Just when we're trying to form civilian government entities and gain cooperation from the populace, they're accusing us of injustice and negligence. The word on the street is we're heartless bastards who don't care that the German population are getting butchered. They'll turn more to criminal elements and underground Nazi revivalist groups."

Major Bolton, the civil affairs director, said, "Maybe the fact that an American nurse was the latest victim will help calm things down."

"Major Bolton is right," Major Littleton said. "This development could help civilian relations. But if we replace Mr. Collins now, we'll appear to have suddenly thrown everything we've got into this investigation now that an American nurse is the victim. We'll be proving their point: that we didn't really care until it was one of our own."

Mason felt disgusted. These two gutless pricks only saw the dead girl as a political pawn. He felt a renewed respect for Colonel Walton when the colonel said, "This conversation is degrading to the poor woman who suffered and died. I will not stand by and see her corpse used as a public relations tool."

"Now, see here," Major Bolton said, "I was simply stating a fact—"

"That's enough, gentlemen," General West said. "Everyone here is stunned and saddened by Lieutenant Emily O'Brien's death, and no one means disrespect to her memory. But perception is important. We can't ignore that any radical change in this investigation could inflame German misconceptions. If we intend to build a democratic Germany then we need to lead by example." He signaled for General Jenkins to continue the sentencing.

"Mr. Collins, you are to remain as the lead investigator, but I'm giving you one week to solve this," Jenkins said. "If you haven't done so, or damn close to it, I'm pulling you out. Are we clear?"

"Yes, sir."

"I want daily reports. I want to see forward momentum. If there is anything that you need, within reason, run it through Colonel Walton. He will immediately forward it on to me. Get it done."

29

He rode beside the wagon driver. The wooden wheels clattered over the cobblestones of the narrow alley. They traveled the short distance and entered a courtyard. In front of them, three stories of outer brick wall were all that remained of the shoe factory, and to the left, three single-story outbuildings.

The wagon stopped in front of the last outbuilding in the row, and the driver and he climbed down. In the back of the wagon lay several crates of junk metal and the main prize, a twisted carcass of a motorcycle. While the driver unloaded the crates, he unlocked a small reinforced door and entered the building. With a loud clank of sliding bolts, the wide double doors swung open.

The wagon driver waited by the wagon. "You'll have to help me with this motorcycle, Herr Lang."

Alfred Lang was the name he used in connection with his workshop. "No need," Lang said. He reached up, grabbed a chain and pulled. A steel triangular lift unfolded from the wall above the double doors. Lang wrapped the chain around the motorcycle and pulled the other end. The large pulley and gears did all the heavy lifting.

In a moment, he rested the motorcycle on a metal rolling

pallet. He paid the wagon driver with four packs of cigarettes. An exorbitant amount, but it kept the driver quiet about the delivery.

The wagon pulled away and Lang proceeded to wheel in the collection of scrap metal he had collected from the ruins.

Inside the workshop were shelves of tools and metal parts separated by function and size. Against the back wall sat a partially completed 1905 Altmann steam-driven car. He'd found the rusting car body with most of the engine intact behind a burned-out house just outside of the city. Shelves along the north wall contained pendulum clocks, carved wooden cuckoo clocks, Victrola gramophones and radios, all in various states of disrepair. Also among the items sat his next automaton project: a mechanical magician who made his own head disappear, then, with a wave of his wand, his severed head would rise up from a black box. The outbuilding had been a machine shop associated with the shoe factory, and Lang had managed to repair most of the metal saws, punches, and lathes. A network of strategically placed chains hung down from the ceiling pulley system.

As he turned to retrieve the last crate, he was startled by a barrel-chested man standing in the courtyard. The man had his hands on his hips and wore a big grin. A crime boss before the war, the man had bought his way into the Gestapo and hunted down Jews. Many of the crime bosses had fled or been thrown in the camps during Hitler's reign, but he, along with a number of others, had played the system and now that the Nazis had gone, they had taken over the streets once again.

Lang knew him only as Rudolph, though he was sure that was a false name. Rudolph controlled a large swath of southwestern Munich. There were rival gangs of Russian and Polish displaced persons, as well as American, British, and French deserters, but those gangs were after bigger cash hauls. Rudolph and the few other German gangs knew someday the rivals would have to pack up and leave, so he and the others stuck to the black market and protection. The man was very dangerous, and Lang despised him, but his fate for the moment was tied to Rudolph. He would have to play the supplicant a little while longer.

"Alfred," Rudolph said, "I believe you have something for me." He walked forward with two ex-Wehrmacht soldiers in tow.

"I put the finishing touches on it a few days ago," Lang said.

Lang and Rudolph walked into the shop while the two musclemen waited outside. They stopped in the middle of the workshop, where something sat under a canvas cover. Lang pulled off the cover. Underneath was a 1928 NSU 500cc motorcycle. It looked as close to showroom perfect as Lang could get, relying only on salvaged and black-market supplies.

Rudolph walked around admiring it with his toothy grin. "It's beautiful. You've done an amazing job. How does she run?"

"I would say, better than factory," Lang said, avoiding Rudolph's gaze. "Much of the engine I made or modified myself."

"You truly have talent," Rudolph said. He eyed Lang for a moment. "Why are you so nervous, Herr Lang? Do I scare you that much?"

Lang had done everything he knew to feign nervousness: speaking too fast, twisting the canvas cover in his hands. "I think, Herr Rudolph, that I am working too hard and not sleeping."

Rudolph grunted and nodded to one of his musclemen. The man stepped forward. Lang stepped back as if startled.

"You *are* nervous," Rudolph said. "Are you doing business with one of my rivals?"

"No, sir. Of course not."

The muscleman handed Rudolph a paper sack, and Rudolph held it out for Lang. "The new American military pass and salvage permit. Those are very hard to come by. I had to pay the American clerk a great deal. Therefore, I can only give you two cartons of cigarettes."

"Still very generous, Herr Rudolph."

Rudolph waved for the two musclemen to roll the motorcycle away. "You also have two months' protection, as usual. Just be sure your workshop keeps making me money." Rudolph noticed something over Lang's shoulder. "What is that?"

Lang knew what Rudolph was referring to, the large rectangular object concealed under a black cloth that sat in the back corner.

Rudolph walked toward it. "What are you hiding from me, eh?"

Lang rushed to catch up. "Nothing, Herr Rudolph. I—"

Rudolph yanked back the cover, and parked before him was a black 1928 Mercedes-Benz SSK. Despite the weather-beaten body and torn upholstery, it was still a beautiful automobile.

"This is marvelous," Rudolph said.

"This is a very personal project, Herr Rudolph. I have no plans to sell or barter for it." He actually had big plans for the car, and they included Herr Rudolph. What he needed from the man would cost a fortune in black-market currency, and what better way to reel him in and increase the price than by feigning a deep reluctance to sell.

"Who can afford personal projects?" Rudolph countered. "And what can you do with it, anyway? Germans are not allowed to drive."

Lang shrugged. "It's not nearly ready to be driven yet, Herr Rudolph."

Rudolph shook his index finger at him. "For your own good, I will take this off your hands. You'll be paid very well, I assure you."

Rudolph began walking away. Lang chased after him.

"Herr Rudolph, I don't want to sell it."

"I won't cheat you. And the most important thing is, neither will I steal it. Think of a price, and we can negotiate when it's ready. Good day to you, Herr Lang."

Lang stood outside the double doors, watching Rudolph and his men disappear down the driveway and out of sight. Without the distraction of the outside world, the voices within rose to a shrill hiss. Behind him, in the dark interior, he could feel a shadowy presence. The dread of what he must do made his body let out a great shudder. He'd hoped that by salvaging in the ruins that morning and finding a project to tinker with, the distraction would calm him, but now that he stood near the large doors that stood open like a black maw, he realized that he must come to grips with the inevitable.

Still facing outward, he pulled the double doors closed and locked them with the sliding bolts. He lit a kerosene lantern, closed the single door, and turned to face the center of the room. The lantern threw exaggerated shadows on the walls. The odor of motor oil and the vapors of old fires and mildew overwhelmed the fresh air. And just below those fumes, the scent of blood and death. Or was that his imagination?

In the center of the room, he pulled a chain. The clank of the chain on the geared pulley seemed deafening in the enclosed space. A two-by-four-foot rectangle slab of concrete flooring rose up on one side, revealing steps that lead down to a bomb shelter the shoe factory mechanics had constructed for themselves and the factory executives.

He hesitated at the top of the steps. The lantern light pierced only a few yards of the darkness below. After the other sacrifices his elation had been so great that the task before him served as another phase of the celebration for a well-performed beatification. But this time he had defied the urgings to select a child for sacrifice. He had hastily chosen an adult for beatification to appease the voices, but the ceremony had become an ordeal. Instead of elation, anguish came. The screams, the blood, the horror had given him no pleasure.

Lang reassumed his true identity—Dr. Ernst Ramek—as he

descended the stairs. His legs seemed drained of blood, and his knees threatened to buckle. With each step down, the memories, the visions, the sounds flooded back, immersing him in the very hell he desired to escape. Each descending footfall brought with it a sense memory of those he had taken into the medical research blockhouse at Mauthausen concentration camp, its dark hallway lined with doors, and behind the doors, victims of experimentation, mutilated, sliced open, infected, gangrenous... And none allowed medication to relieve the pain. Every day to walk that hallway and listen to the moans, the pleadings for mercy, the screams of those driven insane by relentless terror and agony. At the end of that hallway—the vision very clear now—lay the operating room, where he'd been compelled to go each day to assist with mutilation done in the name of science.

He had made a pact with evil to save his own skin. What man would say no? A question he had often used to justify those abominations over certain and cruel death. As madness replaced abject horror, the victims' suffering, their blood, their writhing bodies, their pleading for mercy, elicited a kind of carnal passion. Each "procedure" brought lust then despair, excitation then depression in equal quantities.

His feet touched the former bomb shelter's floor, thirty feet underground. A short hallway led to a steel door. He unlocked it and entered a large, square room with an operating table in its center. Pools of black coagulated blood covered the table. Bloodied rags lay scattered around. An open aluminum vat held blood collected from the hole at the foot of the slightly tilted table.

The sights induced another flashback: a prisoner patient writhing on the operating table as one of the doctors sliced through the torso and dug out the stomach. A victim he'd helped select, strapped down to the table and told lies that no harm would come, that the doctor simply wanted to examine her. *For research, you understand?* But the victims suspected the fate awaiting them in the medical blockhouse. They'd heard the rumors, and sometimes the screams. They knew that very few "rabbits," as the Nazi doctors liked to call their subjects, who entered that blockhouse were ever seen again.

Dr. Ramek fell against the wall and covered his eyes. *Please stop.*

He was being punished. All his efforts, all his success could be repudiated. He must obey the urges. He must suffer along with the Chosen One. Only then would the beatification ceremony expunge his sins. He must embrace the anguish, for only then would he be lifted up among the venerated in heaven.

Resolve gave him strength. Excitement and anticipation returned. Past images no longer assaulted him, and his mind cleared. He began to hum an obscure tune from his childhood, as he went about making the room pristine again, preparing for the true and perhaps final sacrifice.

M ason had decided to walk despite the freezing rain
that had started with nightfall. The damp cold
helped revive him after the tedious yet macabre task of
wading through endless written testimonials of ex-concentration camp inmates. As the afternoon had worn on, his
outrage at the grisly details dulled to numb detachment.
Single acts of unimaginable cruelty, which had horrified him
at the beginning, began to elicit as much reaction as a
weather report. How many more testimonies of savagery
would it take before he was so dulled by the suffering that
he lost his compassion altogether, the empathy slipping away,
grain by grain?

He stopped across the street from Laura's hotel and lit a
cigarette, took a puff, then decided he didn't want it. He tossed it
to the pavement, crossed the street and entered the hotel. The
lobby exuded old-world charm: walls of carved wood framing
painted Bavarian pastoral scenes, oak-beamed ceilings and silk-
upholstered furniture. Candles provided most of the light, though
a few light bulbs glowed dimly at strategic places, probably
powered by an army-supplied generator. Two German hotel

employees were in the midst of decorating a Christmas tree in one corner.

Mason continued past the spiral staircase and a bay of elevators and traversed a short hallway that led to the restaurant entrance and the hotel's bar. Plush but tattered sofas and low tables filled the lounge, with a long bar at the far end. Two large fissures spanned the marble floor, the only testament to the violence of the bombs exploding all around the hotel.

He saw Laura sitting at one of the tables. She laughed along with a group of companions: three women and two men in civvies and two men in uniform.

Mason removed his hat but remained where he was. He hoped to attract Laura's attention from a distance. Laura spotted him. She excused herself and joined him.

"I hate to break up your little shindig," Mason said.

"It's fine. My friends and I were just having a little farewell party." She took him by the arm. "I'd introduce you, but four of them are reporters. You'd be like a minnow with the sharks." She led him to a sofa tucked away in a corner. "Did you eat? I'm sure they're still serving."

"I'll order a sandwich or something. Whose farewell party?"

Laura sat and patted the cushion next to her. "I'll give you the whole scoop when you sit down."

A waiter arrived when Mason sat. Laura ordered a martini. Mason ordered a ham sandwich and a double whiskey.

"I bet you had a bad day," Laura said.

"You don't know the half of it."

"I want to know all of it."

"You first."

Laura hesitated then shook her head. "Maybe we'll wait for your whiskey."

"Ah. Ply me with alcohol before giving me the news."

"Something like that."

The waiter brought the drinks and promised to bring the sandwich in a few minutes. Mason and Laura clinked glasses.

"Here's to new horizons," Mason said and held up his whiskey. "You're going to have one juicy story by the time this case is finished. But you might have to convince someone else to tell the rest. Your boyfriend, Jenkins, has given me one week to solve it or I'm out."

"He's not my boyfriend. We called it quits a few days—" She stopped. "What do you mean, you've only got a week?"

Mason told her about the meeting with the brass that afternoon, then about how everyone was stunned and distressed over Albrecht's suicide and the cathedral murder scene. "Now the entire army brass is breathing down my neck. They've given me one week. And for some goddamned reason, I fought to stay on this investigation. I don't know why. So we can go through the motions of solving this case while we wait for the next victim."

"If they boot you off, that's one thing. There's nothing you can do about that. But you need to give it everything you've got. Then, if you don't solve it, you can walk away knowing that you did all that was humanly possible. Otherwise, you're going to carry a big weight around on your shoulders."

They both fell quiet when the waiter came back with the sandwich. Laura snagged one of his limp fries. "The German cook hasn't mastered the art of french fries yet. Cooks them like they do all their potatoes."

Mason took a bite of his sandwich. "Let's talk about you. Why did you break up with the general?"

"Maybe it's time I really got to know the lowly GI."

"You'll enjoy the novelty… for a while."

Laura picked up a french fry and threw it at him. "That's just a form of conceit. It doesn't suit you."

"A cop and a reporter…" Mason rubbed his chin and feigned a thoughtful pause. "Well, they said man would never fly."

Mason saw her expression change in a split second from confident to vulnerable.

"Laura, what is it?"

Laura tried to smile at him, but it turned lopsided. "I'm leaving in a few days."

Mason was aware of Laura probing him with those intense blue eyes, but he'd lost track of what his face was doing. He felt like he'd been punched in the stomach. "Leaving for where?"

"Berlin, first."

"For good?"

Laura shrugged her shoulders. "I don't know. The story I told you about when we first met—getting an angle on the black market?" When Mason nodded, she continued. "I've been doing a whole piece on it, and I've made a few contacts—German and American—who run sizable operations."

"Laura, that's dangerous work."

"I've been in dangerous situations before. I can handle myself."

"Haven't you had enough of people shooting at you? Not enough thrills for one lifetime? No, sir, not you. You can't stand to be away from it."

"Look who's talking."

Mason had no argument against that, and they fell into silence for a moment.

Finally Laura said, "One of my contacts has connections with a major ring that operates out of Berlin. Those people have their hands on everything. Their principal line of supply is a route that comes up from Italy into Austria, through a small town called Garmisch-Partenkirchen, into Munich, and on to Berlin. My contact is going to help me get in touch with someone in Berlin."

"Are you going to share whatever you find out with the police?"

"A reporter is only as good as her confidential sources."

Mason was about to say something, but Laura went on. "Look, some of the stuff they're into is despicable, but it's mostly coal, fuel oil, food—"

"Drugs."

"No doubt. But I promise that if I learn of anything that harms innocent people, and if I've got hard evidence, then I will contact the police."

"When you do that, make sure you're far away."

Laura nodded and looked away for a moment. "That's why I'm not sure when, or if, I'll be back."

"I wish you'd leave this kind of thing to the police."

"You said it: Dangerous assignments are my way of thumbing my nose at my parents."

"I'm being serious this time. You've got to be careful."

A smile spread across Laura's face. She leaned over and kissed him. To Mason, the room seemed to disappear. Nothing else existed, but only for a moment.

Laura broke the kiss and fished for something in her purse. "I won't be leaving for four or five days." She laid whatever it was on the table and slid it over while covering it with her hand. "Why don't we make the most of it?" She stood and walked away.

Mason watched her go then looked down. Laura had left a note with her room number.

A few minutes later, Mason entered Laura's room. The only light came from the fireplace. Laura stood up from the bed and met him halfway across the room. Mason lifted her chin and kissed her hard. Their lips never separated as they pulled off their clothes, gently at first, then frantically as if they couldn't get them off fast enough. They stood next to the fire, their hands caressing and probing. With Mason's passion came the bliss of forgetting. Only her body, her moans of pleasure mattered. He grabbed the quilt off the bed even as they embraced. He wrapped them both and lowered them to the floor. While making love, he felt an intense relief, precious moments when nothing pressed on his mind and his body felt weightless. For a few moments, he could push aside thoughts about how it would all flood back again.

The ocean always falls away before the tidal wave roars ashore.

Mason sat at the phone struggling to hear the War Crimes Commission lawyer over the din of the operations room. He turned in his chair and waved for the others to tone it down, but no one noticed. The operations room had blossomed: They now had five phones and four rows of tables with his team of investigators and ten army clerks answering the constantly ringing phones or bustling around the tables sorting through piles of documents. The extra phones, tables, and clerks were there thanks to Wolski's skills at "procurement." Mason had no intention of asking Wolski how he had pulled it off, but he suspected that at least half of the procurement had been misappropriated from Colonel Walton's provisions and staff.

"What was that, sir?" Mason said into the phone. He listened. "I know the Russians have agreed to participate in the Nuremberg trials. I simply want you to *mention* to Herta Oberheuser's lawyer that a combined Polish-Russian tribunal is *petitioning* for the Ravensbrück prisoners to appear in a separate trial in Poland because of atrocities perpetrated on Polish women."

Mason noticed Wolski hovering next to him and he held up his hand, telling him to wait. "That's correct. It's a ruse to get her to talk. I'm sure she's holding back information we need for our murder case…. Yes, you've heard about our case, then. So you understand the urgency. The Dachau camp commander told me she's getting panicky about the trial, and I'm counting on this disinformation to push her over the edge and cooperate with us." He listened. "Good. I appreciate this, sir." Mason hung up the phone and turned to Wolski. "They've agreed to do it."

"Hopefully we can piggyback her with Dr. Blazek tomorrow."

"Tomorrow? When did you hear this?"

"Colonel Walton just called to say that JAG is getting Blazek up here to visually identify Mauthausen guards and provide an oral statement. He arrives tomorrow at Dachau. They were going to bring him up here anyway, but they moved up the date for us."

"That's good news. We can go at both of them about that German prisoner doctor, the Healing Angel. That name has popped up a couple of times with a description of being tall and broad-shouldered."

Cole came up to the table and laid out a short stack of files. "This is what we've got so far on the night passes for German civilians. It's all the potentials we've been able to match up from identity papers. Of these forty, fifteen have been reported by checkpoint MPs as using wagons. Freight mostly. Some for salvage operations."

"Check them out right away."

"It's just me, sir. Mancini had to team up with Timmers and MacMillan to help check out the hundreds of sightings we've been getting from citizens."

"Not one of those sightings has amounted to anything so far," Wolski said.

"We can't ignore them," Mason said. He split the stack and handed a portion to Cole. "Team up with one of our MPs. You take half and we'll take half."

Mason stood and said to Wolski, "Let's go."

"You know this is a long shot."

"O ye of little faith."

WOLSKI PARKED THE JEEP ON A SHORT STREET LINED WITH damaged warehouses and factories. In front of them stood an arched brick entrance with large wooden doors. Rising above the enclosure, they could see the ragged remnants of a factory.

"You sure you got the address right?" Mason asked.

Wolski checked his notepad. "That's what it says, right here. Schwanthaler shoe factory."

They both climbed out of the Jeep and approached the closed doors. Mason banged on the doors with his fist.

"Maybe it's a bogus address," Wolski said.

Mason pounded harder. The doors rattled from the force of his blows. When they received no answer, Mason gave the doors a swift kick.

"Don't take it out on the door. You've wanted to hit something all day. What's eating at you, Mr. Grouchy?"

"You going to put a 'sir' in there somewhere?"

"Mr. Grouchy, sir."

Without taking his eyes off the doors, Mason said, "Laura's leaving Munich. Possibly for good."

"What? You're just going to let her leave?"

"She's doing her job. What am I supposed to do, put her in handcuffs?"

"You better think of something. Snag that girl and live happily ever after."

"Well, thanks, *Miss Lonelyhearts*, I'll keep it under advisement."

Wolski was about to say something, but Mason whirled around to face Wolski. "For your own safety, stop right now."

Wolski raised his hands in surrender. He stepped back and looked at the ruins beyond the gate. "You really think this is going to lead us anywhere? How many guys with night passes supposedly fitting the description have we checked out already?"

"Four."

"I know how many. And it's five, including the ex-soldier with one arm and a guy that looked like he was about a hundred. Whoever filled out their physical descriptions had to be drunk."

"If you want to go back to headquarters and go through more camp documents…"

"No, thanks."

They turned at the sound of horse hooves on the cobblestone street. At the end of the block, a wagon carrying two men had just turned the corner. As the wagon completed the turn, the passenger put his hand on the driver's arm. The driver stopped the wagon. The men were too far away to see their faces, but the passenger sat very tall on the buckboard. A tense moment passed. Mason was about to pull out his gun and approach the wagon when it started up again.

"That was a little suspicious," Wolski said.

Mason watched the men carefully, alert to any sudden movement. When the wagon got closer, Mason saw that the passenger was indeed a tall man in his thirties. The driver looked to be in his late sixties. The driver finally reined in his horse and applied the hand brake. While Wolski took hold of the horse's reins, Mason came up to the passenger's side and showed his CID badge.

"We'd like to talk to you, sir. Could you please step down from the wagon?"

"You too, sir," Wolski said to the old man. "Please step down and stand against the building."

The tall passenger climbed down. "You are police? Have I done anything wrong?"

While Wolski questioned the driver, Mason introduced himself and Wolski. "Can I see your identification?"

Lang handed over his papers. Mason studied Lang's face against the photograph on his identification paper. According to his papers, he was forty, though he looked younger. He had that German poster-boy chiseled jaw and thrusting chin, his good looks marred only by thick glasses that magnified his cow eyes. He stood three inches taller than Mason—not a giant, but tall by European standards—and he definitely filled out his tattered and oil-stained brown overcoat. His large hands had scratches and his fingernails were full of dirt and grease. Not the hands of a surgeon. Though, Mason thought the killer didn't need clean hands for what he was doing to his victims.

"Why did you have the driver stop at the end of the street when you saw us, Herr Lang?" Mason asked.

"I didn't know you were American policemen. When I saw two armed men in uniforms standing by the gate I panicked. I can only explain my fear, well, it sounds foolish…."

"Try me," Mason said.

"For ten years we Germans lived in fear of the SiPo, the Nazi security police—"

"I know what the SiPo was."

Lang waved his hands and sputtered, "Not that I think you nice gentlemen are SiPo. But from a distance and seeing you two in uniforms and armed, I was suddenly back during Hitler's Reich. It is a foolish thing, I know, but after so many years of living in fear…."

"Was there something you did that made you afraid of the SiPo?"

"Nothing criminal, if that's what you mean. I was a Social Democrat, and I, among others, protested against Hitler taking full power, and I…."

Mason lost patience listening to the same old history lesson—

the tried-and-true "I was against Hitler" defense he'd heard a hundred times. He wondered if Lang's story, like many others', was scripted and rehearsed. Despite the man's shabby clothes and filthy appearance, he struck Mason as more professorial than laborer. The man's papers seemed in order, though for a hefty price legitimate papers could be obtained from unscrupulous U.S. authorities. Some guys were getting rich off selling under-the-counter papers, especially the category five denazification card certifying the bearer as a "Person Exonerated" (though most Germans referred to it derisively as a *Persilschein* after a well-known laundry detergent—a veritable whitewashing of past Nazi sins.) Despite the derision, it was the most sought-after document, as it kept them out of prison and gave them the right to work and better ration cards.

"How long have you been in Munich?"

"Most of my life. Until I was conscripted into the Wehrmacht."

"What did you do in the Wehrmacht?

"I was a chief mechanic in the Third Panzergrenadier Division. Tanks and armored cars were my specialty. I became quite proficient—"

"Do you have your army papers?"

"My *Soldat Buch* and other papers were confiscated when I became a prisoner of war."

"Do you live here?"

"Could you explain to me why you are asking all these questions?"

"We are investigating a series of murders, and you have physical characteristics that match descriptions of the suspect."

Lang froze, his mouth forming a small O. He finally muttered, "Oh, dear. But I have nothing to do with these murders."

"You see why answering all our questions is important?"

Mason began to notice that, for all Lang's stammering and

glib patter, his body expressed the opposite: no nervous tics, his eyes fixed, his breathing steady. Mason had learned the physical signs of a man who felt cornered or feared being caught, but Lang seemed to feel nothing. A void behind a theatrical face.

"I'm sorry," Lang said. "What was your question?"

"Do you live here?"

"Yes. Unfortunately, my residence was destroyed, but I do enjoy the quiet this situation provides me. It is also my workshop."

"You know, for all your appearance as a humble junk collector, you sound pretty educated, Herr Lang."

Wolski instructed the old man to stay where he was and joined Mason. Lang took a step back when he noticed Wolski.

"This is not my chosen occupation," Lang said. "The war changed that. Now I do what I must to survive."

"What were you before being drafted into the army?" Wolski asked. "An engineer? A doctor, maybe?"

Lang turned his upper body to face Wolski. "Do you like the idea of a German professional fallen from grace because of the war? Does that make you feel superior?"

First, he's the humble junkman, now an indignant member of the upper class. Mason couldn't quite figure the man out. Something about him didn't fit, but Mason had no more than a vague notion of this, like a faint disturbing odor.

"You didn't answer his question," Mason said.

"I worked as a factory supervisor for Mercedes-Benz while studying industrial engineering at the University of Kassel. Have I adequately answered the question?"

"There's no way for us to know, Herr Lang. Just so our minds are at ease, why don't you show us your workshop?"

"Of course," Lang said and pulled out his keys. As he unlocked the doors, he said, "You will find all is in order. Perhaps then you will stop this harassment and leave me in peace."

"That depends on what we find."

Lang pushed open the doors. Mason gestured for Lang to go first. Wolski instructed the old man to follow them, then he caught up to Mason. "The driver's papers check out. Got his name and address. He said that Lang rented him and his wagon for the day. I checked the back of the wagon. Just a bunch of beat-up auto parts and the rusted guts of some radios or something."

When they entered the courtyard, Mason took in the shattered and burned shoe factory. "Your workshop is here?" Mason said. "Good place to do things you don't want anyone to know about."

Lang fished the keys out of his pocket and unlocked the single door. "You shall see why I chose this place."

Lang opened the door, and Mason pushed in past him. Wolski followed Lang inside while keeping a hand on his pistol. Lang opened the big double doors. The blue-gray light of dusk poured into the center of the room, but still left the corners in shadow.

"Stand just outside the doors, please," Wolski said. "And no sudden moves."

"Why do you treat me like a criminal? I have done nothing wrong, and I resent the intrusion—"

"Shut up," Wolski said, and pointed to a spot outside the doors. "When I said *don't move*, that meant your mouth, too."

Lang complied. Mason and Wolski made a slow search of the workshop with their flashlights in hand. They first checked out the 1928 Mercedes-Benz, which was partially covered by the black cloth. Wolski pulled off the cover the rest of the way and whistled in admiration, then he and Mason checked the interior for anything suspicious. The Altmann car was next, then they wove through the shelves, examining the various tools, automobile parts, and clock mechanisms.

"The owners don't mind that you took this place over?" Mason asked.

"Am I allowed to speak?"

"Only to answer questions," Wolski said.

"The original owner was Jewish. He was forced to give it away, and a group of Nazi officials took it over. I imagine they are either dead or in detainment camps. I knew about this machine shop, as a friend of mine used to work here."

"Did you fix all these clocks and things?" Mason asked.

"Of course. I found everything in unclaimed ruins. They were worthless before I repaired them."

Mason examined a brass torsion pendulum clock under a glass dome. "My grandmother had one of these," he said to Wolski. "When I was a kid, I'd stare at it for hours." He looked at Lang. "You do very nice work."

Lang bowed his head. "I am fortunate to have a skill that helps me survive."

Wolski called Mason over, and Mason looked where Wolski had trained his flashlight beam. On the floor in the corner lay a small mattress with rumpled sheets. It confirmed Lang's story about sleeping there. They both surveyed the shelves of Lang's repaired objects. On the last turn, Mason saw a long narrow object under a canvas cover. He and Wolski stepped over to it, and Mason pulled off the cover. Underneath sat a half-built Horex motorcycle.

Wolski whistled. "You did this?"

"Why do you keep asking me this? Yes, it was just a twisted hunk of metal when I found it, but parts are difficult to find. It will take me a long time to finish that project. The clocks and radios help me to eat, but cars and motorcycles are my passion."

Mason and Wolski continued to scan the darker areas with their flashlights. Nothing seemed suspicious, and Lang didn't look nervous at all about them searching his workshop.

In a corner of the workshop and out of Ramek's hearing, Wolski said, "Another dead lead."

"I don't know," Mason said. "There's something not right

here, but we've got nothing to go on, except that the hairs on the back of my neck are sticking up."

"Maybe you should see a doctor about that."

"No, they've rarely let me down. We'll ask Becker to have one of his men keep an eye on this guy. Let's get out of here."

Mason walked up to Lang and stood directly in front of him. He leaned in as if to catch a scent of guilt while watching Lang's eyes. "I'm not convinced you're who you claim to be. We'll be watching you. Have a good evening, Herr Lang."

~

DR. RAMEK, A.K.A. ALFRED LANG, WATCHED THE TWO detectives drive away. He pulled off the thick-lensed eyeglasses and tried to rub away the strain that element of his disguise inflicted upon his eyes. He could still smell the stench of their presence. He felt physically violated, sodomized by their prying gazes, their superior tones, and their demeaning questions.

The criminal gangs and the German police, even the loathsome populace, could cripple his path to ultimate salvation, but no one wielded more power, and thereby posed a greater danger, than a police detective of the occupying army. He would have to devise a way of dealing with this interloper.

"No, Investigator Collins, I will be checking in on you."

M ason had to walk a gauntlet of cold stares directed his way from the MP guards and the protesting citizens. For a second day, the crowd of protesters had gathered for a daylong silent vigil in front of Mason's headquarters, and a handful of MPs had been given the miserable duty of standing out in the freezing rain to keep the protesters to the opposite side of the street.

He made his way up to the operations room. Most of the investigators were out of the building checking up on tips or reported sightings, and the brief calm gave Mason the opportunity to go through the documents set aside for his review: a too-short list of potential witnesses; witness affidavits from Mauthausen but nothing conclusive; Counter Intelligence Command bulletins of newly captured Nazis. There was also a CID report about a private who had raped and murdered two elderly German ladies, a husky twenty-two-year-old who had a penchant for slicing them up afterward. Mason was sure the private had nothing to do with his case, but he had sent Wolski over to check it out.

He felt someone hovering behind him and turned. A corporal

stood by the door with his eyes fixed on the horrific crime scene photos.

"What is it, Corporal?"

"The colonel wants to see you, sir. He's hopping mad about something."

Mason thanked the corporal and descended the stairs to find Colonel Walton waiting at his office door.

"On the double, Collins."

Mason trudged into the office. Colonel Walton closed the door and marched over to his desk. He held up a newspaper. "Someone leaked details of the murders and the investigation to the *Washington Post*. And you want to know who? The woman who wrote that article about your exploits during the riot."

The shock hit Mason like a heavy blow, and he stopped listening to the colonel. He could feel his face turn red with anger. Laura had betrayed her promise. A second later, Colonel Walton's continuing rant reached his ears....

"The article goes on to blame the army for returning too many experienced troops home, leaving green recruits and reprobates led by bottom-of-the-barrel officers as an occupying force. It draws the conclusion that if the army can't solve a simple murder case in a country under martial law, then what's going to happen when bigger problems arise." He slammed the paper down. "You see where this is going? Third Army brass is taking the heat from USFET and the Pentagon, and they're passing it on to me. I'm getting handed my balls because of this one case. Your case."

Mason remained silent.

Colonel Walton sat and jerked his chair forward, as if mauling the chair was a substitute for what he wanted to do to Mason... or Laura. "Five days left and you still have squat. What are you and half my squad of investigators doing out there?"

Mason started to answer, but the colonel waved for him to be quiet.

"Don't answer that." The colonel let out a tired sigh. "Look, I've done police work in my time, and I know how tough an investigation can be. Giving you a week was unrealistic, but your failure is my failure, and I don't need a black mark on my record...." He clamped his jaw tight enough for the muscles to bulge. "I'm trying to stay calm, but my ass is on the line." He grabbed Mason's daily report from the previous and waved it. "I'm tired of telling you to get things done. I'm tired of sending in your paltry reports. I want some meat. Something I can show to keep the hounds from nipping at my heels. Lie if you have to. Just—"

Colonel Walton stopped and took a few deep breaths to bring his rage down a few notches, giving Mason time to do the same. Colonel Walton opened a side drawer, laid out two shot glasses, and went to the file cabinet. He opened the top drawer then slammed it closed. "Who keeps stealing my goddamned scotch?" He marched back to his desk and held up Mason's report again. "You know what 'embellish' means? That's what I want you to do to these reports. I want them to read like a fucking dime detective novel. If you want to stay on this case then give them something that'll make their dicks twitch."

He dismissed Mason with a backhanded wave. "That is all."

Mason turned to exit, but the same corporal blocked his way. "What is it this time?"

"A message came in from Major Rivers at the Dachau detainment camp, sir." He referred to his note. "A Herta Oberheuser wants to talk to you. She says she has more information about your case. Major Rivers said that if you don't make it over there this morning, all bets are off—whatever that means."

Mason turned back to Colonel Walton. "Sir, I need new travel orders to go to Dachau this morning. Wolski and I had planned to go over there this afternoon to interview a Dr. Blazek, but it looks like Herta Oberheuser might be ready to talk."

"You think she's really going to give it up this time?"

"I had JAG let it out that the Poles and Russians want to put her on trial."

"You what?"

"You told me to lie, sir."

Colonel Walton yelled for his assistant. "Pantina, get your ass in here."

"I need a new one for Wolski, too," Mason said.

"Where's *he* been? I wanted to see him this morning."

"I sent him to 508th headquarters to check out a report. I'll go by and pick him up on the way."

"He's lucky I don't issue him travel orders to the stockade for stealing my scotch." At Mason's look of surprise, Colonel Walton said, "I know more about what goes on here than you think."

"Yes, sir."

"All right. Go get some results." As Mason turned to leave, Colonel Walton said, "Remember... those reports. Embellish."

Ten minutes later, Mason exited headquarters by the main entrance. The silent protesters were still there. In fact, the number had increased considerably. He gave them a parting glance as he climbed in a Jeep the motor pool had brought around for him.

It revolted him to be close to so many wretched creatures, packed in as they were on the sidewalk. They held signs of protest or simply stood in silent vigil. But even in their silence, he could hear the cacophony of their beating hearts, their rasping breaths, the blood running in their veins. Though all wore heavy coats, he could sense their warm flesh, and he fought the urge to remove the scalpel from his pocket... *Flesh is your canvas, organ and bone your marble.* The urges overwhelmed him and made him shudder.

The man closest to him turned to him and smiled. "It is very cold, yes?"

The sudden attention sent a pulse of panic through him. He dived into the crowd, using his shoulders as a wedge and forcing his hands deep into his pockets lest he succumb to the temptation to cut his way through them.

Near the front of the crowd he stopped. The man he had been waiting for just emerged from the triple-arched entry. Ramek watched his nemesis briefly scan the crowd and nod to an American MP. Ramek pushed his way to the front as the man climbed into the waiting Jeep.

He stopped. This was neither the time nor the place....

But a new plan formed in his mind as he watched Investigator Collins drive away.

"You guys really stirred things up around here," Major Rivers said as Mason and Wolski entered the administration building. Major Rivers, Dachau's camp commander, had deep-set eyes framed by thick black eyebrows that arched high on his forehead like exclamation points on his scowl. Rivers led them down the hallway to the interrogation room as he talked. "I don't know how you started the rumors, but half the prisoners think that the Russians are coming to get them. I've been inundated with calls from the prisoners' lawyers trying to find out what's going on."

"The message was only intended for Herta Oberheuser, sir."

"Yeah, I found that out only after putting in a few high-level calls. I've held off quashing this rumor until you've had a chance to talk to the evil witch of Ravensbrück, but I'd appreciate if, in the future, you inform me of your plans before starting a panic."

"I apologize about the inconvenience, but I'm running out of time and need results. I really want to thank you for all your help in this case. General West will appreciate it too."

At hearing that last remark, Rivers took a more conciliatory tone. "My help isn't going to amount to much now. They'll clam up tight once they catch on to your ruse."

They stopped at the closed door of the interrogation room, and Mason said, "It'll be worth the gamble if Oberheuser talks."

Major Rivers risked one more scowl before walking away. Mason looked at Wolski. "I *hope* it's worth the gamble."

They entered the small interrogation room. The two escorting MPs stood guard on each side of the door. Mason asked them to wait outside, and the guards complied. This time Dr. Oberheuser and her lawyer were already there. The lawyer peeked over the top of his newspaper and nodded from his chair in the corner. Oberheuser waited in the chair facing the blank wall.

"May I have a cigarette, please?" Oberheuser asked without turning around.

Wolski handed her one and lit it for her. He then took his place by the window. Mason sat opposite her. She looked smaller and frailer than the last time. Her face expressed defiance, but her hands fought with each other on the table surface.

"I'm glad you agreed to talk with us," Mason said. "We'd like to know about the German prisoner doctor you mentioned. The one who the inmates referred to as the Healing Angel. What can you tell us about him?"

Oberheuser remained silent and gave no indication that Mason was in the room.

"Dr. Oberheuser?"

Herta looked up at him. "Frau Doktor Oberheuser. We are not friends."

"Frau Doktor, now that you've had some time to think over our last conversation—"

"You said that if I gave you information, you would file a favorable report to the prosecutor's office."

"Yes. Showing compassion for the innocent victims and a willingness to cooperate can help your defense."

"I do not wish to be handed over to the Russians. I don't want to be hanged."

"We'll do our best to help you avoid them, but—I'm being honest with you here—your sentencing is not up to me."

Oberheuser's frown deepened. She noticed her battling hands and dropped her free hand to her lap. "I want to be clear that anything I say will not implicate me in any way. I will only tell you things that cannot be used against me."

"Whatever you tell us about your activities stays in this room," Wolski said.

"What I told you before, that I hardly knew the German prisoner doctor, wasn't quite correct."

"Why don't you start with his name?"

"Dr. Ernst Ramek."

Wolski wrote it down, and Mason asked, "Could you describe him for us?"

Oberheuser took a long drag on her cigarette. "I..." She paused. "Maybe this was a mistake."

"I believe part of you wants to come forward because you know these killings are wrong," Wolski said. "You became a doctor to save lives. German lives. And this killer is murdering fellow Germans."

Herta chortled. "Do not patronize me, Mr. Collins. I give you information, and you save me from the Russians. Though I think you are lying about that, what choice do I have?"

"Then don't tell us anything and go back to your cage. It's up to you."

With a smirk of superiority, Oberheuser fixed her gaze at the wall.

Mason stood. "We're done here. Guard!"

Oberheuser stiffened. "No, wait."

The MP guard opened the door. Mason signaled him to go back outside. He sat again and waited for Oberheuser to speak.

"He was as you described. Tall and broad-shouldered. Though very thin."

"Anything else about his appearance?"

The woman shrugged. "After a year of slave labor anyone looks like a skeleton. He always looked sickly to me. He had this long stare and hollow eyes."

"What about hair? Scars or deformities? Glasses?"

"Brown hair, brown eyes, no glasses, no deformities that I know of."

"Did he tell you anything about where he came from? Family? Friends? Was he a deeply religious man?"

"We never talked except for my instructions during procedures. I had no interest in him other than his skills as a surgeon."

"So, this man, Ramek, assisted you in your experiments?"

Oberheuser nodded.

"Can you tell us why he was put in the concentration camps?"

"I have no idea. All I know about his history is that he had worked as a slave laborer at Sachsenhausen for a year before arriving at Ravensbrück."

"And where was he transferred after his stay at Ravensbrück?"

"Mauthausen."

Wolski flipped through his notepad. "Kiesewetter took him on to Mauthausen?"

Oberheuser nodded again.

"Okay. What else do you remember about him?"

"I found it amusing that most of the other inmates considered him a gentle and kind man. A savior. That's why they called him the Healing Angel." She let out a soft chuckle. "Yet he operated with a certain... glee. You see, he could manipulate subjects into believing that he was there to help and protect them. That the procedures were for their own good. He could get them to lie down on the operating table despite the camp rumors to the contrary."

"Did he ever go beyond what was required?" Wolski asked. "We're asking this because we want to feel confident that this is our killer. Anything you could tell us about his behavior could help us."

Oberheuser took a puff as she thought. "After we had performed several procedures together, I noticed he became sexually aroused during the operations. He seemed to go into a trance, though his methods were still very good. Very meticulous. I grew to respect his work, but as an individual he disgusted me. And later, after I had moved on to other studies, I heard he had, at times, gone too far—performing multiple amputations or separating a subject's entire pelvis and legs. He would operate with incredible intensity, and then once the procedure was finished, he would fall into a kind of despair."

"Did he ever perform these operations on subjects without anesthesia?"

"Never. What would be the point? All our studies were conducted to discover better ways of treating wounded soldiers."

"Any rumors of him performing other types of operations without anesthesia?"

Oberheuser crushed out her cigarette, and Wolski offered her another. After he lit it for her, she said with a quiet and unsure voice, "None that I had anything to do with."

"Then he may have."

"He assisted Dr. Kiesewetter in several studies. What they did or how they did them is none of my affair. I will not substantiate rumors."

"Then there were rumors about Kiesewetter and Ramek operating on subjects without anesthesia?" Wolski asked.

"There were always rumors. But I will not tell you something I did not see with my own eyes."

"How long did he stay at Ravensbrück?"

"To my knowledge, nine months. Like I said, he followed Dr. Kiesewetter to Mauthausen. In early 1944."

"Was it usual at Ravensbrück for SS doctors to take prisoner doctors with them when they were transferred?"

"Yes. However Dr. Kiesewetter seemed to rely heavily on Ramek. Who knows? Maybe they both had erections while operating and then simultaneously ejaculated at the moment of the subject's death, like some depraved men's club."

Mason leaned forward and looked into her eyes. "Frau Doktor, I hope you're not telling us fairy tales just so you won't be turned over to the Russians."

Oberheuser glared at Mason. "I have far more to lose if you discover I am lying. And how can I be sure that once you're finished with me you won't hand me over to the Russians? Or that you're lying about that favorable report?"

"We'll do what we promised, Frau Doktor," Wolski said. "The Judge Advocate's office assured us that they will deny the Russian petition in exchange for talking to us. We will also submit the favorable letter today."

A three-way staring contest lasted a few moments until Wolski asked, "Do you have anything to add?"

The doctor crushed out her cigarette into the ashtray and stared at the table. Her hand shook and her eyes watered. She shook her head and used the table for support as she stood. Her lawyer moved over to the table to help steady her. Wolski walked over to the door and knocked. The two MPs entered, and Mason watched as this now-broken woman allowed the guards to attach her shackles and lead her away.

Wolski feigned a shudder of disgust. "She was more disturbed by the idea of two doctors ejaculating than them cutting open a live patient."

"Aside from her twisted mind, do you think she's telling the truth?"

"You saw her eyes. She was back there in the camp, reliving all the madness...." Wolski shuddered again. "She was telling *her* truth, anyway."

"Now we get to hear from an inmate, Dr. Blazek. Another truth, another camp, and another nightmare."

33

A t three o'clock, Mason and Wolski were led to a two-story house just outside the Dachau camp enclosure, reserved for the camp commander and visiting war crimes lawyers and investigators. They waited in the front foyer where the escorting sergeant had left them. A tall, lanky JAG captain with a bald pate and wire-rimmed glasses slid open the living room pocket doors, entered, and closed them again. He introduced himself as Arnie Patterborn.

"Dr. Blazek is ready for you now. But just a few ground rules. It took him four months in a hospital to recover, and he's still weak. You name a disease and he had it when Mauthausen was liberated. This trip, our deposition, and identifying the camp perpetrators has taken a lot out of him. So try to make this as brief as you can. If he drifts off subject, which he tends to do, then gently get him back on track. We still have to return him to Prague this evening. The Czechs don't want us to keep him overnight, and I don't think they'll be too happy if they know he's being interviewed in a criminal investigation. I'll be in the room with you, and if I determine you're pushing him too hard, then I'll cut it short."

Mason and Wolski agreed. Patterborn slowly slid open the doors like stage curtains opening on a somber play. The living room curtains were drawn halfway. The reduced incoming daylight and the mahogany paneling made the room quite dim. Blazek sat in a wheelchair with a blanket across his lap. Mason knew the man was in his late forties, but he looked sixty-five. His white hair topped an angular face made more so by his sunken cheeks and white goatee.

Patterborn introduced them.

"Forgive me, gentlemen, for not greeting you properly," Blazek said. "My heart and kidneys are not what they should be." He spoke perfect German with a thick Czech accent.

Mason and Wolski sat on a sofa facing Blazek. Patterborn took a chair off to one side.

"We're very happy you're willing to talk to us, Dr. Blazek," Mason said.

"Captain Patterborn told me all about your investigation. A terrible thing. Terrible."

"We hope our questions won't be too tough on you, bringing up bad memories and all," Wolski said.

"The memories are burned into my psyche. Your questions will have no effect on their constant presence in my mind."

"We understand you were a prisoner doctor at Mauthausen," Mason said. "We're hoping you might be able to give us information on a possible suspect."

"The murderer. Yes…" Blazek paused a moment, as if to summon his memories. "I was at Mauthausen from the summer of 1942 until liberation this past May by your American army. Though I was a psychiatrist before my internment, I had practiced enough medicine to be chosen to work as a prisoner doctor. I was on block twenty-six in logistics and block thirty-two for convalescing inmates."

"Did you know a Dr. Ernst Ramek, a German prisoner doctor?"

"My, yes. Toward the end of '44 we were housed in the same block. We shared many talks together, whispering in the night. Dr. Ramek had a very troubled soul."

"How do you mean?"

"We all—'we' meaning the prisoner doctors—felt a certain amount of guilt about working with the SS doctors. We were better fed, better housed, and spared the appallingly brutal labor. We survived by agreeing to work for sadistic thugs. Administering medical care to inmates, while knowing that if they recovered, they must once again suffer in the quarries or the underground factories. We all to some degree made a pact with the devil for the chance of survival. Do not misunderstand me; we all lived with imminent death, hour by hour, day by day. We risked the nightly beatings and random murders by the kapos. We suffered from malnutrition and, in my case, contracting any number of diseases...."

Mason interrupted Blazek to bring him back to the question. "And Dr. Ramek? All of you suffered, so why do you say that *he* had a troubled soul?"

"He never told me details of his participation, except to say that he assisted in savage, inhuman medical experiments. So his guilt, the guilt we all share, was amplified a hundred-fold."

"But he wasn't the only prisoner doctor forced to assist in experiments like that," Wolski said.

"Ah, but layered with his guilt, he admitted to fantasies and arousal in the act, only to be devastated afterward. I believe he was a troubled man before his internment. Being forced to participate in those experiments unleashed repressed feelings. Flights of fancy as a boy or adolescent, normally repressed, suddenly collided with reality."

"Another witness who knew him claims that he started out as a kind and respected prisoner doctor," Wolski said.

"Yes, he was kind and gentle to other inmates. He was never a monster. He simply lost his soul and, consequently, his sanity. I witnessed many inmates who, when faced with such terror and depravity, teetered on the edge of insanity. Dr. Ramek became trapped in a mental cycle of fantasies, desire, performance of the act, then the crushing disappointment that his fantasies had not been realized."

"So, as long as he needed to fulfill his fantasies, he'd go on killing," Mason said. "Like the man we're hunting in Munich."

For a time, Blazek fell silent. "During my long recovery, I've had time to consider the many men placed in the extreme environment of Mauthausen. The men who performed unimaginable cruelty... and the victims. What brought each to that point, and how does one go back to a normal life? How could a camp guard or a kapo or an SS doctor who for years performed inhumane acts, settle back into normal society? There must be a dissociation between the two experiences, creating a duality that preserves the psyche. Dr. Ramek, and perhaps your murderer, could not maintain that duality, leaving them unable to recover from their experiences."

"What if I told you that we believe Dr. Ramek and the Munich killer are the same person?" Mason asked.

"The same? Oh, no, that is not possible."

Mason and Wolski exchanged looks of surprise. "How is that, Doctor?" Wolski asked. "They both fit the physical description and their methods of killing."

"It is not possible because Dr. Ramek is dead."

There was a moment of silence as Mason and Wolski exchanged looks, the ticking of the clock on the mantelpiece the only sound.

"Are you sure?" Mason asked. "Perhaps he was transferred without your knowledge?"

"When news arrived at the camp that the American army was approaching, the Nazis tried to cover up the worst of their crimes. They destroyed documents, tried to burn all corpses and killed many who witnessed the worst of the medical experiments. SS guards rounded up inmates who'd worked in the gas chamber and the crematoria, as well as many medical personnel, and shot them. They entered the block where Ramek worked and killed the prisoner staff—the medics, the radiologists, the pathologists—all of them. Many of the Nazis guards then fled in the night before the American troops arrived."

"Did you actually see the killings in Ramek's block?" Wolski asked. "Or see Dr. Ramek's body?"

"No, but no one could have survived. Many of the bodies were burned, so identification was impossible."

"But you can't be sure that Ramek was killed," Mason said.

"I can't be sure, but I never saw him among the survivors."

Mason couldn't believe they'd come this close to identifying the killer only to learn they were following another dead end. It had to be the same man. "Maybe he was afraid of reprisals by the other inmates, because he worked with the camp doctors, and he slipped away after the guards had fled and before the camp was liberated."

"It is possible, but I believe I am the only surviving inmate who knows the truth about his activities. And I was not going to condemn the man. He suffered as much from the Nazi killing machine as anyone. If he had survived, why would he evade his liberators and risk capture by the retreating Germans? They would surely have killed him to cover up their crimes. No, gentlemen, I doubt very much they are the same man. I'm sorry if I disappointed you."

Mason and Wolski fell silent. Both were at a loss for words.

Patterborn broke the silence. "I think Dr. Blazek has had enough for one day." He stood to signal that they were done.

Mason ignored him. "Dr. Blazek, could you please give us a physical description of Dr. Ramek?"

"Gentlemen, please," Patterborn said. "I must insist—"

Blazek raised his hand. "Mr. Collins would not be a good policeman if he took no for an answer."

Patterborn looked at his watch and sat on the edge of the chair.

"I want you to keep one thing in mind," Blazek said. He gestured to himself. "I was a healthy and physically fit man before my three years in the camp. After six months, I wager my own family would have had trouble recognizing me. Doctor Ramek had been in camps for three years. Having said that, Dr. Ramek, as you know, was very tall with long legs. He had a strong jaw and chin...." Blazek looked away and appeared to drift off.

"His hair? Did he have any scars or features that stood out?" Mason asked.

"Brown hair, I believe, though we all had our heads shaved to help control lice. No scars or features that were remarkable. Long, powerful arms and big hands for a surgeon. He was quite strong even in his weakened state. He always joked that he got his height from his mother's side... the Lang family."

Blazek chuckled at the reference, but Mason and Wolski were stunned into silence. The junkman—Alfred Lang!

"You see?" Blazek said, mistaking their silence for lack of understanding. "*Lang* in German is 'long.' Lang? Tall? The tall side of the family?" Blazek fell silent and gestured to Patterborn. "I think it's time to say *Auf Wiedersehen* to these two nice gentlemen".

Mason wanted to rush out of there and immediately call headquarters. Instead, he stood and offered his hand. "Thank you, Dr. Blazek. Your information has been a great help."

"Good luck, Mr. Collins. I wish you all the best."

Wolski did the same, then followed Mason out the door.

They were almost at a dead run as they reached the gates; a rash act running at armed guards and the entrance to Dachau, but Mason couldn't help himself. He had to call headquarters and get every CID investigator and MP available to surround and descend upon Ramek's workshop.

34

A nerve-wracking forty-five minutes later, Mason and Wolski pulled into the shoe factory courtyard. Wolski squeezed the Jeep into the midst of what seemed to be their head-quarters' entire contingent of vehicles: Jeeps, sedans, and troop carriers. MPs and twenty-plus German police searched surrounding buildings or controlled the growing crowd of onlookers.

Mason and Wolski raced through the snarl of vehicles and humanity. They both skidded to halt in front of the open doors of the workshop. The workshop lay empty except for the larger machinery and empty shelves.

"Son of a bitch!" Mason said. He saw Timmers emerge from the workshop and rushed up to him. "Did you find anything?"

"Whoever was here cleaned the place out pretty good," Timmers said. He then thrust his thumb toward the remaining workshop machines. "Techs checked for fingerprints, but it looks like he wiped down the machines." He pointed to the open trap-door. "Wanna check out the dungeon?"

Mason felt like he'd been hit in the stomach and couldn't catch his breath. He looked at Wolski, and Wolski appeared to be feeling the same thing. They'd had Ramek in their hands, *and* in the place where he had butchered his victims. They had stood in the workshop, while Ramek's chamber of horrors lurked just below their feet. And they had walked away.

Timmers headed for the trapdoor, oblivious to their reaction. Mason pushed down his frustration and anger, and then gestured for Wolski to come along. They followed Timmers down the cement stairs.

"Forensics and an evidence team are down here now," Timmers said. "I had to come up for air. It's nasty down there. You're not gonna believe what we found."

The three investigators wove past crime-scene techs and MPs in the long corridor and entered the twenty-by-twenty-foot space. The stagnant air stank of mildew and chlorine. Seeping moisture and black mold stained the low ceiling and walls. In this fetid gloom, it was Ramek's operating table that chilled Mason's spine. The eight-foot-long table with a thick wooden top and metal support sat in the middle of the room, with leather straps hanging from the sides. A lieutenant from forensics and an evidence tech stood over the table, examining it carefully.

"They found traces of blood and a few bone chips," Timmers said. "It's not a real operating table. It looks like it came from a slaughterhouse or something." He led them over to the table and knelt, shining his flashlight underneath the table.

The idea that Ramek had sliced open his victims on a butchering table was not lost on Mason. He forced his legs to move and approached the table. He knelt and looked where Timmers aimed his flashlight. A metal label had been affixed to the wooden underside with a serial number.

Mason read the label. "MGF GmbH, Munich."

"Inspector Becker checked it out for us," Timmers said. "It's a company that manufactured equipment for slaughterhouses and meat-processing plants. They switched over to war production in '39."

"This was probably salvaged from one of the damaged factories," Mason said as he stood. "We'll access the manufacturer's files and see who they sold this table to."

The nightmarish scene had so transfixed Mason that he hadn't noticed Inspector Becker standing in a corner of the room, staring at something on the floor. Just above his head, a pipe hung from supports fixed in the concrete ceiling. Mason walked over and greeted him, then flicked on his flashlight and trained it on the spot where Becker had been staring.

"Bloody rags and two buckets full of blood," Becker said, then indicated the suspended pipe. "This must be where he hung the bodies to drain them of blood."

Both of them stared at the contents in a moment of silence. Mason felt a chill imagining the macabre scene.

"Wolski and I interviewed this man," Mason said in a soft voice. "We were here, at his workshop. We questioned him, and we let him go."

Becker nodded. "I wonder how many times I have done the same thing, whether from ignorance or lack of evidence. I, too, let a murderer slip through my fingers because I had the wrong information."

Mason said nothing, but he appreciated Becker's words. "We just came from Dachau. Herta Oberheuser gave us his name: Dr. Ernst Ramek."

Becker looked at Mason. "Then some good news. My team and I can now check city and state records, medical records, perhaps even his SiPo arrest record."

Mason nodded. "Wolski and I will get with a sketch artist and have Ramek's portrait drawn up."

"We are closing in on him."

"There's something else you should see," Timmers said. He

led Mason, Wolski and Becker to the opposite corner where a narrow door opened up into a second room of the same size. "Looks like he spent some time down here." He pointed to a cot, a small table, and chair that were placed near a wood-burning stove. A tech was trying to lift fingerprints off the stove surface.

"He had the stove vented up to the roof," Timmers said. "Looks like he'd planned to stay here awhile." He swung the beam of his flashlight to the facing wall. "This is what I wanted to show you."

They walked over to a set of metal shelves containing packaged medical supplies and surgical tools: saws, retractors, cotton bandages and rags, scalpels, suture needles, and two bottles of diethyl ether.

"Right out of some Frankenstein movie," Timmers said.

"This stuff is all U.S. Army issue," Mason said.

"Not sure why he left it all behind."

"Maybe he ran out of time," Wolski said.

"Or maybe he couldn't risk being caught with U.S.-issued medical supplies," Mason said. That got Mason thinking. "He couldn't have found or stolen all this. He must be using the black market to buy them."

"And he'll need more if he wants to keep going," Wolski said. "If we can find out who his supplier is, we put surveillance on him and see if he shows up looking to buy."

Mason turned to Becker. "Put together any information you have on black marketers, especially in medicine, and we'll do the same." He decided not to mention Laura's possible inside information on black marketers, but made a mental note to talk to her when he found a spare moment.

"I will take care of that right away," Becker said and left.

"We're still waiting on a genny and lights," Timmers said. "Who knows what else we'll find when that happens."

"Any witnesses?" Mason asked.

"No one yet."

"When we were here, he had a ton of stuff up top," Wolski said. "He had to have made several trips in a wagon to get it all out."

"You guys were here?" Timmers said. "You had him and let him get away?"

"If you'd read my daily report the way you're supposed to, you'd know that."

"Damn, what's the colonel gonna say?"

"Forget what the colonel's going to say. Ramek hired a driver the time we were here. Wolski has the driver's name and address. Get Cole and Mancini to pick him up. Then get a couple of teams together and find out if anyone within a four-block radius spotted a wagon loaded with radios, clocks. He even moved two goddamned cars and a goddamned motorcycle!"

"Okay. You don't have to yell. I ain't the one who's gonna jump down your throat."

Mason jabbed his finger toward the exit, and Timmers trotted off.

"At least we know his face, his name, and his alias," Wolski said. "Plus, we've shut him down for a while. He's going to have to acquire equipment and find another secure location. That's going to take time."

Mason looked around and cursed under his breath. "If he hasn't left town."

Mason and Wolski emerged from Ramek's torture chamber and stepped outside the workshop. Mason looked up at the surrounding ruins, the dark windows staring like sad eyes.

Wolski said, "If he needs to keep on killing without a break, then he'll be desperate. He's bound to make a mistake. We'll get him."

"He left the buckets of blood and rags for us to find. To taunt us. He *planned* for this. He could be looking down on us right now from one of these buildings, enjoying his triumph. He'll be up and running in no time."

"Sir, you'd better see this," an MP said to Mason. He stood among the jumble of vehicles. His blanched face was enough to prompt Mason to hurry through the cars behind the MP without question. He stopped three paces from the Jeep that had brought Wolski and him to the workshop. The back of the passenger's seat, the seat Mason had sat in on the way over, was slashed to shreds and smothered in crimson, coagulating blood.

THE THRILL HAD BEEN WORTH THE RISK. HE HAD JEOPARDIZED everything to get close enough that he could have easily slashed the investigator's throat. In the chaos of MPs and German police, no one noticed him brush past Investigator Collins while fingering the scalpel he held deep in his pocket. And how simple it had been to slip in and out of the shoe factory courtyard wearing a German police uniform and carrying the forged identity papers attesting to his membership in the Landespolizei as a newly transferred *Wachtmeister*. He had acquired this new disguise in his final trade with Rudolph for the Mercedes. But the greatest prize in the trade, and the one Rudolph had the most difficulty obtaining, was an American military police uniform. If he were careful enough, he could blend or move about the city with impunity. He might even be among the squad of German police who would find the slashed bodies of Rudolph and his clumsy bodyguard. Departing the chaos of the factory had been just as easy, blending in with the rest of the green-uniformed *Landespolizeien*, and then slipping through the small crowd gathered to watch the spectacle. Just another *Wachtmeister* moving out to search for witnesses.

Now he stood on the edge of the vast site where demolition

crews dumped the rubble collected from so many of the ruins. His eyes were fixed on a blazing pyre, and he wept as he watched his collection of clocks and radios, the Horex motorcycle, and the Altmann car, his labors of love, go up in flames. He had spared a few of his favorite objects from the flames, but the rest could not be left for the masses to pilfer, the greedy, undeserving creatures that would plunder his treasures. No, he could not face that. They would return to the ashes from which they had emerged. Let their remains rise up to the heavens, as he would do one day soon.

In the distance, a fire truck blared its siren. He let out a shriek of anger, and his body shook. That American detective had violated his sanctuary. He would have real revenge.

He turned away from the blaze and slipped into the shadows.

Thirty minutes later he was home. He changed out of his uniform and put on his street clothes. This day was worthy of a diary entry, and he sat at the small table in the dark room. Yes, he had lost his treasures, his place of sacrifice, and some of his medical equipment, but today's entry would be filed with more triumph than defeat. He could now approach without detection and kill the vile detective when the time was right. All that remained was the method.

He must think. Weigh his options. The voices would do anything to keep him from escaping their torment. The obstacle must be removed. As Rudolph and his bodyguard had been. The crime boss had become too curious about his request.

"Why would a humble tinker want police uniforms?" Rudolph had asked. "What have you got going on the side?"

Rudolph had threatened to withhold the uniforms. Clearly, he'd begun to suspect Ramek was hiding something sinister. The bodyguard had been fooled by Ramek's act of timidity. Killing both of them had been so easy.

The rest of Rudolph's crew would be looking for him. The police manhunt would intensify. He was doomed either way, but that was the price for ascension. But ascension, he now realized, could only be achieved by making the ultimate sacrifice. It would involve the suffering of a true innocent. He saw it clearly now: It would be like Abraham preparing to sacrifice his son. Only his willingness to obey, his duty performed up to the final act, could compel God to stay his hand and deliver him to the kingdom of heaven.

But it began with the selection. And now, Ramek knew, his final Chosen One must be the ultimate symbol of innocence... a child.

R amek's wagon driver, Herr Winkler, sat across the table from Mason. He turned his battered Tyrolean hat in his hands and stared at the table's scarred surface. A number of the third-floor offices had been transformed into interrogation rooms to accommodate the large number of interviewees swept up after the raid on Ramek's workshop. The entire floor buzzed with activity.

"I only met him that one day, Herr Inspektor," Winkler said.

"Had you seen him around your neighborhood?"

"Never." Winkler looked up at Mason with wet eyes. His lips trembled; he looked like he expected to be shackled and taken to prison at any moment. "My family, my friends, will be very angry with me for helping this killer."

"I won't tell if you don't, Herr Winkler. Did he say anything about where he stays other than the workshop? Family? Friends? Anything about his past?"

"We spoke very little, sir." He put his hands on his cheeks. "To think I sat next to this man for six hours. Every time I think about it…."

"Have you heard any other wagon drivers or livery owners speak about him?"

"Only rumors of a man who paid very well to hire a driver and wagon. But no one I know has ever dealt with him. Please, sir, you are not going to arrest me, are you?"

"No," Mason said and pushed a notepad and pencil across the table. "I want you to write down all the places you visited with Herr Ramek, and what you did there."

Mason sat back and watched Winkler take up the pencil and begin to write. Becker's teams had already questioned the known livery stables. A couple of them had rented a wagon and horse to Ramek, but they all said the same thing as Winkler: Ramek used a different name each time and paid amply in cigarettes and cash for their services. He stood and stretched to get the kinks out of his back, then turned to the MP standing next to Winkler. He said in English, "When he's finished, let him go."

He stepped out into the hallway just as one of his investigators, Curtis, came up to him.

"The deputy chief of the Munich Fire Department just called," Curtis said. "They had to put out a fire at one of the rubble yards." He looked at his notes. "They found a big heap of burned items: clocks, radios, phonographs, auto parts, a motorcycle, and an old jalopy. He thought you'd like the info."

"Now we know what Ramek did with all the objects at the workshop. You and Pike go over there and see if you can pick up his trail."

Mason slowly passed the other interrogation rooms as he thought about what this meant: Was Ramek planning to leave town? Spread his terror to other cities? Forget the army brass's deadline; they would have to move faster than that if they hoped to catch Ramek now.

Mason paused by an interrogation room where Becker was

interviewing a black-market drug dealer. Despite the dealer's ignoble status as Becker's paid informant, the two of them were in the midst of a yelling match in rapid-fire Bavarian dialect. Mason could understand only a few short phrases. He watched their hands and facial expressions for a few moments and felt satisfied that Becker was wearing down his opponent.

Mason stopped outside the operations room. He wanted to take a second of quiet before entering the fray once more. Phones rang; clerks scurried. Cole and Mancini moved down a line of black market "vendors" caught in the series of raids, asking them questions and showing them the sketch of Ramek. He rubbed the exhaustion from his face. It was close to seven p.m., and they'd been going non-stop since the workshop raid. Sandwiches had been ordered, but they hadn't shown up yet. At some point, he would try to break away and track down Laura. He hated to admit it, but he'd been putting it off because he was still steamed about the article in the *Post*.

Mason heard footsteps and turned to see Colonel Walton walking toward him. The last time Mason had seen Colonel Walton was before the trip to Dachau that morning, and he knew the colonel would be fired up after another army brass meeting. He met the colonel halfway down the hall so they would be out of earshot from the rest.

"I've just come from another joyful meeting with General West and his merry band of henchmen, in which I had the dubious honor of explaining why you let Ramek slip through your fingers. General West blew a gasket, and I had to take the brunt of it." Two clerks rushed past, and Colonel Walton stopped to watch them. "That brings me to my next point. I've noticed a distinct absence of office furniture, telephones, and clerks in the main squad room."

Just then, Wolski exited his interrogation room. He tried to head casually in the opposite direction, but Colonel Walton had spotted him. "Well, Warrant Officer Wolski. Let me gaze upon the man responsible."

Wolski reluctantly joined them.

"Resourcefulness can be an asset, but not when it means looting my squad room. And we're going to have a long talk about the consequences of stealing a man's scotch." When Wolski offered no explanation, Colonel Walton said, "We'll deal with that later." He turned to look at both of them. "So, you two are having a busy day. But I wonder how raiding the black market is the best use of your time. By my count, you have just a few days left before the full weight of army brass comes down on your heads."

"We're following simultaneous leads—" Wolski said.

"Simultaneous?" Colonel Walton said, pretending to be impressed. "Well, then, my mistake. You boys have it all under control."

Wolski looked flustered, but he continued. "We have a team working with German police following up on census and university records, bank and tax records, voting registration, doctor's license, camp records—"

Colonel Walton stopped him with a raised hand. "Besides the war messing up the German filing system, whatever old records you find on Ramek aren't going to help track him down."

"Our squad of MPs and the Landespolizei are distributing the sketch of Ramek," Mason said. "Also, the *Stars and Stripes* and the German press will print his sketch in tomorrow's newspaper. Reporters have been calling most of the evening, asking for a statement."

"I'll take care of that," Colonel Walton said.

Mason was more than happy to let him. He only wondered if Laura had been one of the eager callers. "Becker dug up Ramek's Gestapo arrest record. They went to the address, but it was destroyed in the bombing raids. Shouldn't be too long before we have the location of his family's home. Also the former prisoner doctor, Blazek, said, Ramek's mother's maiden name was Lang. We're checking up on those records. We know the father died in '32. Meanwhile, we're contacting all the German medical and surgical supply houses."

Wolski cleared his throat and said, "Actually, sir, we were hoping you could allot us just a few more men and Jeeps."

Colonel Walton's expression stopped him from going any further. "You can't be serious." He took a deep breath. "Use more German police."

"We're already doing that, sir," Wolski said. "They've augmented our manpower but—"

"'Augmented'?" Colonel Walton said, interrupting. Pointing to Wolski with his thumb, he said to Mason, "This guy's going to go places, using big words like that."

Wolski, undeterred, said, "But the Germans can only spare so many men."

"Probably because they're doing other police work." Colonel Walton gave them a sly smile. "You can have Havers and a bicycle." He walked away obviously delighted with his retort.

Timmers and MacMillan came down the hallway while removing their overcoats. "Checked all the legit medical and surgical suppliers. No records of a Dr. Ramek, Mendel, or Lang buying from any of them."

"He could have used another alias," Wolski said.

They all exchanged looks; no one wanted to hear that.

"Any food come yet?" Timmers asked.

Mason shook his head. "Go help Cole and Mancini in the operations room."

Timmers and MacMillan looked annoyed at the prospect of a long night and nothing to eat.

Becker came out of his interrogation room. "You both need to hear this."

Mason and Wolski followed Becker into the interrogation room. The informer, Weber, looked very satisfied with himself, leaning back in his chair with his arms crossed and sporting a big smile.

"Tell them what you told me," Becker said to Weber.

Weber rubbed his index finger and thumb together.

"You'll be paid," Mason said.

"I know of one person who deals in black market medicine. Heinrich Kessler. He's a member of a very bad gang...." He shook his head with disapproval. "Very bad. They deal in diluted penicillin and phony baby formula. They steal medical supplies from hospitals. Kessler is small potatoes, but he's a blowhard, always exaggerating his own importance. And he talks too much. Even for me, he talks too much. He keeps going on about making it big one day—"

"Get to the point, Weber," Becker said.

"He tells me about forming a partnership with an American gang member. I don't know this man, but he supposedly sells hard-to-find medicines in large quantities, hospital equipment, and surgical supplies."

"Where can we find Kessler?"

Weber shrugged. "He seems to move around: one place one week, another the next week. We haven't talked for some time—two weeks, maybe, so I'm sorry, I don't know."

"Tell him the rest," Becker said.

"The last time we spoke, he said he was talking to an American reporter. A very beautiful one, at that." He gave them a big, lecherous smile.

～

MASON TOOK A STEP INTO THE PRESSROOM, WHICH accommodated a large portion of the U.S. Army-certified war correspondents. It resembled any pressroom of a medium-sized newspaper with the bustle of reporters, the cacophony of voices, the clack of typewriters, and the ringing phones. The only difference was the number of men and women in uniform. He scanned the room for Laura. Mason recognized one of the women who had been partying with Laura at the hotel. She looked up at him as she talked on the phone and pointed toward the hallway.

Mason stepped back out and spotted Laura emerging from another office. She saw him and smiled. The smile faded when she noticed his expression. She clenched her jaw, marched up to him, and took him by the arm.

"Come with me," Laura said.

She led him to an empty office and shut the door a little too hard. She whirled around and crossed her arms. "Now, before you go off on me about the article in the *Post*, I have a few things to say."

"I'm not mad about the article; I'm mad because you broke your promise."

"Did you read it?"

"My commanding officer summed it up pretty well while chewing me out."

"I thought so. Do you read anything other than comic books? I didn't break my promise. There's nothing in the article that anyone doesn't already know."

"Except you're the one to give it to a national newspaper."

"I got fed up with the army censoring the press. I was mad at the brass for giving you only a week to solve a case that any police department would have a tough time solving. Their arrogance and stupidity drive me crazy. And your argument that it might give the killer information is irrelevant since the *German* killer isn't going to pick up the latest edition of the *Washington Post* at his local newsstand." She made a move for the door.

"Heinrich Kessler. Do you know him?"

Laura froze for a moment, then slowly turned to face Mason.

"Is he your black market contact?" Mason asked.

"I won't answer that."

"You didn't say no, so I'll take it as a yes."

"Take it any way you like. I'm not going to give up a confidential source."

Mason took a step forward, looking in her eyes as he did so. "Kessler is part of a gang that deals in diluted penicillin and phony baby formula. They steal medical supplies from hospitals then turn around and sell them for sky-high prices. They screw over the sick and the dying, infants and kids, for a profit."

"How do you know all this?"

"One of Inspector Becker's informers is at headquarters right now. He told us all about it. He identified Kessler, but doesn't know where he is. We need to find him. He may have information that could lead us to Ramek, the killer." He took another step closer. "You said that if you knew anyone committing those kinds of crimes you'd come forward. I need to know where to find him."

"My contact is just a low-level operator in a much bigger machine. If I can get inside, I might be able to learn enough to crack open the entire gang. Really shut it down. You think the army would be able to do the same thing? If I give him up, it will blow my only source of inside information."

"We'll make it look like a routine black market sweep and pick him up that way. He'll never know how we found him, and he'll be back out on the streets. Your investigation will hardly skip a beat."

Laura thought a moment while glaring at Mason. "A reporter and a cop. What a silly idea."

"Laura...."

"I don't know where he lives, but we've met a number of times at Gärtnerplatz. He's usually there in the evenings until curfew. You'd better hurry if you want to catch him."

Mason walked around Laura and opened the door. "Talk about arrogance and stupidity," he said. "You're in way over your head this time, and you could get yourself killed." He left without waiting for a response.

All eyes in the precinct turned toward the uproar coming through the front entrance. A runt of a man, soaked to the bone, yelled as he struggled against Wolski's grip. Only a handful of the MPs and officers could understand his Bavarian dialect, but the spectacle of this wiry, bug-eyed man being half-carried by an equally rain-soaked giant amused everyone. Mason and Becker brought up the rear. They all stopped just inside the door and the investigators shook off as much rainwater as they could.

"If you don't shut up for one minute, we *are* going to torture you," Mason said.

"Help! I will be tortured! American soldiers beat innocent Germans!"

The crazed man had switched to High German to make himself understood, but he'd neglected to notice that the building was full of American soldiers. Wolski and Mason grabbed his arms and started dragging him toward the stairs, with Becker solemnly taking up the rear. All the way up the stairs Kessler cried for help and declared his innocence. Once at the door to an interview room, Wolski tossed Kessler inside. Kessler let out a scream and bolted for the hall, but Mason dragged him back in and shoved him into a chair.

Kessler was a gaunt man with circles under his eyes so dark it looked like someone had given him double black eyes. Sweat and raindrops poured off his face in equal amounts. He clasped his handcuffed hands together to keep them from shaking, staring at them as if willing them to stop. But, as if he were trying to hold down a jackhammer, the trembling traveled up his arms making his torso shake.

Under his breath, Mason said to Becker, "Looks like he's a junkie in need of a fix."

"Offer him his freedom for the information. I won't object."

"Are you sure?"

"A man like this will not stay out of trouble for long. I am sure we will get him in the very near future."

The half-crazed man muttered at the table in Bavarian dialect. Mason could only catch a couple of words, something about rights and animals. Mason slapped the table. "For the purposes of this interview, Herr Kessler, you will speak in High German."

"I have been denied my rights," Kessler said. "You Amis are treating me like an animal. I have done nothing wrong!" He finished his sentence with a shriek.

"Selling morphine and amphetamine pills is a very serious offense," Becker said.

He jerked his thumb at Becker. "Why must he be here?"

"Because, Heinrich, we're not supposed to arrest German nationals without Landespolizei supervision."

"How do I know he's not ex-Gestapo? Or his comrades. I might get my throat cut—"

Becker grabbed Kessler by the lapels and lifted him from his chair. It was the first time Mason had seen Becker lose his cool, and he was surprised at the older man's strength.

"You piece of filth, I was never Gestapo. It was snitches like you who turned innocent people in to the Gestapo pigs so you could make a profit." He threw Kessler back into the chair.

Kessler jerked his head as he looked at the three detectives as if searching for a friend among them. He received only grim looks in return. "Please, sirs, I wasn't selling anything. You can't prove I was. You found nothing on my body."

Mason lifted Kessler's knapsack that he'd placed on the floor. "What do you call this?" He opened the knapsack and rummaged around. "Packets of morphine, amphetamine pills, syringes, packs of needles—"

"That's not mine! Someone dropped it in front of me!"

Mason wondered if Kessler always ended his sentences with a shrill wail. "I bet if we examine the contents, we'll find your fingerprints all over this stuff."

"Somebody must have taken my prints and put them in there. They came in while I was sleeping and took them."

"I hate to inform you, Heinrich, but that's not possible."

Kessler grabbed his head and banged the table with his elbows. "Not true. Not true."

Wolski moved over to stand just behind Kessler's chair. Kessler hunched into the table and covered his head with his hands. "We know you were selling those things," Wolski said. "You can go to prison for twenty years."

"No! Those drugs are not mine! If I go to prison, I'll die."

Kessler's shrieking was giving Mason a headache. "Maybe we're wrong. Maybe he gave these medicines to sick people. People in pain or needing energy to get through their day."

"Is that what you were doing, Herr Kessler?" Becker said. "Giving medicine to people who needed it?"

Kessler sat up. "Yes, I was doing that. Giving medicines to sick people."

"You see? This man isn't the lowlife scum we think he is. He's a good Samaritan, giving relief to the sick and injured."

Kessler raised his head, his whole body shaking now. "Does that mean you'll let me go?"

"Illegally distributing narcotics and stolen medicine is still a crime," Mason said. "I bet if we turn you over to Oberinspektor Becker, he'll put you away for the full twenty."

Kessler's mouth popped open in a silent scream. Mason let his paranoia stew into a frenzy. "Please, sirs, I cannot go to prison. I'm a sick man. My health, you see?"

"You have an alternative," Becker said. "Give us information, and maybe we can arrange something."

"Yes, an arrangement. Yes, I'll do that." He stopped. His eyes widened with sudden realization. "You want me to be an informer?" He shook his head violently. "No. If they find out, they will kill me."

Wolski leaned on the table next to Kessler, dwarfing the smaller man. "The alternative is prison. In there, you'll die a thousand times."

Kessler played with his shaking hands. Then his face brightened. "Before you tell me what you want of me, we should negotiate price." He counted on his fingers. "Day of lost sales at the markets, one copper who brutalizes me, psychological damages—"

Mason counted on his fingers, "Asking Oberinspektor Becker not to arrest you, avoiding twenty years in prison...."

"Okay, okay," Kessler said, and he plastered on his best salesman smile. "What can I do for you gentlemen?"

"We want to talk about your new partner," Becker said. "The American selling hospital equipment and surgical supplies."

Kessler shrank in his chair. Obviously, he didn't like where this was going. "Surgical equipment? I don't know anyone who sells such things."

Becker pulled out his handcuffs. "I am finished listening to this animal. Herr Kessler, you are under arrest—"

"No, wait! I only know one person. But, please, don't ask me to tell you who. He is connected to a very dangerous gang. They will kill me if I tell you."

"They won't know it's you," Mason said.

"They will. They will find me and kill me."

"You're forgetting our arrangement. You give us information, and Oberinspektor Becker here doesn't throw you in prison."

Wolski leaned on the table, his mouth by Kessler's ear. "And if you get thrown in prison, we'll have Oberinspektor Becker spread the word that you're a child molester. Guys bigger than me will ravage you and beat you over and over again. You'll spend the rest of your days in a bloody pulp with an asshole as big as my fist."

"All right!" Kessler cried out with his characteristic shriek. "His name is Frank Wertz. He sells on the street, but he is a member of a very dangerous gang of American deserters and Russian and Polish refugees."

Mason laid a sketch of Ramek on the table in front of Kessler. "Have you seen this man buying from Wertz?"

Kessler studied the face for a moment. "I think so. A big man, yes?"

Mason leaned on the table. "What do you know about him?"

"Very little, except that he has some influence with some crime boss, so he receives special privileges. Wertz sometimes delivers to him."

Mason and Wolski exchanged glances. "Where?" Wolski asked.

"Do you think they would share such information with me?"

"We want to meet Wertz, and you're going to point him out," Mason said.

Kessler's jaw dropped.

Wolski held his fist in Kessler's face, then made an obscene gesture. "Remember, Heinrich...."

Kessler dropped his head onto the table. "Why is life so cruel to me?"

"Ask that to the people you sell diluted penicillin to," Becker said.

~

MINUTES LATER, MASON, WOLSKI, AND BECKER EXITED THE interrogation room and descended the stairs to the squad room.

"Since Wertz won't show his face until tomorrow morning, we'll keep Kessler locked up overnight," Mason said to Becker. "You can do whatever you want with him once we're finished."

"I will honor the agreement. He will be free to go. For now. Good night, gentlemen."

Mason and Wolski returned the farewell and watched Becker leave.

"How about a shot before calling it a night?" Wolski asked.

"You're on."

Wolski sneezed, his whole body convulsing from the effort. "God damn it. I can't get a cold. I promised to take Anna to the OMGB Christmas dance tomorrow night."

"Having a cold doesn't make you concerned about giving this investigation your full effort?"

"My full effort's what gave me this cold."

As they walked to Mason's office, Wolski said, "When I was sick as a kid, my dad would give us shots of hot bourbon and honey. Don't know how much good it did the cold, but it sure did him good."

Mason didn't hear Wolski. He was fixed on the foot-high object wrapped in brown kraft paper sitting on his desk. Since

Timmers had a clear view of Mason's office door, Mason stopped at his desk.

"Tim, did you see who brought in that package on my desk?"

Timmers lifted his tired gaze from his paperwork. "An MP. He asked where your office was then dropped it off and left."

"Did he say what it was about?"

"Nope."

"What time?"

"About an hour ago. Before you guys got back."

Mason and Wolski walked into the office and stared at the package.

"Could be something sent down from the war crimes records office," Wolski said.

"There's nothing written on the outside. Usually, those have destination and official labels plastered all over them."

"Maybe it's a bomb from one of your admirers."

Mason gave him a look of rebuke. He leaned over and put his ear to the package. No sound from inside. He lifted it and turned it on its side. Something metallic rattled.

"Bombs don't rattle," Wolski said. "Could be from Laura. Open it."

Mason placed the object on his desk. He delicately unwrapped the paper and revealed a mahogany and brass pendulum clock. Mason was puzzled at first. He couldn't think of who would send him such a beautiful gift.

Then he remembered the workshop, and Ramek, and having admired the exact same clock. He suddenly felt very cold.

"God damn. Look at this," Wolski said.

Wolski held up the kraft paper. Written on the underside, in large block letters:

YOU MUST WIND IT. I DIDN'T WANT YOU TO THINK IT
WAS A BOMB. A TOKEN OF OUR BRIEF YET

INTERESTING ENCOUNTER, AND A REMINDER OF LIFE'S FLEETING TIME.
DEATH IS JUST AROUND THE CORNER

With a swipe of his forearm, Mason batted the clock against the wall. It shattered and fell in pieces on the floor."

M ason looked at his watch again then scanned the square. He sat in an army sedan, with Wolski behind the steering wheel. Kessler hunched low in the back. Across from where they were parked on Paradiesstrasse, they could survey the square formed by five intersecting streets that lay on the southern tip of Munich's immense park, the Englischer Garten. Three hours, and still no sign of Wertz.

From what Mason could see, not much of the park had been spared. Bombs had shattered the decorative pavilions, splintered the trees, and left behind craters in the place of flowerbeds. But it was a good place to conduct black-market trading: populated, but not too much so, with wide lines of sight and a large five-street intersection providing multiple escape routes—not to mention the vast park itself.

Several "vendors" traded their wares on the square and by the park entrance: two separate women with racks of clothes emptied from closets, a butcher hawking questionable meat, lone individuals selling jewelry displayed by opening their overcoats. Behind them, in the park, people hacked away at fallen trees for firewood.

The easy pickings had already been taken; now an intrepid few attacked the large branches and trunks.

To the left of the square, Timmers and Pike, dressed in civilian clothes, milled on a corner of the park entrance. Four other investigators of his team were occupied in other parts of the city following up on reports from eyewitnesses, so Mason had no other choice but to take Colonel Walton up on his offer to use Havers.

Mason glanced to his right, where MacMillan and Havers sat at one of the sidewalk tables of a café. Havers was supposed to be using a newspaper as cover, but he kept eyeing the square, or he would get up and pace before MacMillan could urge him to sit again.

"I'm hungry and I have to pee," Kessler said.

"Shut up," Mason said.

"That's the first two words I've heard you utter since we got here," Wolski said.

Mason glowered at Wolski, then went back to watching the plaza.

"You can't let Ramek leaving that clock get to you."

"You going to tell me now that it's no big deal? He's thumbing his nose at both of us. We're flailing around, totally blind, trying to find this guy, and he walks right into a building full of cops and plops it on my desk."

"I suppose you're pissed off about Laura, too."

"That subject is off-limits."

"I've got to pee," Kessler insisted.

"What are you, five years old?" Mason said. "Get out on the blind side of the car and pee in the gutter."

As Kessler got out of the car, Wolski said, "Don't pee by my door. I don't want to step in it."

In the middle of relieving himself, Kessler stifled a cry. He ducked down and peered through the sedan windows. "There he is. Green coat and brown fisherman's hat."

To his right, Mason spotted Wertz crossing Lerchenfeld-strasse. Wertz looked to be in his mid-twenties and walked with an athletic gait. He kept checking his flanks as he entered the square and headed for the park.

Mason got out of the car and removed his hat. That was the signal for the others. Wolski told Kessler to hide in the backseat. "Don't go anywhere," Wolski said, then he followed Mason across the wide intersection.

Timmers and Pike were doing the same thing, entering from the west to cut off Wertz's potential escape into the park. MacMillan was waiting until Wertz passed him, but Havers got up too soon. Wertz whirled around. Havers froze.

Mason and Wolski broke into a run. The other team did the same thing. MacMillan shot up from the table and charged, but Wertz pulled out a nine-millimeter pistol from his pocket and fired. MacMillan jerked from the pain and went down. Civilians screamed or ran for cover. Havers remained frozen as Wertz fled down a small street branching off from the intersection.

As Mason rushed past Havers, he yelled, "Help MacMillan."

When Mason and Wolski reached the street, Wertz had a fifty-yard lead. Both sides of the road were lined with ruins and rubble that lay in piles at the base of collapsed buildings.

Mason and Wolski had their pistols out. "CID! Halt!"

Wertz put on a burst of speed and leapt over a heap of rubble, but his foot landed on loose gravel and he slipped and fell on his side. He scrambled behind a heap of bricks and fired his pistol. The bullet whizzed by Mason's ear. Mason and Wolski dived to opposite sides of the street and took defensive positions. A silent standoff ensued, a sharp contrast to the explosion of the gun. In the distance came the wail of sirens. To keep Wertz pinned in place, Mason aimed for the bricks at the top of the heap protecting Wertz. He shot twice. The bricks shattered into dust.

Apparently judging the risk worth it, Wertz jumped to his feet and ran. Mason and Wolski chased after him. Fifty feet later, Wertz turned again and fired. Mason dropped to the street and aimed. Before Wertz could turn to run again, Mason pulled the trigger.

The bullet smashed into Wertz's thigh. He screamed and fell face-first onto the pavement. Mason and Wolski raced up. Wertz tried to reach for his pistol, but Wolski kicked it away. Timmers and Pike arrived seconds later.

"We've got this," Mason said, out of breath. "Help MacMillan. If you can't get an ambulance, take him yourselves."

"What about him?" Timmers asked, pointing to Wertz. "He's gonna need—"

"We'll take care of him. Now go!"

Timmers recoiled as if he'd been slapped in the face. He looked at Wolski for a moment, then took off with Pike. Mason turned his attention back to Wertz. The bullet had passed through his thigh, taking a chunk of leg with it. Mason looked around. There were a few curious bystanders at both ends of the street.

"What are you thinking?" Wolski said. "He could bleed out if we don't get him to a hospital."

Mason leaned over Wertz. "You hear that, Wertz? If we don't get you to a hospital you're going to die." Wertz could only moan. "So the sooner you talk, the quicker you'll get your sorry ass to a hospital."

"Chief, don't do this," Wolski said.

"Shut up. This asshole just shot a cop. And he tried to do the same to us. He is gonna talk. Right here, right now."

Mason flipped Wertz on his back. He pulled out the sketch of Ramek and held it in Wertz's face. "You sold surgical equipment to this guy. Dr. Ramek. I want to know where he lives."

Between gasps for air and spasms of pain, Wertz said, "I don't know what you're talking about."

"You want to bleed to death, huh, Wertz? Start talking or we're going to walk away and let you bleed out."

"I swear I don't know him!"

MP and ambulance sirens echoed in the narrow street as they pulled into the square. Mason was desperate. He ground the toe of his boot into Wertz's wound. Wertz screamed.

"Chief, come on—"

Mason dug his boot deeper into Wertz's gaping wound. Wertz cried out, almost squealing.

"You tell me where I can find Ramek, or I'm going to keep doing this...." Mason put the full weight of his body behind his boot.

Wertz screamed and held up his hands for Mason to stop. "All right. Just stop." He took a few gulps of air. "I made some deliveries. A couple of times. He had some kind of machine shop...."

Mason raised his foot to strike. "That's not good enough. Not a shop. Not his favorite hangout. We need a residence. His house."

"All right! He has a house. On Landsberger Strasse. I don't remember the number. Two seventeen, or something. White brick with red shutters." His face had gone white from blood loss and pain. "Now, please. Get me to a hospital!"

A Jeep and ambulance pulled up behind Mason and Wolski. Two medics went into action, applying sulfa powder and a tourniquet. A large pool of blood had formed around Wertz's leg, and he had become still, his eyes glazed, his skin shading to gray. Mason watched in silence as the medics put on a pile of gauze and mounted Wertz onto a stretcher.

"What's his status?" Wolski asked.

One of the medics said, "He's lost a lot of blood, and he's in shock. If we get him back in time, he should live."

Wolski shot a hard look at Mason and walked back toward the square. Mason sprinted past Wolski and up to where MacMillan had been shot. Havers sat at the café table, his eyes fixed on MacMillan's spilled blood. The ambulance had already taken MacMillan away.

"Is Mac going to be all right?" Mason asked Timmers.

"He got hit in the chest. A clean exit wound, but it collapsed his lung. He's pretty bad." He turned his head toward Havers. "If this asshole hadn't screwed things up, no one'd be hurt."

"That's enough," Mason said.

Wolski walked up. "Are we going after Ramek?"

Mason nodded. "We'll pick up some fresh bodies then get Becker and a German team to go with us."

"What about Havers?"

"Tell him to go back to headquarters. I don't want to talk to him right now."

"Why? You might torture him, too?"

"If you're getting squeamish, just let me know. We'll get you off the street and behind a desk." When Wolski didn't respond, Mason said, "Let's get moving. Now we know where this bastard lives."

The neighborhood could have passed for any American middle-class suburb: one- and two-story houses on tree-lined streets, a peaceful setting spared by the ravages of war. Mason and Becker sat in an army sedan with a clear view of Ramek's house. They were parked a hundred feet down on a street that formed a T intersection with Ramek's street. Mason checked his watch for the umpteenth time, then scanned the house with his binoculars.

The Handie-Talkie crackled, and Wolski's voice came over the handset. "One pedestrian coming your way. Long, blue coat and black hat. His back is to us, so I couldn't get a good look at him."

Mason acknowledged and they waited. Wolski had opted to team up with Timmers, and they were parked at the far end of Ramek's street. Pike and two MPs had stationed themselves at one of the main approaches to Ramek's street, with Mannheim and four German police covering a second approach and the back of the house.

Moments later, the pedestrian came into view. Mason sighed and dropped his binoculars. "Not our guy."

"Ramek knows we've discovered at least his workshop alias," Becker said. "He may have even heard of Wertz's arrest. In all probability, he will stay clear of this house."

"Yeah, I figured that. You can't blame a man for hoping. We've been here for five hours. It'll be dark soon. I say we take a look around, then post a couple of surveillance teams just in case he tries to sneak back."

Becker nodded. "He may have to come back for something that is vital to him."

"Yeah, maybe he forgot his toothbrush." Mason said into the Handie-Talkie, "It's time to go in. You all know how I want this to go down: Approach on foot, safe and quiet, on the off chance that he's hiding out in there."

Silently, Timmers and Pike with a team of MPs sprinted toward the back of the house to join a team of German police. Mason and Wolski, along with two other MPs sneaked up to the front door, while Becker, Mannheim, and four German police officers fanned out along the front lawn.

When everyone was in position, two German police officers came forward. One had a sledgehammer. Mason nodded, and with one strategic swing, the sledgehammer hit the latch and the door flew open. Mannheim and the German officers charged in first. Mason, Wolski, and Becker came in behind them.

The German police yelled a warning—"*Polizei!*"—as they advanced into each room. Mason, Wolski, and Becker stayed in the living room, which only contained a few rows of chairs and a desk in the corner.

Mason scanned the area while waiting tensely. Protocol was for the German police to make any arrest. With each successive search of a room, the German officers called out, "*Klar!* ... "*Klar!*"

Mason couldn't stand it any longer. "The hell with this." With Wolski and Becker right behind him, Mason dashed into the next room. They found themselves in a typical doctor's examination room.

"Ramek was still practicing medicine?" Mason asked aloud.

They went from room to room and, while all had clean, modest furniture, they lacked any personal touches: no pictures or knickknacks of any kind; aside from the living room, the place was more like a furniture store showroom than living quarters. Mason and Wolski stopped in the kitchen, and again showroom clean but void of pots and pans.

"Does this guy even eat?" Wolski asked. He opened the pantry. "Look at this." He grabbed a can out of the pantry and tossed it to Mason. "Almost exclusively old Wehrmacht rations. I could barely eat army rations when I had to, and he does it by choice."

Mason examined the label. "Conserved pork meat. He must have salvaged this stuff from somewhere around the city." A thought came to him. "That butcher's table in Ramek's workshop. The manufacturer said those kinds of tables were sold to meat-processing plants, right?"

"Yeah, the manufacturer said those kinds of tables were sold to five meat-processing plants in and around Munich, but they couldn't say which one it came from."

Mason nodded. "I bet it's from the one that made these rations."

Excited voices erupted from a room off the kitchen. Mason and Wolski rushed into the room and saw two German police trying to open a reinforced door. One of them called for the sledgehammer. Someone passed the hammer down the line. It took three blows to break open the door. Beyond was a small dark bedroom with the windows boarded over and blackout cloth attached to the boards. With guns drawn, the German officers charged inside the room. Mason and Wolski entered right behind them and looked around with their flashlights. No

Ramek, only a writing desk, two chairs, and a full-length mirror.

Mason had been almost certain they wouldn't find him, but it still was a crushing disappointment. Becker and the German officers filed out, leaving Mason and Wolski alone in the dark. In the adjoining room, Mason heard Becker giving orders to his men to interview the neighbors. Wolski started to search through the small writing desk, while Mason walked up to the wood-framed full-length mirror that stood on a throw rug in the middle of the room.

"Strange," Mason said. "The top third of the mirror has been painted over."

"The desk doesn't have much. Pens, blank paper, some office supplies in the drawers."

Timmers and Pike came into the room out of breath. "We rummaged around out back," Timmers said. "No garage or other structures. Looks like he never went out there much. No signs of fresh graves."

"We checked the basement, too," Pike said. "Nothing down there but a bunch of junk."

"Look at this," Mason said. He had the flashlight trained on a small carpet that lay in front of the mirror. "Seems to be blood-stains." He squatted and touched the spots. "They're not fresh."

Mason lifted a corner of the rug, revealing a partial print of a shoe. He pushed the mirror to one side and pulled the rug away. Underneath was a trapdoor. They gathered silently around and drew their pistols. Mason lifted the small ring handle recessed in the door and looked up at the others. "Ready?"

The others nodded. Mason yanked the trapdoor back. Silence and darkness in the space below. Flashlight beams searched the hole. Wooden stairs led downward. The smell of dank earth flowed into the room.

Mason yelled down. "Ramek? Your house is swarming with

police. There's no escape. Come out with your hands up. Ramek?"

Nothing.

"In the good old days, we'd've tossed a couple of grenades down there and been done with it," Timmers said.

With his flashlight in one hand and pistol in the other, Mason took a tentative step. He crouched low and slowly descended. His body tensed without his volition, as if preparing for the explosion of gunfire and a bullet slamming into his leg. Halfway down, he could see most of the center of the room. He braced himself, jumped, and landed on the dirt floor with his gun and flashlight up and ready to shoot.

Nothing obscured his view, and there was nowhere to hide. "Clear," he said with a dispirited voice.

While the others clambered down, Mason concentrated on the room's contents. The twenty-foot-square space of dirt walls had probably been a root cellar at one time. Used candles sat everywhere: on the floor, in small holes dug into the walls, and clustered on a long, narrow table. In the middle of the table, surrounded by more candles, Ramek had placed a tall crucifix. Framed pictures of saints dotted the walls behind the crucifix.

"Looks like some kind of shrine," Wolski said.

"To your left," Mason said.

All turned. Ramek had created a baptismal cross of wooden planks painted black. The planks were a foot in depth and the arms spanned six feet end to end. It was mounted slightly off the floor, making it higher than Mason's head height. At the ends of the eight points of the cross, alcoves had been fashioned, and in each alcove was a large glass specimen jar. Each jar contained a different human organ. In the very center, a ninth alcove held a specimen jar containing a human heart.

"There's a light switch, here above the table," Pike said behind Mason. He turned the rotary switch, and the cross lit up.

Ramek had installed lights behind the entire cross and it created an eerie glow in the dark space.

"The sick bastard," Timmers said.

Mason approached the wall and examined the jars. "The brain is in the top jar. Lungs, kidneys, intestines...."

"Probably the poor nurse's remains," Pike said.

"None of the victims had their brain removed," Mason said. "Where did he get that?"

"There's obviously a victim we don't know about," Wolski said.

Becker and Mannheim came down the stairs. "One of the neighbors—" Becker stopped when he saw the alcoves. "*Gott im Himmel....*"

"Ramek's shrine," Mason said, then he turned to Timmers and Pike. "You two get the crime scene techs and forensics out here. The rest of you search for trapdoors or false walls throughout the rest of the house."

They spent another two hours searching the house, but found nothing that might indicate where Ramek was now or what he planned to do next. Mason and Becker exited the house and stepped out onto the front lawn. The fresh air and cold sunlight broke the nightmarish spell of the root cellar.

Mason turned back to look at the house. "I can't figure the mirrors. Every one of them has a portion masked out. I stood in front of them, and you can't see your face. For the smaller ones, I figured at his height, he wouldn't be able to see his eyes."

"Very curious, indeed," Becker said.

Wolski exited the house and joined Mason and Becker. "So far, we haven't found any ledgers, letters, or a diary. If he kept one."

Becker said, "What I was about to say in the cellar, one of the neighbors says she saw Ramek... she knows him as Dr. Schiller."

"Another alias?"

Becker nodded. "She saw him last night exit the house with two large canvas bags."

"By the looks of his exam room, he left in a hurry. He made a big mess in there, grabbing everything he could jam in those bags."

"He didn't take many clothes, either," Wolski said.

Mason and Wolski shared an unspoken acknowledgment about what that meant. Ramek had no intention of running and every intention of killing again.

"Let's go check out those meat-processing plants."

"Now?" Wolski asked.

"He got the butcher table and army rations from one of them. He could be using it as a hideout."

"It's going to be pitch-black in an hour."

"It's the only lead we have right now, so unless you can think of something better to follow up on, we're searching the plants."

MASON, WOLSKI, AND BECKER, ALONG WITH FOUR GERMAN policemen, approached the lone security guard for the Lindenberger meat-processing facility, though what the man actually guarded was a mystery to Mason. Like most of the surrounding buildings in the complex north of Munich, the two that made up the processing facility were nothing but shells. The sun lay on the horizon behind heavy rain clouds, obliging everyone to use flashlights.

After brief introductions, the guard led them through the main doors to the plant.

"I'm not sure what you're expecting to find," the guard said. "Most everything that wasn't nailed down has already been salvaged."

Indeed, only the machines beyond repair and the debris from

the collapsed roof remained on the factory floor. Mason thanked the guard and said they would have a look around anyway. The guard shrugged, then left them to their task.

"Exactly the same as the other two processing plants," Wolski said. "Ramek wasn't the only German to salvage the Wehrmacht rations for food. I told you this was a waste of time."

"Your lack of enthusiasm is disturbing," Mason said sarcastically, but Wolski ignored him.

Adding to Wolski's foul mood, a cold rain began to fall.

Mason pulled his collar tight around his neck. "We're here. Might as well look around."

They spread out in a line and proceeded to search the expansive factory floor. Gusts of wind howled through the building's glassless windows. Everyone bent forward against the driving rain.

"These remote factories *do* make an ideal place for Ramek to bring his victims," Becker said.

"Yeah," Wolski said, "this one and about a thousand others."

A ten-minute search brought them to the far side, and they descended the stairs to the sub-level. As on the floor above, much of the metal and small machinery had already been removed, leaving only the large furnaces, the heavier can-manufacturing machinery, and traces of the overhead conveyor system. The group spread out again and searched the area with the beams of their flashlights. The darkness and cascades of rainwater made the going slow, but in twenty minutes they reached the opposite wall. They gathered by another set of stairs, and each man shook his heads to say he'd found nothing. Then they repeated the process in the shipping and receiving building, remaining silent as they did so; it had been a long, frustrating day, and the foul weather threatened to sap their resolve.

"Let's call it a night," Mason said. "We can do the last two plants tomorrow."

"You mean when we can actually see something?" Wolski said with bitterness behind it.

Mason decided to let it go. Wolski had been sullen since the incident with Wertz. And the series of setbacks had worn on all three of them. They needed an evening's break.

As Mason led them through the rain and toward the vehicles, he fought grim thoughts of Ramek still out there somewhere, always one step ahead, and stalking his next victim.

39

Mason attacked the helpless typewriter keys with increasing violence. He sat in his office typing up his daily report: a series of actions that ran long on detail and short on results. He also had to file a preliminary report on his shooting of Wertz. Preliminary, meaning a pile more to come, since the man was an American soldier, and then an inquest with army lawyers. The whole process took much longer than usual, his train of thought constantly drifting to images of the day playing out in his mind.

A welcome moment of calm had descended on the squad room. Most of the investigators were out on assignments or finished with their shift. In the otherwise quiet squad room, Mason could hear Wolski typing. He got up and sauntered up to Wolski's desk. He pulled over a chair and sat.

Wolski's gaze never left his typewriter. "What do you want?"

"I wanted to see if you're feeling okay."

"Right as rain," Wolski said in a deadpan tone.

"Good. Then you won't mind if I sit here awhile."

"If you want to get something off your chest, there's a bartender down the street who'll listen. Even pretend he cares."

"You've seen what that killer does to his victims. I'm not going to let an asshole who sells bad penicillin and cut baby formula get in the way."

"You made that pretty clear."

"I told you when we first met that homicide isn't like anything else. You've got the makings of a good investigator, and you might as well know right now that sometimes you have to push the boundaries to make a case. I've never taken a bribe, leaned on an innocent interviewee, or tampered with evidence to get a conviction. But if I know a guy is a lowlife who has information, I'm not above beating it out of him. And Wertz shot a cop."

"Maybe I'm not that kind of guy."

"We're the only ones standing between a homicidal maniac and innocent victims. And when you're on the job, people have the right to expect you to catch the bad guys. It's not like what you read in the detective comics or see in the movies. It's the real thing, and it can get ugly."

"You don't need to lecture me. I know what the score is. You're the best detective I've ever worked with, and maybe I had too high expectations. A cop who could get results using his brain and not his muscle. I don't want to get to the point where it tears me up enough to beat on a guy even if he is a lowlife."

Wolski fell quiet, and Mason let him mull things over while they both stared at nothing in particular.

Finally, Wolski said, "The army's offering courses in criminal justice and law. I'm going to finish this case with you then I'm going to sign up. Maybe after that, I'll see if I can get into law school. Colonel Walton's already set it up for me."

"Sounds like a plan." Mason pulled out a cigarette and lit it to mask his disappointment. "I hope I didn't push you into becoming a lawyer, of all things."

"Nah. I've been thinking about it for a while. I think I prefer to work the other side of the justice system. You bust 'em and I'll convict 'em."

"I bet you'll be good at it."

Wolski gave him a halfhearted smile. "Thanks."

"I mean it...." The telephone ringing in his office distracted him for a moment. He tried to ignore it. "No hard feelings? I'd like to think we can still work together and find this maniac. I'd also like to think we could be friends."

Wolski gave him a sly look. "I noticed you don't have too many friends."

"Consider yourself a charter member in an exclusive club."

"We work together, but no more torture. You do, and I have the right to break your jaw."

"Done."

The telephone continued to ring. Mason hauled himself from the chair while mumbling a few obscenities. He walked slowly to his office, hoping the ringing would stop before he got there. No luck. He picked up the phone. As he listened to Becker, he fell into his chair and let out a tired sigh.

Manganella parked the Jeep in front of Laura's hotel. "Good luck in there."

Mason thanked him. "For once I'm glad you drive like a maniac." He jumped out of the Jeep and headed for the hotel entrance.

Before he could pass through the hotel door, Laura came out. She wore street clothes and a heavy wool coat. "Laura—"

Laura blew past him, stepped up to the curb, and hailed the single waiting taxi. Just as the taxi pulled up, Mason slipped in front of her and opened the front passenger's door.

"She changed her mind," Mason said to the taxi driver. He

threw some money on the seat. "Drive yourself anywhere you want. Beat it."

The taxi drove off, leaving Laura by the curb. "What did you do that for?"

"We need to talk."

Laura turned and walked down the street at a fast clip. Mason caught up with her.

"I've got an appointment," Laura said without looking at Mason. "Now I'm going to be late."

"It's to meet Kessler, isn't it?"

"None of your business."

"Kessler's dead."

Laura kept walking but her pace slowed to a crawl. She looked at the pavement and said nothing.

"The German police found him in Gärtnerplatz," Mason said. "His throat was cut."

Laura stopped. "I was afraid of that when he didn't show up this afternoon."

"You went there this afternoon?"

Laura finally looked at Mason. "You and I are to blame for his death."

"We swept him up in a raid. We picked up a number of people. No one should have suspected..." He decided that wasn't the right tact. "Laura, Kessler was beaten and tortured before they killed him. They'll know about you."

"My college wit and debutante charm are failing me right now. All I want to do is cuss you out—" She groaned and turned in place, taking deep breaths to control her temper.

"If the gang put it together this fast and took Kessler down, then they suspected him long before we snagged him. This could have happened to him regardless. And it might have happened to you if you'd been with him. I said you were playing a dangerous game."

Laura took off toward the hotel, and Mason had to catch up again.

"Berlin is out now," Laura said.

"I'm going to see that you get protection."

"I don't want protection. I want the story."

"Wolski knows some MPs who'd be great for you. They'll do it on their off time for some extra cash—which I'll take care of."

Laura had stopped listening and talked more to herself than to Mason. "I know enough to pick up the trail in Garmisch. There are some guys I know down there...."

"God damnit, Laura, what am I going to do if you get killed?" Mason surprised himself by saying it.

That stopped Laura and she made a weak smile. "Selfish, but the sentiment's there." Her look turned inward as if she struggled with a host of emotions. "The last time I talked to Kessler, he was afraid they were onto him. I think he was trying to redeem himself by giving me information. I used that and probably pushed him too hard. I know he was a drug dealer, but I can't help feeling bad for him."

She looked at Mason with moist eyes. Mason said nothing, letting her come to terms with all that had happened.

"Laura, you need protection. I'll arrange it without your approval, but it'd work better if you go along with it."

Laura thought a moment, then nodded her head. "All right," she said in a weak voice.

"Go to your room and stay there. Tell the hotel guards and staff not to let anyone but me come near your room. I've got a couple of things I need to do, then I'll be back."

❧

MASON REACHED THE FOURTH FLOOR OF MUNICH'S U.S. military hospital, the 98th, where the slain American nurse had worked. Everyone he passed seemed on edge or on the verge of tears. Mason stopped at the nurses' station and asked for Lieutenant MacMillan's room.

"We're asking visitors to stay only a few minutes," the nurse said. "He already has two visitors. Don't tax him too much, okay?"

"How is he?"

"He came out of surgery a couple of hours ago," the nurse said in a bored monotone. "The surgeon thinks he'll be fine. The bullet grazed the nerve center in his shoulder. He can't feel or move his right arm. As soon as he's stabilized, he'll be transferred to the Frankfurt hospital for further treatment."

"Will he get the use of his arm back?"

"Do I look like a neurosurgeon to you?" She let out a tired sigh, as if fed up with dealing with stupid questions.

"The room number, if that's not asking too much?"

She gave him the room number, and Mason found it moments later. He knocked and entered. Colonel Walton stood by the bed, hat in hand, talking to MacMillan. Havers sat in a chair in the corner and avoided eye contact.

Mason stepped up to the bed opposite Colonel Walton. MacMillan slowly turned his head, looked at Mason with half-lidded eyes, and gave him a feeble smile.

"I talked to the nurse," Mason said. "She says you're going to be fine."

"I guess so. I can't feel my right arm, though."

"I bet it's just the shock. I had a buddy who was hit in the hip, and he couldn't feel his ass for about two weeks. You can imagine the problems he had to contend with."

MacMillan laughed, then grimaced. "I heard you got Wertz, at least. He gave up Ramek's address...." His eyes started to close. "Hope it was worth it."

Mason could feel Colonel Walton's stare as he leaned into

317

MacMillan. "We're going to get this guy," Mason said. "You did good, Mac. You saved another man's life and helped crack this case."

He didn't know if MacMillan heard. MacMillan's eyes fluttered in an attempt to stay open, but finally gave up the fight.

Colonel Walton leaned in and spoke softly to MacMillan. "I've got to be going. Take care of yourself, son." Then, as he moved for the door, he said to Mason, "Collins. Out here."

Mason joined Colonel Walton in the hallway down from MacMillan's room.

"You nearly got a man killed today, and for what? An empty house. Another miss. These investigators are good men, but they don't have the field experience for potentially dangerous situations. I want you to remember that the next time you concoct a scheme to take down a desperate outlaw. Furthermore, there's a story that you refused aid to a wounded suspect and subsequently tortured him. Screams were heard after the man had gone down."

"He was in pain—"

"Bullshit. The man is a scumbag, but that doesn't give you the right to torture him. In public, no less. How far are you willing to go, Collins? The end does not justify the means. Not in my book. So, I'm asking you, how many are you willing to put in harm's way to get what you want? Never mind justice or the law." He spun around and walked away without waiting for an answer.

Mason was glad Colonel Walton denied him the opportunity to respond, because he might have answered truthfully.... *I will do whatever it takes.*

M ason walked out onto the streets again. The heavy rain had finally stopped, but the temperature had dropped to freezing, making the still damp air chill him to the bone. He stopped at his place first. Captain Shaw and his poker group were already drunk when he arrived. From his room, he collected an armful of chocolate and cans of potted meat he'd bought at the PX a few days before.

Twenty minutes later, he approached the ruins where the orphans took shelter. Kurt and his younger companion Dieter squatted by the entrance smoking cigarettes. As soon as they saw Mason they pinched off the hot crowns and put the remaining stubs in their pockets.

"I thought I told you not to smoke." They both looked at the ground. "I was bringing you some things to eat, but I guess you don't need them. You're smoking what you could use to buy food."

Hearing Mason's voice, the other children piled out of the opening to see what he'd brought.

"We only smoked a couple," Kurt said. "Besides, we have lots of cigarettes."

"A man brought us two cartons," Ilsa said. "We're rich!"

"You've got to make them last. I can't be bringing you food all the time, so you've got to save them for when winter gets real bad—" He stopped. "Where's Angela?"

"A man came and got her," Kurt said.

"What do you mean? What man?"

"He's the one who brought us the cigarettes," Dieter said.

Mason's stomach twisted into knots. Neither war nor peace had stopped pedophiles from preying on helpless children. His heart began to race. He squatted and tried to show calm. "Tell me about this man. Did he just take her?"

"No, he said he was her father," Kurt said.

"Did Angela say this, too?"

"The man said he'd been in the war a long time, and that Angela was a baby when he went into the army."

Mason looked from face to face, their expressions of guilt and worry only worsening Mason's growing dread. *Stay calm and go easy on them.* "That's not what I asked. What did *Angela* say?"

"The man was strange," Ilsa said. "I didn't like him."

"Sometimes war can make people a little strange, but they get better," Mason said to allay Ilsa's fear. He turned to Kurt and Dieter for a more direct answer.

"I think she was too afraid to say anything," Kurt said. "And he didn't even know her name."

Fear clutched at Mason's heart. "Exactly what happened? Tell me everything."

"He was just standing on the other side of the street, watching us. For a long time. Then Angela came back from begging near Saint Paul's Church."

"That's when the man came across the street," Dieter said.

"What did he do then?"

"He tried to talk to Angela, but she wouldn't say anything,"

Kurt said. "Then he asked her name. When we told him, he started saying weird things we couldn't understand."

"Angela wanted to go inside, but the man said he was her father," Dieter said. "He said he'd come to take her home."

"And he said he was away in the war?" Mason asked.

They nodded.

"Angela said her father was dead," Kurt said. "Her mother told her."

"But he kept saying she was wrong and he wanted to take her home and take care of her," Dieter said.

"Did he force her to go?"

"No," Kurt said. "He just kept saying he was her father. He even started crying. I guess Angela felt bad or something and finally decided to go with him."

"He gave us chocolate and the cigarettes," Dieter said. "He told us not to tell anyone."

Mason felt he would explode with panic and rage, but he had to keep his cool for the kids. "Okay, now. Think back. Picture the man in your mind and tell me what he looked like."

"Real tall," Kurt said.

"He was like a giant," Ilsa said. "He scared me."

Mason scrambled around in his back pocket and found the piece of paper. He unfolded it with shaking hands, knelt among the children, and held up the artist's sketch of Ramek. The question stuck in his throat.

"That's him," Kurt said. "He's the one who took Angela."

Ice-cold fear shot through Mason. Why hadn't he connected the dots before? Ramek chose victims with limps, and Angela mirrored the victims of the very experiments Ramek had performed at Ravensbrück. Mason leapt to his feet and he ran. The direction didn't matter. It was only to get far enough away from the kids before he yelled at the heavens.

IN MASON'S EXPERIENCE, CLAIMS THAT LARGE QUANTITIES OF alcohol numbed the brain were not accurate. The mind could simply not concentrate on two things at once, so moving through space without injury, and in his case not being arrested by MPs for public drunkenness, occupied his consciousness. The rage and, with it, grief, still lay in wait behind a thin veil, but for the moment inebriation relieved the crushing emotions.

He received a few disapproving or cautious looks from the guards at the entrance and the people milling around the hotel's lobby and front bar, but none took any initiative to stop him; a drunken soldier was not an uncommon sight. Forgetting the existence of the elevators, Mason struggled up four flights of stairs. The room numbers on the doors defied readability, so he counted three doors to the left. Using the door frame for support, he knocked. The peephole darkened then Laura flung open the door.

"It's about time—" She stopped after having a better look at him.

Mason staggered past her and used a chair to steady himself. Now that he'd reached his objective safely, the sorrow welled up from his stomach.

Laura came into view. "You've got a lot of nerve showing up drunk out of your mind."

Mason didn't answer. He couldn't. Laura's face, her voice, broke the last barrier of control. His eyes burned. His cheeks felt wet, and Laura's expression changed to concern.

"What happened?"

Mason still couldn't talk. She came to his side and put her shoulder under his.

"Come on. Let's get you into a chair before you fall down."

She helped him sit in one of the upholstered chairs and crouched next to him. "Tell me what happened."

"I got hammered."

"I can see that. Why?"

"I needed a break, is all."

"Stop being cute and tell me what happened."

"Ramek, the murderer, he abducted the crippled orphan girl, Angela."

Laura covered her mouth and stood. "Oh, my God." The shock pushed her back two steps and forced her to sit on the edge of the bed.

"You can see why I had a few too many drinks."

"How could he do that to a little girl?"

"There's nothing I can do to stop him. I'm completely goddamned helpless."

"Are you sure Ramek has her?"

Mason told her about going to the orphans' makeshift shelter and what the children had told him. "I showed the kids the sketch of Ramek and they ID'd him. We raided Ramek's house today, so I drove over there, hoping the surveillance team had spotted him. Ramek hadn't shown up there, so I called in an additional team to keep watch. Then I went to headquarters to have a sketch of Angela done. I guess I lost it after that. Barking orders like a madman. I realized I wasn't doing any good the way I was, so I ended up wandering the streets trying to come up with a way to find him. Something I hadn't thought of. There has to be something I've overlooked." He grabbed the arms of the chair and squeezed them.

Laura came over and crouched in front of him. "Stop punishing yourself. You're doing the best you can."

"Don't patronize me."

"Well, what do you want to hear? You're worthless and incompetent? It's all your fault that these people died? You're in over your head, and a really good CID investigator would have solved it by now? There. You feel better?" She paused. "I don't believe this is because it all got to you. There's something else, isn't there? Something you're not telling me."

Mason looked at her, but he couldn't hold her gaze.

"Is it because Ramek took a child? It's the worst thing I can imagine, but for you to be so distraught, almost unhinged. You're acting just like a father who's lost his daughter."

The first time Mason had seen Angela she had struck him like no other orphan girl had since the end of the war. She looked so much like the other one....

"What is it about her?" Laura stood and shoved his shoulders. "Answer me."

Mason leaned his head back and looked at the ceiling. He'd resolved never to speak about it to anyone and tried to bury it deep within, but it had only festered there, in a dark corner of his mind. Maybe tonight, and with Laura, he could face it down. As he conjured up the memories that he'd worked so hard to suppress, he relived the biting cold, the raging fever, fire and ice torturing his emaciated body, the delirium from the starvation and disease, the constant fear of collapsing onto the snow-covered ground to freeze to death or be dragged off into the woods and shot in the back of the head.

That's why I did it, right?

"You've heard about the death marches from the POW and concentration camps?"

"Yes. I interviewed a couple of soldiers who'd been forced on a march."

"I've never told anyone, but I was on one of those marches."

"You? I thought you were liberated at a POW camp at Moosburg."

"That's where I was liberated. I first spent two weeks at a sub camp of Buchenwald, but then a Wehrmacht colonel took exception to the way I and a couple of others were being treated. He arranged for us to be transferred to a stalag near the Polish-Czech border. We were already half-starved and weak when we got there, but not ten days later, the guards broke us into groups of three hundred and forced us all to march out of the camp before the Russian army could liberate us."

"The Russians were already that close?"

Mason nodded. "We could hear their artillery in the distance. I don't know how many hundreds of kilometers we walked in the snow and blizzards, and by all accounts, that was one of the coldest winters in a century. Plus, our group was led by a real nasty son of a bitch. The prisoners who couldn't go on were left by the side of the road. If a man collapsed or refused to go on, many times the guards would beat him or drag him into the woods and shoot him. Mile after horrible mile, stepping over the frozen bodies of other soldiers, I kept waiting for my turn. Then, about four days into the march, a couple of Russian fighter planes thought we were retreating German soldiers and strafed our column. A group of us took advantage of the attack and ran off into a thick pine forest."

"You escaped? Did you honestly think you could survive in the countryside in the middle of winter without food or shelter?"

Mason shrugged his shoulders. "We knew we didn't have much of a chance, but we all thought that escape was better than dying on that road like an animal. I don't know what happened to the others. We got separated. Then I heard gunfire, and I ran like a crazed man. I ran until I couldn't run anymore. I finally collapsed against a tree and waited. I waited for death. I'd given up."

Laura put her hands on his and looked at him with such intensity that it urged Mason to continue.

"I don't know how long I laid against the tree. I was delirious and already feeling that calm they say you experience when you're freezing to death. But at some point, I became aware of a little girl of about ten kneeling next to me and hugging me. She was dressed in rags and more emaciated than I was. At first, I was so delirious that I thought she was an angel coming to save me or take me away. The funny thing is, she was looking to me to save *her*. She clung to me like I was her protector. She was so scared and sick and helpless that it brought me out of my stupor. Suddenly I had a responsibility to take care of this kid. It gave me the strength to keep going, to get us out of that hell and live."

"Where did the girl come from?"

"She was a Pole from one of the concentration camps, a subcamp of Auschwitz, I think."

"But what was she doing in the middle of those woods? She escaped a death march like you did?"

Mason nodded. "There was a road that ran parallel about a mile from the one I had been marching on. The inmates of the camp, mostly Polish Jews, were being marched west like we were. The girl —Hana was her name—took me to a spot where hundreds of corpses lay in the road. It was horrible. From where I stood on a straight length of road, corpses stretched to the horizon. Women and children, mothers still clinging to dead infants, all frozen, either dead where they fell or shot in the head. This girl's mom was among them."

Laura covered her mouth. "How did Hana escape?"

"She played dead. And for some reason the Germans didn't make sure by shooting her. I got that much out of her because she spoke a little German. I decided to head east and try to intercept the Russians. We went on for days, sticking to the woods. I had no idea where we were. I have no idea how I kept going—nothing to eat, frozen to the bone. But trying to save her had saved me, and she became everything to me…."

Mason stopped, unsure he could continue. Laura said nothing, letting him tell it in his own time. He reached for his pack of cigarettes but found it empty. He crumpled it and threw it into the fireplace.

"I lost track of the days we were out there—maybe three or

four. Then one day before dark, we came to a farmhouse. I was desperate. We hadn't eaten a thing, and we were caught in a blizzard. She begged us not to go to the farm, but I had to take a chance. I knew we couldn't live through one more night if we didn't have something to eat and get out of that storm."

"Did the farmer take you in?"

Mason nodded. "Turned out, we had crossed into Czechoslovakia. It was a Czech farmer, his wife, and a daughter about the same age as Hana. We were able to communicate in broken German. They were taking an awful chance harboring an escaped U.S. soldier and a Jewish child. With both German fronts collapsing, the German security forces were resorting to more and more brutal methods to keep things together. Soldiers and civilians were being shot on the spot even if they were just suspected of desertion or treason. By the end of the second day, we were feeling better, and I knew we were putting the family in too much danger. They drew me a map on where to find a group of Czech partisans...."

Mason paused at the memory of it. "But then the Gestapo came."

"Oh, no."

"I don't know if one of the locals reported us, or if they were just making a security sweep ahead of the retreating German army. It doesn't matter."

Mason rubbed his face and sighed. "They herded us out in a field and stood the two girls together. One of the goons stuck a machine pistol to the back of my head and forced me to kneel in front of them. Then they lined up the parents behind me with guns at their backs. The commander paced around, condemning everyone to death for partisan activities and treason against the Reich. We would be shot and the family hanged. I didn't listen. My only thoughts were of regret and shame for failing Hana and destroying an innocent family. I prayed for forgiveness, while I readied myself to die.

"Then the commander shoved his Luger into my hand. He said, 'I'm in a generous mood today. If you shoot one of these two girls, the rest will go free. But you must shoot one. If you refuse, all will die, including you. If you try to shoot me, or yourself, all will die. Your fate and theirs are in your hands.'"

"What did he hope to gain by making you do that?"

"It was a common thing at all the concentration camps. I saw it all the time at Buchenwald. They'd make fellow prisoners execute one of their own or be killed themselves. It was a way to break them down. Lose all sense of humanity. It worked. Believe me."

He looked at Laura for a moment, hoping that she could possibly understand. But then he knew she could never understand completely. He looked down at his hands as if the memory of it had suddenly materialized. "I just stared at that Luger. All I could think about was the terrible things it could do to a little girl's flesh and bone and it made me violently ill. I felt disgust, guilt, terror, rage. The girl was crying. The parents were crying. Hana just stood there, staring at me. Passive. Ready."

Mason summoned the courage to look in Laura's eyes again. "You have to understand. I had no choice."

Laura kissed the palm of his hand, but he withdrew it. He didn't deserve the kindness, and it would weaken his will to continue.

"As I stared at that pistol, I was vaguely aware of the commander yelling orders for me to choose or I would die. Then everything went quiet for a moment, except for the girl and her parents sobbing. From behind my back, the commander ordered his man to shoot me. The gun barrel pressed into my skull. I heard him pull back the charger. Then—boom. A gun went off just by my head. My whole body convulsed expecting the impact of a bullet. Every nerve in my body fired, and I nearly blacked out. A second later, two other goons forced the farmer and his wife to their knees. The commander told me that if I didn't decide by the count of five, they would die.

"Hana and I locked eyes. She muttered in broken German that she wanted to join her mother. She would die to save the others. This brave little girl begged me to shoot her. She seemed at peace and silently forgave me. God...."

Mason took a deep, shuddering breath and wiped a tear from his cheek.

"I aimed the pistol and prayed that my shaking hand wouldn't make me miss and only maim her or cause her pain. With all my will, I steadied my hand and aimed through my tears... I pulled the trigger."

Laura gasped and backed away.

Mason kept his gaze on the wall. "I fired into the ground. I couldn't do it. I couldn't shoot a child. The commander shouted orders, and then I was struck in the head by a rifle butt."

"But why, after all that, did he save you?"

"The commander thought it was great fun to lead me on when he never intended to shoot me. I was to be in a prisoner exchange with a group of Czech partisans. The partisans had captured some high-ranking German officer, and since I was an American intelligence agent the commander thought I would be a valuable bargaining chip. I was turned over to a Wehrmacht battalion coordinating the exchange, but it never came off."

"Thank God for that."

In his worst moments, Mason had believed the exact opposite. After a moment of silence, he said, "There's one image from that day that will stick with me all my life. I came to just as the Gestapo goons started to drive me away, and the commander forced me to look back. In the field, Hana lay dead with her blood staining the snow. The farmer and his wife were dead, too, shot through the head. And the farmer's little girl stood frozen with shock, staring at nothing, all alone in the field. The commander leaned next to my ear and said, 'You see what you did? You've killed them. And you've made an orphan of that little girl. I doubt that she will survive. You did all that.'"

For what seemed like a long time, Laura said nothing, did nothing. Finally she wrapped her arms around him and laid her head on his chest. Mason was aware of it, but felt nothing. In his mind, he was still back in the truck that took him away from the farm, looking upon the lone young girl in the blood-spattered snow with her parents and Hana lying dead at her feet.

He would go on, as Hana had inspired him to do in the forest. He would go on. Someday he would find the Gestapo commander. And maybe someday he might find the farm girl and ask her forgiveness. He could no longer ask for Hana's.

And now there was Angela....

He wept. The tears blurred his vision. The surgical instruments seemed to undulate in the watery distortion. Now he understood the power and meaning of supreme sacrifice. Ascension required the greatest of ordeals. Only by plunging into the abyss could one then soar to heaven.

Behind him, the girl, gagged and bound to the table, burbled with sobs only to then choke and gasp for air. Each utterance made him shudder. He had already violated one of the ceremonial canons... the gag. Though he was in a secure basement, there was still a risk the screams could be heard.

That was the logical reason. But he also knew he could not bear to hear her screams, her pleading for mercy. Not from an angelic child. The required task was abhorrent enough without having to bear the angel's screams.

Oh, God, and thy flock of fallen angels, why must I do this?

The wail started deep in his gut and rose with a burning fury until it exploded out in a howl. He yanked up the sleeve of his surgical gown and thrust the tender part of his upper arm over the flame of the gas lantern. As his skin began to scorch, then blacken, the ecstatic pain calmed him.

He pulled his arm away just as the flesh began to crackle. The searing pain swept away his desperate thoughts, the guilt, the shame and repugnance. He lowered his head and prayed.

The discovery of this angelic child had been the culmination of a long and difficult path. At Ravensbrück, the surviving victims of the experiments had emerged from the medical block like souls risen from the dead, testaments of his heinous deeds. They limped through the camp, and they disgusted and terrified him. Yet, at the same time, they inflamed his urges, inflamed his groin, his desires, and he had managed with extreme care to murder two of them.

During several months after the war, recovering from illness and seeing to daily survival had superseded all else. With time, he'd returned to practicing medicine, but the memories, the urges never left him. Then an event occurred in an unexpected way. A doctor at a clinic in the Bogenhausen district, whom he had encountered at random, looked strikingly like an SS doctor at Ravensbrück, and, in what was surely a divine manifestation, the doctor walked with a pronounced limp. To embody both surgeon and victim overwhelmed him with desire. Without a second thought, he had killed the doctor instantly, mutilated his corpse and buried him in a field.

To his surprise, he had felt more remorse than joy, yet at the instant of killing he had sensed a cleansing of sins, a lifting of his spirit toward heaven. It was then that he realized that to expiate sin required profound suffering. It would require surrogates. These surrogates would endure the same experiments he had performed in the camps. Each surrogate would be offered up to God in a glorious ceremony.

He had found his path to absolution. And a perfect angel had been brought to him.

He lifted his head from prayer and took deep breaths. His hands no longer shook. He was ready now.

He turned to look at the child on the metal table. She was naked, but he felt nothing sexual at the sight. She elicited in him adoration, exaltation. Even her name… *Angela.*

He took the lantern in one hand and, with the other, rolled the tray of instruments up to the table. He poised his scalpel in his gloved hand and scanned her body. He started at the feet and moved his gaze upward. Her single foot and legs trembled and struggled against the straps. Her stomach and lungs heaved. Her breasts, not yet blossomed to womanhood, retained the vision of innocence.

That was where he would begin.

He lowered the scalpel toward a point just below the clavicle. Then against all resistance to temptation, despite the warnings of the voices, he looked. He looked at her face, into her eyes. Her terror had transformed her angelic vision. Her blue eyes, flooded with tears, locked onto his. They dug deep into his psyche, ripping away the illusion.

Before him was a living child, just a child, with tears and snot and crooked teeth. The flush in his groin and abdomen dissipated. The transfiguration from human to saintly angel vanished.

He fell to his knees and clasped his hands, his face level with the child's body. He could smell her humanness, the odors of sweat and urine and defecation.

He bowed his head and prayed for strength and mercy.

Corporal Manganella stopped the Jeep in front of Asamkirche on Sendlinger Strasse. Mason had expected to see at least two of his investigators and a team of MPs, but they were nowhere in sight. Becker waited by the church's entrance with four other German police.

"Where are our guys?" Mason asked Manganella. "They were supposed to rendezvous with us here."

"Don't know, sir. I did hear a call over the radio recalling a number of the guys back to headquarters. Could be they're checking on a hot tip. We've been flooded with calls since the morning papers have come out with Ramek's picture."

It had just turned ten on Sunday morning—at least ten hours since Angela's abduction. Mason had called for his teams, along with Becker and his men, to stop by every church in the city to canvass the congregations with the sketches of Ramek and Angela. Mason had already visited three, and Wolski was to hit another three. There were too many churches to cover quickly without splitting up.

Mason climbed out of the Jeep and joined Becker.

"Mass has just finished," Becker said. "My men are talking to the congregation now."

Mason could easily see into the ornate Baroque church, as an Allied bomb had sheared off the front of the building, leaving most of its interior exposed. He removed a map from his breast pocket and unfolded it on a worktable set aside for repair of the church. On the map the city had been broken down into grids with small areas shaded in different colors. He indicated points within the grids. "I've been to these three churches. Nothing definitive. Wolski is covering these three in Schwabing."

"My teams are now spreading out to churches outside the city center," Becker told him. "I have men distributing sketches and canvassing the markets, train stations and tram stops. We performed a full search of the entire grid surrounding Ramek's house and the western warehouse district. Other forces have covered areas here and here. But that still leaves around seventy percent of the city, not including many suburbs. About one hundred and forty square kilometers."

"And sixty percent of that is either ruins or just plain rubble," Mason said.

They fell silent, awed by the enormity of the area left to search.

A German policeman came up to them. "Herr Oberinspektor, we have someone who may have seen Ramek and the girl."

Mason and Becker followed the policeman into the church. An elderly woman dressed in her threadbare Sunday best waited for them inside the narthex. Mason found it disturbing that she happened to be standing underneath a gold-colored sculpture of a skeleton that appeared to be menacing a robed child with a large pair of shears.

Becker introduced them in a soft, baritone voice. "Frau Siegel, could you tell us what you saw?"

"I couldn't see their faces," the woman said.

"Yes, ma'am," Mason said. "What *did* you see?"

"Around two a.m. I noticed a tall man in a long, dark coat carrying a crippled child. I said to myself, what is a man doing carrying that poor child in the streets at two A.M.? I didn't think anything else about it until that policeman showed me the sketches. Then I realized it must be the killer."

"Could you describe the girl for us?" Mason asked.

"It was dark, you understand. I didn't see her face, but I am sure that she was missing her left leg. The poor girl, I—"

"Where was this, ma'am?"

Frau Seigel looked startled by Mason's sudden interruption. "On Holzstrasse, where I live, of course. You know, when you get to be my age—"

"Yes, ma'am. Can you tell which direction they were heading?"

"South, toward the canal."

Mason hesitated with the next question, but he had to know. "From what you could tell, did the girl look okay?"

"She was alive, if that's what you're asking," Frau Seigel said, a little annoyed at Mason's impatience. "I know, because I heard her crying."

They thanked Frau Seigel and returned to the map outside the church. Mason drew out a rectangular area south of their location. "To start with, we'll spread out a search from here, west to Lindwurmstrasse and east to the river, just down to Kapuzinerstrasse."

"That could take days," Becker said.

A Jeep pulled up behind them, and they turned to see Wolski drive up and climb out. He met them at the table.

"Anything?" Mason asked.

Wolski shook his head. "Everyone wanted to help so much that they were making things up. But listen to this, I went by the Frauenkirche and Saint Michael's, but our teams were gone. No one is watching those churches. Mass had already let out, so I don't know if any of them canvassed the church-goers or not."

Manganella called over to them. "I heard something over the radio, sirs. Colonel Walton recalled all our detachment's investigators except you guys back to headquarters for some big operation."

"He did what?" Mason said. "He knows that's going to screw us." He turned to say something to Becker, but Becker beat him to it.

"Go," Becker said. "I will organize the search."

Mason tapped Wolski on the arm and rushed for the Jeep. "You're coming with me to make sure I don't murder a superior officer."

MASON AND WOLSKI ENTERED THE SQUAD ROOM JUST AS EVERY CID investigator and MP staff sergeant poured down the stairs from the third floor. They talked excitedly or barked orders to their subordinates. Colonel Walton led Timmers and Pike to a table and started giving instructions as he pointed to areas on a blueprint spread out on the table surface.

Mason and Wolski rushed up to Colonel Walton. "Colonel, what's going on?"

"They've got us going out on this raid," Timmers said, indicating the blueprint of the immense refugee camp for displaced persons a few miles outside of Munich.

"What raid?"

"The raid on this DP camp," Colonel Walton said. "All available personnel are ordered to go."

Colonel Walton walked toward his office, and Mason followed close behind.

"You're taking my investigators?"

"Last time I checked they weren't your investigators."

"Colonel, I need all my guys to go out on a search for Ramek and the girl. We just found a witness who saw them last night near Sendlinger Tor."

"This is a battalion-wide raid. We need everyone we've got. That perp you brought in, Wertz, gave up the gang's hideout. The gang is heavily armed, so we're going in with even heavier ones. You're lucky I'm not shanghaiing you and Wolski."

"Colonel," Mason almost shouted, "we've got to move on this abduction."

"You're hoping by some miracle that you'll find one crippled girl in an ocean of rubble. The entire battalion wouldn't make a difference." Colonel Walton slipped on his overcoat and pointed his finger at Mason. "And don't you raise your voice to your commanding officer. This is still the United States Army. You will respect the rank."

Wolski stepped in between Mason and Colonel Walton. "Sir, we know that from the time Ramek abducts his victim to the actual killing is between twelve and twenty-four hours. There's still the possibility we could track them down before he kills her."

"Then tell your partner here to stop hounding me and hit the pavement."

Colonel Walton started to leave, but Mason cut him off, putting his face in the colonel's. "Your raid can wait a few hours. That girl can't!"

"Orders for this raid came from the top," the colonel said. "This camp is a haven for criminal activity—" He waved his hands. "I don't have to justify myself to you. Now get out of my way before I have you arrested."

Mason was too crazed to move.

"You're goddamned bucking for a court-martial, Collins. You want to have the entire battalion running around looking for this girl, when, based on your previous track record, the only way you're going to find her is after her butchered carcass is strung up on a church wall."

Mason balled his fists, but Wolski trapped his arms and pulled him across to the other side of the room.

"I'm having you drawn up on charges," Colonel Walton said with a growl, though he clearly looked rattled.

"Colonel, please," Wolski said. "May I respectfully submit, sir, that what you said was way out of line. And Mr. Collins is under a lot of strain. This butcher has gotten under all our skins, sir. Please."

Colonel Walton stared at them a moment, then said, "Get the hell out of my sight, both of you."

Wolski released Mason, and they left the office. A moment later, Colonel Walton stormed out. A flood of men followed him down the stairs, leaving the squad room virtually empty.

Mason and Wolski entered Mason's office. Mason dropped in his chair and caught his breath.

"You nearly shot yourself in the foot with that crap," Wolski said. "If you'd have hit him, he could have thrown you in the stockade for years. Then there'd be no investigation at all."

"You didn't convince him to let me off the hook. He keeps me on the case, but hamstrings me by reallocating my manpower. That way, if the case falls apart and the brass boots me off, he avoids the blame."

"You play the hand you're dealt. That's it. Bottom line is, we've got to find that girl and stop Ramek. You've got to clear your head."

Mason took deep breaths in a struggle to calm down.

"You don't have to worry about Laura, at least," Wolski said. "I found some sharp guys who will keep her safe."

Mason nodded. "Thanks. I hate saying it, but I can't wait for her to get out of town." He reined in his worries about Laura. The search for Angela would need all his attention. "How many men do we have left to search for Angela?"

"Today? You and me. Maybe two MPs. The raid has taken just about every other warm body."

"The DP camp raid will probably take most of Becker's men, too."

Mason's phone rang. He answered, "CID, Collins." He listened. "When?"

Mason felt so excited that he slammed the phone down onto the cradle. "That was the MP station. An MP who just came on duty recognized the girl from the sketch we dropped off earlier. He and his partner picked up a girl matching her sketch and description around three this morning. She was naked and in shock, but not physically harmed. They dropped her off at the LMU hospital. Get someone to go pick up Becker. I want him in on this."

O n the pediatrics floor of Ludwig Maximilians University
hospital, Mason, Wolski, and Becker were directed to the
child recovery center. The "center" was a large room with twenty
beds, each sectioned off by side curtains. A German police
sergeant sitting at the foot of Angela's bed shot to attention and
saluted as Becker approached.

"This is definitely Angela," Mason said.

Angela lay under a thick blanket up to her neck with her right
arm exposed for an IV drip. Her thin face was more gray than
white. Her blank eyes stared at nothing.

A doctor attending an emaciated boy furrowed his brow at the
disturbance and marched up to them.

"This is Dr. Riesler," the sergeant said.

"Who are these people?" Dr. Riesler asked.

Mason, Wolski, and Becker introduced themselves and
explained their connection to Angela. The information seemed to
satisfy Dr. Riesler, and they gathered around the bed.

"Has she said anything?" Mason asked.

"She's in a state of shock and has not been responsive to

stimuli since the American police brought her in. She was also hypothermic and dehydrated. She's obviously suffered extreme psychological distress. Though physically she's recovering, only time will tell about the state of her mental faculties."

"How long before she's responsive?" Wolski asked.

"Assuming she hasn't sustained any profound psychological damage, she could come out of her stupor at any time. It rarely lasts more than a few days. She might respond better to a family member."

"She's an orphan," Mason said.

"We don't even know her family name," Becker added.

"What a pity," Dr. Riesler said. "There are so many orphans." A thought came to him. "Perhaps a friend or close companion. Someone she feels safe with could possibly get her to respond."

As soon as the doctor said that, Mason knew what he had to do. "You two stay here. Talk to her. I know someone who might be able to help." He left Wolski and Becker to wonder where he was going in such a hurry.

IT TOOK ALMOST AN HOUR FOR MASON TO PERSUADE KURT TO trust him enough to leave the safety of the shelter. Kurt was suspicious of most adults, especially those in uniform. Nurses and doctors terrified him, so just getting him to enter the hospital required another ten minutes of negotiations. Mason enjoyed his role as Kurt's guardian and protector, and by the time they had reached the pediatrics floor, Kurt had glued himself to Mason's leg. As soon as Kurt breached the door to the recovery center, he locked his feet when he saw Becker and the uniformed German policeman.

"It's all right," Mason said. "They're here to protect Angela."

"They won't take me away?"

"No. I promise."

Kurt stayed behind Mason's thigh all the same until he saw Angela. He sprinted the last few yards and stood by her bed, staring down at her.

"Angela, it's me, Kurt." No response. "When's she going to wake up?"

"Like I told you before, we hope when she hears your voice and knows you're here it might make her feel better."

"What happened to her?"

"The man who said he was her father really wanted to do bad things to her."

"She escaped?"

"We don't know."

Dr. Riesler watched from across the room. A couple of nurses hovered nearby.

"I think she escaped," Kurt said, keeping his gaze on the little girl. "She was brave and fought him off."

"Maybe."

Angela shuddered once then exhaled. A tear formed in the corner of her eye.

"Angela, come on, wake up. I'm really happy you're okay." Kurt looked up at Mason. "Can I touch her?"

Mason nodded, and Kurt used the back of his hand to stroke her cheek. Angela blinked.

"I think she's waking up!" Kurt said.

Mason put his finger to his mouth, warning Kurt not to yell.

Angela's eyes widened from an unseen fear. A low moan emerged from her throat and then she gasped as if remembering the terror. On impulse, Kurt hopped on the bed. Remaining on his knees, he held her cheeks and leaned in, his face close to hers.

"It's okay, Angela, I'm here. There's no bad man. You're safe."

Mason was impressed by Kurt's sudden expert bedside manner. Kurt spoke gently but with authority. Angela's breathing calmed and she stirred.

"Maybe we should step back," Mason whispered. "Three big men hovering over her...." He gestured for the others to move.

They stepped back a few feet and watched Kurt do his magic. Angela whimpered and pulled her free arm out of the blanket to hug Kurt.

"That man..." Angela said. "He lied. Oh, Kurt, it was horrible."

"You're safe now. You're in a hospital. There are police here to protect you. He can't get you anymore."

Angela saw Mason and his companions for the first time. "You remember the American policeman?" Kurt said.

To Mason's relief, Angela looked at him with a calm, neutral expression—the expression she usually gave him, the expression of a child who had lost her parents, her leg, everything. Mason took a chance and stepped forward.

"Hello, Angela. You've been a brave girl. I'm so glad you're okay."

"A man..." was all she could get out before collapsing into sobs.

Kurt tried to comfort her. The doctor came over when he heard Angela cry.

"She should rest. If you make her talk it might be too much for her."

Mason said in a low voice, "Doctor, the murderer who butchered those people is the one who took Angela. I don't know how she managed to survive, but if we could just get her to tell us where he took her, we might be able to capture him."

"If you push her too hard she might suffer too much mental trauma, and you won't get anything at all. Also, I must advise you that many people after suffering such a mental shock have anterograde amnesia. She may not remember a thing from the recent past. In the interests of the girl's health, I must ask you to give her some time to recover. Maybe in two or three days."

"Two or three days? Doctor, the killer could move on by then. He may have just discovered she's gone. He'll find another place to cut up his victims and start hunting another child. I'm sure you don't want that to happen."

"Of course not, but—"

"How about if I have the boy ask her the questions? I'll tell him to avoid asking about the traumatic details of the abduction. I just need to see if she can identify the place the killer took her."

Riesler thought a moment. "If you limit it to a few questions and have the boy ask them."

Mason stepped up to Kurt, who sat on the bed holding Angela's hand. In a hushed tone Mason said, "Kurt, can you hop off the bed for a moment?"

"Don't make him go," Angela said.

"He'll be right back. I promise."

Mason led Kurt away from Angela's bed and squatted to be on Kurt's level. "I need you to ask Angela a few questions. It might be really hard for her to remember what happened, but we need to find out where the man took her. Then we can go capture the man and put him in jail. Do you understand?" Kurt nodded. Mason continued, "Don't rush her and be gentle. And don't ask her anything but where she was."

"I can pretend I want to know so I can tell the others how brave she was."

Mason smiled at the boy's insight. "That's a good idea. I'm going to step away so she isn't afraid to say anything. Try to remember every detail of what she tells you. And take your time."

Kurt crawled back on the bed. Mason joined Becker and the doctor in the middle of the aisle. He could hear Kurt speaking in a tender voice.

"The doctor and I were speculating as to whether the girl escaped, or he let her go," Becker said.

Dr. Riesler nodded. "From what Herr Oberinspektor Becker tells me about this man, it seems impossible that a twelve-year-old girl could escape."

"If he let her go, then perhaps even he has limits," Becker said.

"Whatever the reason," Mason said, "if he's taken one child, then he could go after another. And my guess is he won't let the next one go."

Wolski entered the room from the hallway at a fast pace. "I used the nurses' station phone to call the MP station. I talked to the MP who found her. He said she was limping along with her crutches like a zombie, but going at a pretty fast clip. She was heading south a block from the train tracks on Tumblingerstrasse."

"And she was totally naked?"

"Yeah, he verified that."

"How long could she go before succumbing to hypothermia?" Becker asked Dr. Riesler.

"It never got much below freezing last night, and I'm sure her flight instincts pumped her full of adrenaline. My best guess would be no more than an hour before exhaustion and the cold would get the best of her."

"Have you got your map with you?" Mason asked Wolski.

Wolski pulled out a map from his coat and folded it so that it showed that section of Munich.

"She might get three miles at her speed," Mason said.

"She was delirious, so she could have changed directions numerous times, or gone in circles," Wolski said.

"Ramek must be further south than we thought. We'll start the search between Theresienwiese and the Isar and work our way south."

"It is still a very big area to cover with our limited forces," Becker said.

Mason turned at the sound of Angela weeping softly. Kurt tried to comfort her.

Dr. Riesler glanced at Kurt and Angela then signaled for a nurse. "I'm giving the boy about one more minute, then I must insist she rest."

Kurt didn't need the extra minute. After promising Angela he'd be right back, he came over to the group.

"Did she say where the man took her?" Mason asked.

"She doesn't know."

Mason felt the weight of disappointment. "Does she remember the street?"

Kurt shook his head. "She's never been in that part of the city. She said it was a big building that was bombed. It looked like a giant's kitchen."

"Do you know what she meant by that?"

"Huge machines and giant ovens. The man took her into a basement with long hallways and into a room with the scariest ovens she'd ever seen."

"Did she describe the rest of the building?"

"No, but I can ask her."

"That's enough questions," Dr. Riesler said. "Please, gentlemen, I must insist."

"Just one or two," Mason said. "We need to get a clearer picture—" He stopped and turned to Wolski and Becker when an idea came to him. "Ramek's operating table from the workshop and the army rations in his house...." He looked at Wolski's map. "One of the plants we were to search today is near that area, right?"

"Yes," Becker said excitedly. "Just east of where the officers picked up Angela, there is a large complex that processed and canned potted pork rations for the German army."

Mason dropped to one knee and held Kurt's arms. "You did a great job, Kurt. I'm proud of you. Take care of Angela. Okay? We're going to get the man who took her."

Through his binoculars, Mason scanned the immense meat-processing plant. The plant's three buildings formed a U shape and took up a two-by-three-city-block rectangle. The open end of the U provided the main access for delivery trucks and a small parking lot. Though most of the outer walls remained intact, he could see an interior filled with a tangled mass of blackened metal and broken concrete.

Wolski, Becker, and Mannheim stood next to Mason, each with his own binoculars.

Wolski whistled. "A hundred guys could hide out in that place. Our twenty-eight are just going to get swallowed up."

"We go with what we've got, since Colonel Walton refused to request infantry backup. He's afraid he's going to look bad if Ramek isn't in there."

Corporal Manganella's Jeep pulled up behind them, and Lieutenant Edwards, the engineer, jumped out. He came up to the group and unfurled a blueprint across the engine hood.

"This is all I could get on short notice," Edwards said. "It's the main complex layout." He pointed to the largest of the three buildings. "This is the processing facility with the main offices above. There are two sublevels with machinery and maintenance corridors. In fact, there's a whole network of maintenance corridors and tunnels connecting the buildings and the central furnaces."

Wolski pointed to the second-largest building. "That's the canning facility?"

"Canning and packing with can manufacturing on sub-level one. The third building is receiving and cold storage." Edwards looked at Mason. "It's at least five hundred thousand square feet of unstable structures. I know this building. German locals, then the army, tried salvaging operations to recover some of the machinery and raw materials. Both times sections collapsed. Y'all go in there at your own risk."

"That's why your team and the medics are here." Mason pointed to various points on the blueprint. "We'll break up into four teams of six. The teams will enter from the four sides. Have the troop trucks and ambulance drive into the interior courtyard. Wolski and I will take our two MPs and two of Inspector Becker's men into the processing building. My bet is that's where he'll be set up. Inspector, if you could organize your men into three teams to enter the canning facility and the storage building, and you remaining four each take an outside corner and maintain clear sightlines on the four bordering streets. The idea is to encircle the complex and slowly work our way into a tighter circle. Clear up, clear down, then move in, converging on the processing plant. Everyone understand?"

After everyone nodded, Mason said, "Whether the girl escaped or he let her go, chances are he's moved on. I acknowledge that, but I still want everyone on alert. We have Handie-Talkies, but they'll be pretty useless in there. Everyone make sure your flashlights work and you have a couple of flares. Use your whistles only if you spot him. Guns out and eyes sharp. Any questions?"

No one had any.

Five minutes later, Mason and his team entered the processing plant. He sent Corporal Manganella, plus the other MP and the two German police, to search the upper-floor offices of the building while he and Wolski slowly penetrated the maze of the processing facility below. Man-sized meat cutters, saws, and grinders stood quiet in a space that could accommodate two football fields. Suspended from the fifteen-foot ceiling, pipes, conveyor belts, and a system of coffin-sized gondolas wove through the plant. Half of the floor above had collapsed from the bombings, turning an already impossible tangle of metal and concrete into a jungle of rubble and debris.

Wolski made a face and whispered, "Did a herd of buffalo die in here?"

Mason pointed to mounds of black and green rot spilled on the floor. "Looks like bombs hit in the middle of their workday."

The huge holes in the ceiling let in soft light from the charcoal-gray sky, but there were so many shadowy spaces that they had to use their flashlights to sweep the area. They tried to move quietly across the debris-strewn floor, but the men they had sent to the upper floor and the other teams in the other buildings were ignoring Mason's warnings. Mason and Wolski could hear banging doors, loud calls, and heavy footsteps echoing across the entire complex.

"If Ramek didn't know we were here before, he does now," Wolski said.

Mason mumbled curses about the other men's carelessness.

The wind picked up, making the building creak and moan. Somewhere a flap of metal banged rhythmically. Then rain began to fall, the plink of raindrops sounding on metal. They had almost reached the far side when the four men searching the upper offices came noisily down the stairs.

Corporal Manganella breached the doorway first. "No sign of him upstairs, sir."

"Keep it down," Mason whispered back.

Mason and Wolski joined the four others at the stairwell.

"We go down quietly," Mason said. "No talking. Hand signals only."

"What if we see him?" Manganella asked.

"Then blow your damned whistle."

They all descended the two flights of stairs and entered a pitch-black room. Their flashlight beams revealed a large space housing barrel-shaped steam cookers and blending machines; above their heads, a dense metal grate hung just below a web of heating pipes, electrical conduits, and drainpipes.

The group spread out and proceeded slowly, weaving around the heavy machinery. Water trickled through hairline cracks in the floor above, forming stagnant puddles at their feet. The whole setting made the hair on the back of Mason's neck bristle. Doubts about the wisdom of searching this place with so few men began to worm into his consciousness.

A section of the floor grating creaked when Wolski stepped on it. Mason crept closer to him, and they shined their lights down through the metal grid. The tight pattern blocked most of their lights, so they could see only a small portion of the space below.

"What's down there?" Mason whispered.

"Looks like some kind of maintenance access."

The group finally reached a wall that Mason estimated was only a quarter of the way across the building. Mason looked at the others. The six men were stretched out along a fifty-foot line, and they faced two separate corridors. Their faces were barely illuminated by the reflections of the flashlights, but he could clearly see that all of them were unnerved by the oppressive gloom. He signaled for the last three to take the corridor leading to the right. He, Wolski, and Manganella took the corridor that led straight ahead.

The corridor was wide enough for the three to walk abreast, and it continued beyond the power of the flashlight beams. The same metal grating ran down the middle of the floor. Every twenty paces they encountered a doorway, alternating left then right. With each room, they performed the same nerve-wracking procedure, surging into the room two abreast, guns and lights up, never knowing if Ramek waited in ambush. But each search revealed only lifeless giants of metal or mazes of compressors and pipes.

Mason felt it in his feet. The building shuddered. An instant later a deep rumble rolled past them.

Manganella threw himself against the wall. "Christ, what was that?"

"Sounds like something collapsed," Wolski said. "Not in this building, I don't think."

"Sal, go find out what happened and report back to us," Mason said.

"Back that way?" At the sight of Mason's face, the corporal reluctantly turned and walked back the way they had come.

"On the double," Wolski said.

Manganella broke into a run.

"Hope no one's hurt," Wolski said.

Mason felt too conflicted to respond. Was it worth risking lives to be crawling around the bowels of this wreck of a building?

He answered his question by moving forward. A moment later they came to another corridor that led off to the right. Though it was half the width of the hallway they were in, the majority of pipes and conduits branched off in that direction.

"By my reckoning, this main corridor leads to the canning building," Wolski said.

"Sounds about right." Mason nodded toward the narrower corridor. "This one should link us up with the other team. We regroup with them then search the rest."

"Sounds like a plan, O Wise One."

Mason gave him a reproving look, but he appreciated the humor; it helped cut through the oppressive surroundings. They turned into the branching corridor. The suspended pipes and conduits were only an inch above Wolski's head. The same metal grating ran along the middle of the floor but with only a foot of concrete on either side.

They both put as much weight as they could on the concrete, which forced them to slide along the damp walls. A thin stream of water trickled in the tunnel beneath them. Their footsteps on the sandy concrete rasped loudly in the narrow space. After advancing thirty feet, they came to a room off to the right. As before, they swung into the room on either side of the doorframe with guns up. More pipes and compressors.

Wolski signaled for Mason to listen. "Voices somewhere behind that wall," Wolski said. "The other team."

Mason shrugged that he couldn't hear them.

"Old man. Going deaf already?"

"You live through hours of artillery blasts and see how well you can hear," Mason said.

"Hold on to your cane, gramps. We should link up with those guys any minute."

Mason and Wolski stepped out into the corridor again. Mason shot his hand up to stop. He pointed down the corridor another hundred feet ahead. He pushed Wolski's flashlight down to aim at the floor. Then Wolski saw it, too.

The corridor ended, leading to another room. Somewhere in the room, off to the right, glowed a greenish-yellow light. In the distance, beyond the door frame, the ghostly light reflected off a giant furnace.

"This corridor leads to the main furnaces and steam pump room," Mason whispered. "That light wasn't on when we went into that last room."

They crept forward, guns up. Just a few steps later, Wolski's foot made the grate creak. The silence amplified the sound as it echoed off the concrete walls. They waited and listened. Then, hugging tight to the walls, they moved forward again.

A shadow swept across the distant furnace. They stopped. Mason's skin tightened and the hair on the back of his neck stood up as if in warning. A heartbeat later, a tall man stood silhouetted in the doorway as if he had been expecting them. He neither moved nor spoke. Mason and Wolski whipped up their flashlights. The beams struck the man in the face.

He smiled, as if taunting them. Under his long blue coat he wore a full surgical gown, and surgical gloves covered his hands.

Mason registered all this in a fraction of a second, yet he hesitated. His brain tried to comprehend while his skin turned icy cold.

"Ramek!"

Mason and Wolski made quick strides toward the door with their guns ready to fire.

"Don't move! Put your hands up!"

In an instant, Ramek vanished into the recesses of the furnace room. Mason and Wolski broke into a dead run. Mason was faster and he surged ahead.

"Mason, wait!"

Too late. Mason felt the tug of a tripwire at his ankle as he breached the door frame. He heard a metallic clank. At the same moment the lantern extinguished, plunging the room into blackness. Mason spun to his right, gun and flashlight arms rigid. His light flashed across something shiny in a swift, arcing motion coming right at him. An instant later, Wolski burst through the door, slamming into him.

Mason went flying through the air. He heard Wolski scream even as he folded his body to protect himself from the fall. He collided with the cement floor. His flashlight popped out of his hand, bounced then rolled out of reach. As Mason scrambled for the flashlight he could hear Wolski's gurgled fights for breath.

From somewhere in the darkness came Ramek's voice. "The trap was meant for you, but your friend will do."

Mason reached the flashlight and whirled around with the light and gun. He searched frantically for Ramek, but Ramek was gone.

The urges to chase down Ramek or to turn to his friend's aid were both so overwhelming that he remained frozen in a crouching position for what seemed like an impossible amount of time. He trained the flashlight beam on Wolski. Wolski lay on his side, facing away from Mason. His back was covered in blood, and he held the side of his neck as blood oozed between his fingers and streamed onto the floor.

Like a giant scythe, a broad chopping blade that had been hung from an overhead pipe still swayed even after lopping off a huge chunk of Wolski's right shoulder and back.

Ramek's voice came as a haunting echo. "You can hunt me or save your friend."

The voice came from a maintenance tunnel leading to another part of the plant. Out of his mind with rage, Mason leapt up and charged into the tunnel. Six feet in, he came to a ladder leading down into the darkness. He could hear Ramek's heavy footsteps just below him. But he could also hear Wolski's gasps for air and moans of pain.

He hesitated at the top of the ladder. An overpowering voice from within screamed at him to forget Wolski and take Ramek. *Go! You may never have another chance.*

He felt profound shame at the very thought, and it over-whelmed the primal urge to exact revenge. With a deep growl, he fired his pistol three times into the black hole, then rushed back to his partner and friend.

The sight of Wolski sent Mason into a panic. Blood poured out. His shoulder, and a portion of his back and neck, had been cleaved from his body; muscle, bone, and sinew were exposed. Mason blew his whistle and kept blowing it, while he ripped off his overcoat and pressed it against Wolski's wounds. Wolski convulsed from the shock and loss of blood.

Mason dropped his whistle and screamed for help. He didn't know what else to do. Wolski's nearly severed arm bled the most, but applying a tourniquet would do nothing to stop the flow. How long before anyone could find them in this maze of turns and dead ends?

Finally, the sounds of voices and running footsteps echoed into the room. Relief flooded over Mason. He couldn't tell from which direction they were coming, but he prayed the medics were with them.

A moment later, Becker, six German police, and the medics emerged from the same tunnel that Ramek had used to escape. Mason had never felt so happy to see Germans in uniform as he did now.

Mason whispered in Wolski's ear, "Hang on, buddy. We've got help. Hold on."

The two medics crouched by Wolski and pulled away Mason's now blood-soaked coat. For the first time in years, Mason felt the urge to vomit. He heard Becker's voice through the swirl of emotions and it suddenly calmed him.

Becker repeated the question. "How did this happen?"

Mason reminded himself that he was still in command and

had to regain his self-control. He gestured at the swinging blade. "Ramek's booby trap."

The medics called for more light. Several flares popped and illuminated the room in orange and red. One of the German officers found Ramek's lantern. He lit it and held it high for the medics.

"Ramek used that lantern to lure us in here," Mason said to Becker. "We ran in like a couple of bugs to a flame."

"Ramek was here?"

"He escaped through the same tunnel you used to get here."

"Impossible. He'd barricaded the access to the storage building. The engineers had just cleared the barricade when we heard your gunfire. He couldn't have escaped that way."

"Have some of your men check out an alcove just inside the entrance. There's a ladder leading down to a maintenance tunnel. That's where Ramek went."

Becker shouted a few commands, and four of his men ran into the tunnel. He called after them to be careful and watch for traps. Then he turned back to Mason. "It's fortunate the two medics were with us. An engineer was injured while removing the barricade. I suspect Ramek booby-trapped that as well."

"He's probably left traps all over this place. Ramek's goddamned house of horrors."

One of the medics said, "We haven't got a spare stretcher. We'll have to use your coat, sir."

"Do it."

The medics had wrapped Wolski in bandages. One of the medics held a bag of plasma high, with the tube attached to Wolski's arm. Mason rushed over and helped lift Wolski onto the coat. Then he and three of Becker's men each lifted a corner of the coat and heaved. They struggled with the weight and entered the tunnel. Mason could hear the four German officers below calling out as they searched the sub-tunnel.

As he helped carry the makeshift stretcher, Mason stared at his partner's motionless body. He had forgotten his training, abandoned discipline, and run headlong into Ramek's trap. And now his partner might die because of it. Only one thing now kept Mason from total collapse: his single-minded craving for revenge.

44

For Mason, hospital waiting rooms were the same all over the western world, and the 98th General Hospital was no different: hard wooden benches, linoleum floors, and the offensive miasma of disinfectant.

It was just after seven p.m. Mason had been there for two hours. He sat leaning forward, elbows on knees, trying to lose himself in the numbing study of linoleum tile seams and heel scuffmarks. He'd been alone in the room most of the time, except for a woman and her young son waiting for news about a major who'd been in a car accident.

In the last few minutes word had come that the DP camp raid, and subsequent shoot-out, was over. Ambulances were on their way with a dozen victims of gunshot wounds. Mason took some comfort in knowing that at least in the meantime, Wolski had been receiving the full attention of the staff of doctors.

Black shoes and a white hospital gown came into his field of view. An image of the meat-processing plant and Ramek standing in the doorway flashed in his mind. He shot to his feet. Ramek wasn't hovering in the doorway, but Dr. Sutter was.

"Chief Warrant Officer Collins," Dr. Sutter said.

Mason stepped up to the doctor. "How is he, Doc?"

"He's stable but still in critical condition. We don't have the expertise or facilities to perform the kinds of surgeries he's going to require...."

"Is he going to live?"

"I can't guarantee anything at this point, but I remain optimistic."

Mason let out a heavy sigh of relief.

"We were able to save the arm, but I doubt he will have use of it. He's not out of the woods yet. My biggest concern is infection. He's already running a high fever. If he makes it, we'll keep him here for a few days until it's safe to transfer him to Frankfurt. They may be able to repair the wounds better than we can. Some of the surgeons there have experience treating soldiers with severe battle wounds. I'm afraid he's in for months of painful reconstructive surgery and skin grafts. That was a shockingly brutal wound. I wager a smaller man wouldn't have survived."

Like me, Mason thought.

Through the plate-glass window Mason saw Anna. She looked at Mason with blood-shot eyes. Mason pointed her out to the doctor. "That's Warrant Officer Wolski's girlfriend. She's the closest to family Wolski has at the moment."

Dr. Sutter stepped out into the hallway and greeted Anna. He took her aside. Mason watched as the doctor repeated to Anna what he'd said to Mason. She shook, tears rolling down her cheeks. Mason wondered if she would still love Wolski even if he had ugly scars and a useless arm. He hoped with all his heart that she would.

Dr. Sutter left Anna alone and disappeared behind swinging double doors. Her arms were folded tight around her shoulders and she looked like a lost child. Mason went out into the hallway to talk to her.

She saw Mason approach. "You monster," she breathed in

German, pointing a finger at him. "It's your fault. He's in there because of you."

Mason tried to urge her into the waiting room. "Anna, please—"

"Don't touch me. I *knew* if he stayed with you something terrible would happen to him. He thought you were such a great man. Mason Collins, the great detective. And look what you did to him."

"He did an incredibly heroic thing. He jumped in front of the blade to protect me—"

"Do you think that's supposed to make me feel better? It should have been you. You should be in that operating room, not...."

She broke into tears and ran down the hallway.

Becker's voice came from behind. "You must forgive her. She is young and feels her new life is at an end."

Mason whirled around. "Jesus, you shouldn't sneak up on me like that."

Becker nodded. "It has served me well in darker times."

"Anna's right. It should have been me. Though I'd have wound up in the morgue."

An announcement blared from the hallway speaker demanding that all available nurses and orderlies report to the emergency entrance.

"The wounded from the DP camp raid are coming in," Mason said, and he led Becker into the waiting room. "You're here, so I take it you didn't find Ramek."

"After you left we searched the tunnel from one end to the other. He disappeared without a trace. He obviously knew that complex in detail and had arranged for a quick escape."

"My guess is he had several. And even if you find out how, it still means he's gone."

Orderlies and nurses pushed gurneys with the wounded into the hallway and past the waiting room.

"Any determination on the organs we found at Ramek's house?" Becker asked.

"Only that they're not from a recent victim. There were signs of decay, so the pathologist estimates that they've been stored in the formaldehyde for months, maybe longer."

A group of CID investigators and MPs entered the hallway and were shooed into the waiting room by a husky orderly. Timmers was among them. He looked pale and tired.

Mason called him over. "What's the toll?"

"One dead MP—Powell. Four more seriously wounded. None of our guys, except Pike. A bullet grazed his shoulder. They're treating him downstairs."

"Did you hear about Wolski?"

"Are you kidding? That story burned through the battalion."

Mason repeated what Dr. Sutter had said about Wolski's condition. Timmers had trouble looking into Mason's eyes. It confirmed what Mason suspected: The blame fell directly on him.

Colonel Walton wedged his way through the crowd and homed in on Mason with a contemptuous glare. "We need to talk. Follow me." As he turned, he said, "You, too, Timmers."

When Colonel Walton moved toward the door, he revealed Havers standing just behind him. Havers wore a satisfied grin. Mason wanted to knock out his teeth. Mason's tempered really flared when he noticed Havers was following behind Colonel Walton like a loyal dog.

Down the hallway, Colonel Walton led Mason, Timmers, and Havers into a small office. Mason faced Colonel Walton, with Timmers and Havers standing off to one side.

"You screwed up on this one, Collins," Colonel Walton said. "You went in there ill-prepared and undermanned and got people seriously injured. No one died on your watch, but I consider that a damn miracle. From where I stand, Ramek's playing you. Even to the point where he's got you charging right into his trap. Then to add the biggest turd onto an already steaming pile of turds, you lose the suspect. *Again.* This has gone on long enough."

"Colonel—"

"I don't want to hear it." Colonel Walton took a deep breath before continuing. "I acknowledge the progress you made. Some dubious leads paid off. But then you went off the rails." He stiffened, taking on an air of formality, as if the previous words of praise had been calculated to soften the coming blow. "I asked Mr. Havers and Mr. Timmers here as witnesses. Chief Warrant Officer Collins, you are hereby suspended from active duty."

"Colonel, I have three days left on General West's deadline. At least give me the three days! We've shut him out of his house and his two places of killing, eliminated his black-market suppliers, and we've plastered his face on every street corner and newspaper. We went from nothing to that in two weeks, and you want to cut this investigation off at the knees to mete out punishment—"

"Your price is too damned high. Your badge, please, Mr. Collins."

Mason stared into Colonel Walton's eyes for a moment before removing the badge from his pocket and handing it over.

Colonel Walton returned Mason's hard stare. "You're on suspension until I figure out what to do with you. Timmers will take over the case."

Mason nodded. "Mr. Timmers would be my choice. He's been on it almost from the beginning."

"It's only temporary. The upper brass wants a new perspective."

"What? You can't let them do that. How about for once fight for your investigators? Fight for your squad. That's what a good squad commander is supposed to do."

"You say one more word, and I will not only have you kicked out of the CID but see that you're court-martialed and get drummed out of the army. It will be Chicago all over again for you, except this time you won't even be able to write up parking citations in Mongolia!" Colonel Walton headed for the door, but just before exiting he said, "Your final task on this case is to write your report on this latest fiasco. Put it on my desk by oh-seven-hundred, then get the hell out. If I get so much as a hint that you're sticking your nose into this investigation, I'll throw you in the stockade."

Colonel Walton left, with Havers following close behind.

"So you know," Timmers said, pausing before he left, "Colonel Walton fought to keep you on. The order came from the top."

IT TOOK A LONG TIME BEFORE MASON'S LEGS WOULD MOVE. As he walked down the hospital hallway for the exit, he passed the waiting room. He saw Timmers in there, talking to some of the other investigators, and the murmur of conversation stopped. All eyes followed him until he was clear of the window.

Becker met him outside the swinging double doors. Mason stopped but didn't look at him.

"I've been suspended," Mason said.

"Yes, I heard."

"You'll be working with Timmers for now."

"Your superiors have made an unwise, even reckless decision."

"Funny. That's what they've said about me."

"If there's anything you need…."

"Yeah, there's one thing you could do for me. Could you take care of Kurt and Angela? Make sure Angela gets good care and that Kurt can stay as long as he needs."

"Of course. I know some individuals who might be able to take care of them all."

Mason thanked him and they shook hands.

"If you wish, I could keep you informed of any progress," Becker said.

"How about I continue to keep you informed?"

"I don't follow you."

"You didn't think I was going to stop just because they suspended me, did you?"

Mason bounded down the stairs before Becker could lecture him about the pitfalls of going renegade.

45

For the next three and a half hours, Mason wrote up the daily action report as Colonel Walton had commanded. He wasn't a slow typist. Colonel Walton had asked for embellishment, so that was what Mason gave him: the painstaking minutiae of the facts, the decisions, the processes, and what he considered a dereliction of duty if he had failed to pursue the processing plant lead, but most of all, the bravery of the men involved, particularly Warrant Officer Vincent Wolski.

He dropped the thick report in Colonel Walton's in-basket, and, in tribute to Wolski, he used his knife to break into the colonel's file cabinet and pulled out one of his prized bottles of scotch. He raised the bottle in a toast to Wolski and took several long gulps.

Manganella had offered to drive him to Laura's hotel, but Mason preferred to walk in hopes that it would clear his mind. He wanted to think things through in the silence that snowfall brings. The thin layer of snow crunched under his footsteps, and he welcomed the bracing air. Halfway to Laura's hotel, he started to question the wisdom of declining Manganella's offer. The cold had crept into his bones and flared the wounds from the previous winter's frostbite. He turned down Platzl and passed the infamous Hofbräuhaus am Platzl, the beer hall where Hitler had made frenzied speeches attacking the Jews. Behind him an MP Jeep rolled past, which gave Mason a sense of satisfaction that they had finally listened to him and started putting MP patrols on the smaller streets and not concentrate the entire allotment of manpower to the main arteries. He even saw an MP on foot ahead of him stroll to the end of the narrow street and turn the corner.

Moments later, Mason turned the same corner behind the MP. Then it occurred to him: That MP had apparently been patrolling alone, when normally they worked in pairs. This thought rang an alarm just as he heard quick footsteps in the snow behind him.

As he turned, a dark shadow loomed over him, then his head exploded in pain. Electrical shockwaves coursed through his brain. A white, searing light flashed behind his eyes. His legs threatened to buckle as he retreated backward, hoping to gain some distance while he struggled to recover his sight.

He heard the footsteps come at him. He reached for his pistol, but another flash of pain in his wrist made him drop the weapon. His vision cleared in time to see Ramek standing over him with a scalpel in one hand and a blackjack in the other. With his long arm, Ramek swung the scalpel at Mason's neck. Mason tried to grab the arm, but he was too stunned to be accurate. He managed to protect his neck, but the blade slashed across his forearm. The ripping of fabric accompanied the searing sensation in his arm. He pushed away the pain and readied himself for the next blow, but his head still spun out of control, blood blinded his left eye, and his legs refused to obey.

Ramek tried a backhanded sweep with the scalpel, aiming again for Mason's neck. Mason ducked away from the swing, then caught the arm as it arced away. He fumbled for a lock grip on Ramek's wrist, but Ramek was too quick. That powerful arm came back. This time, though, Mason took control of Ramek's arm, and he used Ramek's momentum to force the arm around. He pushed with all his strength. The scalpel sank into Ramek's shoulder. Ramek growled in pain, but instead of recoiling, he brought the blackjack across Mason's head. Mason stumbled back and raised his arms in defense, but the blackjack struck him again.

The blow sent Mason reeling backward and he fell to the sidewalk. He summoned his remaining strength and forced himself up to his knees. He braced for the next impact. But instead, through the haze of his shock he suddenly became aware of headlights and the roar of a Jeep engine.

From somewhere in the distant shadows, he heard Ramek's voice. "We're not finished, you and I."

THE NURSE CLOSED THE GASH ON MASON'S ARM WITH A FINAL stitch. Mason sat on a chair in a curtained-off area of the hospital's emergency room. The nurse had already stitched his temple and applied a bandage there. He had a bandage behind his right ear, a black eye, and a black bruise on his jaw. The sharper pains had subsided, but from the waist up he felt like one big throb.

The doctor entered through the divide in the curtain with an X-ray. "You have one thick skull. You've suffered a mild concussion, but nothing's broken. Can you wiggle your fingers?"

Mason did so. He had complete feeling and mobility in his hand, though the muscle in his upper arm let out a stab of pain.

"Doesn't seem to be any nerve damage," the doctor said. "You're one lucky man."

Mason had to agree.

"Stay off your feet. If you experience any dizziness or numbness, come back in right away."

The nurse told him to wait for his medications, then she parted the curtains for the doctor and they left. A moment later, Laura appeared, flanked by her new bodyguards. She stifled a cry and ran up to him. He tried to stand, but his head spun, and he dropped to the chair.

She kissed him delicately on the lips. "How are you feeling?"

"Jim Dandy."

"Liar. The doctor told me you have a concussion."

"Doctors like to exaggerate."

"Listen to you. Mr. Tough Guy. That maniac nearly killed you. It must have been terrifying."

Mason had felt more shame than terror at being caught off guard so easily.

Laura pulled over a stool and sat next to him. "I heard about Vincent and what happened at the plant."

"News travels fast."

"Faster than you. I was expecting you hours ago."

"I stayed at the hospital until the doc could tell me about Wolski's condition, then I was at headquarters typing up my last report."

"What do you mean, 'last'?"

Mason tried to smile, but failed. "I've been suspended. I'm off the case."

"I'm sorry."

"Are you?"

"Of course I am." She paused. "Come with me to Garmisch."

"Laura, I can't."

"Of course you can. I'm taking the train for Garmisch tomorrow, and in case you've forgotten, tomorrow is Christmas Eve. What better place to celebrate than in a lovely town in the Bavarian Alps? They've turned it into a resort for the army and military government personnel. There are nightclubs, good restaurants, great skiing. Now that you're suspended, you're not working tomorrow—"

"Thanks for the morale booster."

"That's not what I meant. Now that you're free you can come with me. I'll be snooping around down there for some info on the black market, but most of the time I'll be free. You can be my protector..." She gave him a wink. "My ski buddy. I'm taking the train tomorrow."

"I can't do that, Laura."

"Why not? I mean, look at you. If anyone needed some time off, it's you. You need to take care of yourself. Rest. Heal." Laura pulled back to get some distance and studied his face with probing eyes. "You're not going to even try?"

"I need some time alone to think. Besides, I won't be very good company."

"Oh, come on. Say what you mean instead of hiding behind sullen remarks."

"Okay... I want to kill a man." Finally verbalizing it brought up his rage. "That's all I can think about. This whole thing started out as a cop stopping a murderer, justice for the victims, save more innocents from his butchering, but now it's him and me. Nothing else matters, and it's consuming me. I want to inflict all the pain on him he's dispensed, times ten. You see why I'm not going anywhere?"

"You're still going to try to capture Ramek? Even with all the resources the army could give, he's still eluded you. How can you really expect to do it on your own?"

"Then he's going to keep killing. There's no one to stop him."

"So you'll what? Play the vigilante? That's insane. Look, I know you're upset about Vincent. I am, too. I cried when I heard. But not only are you turning down the most romantic offer you'll ever get, you're risking jail time going against orders on your one-man crusade. You're risking your career in the army—your last, best chance at being a detective again."

"You don't get it. You don't get me." There it was in all its ugly glory. He said it in spite of his best efforts to the contrary. "I'm sorry, Laura, but this is getting us nowhere."

"You're right." Laura was yelling now. "Unless you can stop and see what you're doing to yourself, to everyone around you." She grabbed her purse. "I'm leaving." She stopped at the curtains. "The train leaves at one P.M. I get on that train with or without you. You're not there... then you can go to hell."

She disappeared behind the curtains. Mason stood and held on to the table for support, but he went no farther. He only listened to the click of her heels as she walked out of the emergency ward... and possibly out of his life.

46

"Excuse me, sir, but you're crazy," Corporal Manganella said. "A hot night with Betty Grable wouldn't get me to go in there again."

Mason sat in the passenger's seat, as Manganella steered the Jeep into the courtyard of the meat-processing plant. He had convinced Manganella to drive him over despite his off-limits status.

Manganella parked near the processing building. "What makes you think he'll come back here? He hasn't done that before."

"Maybe I can pick up his trail." When Manganella only returned a look of befuddlement, Mason said, "Look, Ramek had to move his stuff and find a safe place overnight. Right? That takes time. And he used a whole precious lot of that time tracking me down so he could kill me. Plus, he had to nurse that shoulder wound I gave him. I'm gambling he couldn't have gone far."

Manganella processed this a moment and smiled. "I still think you're crazy going in there by yourself."

Mason climbed out of the Jeep. "Thanks for the lift. You'd

better get back before they notice. And remember, don't say a word to anyone."

"What if you get caught by one of those booby traps?"

"I'll be all right."

"I'm not going anywhere, sir. I can't leave you out here all alone. Screw regulations."

Mason smiled. "All right then."

Armed with a flashlight, his personal .38 S&W Special pistol, and a Ka-Bar knife, Mason entered the processing building through a bombed-out portion of the wall. Nothing had changed, except for the invading snow transforming black rubble to white. The rats and pigeons had returned after the day's intrusion. He crossed the expanse and descended the same staircase to the sublevel. The blackness closed in on him. He stopped and listened for any sounds of human activity among the creaks of metal and low moans of the wind. Finally, he turned on his flashlight and surveyed the surroundings, but images of Wolski's wounds kept flashing in his mind. Following the same bearing as the day before, he passed the rusting machinery and found the maintenance corridor.

The chances of Ramek returning to the plant were slim, but Mason felt his heart pound out a fast rhythm against the closed collar of his shirt all the same. Watching for potential traps and listening for any movement, he proceeded down the corridor. The path led him to the same narrower corridor off to the right. He followed it past the last room that Wolski and he had checked. Then, up ahead, the furnace room where the trap had been set. Just before entering, he examined the doorway with his flashlight. There, six inches from the flooring, lay the remnants of the trip-wire. Then, just in front of him, Wolski's blood. Mason's chest tightened at seeing how much of Wolski's blood had spilled out onto the concrete floor.

Mason took a few minutes to explore the furnace room. Like

three rusting beasts, the hulking furnaces sat silently, spreading their tentacle-like pipes along the ceiling and extending out into each of the converging corridors. With a last scan, his flashlight glinted off polished metal behind one of the furnaces. He went around the furnace and came upon Ramek's "operating room." A butcher's table similar to the one they'd found in Ramek's workshop had served as the operating table. The leather straps still hung from the sides, and a rumpled white sheet lay along its length. A rolling cart stood next to the table, void of any surgical instruments. The few shelves and a workbench contained nothing that would indicate Ramek had been there. Ramek had removed all his instruments of torture. Mason didn't need proof, but now it was confirmed: Despite every set-back, Ramek planned to continue his gruesome work.

Mason entered the maintenance tunnel where Ramek had escaped. In the alcove with the descending stairs, he sent his flashlight beam into the hole. Eight feet below, another tunnel. He climbed down the ladder, making as little noise as possible. As far as his flashlight showed, the tunnel continued arrow straight in both directions. A ceramic drainpipe, at least four feet in diameter, ran through the tunnel, leaving him barely enough room to face forward. A thick layer of sludge covered most of the floor. Multiple footprints led off in both directions.

He tried to picture the building plan. From the changes in his path's direction, he estimated that behind him the tunnel led back to the main collection area in the processing plant. In front of him, it must lead to the storm drains or the Isar river.

In the dark underground maze, he quickly lost track of time. He looked at his watch: 9:50. Still three hours before Laura's train left. Mason had spent the entire night awake and thinking. Near six that morning he'd come to a couple of conclusions: He was a damn fool, and that Laura was the best thing to come along in his life. Nonetheless, it was still up in the air whether he would get on the train with her or not.

Mason moved forward, his shoulders scraping against the wall and the drainpipe. He'd never considered himself claustrophobic, but the journey through that tunnel tested his tolerance. The foul stench overwhelmed the still air. Rats scurried away from his flashlight beam. The roof and floor seemed to compress in on him as he went.

At about a hundred feet, he encountered several cracks in the floor, ceiling, and drainpipe. He figured he was under the canning plant, which had suffered the worst of the bombardments. Even at this depth the impacts of one-thousand-pound bombs had ruptured the foundation. The threat of another collapse, burying him in this tomb, compounded this new sensation of claustrophobia.

A few yards farther and the cracks became fissures and breaks. A few minutes after that he had to stop. The ceiling of the tunnel had collapsed. There was no way to continue. He tested the chunks of concrete and jabbed at the earth, but all was firmly in place. This was the end of the line. No trapdoors. No secret passage.

How had Ramek escaped? There had to be another way out. The other direction led back to the processing plant. It was unlikely Ramek could have gotten out that way. There had been too many men converging on the processing plant by that time, plus the men as lookouts on each corner. He must have fashioned several means of escape, and, perhaps one of them might be in the very direction Mason would not expect—beneath the processing plant.

When Mason turned to go back, he stumbled on a chunk of concrete. As he tried to regain his balance, his flashlight struck the drainpipe, creating a hollow sound that reverberated within the pipe. With the butt end of his flashlight, he banged on the ceramic pipe again and listened, a new thought coming to him.

Mason retraced his steps, examining every inch of the drainpipe. It had many small cracks and breaks; occasionally he'd stop and tap in places that looked loose. Thirty feet farther on, he came to a section of the pipe that was riddled with a web of fissures. With one good tap, a manhole-sized portion fell into the pipe. Mason examined the edges of the break. The ceramic looked new, and at several places shards of the cut material had shredded away dark-blue fibers. Ramek had cut through the shattered section of pipe and fashioned the piece so he could reset it upon his escape.

The opening was barely big enough for Mason to squeeze through. He didn't know how Ramek had managed with his much greater bulk, but he was sure Ramek had figured that out long before being pursued.

Once inside, Mason had to bend forward to avoid banging his head. And there, in the sludge, was a set of footprints leading away from the plant. He moved forward, bent at the waist, flashlight up. He tried to close his mind to the suffocating darkness, but the pipe was worse than the tunnel. He'd never experienced true claustrophobia before, but now giant invisible hands squeezed air from his lungs and constricted his throat. Maybe it was the crushing events of the last few days; maybe it was the sheer exhaustion. Whatever caused it, sweat streamed down his face despite the cold. His lungs demanded more air. He quickened his pace, feeling like a desperate man climbing out of a grave. What felt like an hour had only been ten minutes when he saw faint daylight.

Finally, he reached the end and saw that a falling bomb had blown off the drainpipe just before it terminated at the river. He dropped off the jagged edge onto the muddy bank of the Isar River and grabbed his knees. He gulped in fresh air and felt the cold grip of panic subside.

Mason surveyed his immediate surroundings and calculated approximately where he was in relation to the city. A narrow islet divided this part of the river. His side of the river flowed swiftly and had cut into the land, forming a high embankment.

He searched around the base of the drainpipe for footprints, but, except for the last foot before the water's edge, snow covered the riverbank. He then headed south, away from the city, scanning the ground as he went. After a hundred yards, he ran into thick trees and brush growing on the steep embankment. It would have taken Ramek a great deal of effort to push through this natural barrier, and he definitely would have left evidence of the struggle. It had to be the other direction.

Mason backtracked and started the search north of the drainpipe. Here, the way narrowed, the high embankment encroaching on the water's edge, with scrub brush and small trees growing from the sand and mud. The embankment would have forced Ramek to keep to the edge of the water, and Mason did the same. At thirty feet, he spotted a large footprint in the mud where the water lapped the land—the same footprint as in the sludge of the drainpipe.

Industrial buildings lined this side of the river, any one of them an ideal place for Ramek to set up his torture chamber. He could be waiting close by, or deep inside the dense ruins. Even if Mason found more footprints, there would be no way to track Ramek once he hit concrete and asphalt. Almost eighteen hours had passed since Ramek had fled into the plant's maintenance tunnel. Eighteen hours to find a new lair. Mason cursed himself for being there, scrambling along the riverbank, hoping beyond reason that he would find a definitive clue of where Ramek had gone.

He wondered if he should go on and looked at his watch again: 10:25. He still had time to stumble around on a fool's errand... something he was getting used to.

Mason walked on. Twenty yards later, he found another footprint just as the embankment flattened out to a gentle slope. Now he had a choice: continue along the riverbank or head inland. He could toss a coin or rely on instinct. He headed inland.

He moved through thick scrub and sparse saplings. Above the top of the rise, he could just see the upper section of a defunct cement factory. Scanning the area, he spied another footprint at the base of a tree, where its branches had blocked the snow. He was right: Ramek had gone this way. With a little luck....

At the top of the slope he came to a wide field bisected by train tracks. Beyond the field and to his left were flat-roofed warehouses, and a half-mile to his right a blue-collar neighborhood on the fringes of the city.

About a hundred yards down the tracks, a bevy of men worked to repair the bomb-damaged tracks. Mason walked down to the spot and showed the men the sketch of Ramek. They all shook their heads, but one man suggested asking around at a homeless camp near an old hydroelectric plant built over the smaller branch of the river.

A five-minute walk along the riverbank brought him to a camp of lean-tos and salvaged army tents. The occupants, all men, sat around fires or washed clothes in the icy river. They all were gaunt and bedraggled. Some still wore their ragged Wehrmacht uniforms. Not too long before, it had been Mason's duty to try to kill these men, but now he only felt pity for them.

As Mason circulated the camp, showing the sketch of Ramek, the men eyed him with suspicion. Most of them gave the sketch only a cursory glance and seemed more concerned that a U.S. soldier had invaded their domain. Mason took a position at the water's edge to face them and gave them the now oft-repeated speech about Ramek butchering innocent Germans and his job being to stop the killer.

The speech, well-worn as it was, seemed to garner their interest. The men started to talk among themselves, but then a hollow-eyed man stood and limped toward Mason.

"I saw that man last night," the hollow-eyed man said, then pointed south along the riverbank. "He was carrying two heavy duffel bags. I didn't pay much attention. I assumed he was just another homeless veteran. He was snooping around that building, though the building's boarded up." The building he pointed to lay in an open field farther up the track to Mason's right. "Even if he got in, he wouldn't be able to stay. Every ten days or so the police come back and kick out anyone trying to use it as a shelter."

Mason thanked them all and hurried away. A few minutes later, he came opposite the building and stopped. The two-story building lay in the middle of the field near a defunct track, a turn-of-the-century relic that had probably been a maintenance and switching station for the railroad at one time. The brick had turned black with age and years of soot. Boards covered the windows of the first floor, but the broad observation windows on the second story were exposed and either broken or streaked with dirt.

Mason entered the field and crossed the train tracks. With nothing to provide cover, he tried to keep his line of approach to a blind corner, but nothing could prevent Ramek from spotting him if he watched from the shadows of the second story. Bent low and gun out, Mason took quick strides and rushed up to a corner of the building, then stopped and listened. No sound but the wind and a transport plane flying overhead.

Then he saw them: on the ground where the eaves stopped the snow, a whole series of Ramek's footprints.

He sneaked up to a window and tried to peer through the separation in the boards. Too dark inside. Ducking below the window, he moved around to the front and only door. A new padlock had been added to the door's hasp. With every muscle tensed and his finger on the trigger, he kicked the door.

The old wooden frame gave way and the door exploded inward. He charged in with his gun up. He moved sideways, his ears alert to any sound. Sunlight poured through the gaps in the boards and made slashes of light in the billowing dust. Still, too many shadows. Mason turned on his flashlight and scanned the single room. To his left, a narrow desk sat under one window and flanked by shelves of rotting boxes. To his right, one under each window, sat two tables with rags, rusting cans, and papers. Nothing in the space could conceal a big man like Ramek.

He moved up the narrow stairs. The boards protested under his weight. With his gun out, he poked his head above the second-story floor. The space was empty except for a lone table.

Back downstairs, Mason checked the outside again. Several tracks led to and from the door. Inside, Mason frantically swept things off the shelves and tossed crates aside. A metal cabinet sat in one corner, nearly buried in empty wooden crates. He shoved away the crates and yanked open the doors.

"I found you, you bastard."

On the upper shelves of the cabinet lay an assortment of Ramek's surgical instruments and supplies, and on the bottom shelf, cans of food, blankets, and a kerosene lantern. Then he noticed something very odd: On a stool wedged between the cabinet and the wall sat a very large children's toy. No, not really a toy. It appeared to be too sophisticated for that. The two-foot-high rabbit stood on its hind legs and held a violin as if bowing the strings. Why had Ramek thought this contraption was so important? There were a lot of other things he could have brought with him, either to help him in hideous tasks or for his survival. Why this?

Mason would address that conundrum later. The building probably served as a temporary stop for Ramek, and he'd be back to collect his things after finding a more secure location. So, at that moment, Mason had to get ready for Ramek's return. He brushed away his tracks in the snow in front of the building, then closed the broken front door as best he could. After completing those tasks, he stood inside the front-facing window and peered out through the gaps in the boards. How much time before Ramek came back?

Mason checked his watch. A little more than an hour and a half before Laura's train. He cursed. Of all the damn luck. He couldn't let Laura go, but now that he had Ramek he couldn't walk away, either.

With one last glance through the gaps, he walked over to the mechanical rabbit and examined it closely. For Mason, the eerie device conjured up images of something out of a kid's haunted childhood. He felt around the heavy base, then lifted the device from the stool. There, underneath the rabbit, lay a small brass key. Mason inserted the key into the base and turned the key several rotations. The music began. The rabbit bowed the violin, swaying with the music and turning its head. Mason glanced at the door, worried that the noise might alert Ramek to his presence. With the last plucked note, the rabbit stopped. A click of metal and a scrape of wood on wood brought Mason's attention back to the rabbit. A drawer had popped out from the base. Inside the drawer lay a leather-bound book. Mason removed the book and placed it on the narrow desk where a slash of dusty light entered through the wooden slats.

He opened it.

Every page was covered edge to edge in written text. On a random page he read:

NOVEMBER 19, 1945

It is 743 days since the end of my being, since the descent, since the beginning of the black day... oh, how they screamed. The voices taunt us with dreams of their agony. They torment us with the curse of remembrance. ...

Ramek's diary.

47

M ason leafed through Ramek's diary and stopped at the page dated December 22.

... We are being punished. Why did we let the angel go? Oh, God, give us the strength. Our burden is heavy... The forces of evil have sent their agent to hinder us. We have eluded him again and again to carry on our holy mission, but we fear he is not far behind. He is no match for our divine powers or the sanctity of our destiny, but before we can perform again the ceremonies of beatitude and extract all our sins, we must defeat the American policeman!

Then page after page of one word repeated: *Mother, Mother, Mother, Mother...* Then: *Mother watches over our Chosen Ones.*

On another page he discovered a prayer to Saint Michael. It began:

O Prince of the heavenly host, by the power of God, thrust into hell Satan and all the evil spirits who prowl about the world seeking the ruin of souls.

In another, much longer prayer to Saint Michael, and Ramek had underlined one particular passage:

The Church venerates thee as protector ... as her defense

against the malicious powers of this world and of hell; to thee has God entrusted the souls of men to be established in heavenly beatitude.

An idea struck Mason. He opened the diary to the last pages and scanned the entries.

December 23...

Last night.

... It is 778 days since the beginning of the black days...

We rejoice! We have found a second angel, a most perfect Chosen One. They have brought her to us as a great sign. We felt fear at the sight of her. We thought she had been sent back to haunt us, but it is truly a divine sign. She is so much like Mother!

The last entry, a short passage entered that morning, December 24...

Today at high noon, we will have the most perfect Chosen One!

Ramek was on the hunt again, and at this very moment.

Mason checked his watch: 10:55. An hour before Ramek abducted his prey. Possibly even a child who resembled his mother. That meant within twenty-four hours she would be tortured, butchered, and put on display. The only chance to stop Ramek was to determine the victim's identity. If he could do that, there might be a slim chance he could save her and trap him. There was no time to go to headquarters, convince a skeptical Colonel Walton, then muster all available forces. Going to them now would take too much time. It would be too late to do anything but wait until the body was found.

But how could he determine the victim's identity? Someone who looked like Ramek's mother. Mason thought back. No pictures had been found at Ramek's workshop or his house, let alone any of his mother. And the only documents found about her had no accompanying pictures, only the statement: missing, presumed dead.

His mind raced. He tried to summon every scrap of detail. He let the images roll through his mind, but nothing helped. There was the diary, but it would take too long to read everything. He fanned through the diary pages hoping something might stand out. A page swept passed with a large drawing. Ramek had taken up almost an entire page sketching out a baptismal cross. Then written underneath: *The cross Mother wore next to her heart.*

Ramek's written words returned to Mason's mind: *Mother watches over our Chosen Ones.*

He stuffed the diary into his coat pocket and ran out the door.

MASON BROUGHT THE JEEP TO A SCREECHING HALT IN FRONT OF the railroad shed. Manganella jumped out of the passenger's seat.

"He's probably not coming back here for a while, but keep a sharp lookout anyway," Mason told the corporal. "I'll be back, or I'll let headquarters know you're here."

"What if Ramek shows up?" Manganella said.

"You've got a gun, don't you?"

Manganella nodded.

"Watch for his scalpel. He goes for the throat."

Mason raced away, leaving a very nervous Manganella to watch for Ramek's possible return.

Fifteen minutes later, Mason pulled the Jeep up next to the two MPs watching Ramek's house. He moved for the house and called out to the two startled MPs, "One of you come with me."

An MP caught up with Mason and they mounted the steps.

"Sir," the MP said, "I have strict orders not to allow anyone inside."

Mason pointed out his CID bars on his sleeve and nodded for the MP to unlock the door. "What's your name, Private?"

"Wilson, Peter, sir." The MP unlocked the door, then a thought came to him. "Hey, wait a minute." But Mason had already rushed inside. Private Wilson followed in pursuit. "You're the one they suspended. Orders came down that we're supposed to arrest you if you came near this place."

"I wouldn't advise it, Private Wilson," Mason said as he entered the back bedroom. He popped his head back out. "Are you coming?"

Private Wilson came into the room, looking unsure what to do next. Mason lifted the trapdoor and descended the stairs. Wilson followed him down and surveyed his surroundings with a look of horror. "Holy smokes."

In front of Mason, the man-sized cross hung as before, but the center alcove and the alcoves at the ends of the eight arms were now empty. The jars containing the human organs had been taken to the forensics lab. Mason turned to his right and stepped up to Ramek's makeshift altar. He groped behind the altar for the light switch. With a click, the lights behind it threw the cross into vivid relief in the dust-laden air. Mason stepped up to the cross and felt all along the edges of every arm. Nothing. He bent slightly to look into the center alcove where the jar containing the heart had once been. There was nothing inside but the opaque glass diffusing the light from the bulb.

Doubt and disappointment welled up. He was sure there was some connection to this oversized cross and Ramek's diary entries. The heart had to be the key: *The cross Mother wore next to her heart.*

He reached inside the alcove and pushed on the glass. It fell away easily. The harsh light forced him to shield his eyes, but beyond the bulb he could just make out a small hooked lever. He pulled on the lever. With a loud clank, the wood-framed cross popped open on the right side.

"Holy smokes," Private Wilson said, and he drifted up to Mason

Mason pulled on the open edge. The rusted hinges groaned and resisted, but the cross finally swung away. Dirt fell from the edges of the structure, forming a cloud of dust. Both men trained their flashlight beams on a four-foot-high wooden door that had been hidden behind the cross. The door lacked a knob, so Mason tried pushing on it, then putting his shoulder to it, but it refused to move.

"Help me kick it in," Mason said. "On three."

With each kick the door cracked, then buckled, and finally disintegrated. A foul stench made them recoil. Covering their mouths, they trained their beams into the small dirt-walled room.

"Sweet mother of Christ," Private Wilson said. "What is it?"

Mason suppressed a gag and took a step into the room. In the center, mounted on a primitive wooden baptismal cross, was the desiccated body of an elderly woman. Like the other victims, the arms and legs had been severed then attached to the X section of the cross, and the torso had been split open and the organs removed. With one difference: Ramek had sawed open the woman's skull, then fastened it back in place.

The mystery of the organs and the unaccountable brain in the specimen jars was now solved.

"Who do you think it is?" Private Wilson asked.

Mason trained his flashlight on a framed black-and-white photograph of an elderly woman scowling at the camera. "Ramek's mother."

Private Wilson rushed out of the room. While Mason listened to him retch and vomit, he surveyed the rest of the room with his flashlight. On every wall hung framed portraits of Ramek's mother, all with a dour expression, except one: a much smaller tintype photograph of a young woman standing in front of a carnival backdrop, the only one with her smiling. He stepped closer to get a better look. Something about her looked familiar…

Laura. The young woman looked just like Laura.

"No!"

Mason burst out of the room. "Private, let's go. Now!" He bounded up the stairs and ran down the hallway. Private Wilson was a few yards behind him. He blew out the front door and ran for the Jeep. As he climbed in, he yelled to Private Wilson, "Get all available squads to converge on every church in the city center. The killer is going to one of them." He jammed the Jeep into gear and raced off.

S omething was wrong.

   Ramek had waited all morning for her to emerge from the hotel. She'd broken her routine. She usually left the hotel at 9:15 sharp with two male escorts and walked ten blocks to the offices on Odeonsplatz. The plan was to follow as he had done before. Then, when she felt safe at her work and without the guards, he had planned to make his approach.

   There was no way he could have missed her. He had an excellent vantage point: across the street and a few yards down from Maximilianstrasse. Now it was after twelve. How could he have missed the appointed time? He paced in the shadows under the portico of a ruined bank. It felt as if some other being would explode from his body. The force of it pushed against his skin. His skull ached from the pressure.

   This was punishment. He knew it. Doubt threatened to triumph over his resolve. The woman who looked like his mother could be an illusion. Perhaps it was a trick devised by the American policeman. After all, he had first seen her with him. This hunt should have been a holy undertaking, a divine act, but now he felt only a burning lust to violate her, to hear her screams, watch her blood rush from gaping incisions, hear the crack of her ribs, exposing her beating heart. God, he would fuck her limbless corpse!

No! Stop!

He bit deep into the meaty part of his hand, taking away a piece of flesh. The pain, the taste of blood, calmed him. He would need all his clarity and wit to abduct a woman in daylight and on a busy street.

How much longer would he have to wait? It must be done, and it had to be now. Now only hours separated his need. The urges were constant, the ache in his groin more acute. This must be the ultimate beatification, for every step had led him to this point. It must be realized, then he would be free to ascend, free of his sins, no longer plagued by the tormenting voices.

Peace will come.

A black sedan pulled up in front of the hotel. Ramek stepped deeper into the shadows and watched. Laura McKinnon's two escorts got out of the sedan.

She was taking a car. He had to think fast. All his careful planning was now useless. The new situation demanded he improvise. He pulled off his long blue overcoat. Underneath, he wore his Munich police uniform. Suddenly he noticed the blood. The previous night's scalpel wound had seeped through the bandage and stained his uniform. His hand streamed with blood from the bite wound and had left a large streak across his chest. That gave him an idea. He could use it. He smeared more blood across the uniform, then exchanged his homburg hat for a policeman's cap, took a deep breath, and stepped onto the sidewalk.

There she was, exiting the hotel and... carrying a suitcase? She was leaving. It truly was now or never.

Ramek broke into a run, dodging a wagon loaded with rubble. He assumed a servile posture and an expression of alarm. The blood would magnify the urgency. He waved his hands above his head. "Fräulein McKinnon!"

The woman stopped at the base of the steps and looked at his bloodstained uniform with dismay. Ramek ran up. The two escorts flanked her protectively. Ramek stopped at a respectable distance, breathing hard, as if he'd run for his life.

"Fräulein McKinnon?" When she acknowledged him, he said in German, "I have some grave news. Investigator Collins has been seriously injured."

Laura put her hands to her mouth. "What? Where?"

"He was chasing the murderer into a building, but the building collapsed on him."

One of the escorts asked, "Is he being treated? Is he in the hospital?"

"It just happened. My comrades are notifying the American military police and medical services." He turned to Laura. "He is asking for you. I'm afraid he won't survive. It's very serious."

Tears welled up in Laura's eyes, but she gritted her teeth to control it.

The escort looked suspiciously at Ramek. "How did you know to come here?"

"Inspektor Becker is with him. The inspektor works with Investigator Collins, and he told me to come here. He dispatched other officers to her place of work and to search along the streets she uses regularly."

"It's okay, Ben," Laura said. "Where are they?" she asked Ramek. "What's the address?"

"I can show you the quickest route. A small street near Saint Michael's Church."

The escorts hesitated, but Laura was already getting in the backseat of the car. "Come on, you two. Officer, get in front and direct us."

Ben left the suitcase with one of the hotel's MP guards, then returned to the car and eyed Ramek before getting behind the wheel. As Ramek stood at the open car door, a shiver coursed through his body. He dug his fingernails into the wound on his hand to suppress another wave. With one last shudder of anticipation, he took the front passenger seat.

"Straight down Maximilianstrasse, then left on Alter Hof," Ramek said to Ben. "Please hurry, sir. There isn't much time."

Ben hit the accelerator and sped down the street. He threw Ramek a handkerchief for his hand. Ramek wrapped the handkerchief around the wound and squeezed tightly.

"Where is Investigator Collins hurt?" Laura asked.

"A wall collapsed, crushing his chest."

"Oh, my God." She bit on her nails to stifle her crying.

Ben followed Ramek's instructions, weaving through a series of small streets. The pain in Ramek's hand could no longer distract him. He turned to the window and took deep breaths. His body shivered just once. Then he noticed Ben eyeing him with suspicion.

"The shock, you see?" Ramek said.

Ben just grunted and started to turn right at Marienplatz, but Ramek saw that MPs had erected a roadblock to check IDs.

"No, not here." Ramek realized he'd said it too loudly. "It is blocked by excavation and a steam shovel." He directed Ben to take a small street going south and away from Saint Michael's. Ruined office buildings bordered both sides of the street, and only a few pedestrians walked in this somber part of the city.

Ramek looked back at Laura and caught her staring at him.

"You work with Inspector Becker?" Laura asked.

"Yes," Ramek said.

"I met him only once just briefly. I wonder how he would know the streets I use regularly or where I worked?"

Ben looked at Ramek with alarm, his suspicions proved right.

Ramek braced himself and, with his left leg, stamped on the

brake pedal. Laura and the escorts were flung forward. Ramek pulled out Ben's .45 pistol from its holster and shot Ben in the head. Laura screamed as Ramek spun in his seat and shot the other escort twice in the chest. Laura sank into her seat when he aimed the pistol at her, huddling as if waiting for the impact of bullets.

While maintaining his aim, Ramek unlatched his door with his other hand. In English, he said, "Get out slowly. You try to run, I will shoot you."

"You're Dr. Ramek, aren't you?"

Ramek put one leg out of the car. "Remember. Very slowly."

Laura opened her door. Ramek rolled out of the car as quickly as he could, but being that tall in a cramped car, it took too long.

Laura dashed out of the car and ran for a burned-out office building. Ramek rushed to the back of the car and aimed, but he couldn't pull the trigger. It couldn't end this way. She had been chosen. To shoot her would mean failure. He had to take her alive, and only shoot her if he had no other choice.

With a growl, he sprinted after her.

Mason slammed on the brakes in front of Laura's hotel, jumped out, and ran for the door. One of the MPs guarding the hotel called out to him as he bounded up the front steps.

"Mr. Collins?" he said with confusion in his eyes. "I thought a building had just collapsed on you."

Mason stopped just before charging through the hotel's front door. "What did you say?"

"A German cop said so. He ran up to Miss McKinnon and said you were seriously injured chasing the killer when a building collapsed on you. Miss McKinnon, her bodyguards, and the German cop all got in a car and took off to find you."

Mason tried to make sense of it. It took only a few seconds to figure it out. "Where are they headed?"

"The German cop said something about Saint Michael's Church."

Mason could hardly get it all out: "It's Ramek. Ramek's the German cop." He shot down the steps.

"They headed west on Maximilianstrasse," the MP said.

As Mason ran up to the Jeep, he called back to the MP, "Call headquarters and tell them that Ramek is at Saint Michael's Church."

Maximilianstrasse was a wide boulevard, but it narrowed after only four blocks at Max-Joseph-Platz then ended and split off into three smaller streets. Mason stopped the Jeep at the intersection. He was in the old city center, where the tangle of streets still followed the random layout from its medieval past. He had to choose. Ramek could have led them anywhere, dumped the escorts, and subdued Laura. There was no guarantee Ramek intended to go directly to the church. He usually held on to his captives, possibly torturing them before the final butchering. Mason's only option was to head for Saint Michael's and search the surrounding area. The MP at the hotel and Private Wilson at Ramek's would have called headquarters by now, so help would be on the way.

Mason hit the accelerator and took Weinstrasse, the most direct way he knew of to get to Saint Michael's. He turned right on Kaufingerstrasse, the main street leading to the church. Streams of pedestrians, cyclists, trolleys, and wagons impeded his path. After passing the Frauenkirche he saw the MP roadblock. He made a hard left, betting that Ramek would have wanted to avoid the roadblock and guided the driver somewhere into this maze of small streets.

At Färbergraben he made a right. That brought him to a narrow street running parallel to Saint Michael's. He looked to his right and caught a glimpse of the church beyond the piles of brick and stone.

Now where?

He slammed on the brakes. Two women stood in the middle of the street, waving their arms at him.

"Get out of the way!"

One woman ran up to his Jeep, while the other still blocked the road.

"Lady, I have an emergency," Mason said.

"Please. Come quick. Two Americans have been shot."

"Where?"

The woman pointed to a street up ahead and to his right. "They are in a car."

Mason ran into the street the woman had pointed out. A hundred feet down the street, Mason ran up to the black sedan and immediately recognized Laura's escorts. He could tell right away they were dead. "Did you see a woman with a tall German policeman?"

"We only saw a German policeman run into that building." The woman pointed to the eight-story office building next to the passenger's side of the sedan. The building still stood but was nothing but a shell. The two flanking buildings had collapsed in on themselves, making the entire area extremely unstable.

Mason slipped inside the building through the opening where a revolving door had once been. He found himself in a lobby with smoke-stained marble, charred wood paneling, and fallen plaster. A few light fixtures hung by threads. A black sludge from the mix of ash and water covered every surface and excreted an acrid odor.

Fifty feet ahead of him, the entire center of the building had fallen in. Every floor, from the roof to the lobby, had crashed into the floor below. Mason eased up to the edge of the hole and saw that it continued on to the basement. He surveyed the exposed floors above. Nothing moved.

From somewhere above came the sound of running footsteps on rubble.

He had to choose: try stealth, hoping to surprise Ramek, or, in case Laura was still trying to evade Ramek, let her know that help was near....

"Laura!" Mason spun around, looking for a way up. Just off to his right, a staircase. He ran up one flight of stairs.

The sound came again, from higher up. Laura hadn't responded to his call. That could only mean that Ramek was close to her and she was afraid to give away her position.

Mason continued up the staircase. With each successive floor, he encountered more destruction, more charred walls and office furniture. Each floor had the same gaping hole, and it was spanned by wood beams set down by search-and-rescuers who'd had the grim task of removing the dead.

On the fifth floor, Mason stopped on the landing and listened. Silence. Why had she gone up here? It was the worst thing to do. Her panic had driven her deeper into Ramek's trap.

A creak of wood just above his head. The sixth floor.

Mason crept up the stairs, pistol ready. Ramek was armed, but Mason worried only about Laura. If Ramek felt cornered and unable to capture her for his ceremony, Mason was sure Ramek would kill her rather than let her go.

The building fell silent, and he imagined Laura hiding and Ramek stalking his prey. Mason stepped carefully to avoid debris as he climbed up to the sixth floor. He hid behind the return wall at the doorway between the staircase landing and the hallway. He peered around the corner.

On this level, a hallway led to doorless offices. The monotony of black was broken only where fire had stripped the inner walls down to concrete and steel supports. As on the other floors, and eighty feet from where he stood, a few wooden planks lay precariously across the expanse of the gaping hole where the floor had collapsed.

Mason sneaked into the hallway, taking one careful step at a time. His ears strained to hear anything move. A few steps farther, he heard it. Soft sobbing somewhere across the gap. Laura. But where was Ramek? Ramek had to have heard it, too.

Mason took longer strides, checking each room as he passed. Still fifty feet from the hole his foot broke through the flooring.

Floorboards gave way. Wood and plaster tumbled to the floor below.

Laura wailed in panic. Like a trapped animal, she shrieked and shot out of a room on the other side of the hole. She ran for a back stairway.

"Laura!"

Laura stopped, recognizing his voice. She burst into tears and ran recklessly across the planks spanning the hole. Mason tensed with alarm as the planks jumped and bent under the force of her steps. He broke into a trot, eyes alert, expecting at any moment for Ramek to attack.

Laura leapt the last few feet onto solid flooring.

At the same moment, Ramek burst through an adjacent office door and grabbed her from behind. His muscular arm wrapped tightly across her neck, choking off her screams. He used her as a shield and aimed his pistol at Mason.

Mason dived into another office just as Ramek fired. The bullet ripped into the doorframe, dusting Mason in plaster and splintered wood.

"I told you that you and I were not done," Ramek said. "I have been sent a perfect Chosen One. You can't imagine my joy that she is also your lover. Let us leave, or I will kill her, Herr Collins."

"You know I won't let you do that."

Laura screamed in pain. Mason extended his head and gun arm out of the doorway and took aim at Ramek.

"You kill her, and I'll kill you," Mason said. "Now, let her go and put the gun down—"

"I have nothing to lose. You *have*. You will please throw your gun away, or I swear I will kill her. Her head will explode before your eyes... Do it!"

Mason had no choice. He was sure Ramek would follow through on his threat. He tossed the pistol forward. It rattled along the floor and dropped into a fissure, clattering to a stop below.

"Now you will let us pass," Ramek said, and he took a step forward.

"I will let *you* pass, but only if you let her go." Mason poked his head out beyond the doorjamb when he heard Ramek's footsteps.

Ramek fired again, the bullet piercing the wall near Mason's head. Mason ducked inside. He was trapped, and every step Ramek advanced brought Mason closer into Ramek's line of fire.

Quickly, Mason tried to recall all he'd learned about Ramek, from the interviews, from Ramek's own diary, from the basement shrine....

Against every ounce of self-preservation in his body, Mason stepped into the hallway.

"I met your mother, Doctor," Mason said.

Ramek froze.

"You butchered her and lashed her to a cross. How can you expect to go to heaven after doing that to your mother?"

Ramek gripped Laura tighter, but his gun hand trembled. "You know nothing about it!" he shouted, as if the memory of it brought him pain. "She was my first beatification. Through her suffering, she became a saint."

Mason took a step and kept his voice calm. "I know you hear voices, Doctor." He paused to let Ramek process that. "I hear them, too. And your mother whispered a prayer to me: 'O Prince of the heavenly host, by the power of God, thrust into hell Satan and all the evil spirits who prowl about the world seeking the ruin of souls.' She knows it's your favorite."

"That was her prayer," Ramek breathed.

Another step. "She wants you to realize that those evil spirits, the ones that prowl the world, are also the voices that speak to you, and they seek to ruin your soul. She begs you to show mercy, that mercy is the path to heaven. Otherwise, you will never be free from what you've done. Letting this woman go is a first step. Letting her go and delaying your path to ascension will be your greatest sacrifice. A selfless act that will go far in cleansing you of sin."

"You lie!" Ramek jammed the pistol into Laura's temple and released her throat long enough for her to scream. "My mother would never say such things. We must all suffer. We are all vessels of sin and depravity... and it must be cut out!" He squeezed Laura's neck so hard that it lifted her off the ground.

Mason hesitated. Talk of his mother seemed to push him closer to losing what sanity he had left. He took another step forward while desperately thinking of a new tack. "I know you are tormented because you let the little girl, Angela, go."

Ramek stopped breathing.

Another step. "That was an act of mercy. Don't you see? You saved that child. You have goodness in your heart. But the voices want to keep you blind to that. And that is why they had you mask your mirrors, isn't it? To prevent you from seeing the truth? The truth that lies deep within you? This woman, who looks like your mother, was sent to help you back from darkness. I was sent to help you, not destroy you."

"This woman was sent to me by divine grace," Ramek said. "Not by you."

Mason took two steps and opened his arms as if daring Ramek to shoot.

"You remember Dr. Blazek, don't you, Doctor? You two talked in the night and shared your fears and desires in a barrack at Mauthausen."

Stunned, Ramek relaxed his hold on Laura. His gaze went elsewhere, as if remembering.

Mason continued. "Dr. Blazek said that you, like all the prisoner doctors, felt a terrible guilt about working for the SS doctors.

That you survived by making a pact with the devil for the chance of survival. Do you remember that? You were *forced* to assist in savage and inhumane experiments. You were never a monster. You have simply lost your soul."

Another step.

Ramek regained his composure. "You know nothing." He aimed the pistol at Mason and pulled back the hammer. "Not another step further."

But Mason took another step, even as he braced himself for the impact of a bullet. "I can see into your tortured soul. I can see within your mind all the innocents you made suffer at Ravensbrück and Mauthausen. All their suffering..." He took a step. "Remember the innocent people you strapped to operating tables? Doing Dr. Kiesewetter's bidding? They screamed in pain at your hands."

Ramek tensed as if hit by an electrical current. He panted and sputtered incoherently.

"Drop the gun and let her go. God commands it. Your mother begs you."

"I won't... I can't." Tears came to Ramek's eyes and he began to mutter a prayer. His trembling had grown almost out of control. His gun arm began to sink.

Mason saw his chance. He charged.

Ramek tensed and aimed the gun at Mason. "No!"

Mason jumped to his right, and Laura slapped Ramek's gun arm. The gun fired. The aim was wide. Ramek flung Laura aside and fired again. The bullet sliced across Mason's rib cage. It felt as though he'd been hit with a sledgehammer, but his momentum carried, slamming him into Ramek. To Mason it felt like he'd run into a brick wall, and searing pain from his wounded ribs paralyzed him. Ramek stumbled backward, losing his grip on the pistol, and it tumbled into the hole.

Ramek growled and slammed his fist into the bullet wound in

Mason's ribs. Mason's entire body convulsed as if receiving a jolt of electricity. His lungs froze and his knees buckled. Ramek immediately wrapped both hands around Mason's throat. The man had unbelievable strength and held Mason tight to his body, almost lifting him from the floor. Mason struggled to maneuver out of the hold, but the incredible pressure from Ramek's grasp cut off the blood to Mason's brain. He felt his hyoid bone strain under the pressure and it threatened to break. He lost feeling in his legs, and he began to lose consciousness.

A cry from Laura brought him back momentarily, and she struck Ramek across the back with a piece of wood. Ramek hardly reacted to the blow, but it had distracted him for a split second. That brief moment was enough.

Summoning his waning strength, Mason thrust his open hand into Ramek's trachea. Ramek gagged and his grip loosened. Mason then twisted his body and raised his right arm up high. With all the power he could muster, he brought his arm down on Ramek's wrists, breaking his hold. Mason reversed the twist and rammed his elbow into the bridge of Ramek's nose. Mason heard the crunch of bone, and blood spurted from the man's nose.

Ramek staggered in place but seemed impervious to the pain. In a swift movement, he reached around to his opposite pocket and brought his scalpel out, swinging it in a wide arc toward Mason's throat. Mason was ready for it. He ducked the swing and slammed the palm of his hand into Ramek's already broken nose. Ramek recoiled and screamed at what must have been excruciating pain. Stunned, his legs buckled and he dropped to his knees.

Mason began pounding Ramek in the face. Left fist, then right. He couldn't stop. He was turning Ramek's face to a bloody pulp. Ramek slumped to the ground, senseless. He no longer struggled. Blood bubbled from his nose, mouth, and ears.

Mason grabbed Ramek's throat and squeezed. His rage added to his strength.

Ramek tried to strike him, but the blow landed without force. His face turned scarlet. He more blood than air. His struggling became desperate swipes at Mason's face. He grasped Mason's arms, but his strength was gone. His kicking slowed....

"Mason!"

Laura's voice snapped him back.

"Stop," Laura said with such horror and grief that it made Mason ease his death grip on Ramek's throat. The doctor took a desperate gulp of air.

Keeping the man pinned, Mason looked into his eyes. "You're under arrest."

Mason struggled to rise. Laura helped him to stand but, faster than thought, Ramek's foot took out Mason's legs. Mason fell heavily to the floor. Ramek climbed unsteadily to his feet and tottered at the edge of the chasm.

"Only by plunging into the abyss can one then soar to heaven," Ramek said in a calm voice.

With a bloody smile, Ramek dropped backward into the hole. Mason rushed to the edge to stop him, but it was too late. He could only watch as Ramek collided with the edges of several floors before his body hit the concrete floor of the dark basement.

Mason fell to his knees. His head spun and his entire body turned cold. He'd never been so exhausted. Then he became aware of Laura's hands on him, tending his wound as best she could while she sobbed. Her touch, her smell, her face so close to his, brought sudden warmth. And he felt as if he had come out of a dark place.

M ason sat in the passenger's seat, riding in a five-ton army truck loaded with supplies. Both sides of the snow-covered road were bordered by thick pine forest, and in the distance rose the snow-capped mountains of the Bavarian Alps. The truck was the only transport available from Munich. A two-day snowstorm had clogged the roads, delayed trains, but the army deemed the truck, its driver, and Mason expendable enough to send them out anyway. He stared out the window as he thought about the past few weeks.

Mason had stopped a brutal murderer, purged a small patch of earth from madness, and for a heartbeat the world seemed brighter, cleaner after Ramek's death. But the moment quickly passed. The clouds still obscured the sun, the snow still fell, and the people in Munich still starved or froze to death.

The army was left without a clue what to do with Mason Collins—hero or vigilante? The *Stars and Stripes* and the American-controlled German press hailed him as a hero. Colonel Walton wanted to bust him in rank and send him to a remote mountain outpost, but the army brass had dragged him in front of the cameras as the new military police poster boy, then stuck him behind a desk when the dust had settled.

Mason had managed to use his temporary star status to wangle a deal: no remote outpost, no desk job, but instead an assignment to an out-of-the-way German town, where he'd spend his remaining year in the army busting black marketers and wayward soldiers. That suited Mason just fine.

Wolski had survived and was now convalescing at the Walter Reed General Hospital. He was trying to convince the army to let Anna immigrate, and he'd probably succeed because of his wounds in the line of duty and his aid in the dramatic case. He still planned to go for a law degree. He and Mason promised to keep in touch, but Mason knew how those things went.

Mason saw Becker often during his final month in Munich, and they had forged a strong friendship. It gave Mason hope that with men like Becker, Germany would rise from the ashes to become a better country. Together they had located a Catholic foundation that agreed to take in the orphans. Kurt had opted out; he had a good business going with cigarettes (partially funded by Mason), and Mason saw him becoming a successful entrepreneur one day. Angela thrived in her new home, however, as she and the others would no longer have to survive alone in the ruins. Mason vowed to visit them whenever he could.

After Laura and he had spent New Year's in Paris, she had immersed herself in her serial about life in postwar Germany. Mason guessed that charging into the fray at full steam was her way of coping with the trauma of the abduction. And though Mason had objected, she had left Munich to try to pick up the trail of the black marketers. Whether they could overcome their differences, reporter and cop, and see their relationship flourish, only time would tell. Either way, Mason was through with the army, and he planned to go back to the States after his year in purgatory was up.

"Whoa!"

The truck had hit a patch of ice and swerved side to side as the driver tried to keep it on the road.

The driver finally gained control of the truck. "That was close."

Mason settled back in his seat and returned his gaze to the snowy landscape.

The driver was a Hawaiian and went by the nickname "Bubbles." Mason had no idea why; the man was built like a rhinoceros.

"Garmisch is a real nice place," Bubbles said.

"I wouldn't know."

"It never got a scratch during the war. It's like some town you'd see in a kid's storybook. A big ski destination. You like to ski?"

"Never saw the sense in putting sticks on my feet and sliding down a mountain."

Bubbles laughed. "I ain't built for it, that's for sure."

Garmisch-Partenkirchen was going to be Mason's new post. A sleepy town—at least, that was its reputation—nestled in a mountain valley near the Austrian border. Only Wolski and Becker knew the real reason why he had used his temporary clout to go from a high-octane city to a somnolent town: Laura was there somewhere, working her story.

Colonel Walton had been more than happy to approve the plan, sending Mason off with a self-satisfied grin. "You're not going to be able to stir up any trouble down there."

Mason smiled.

We'll see.

Did you enjoy this book? You can make a big difference in my career!

Reviews are the most powerful tools in my arsenal when it comes to getting attention for my books. Like most readers, I'm sure you weigh reviews heavily once you've seen the book's cover and read the description. And without reviews, a reader might move on without giving a new author a try.

That's where you can come in: An honest review of this novel—or any of my other novels—just might be the thing that convinces them to read and discover new stories and authors.

If you enjoyed this book, I would be very grateful if you could take five minutes to leave an honest review on the book's Amazon page.

Leaving a review is easy:
    1) Go to the book's page on Amazon
    2) Scroll down to the reviews section a click the "Write a customer review" button just below the stars rating bars
    3) Select a star rating
    4) Write a few short words (or as long as you like)
    5) Click the submit button

Thank you very much!

BOOKS BY JOHN A. CONNELL

Madness in the Ruins

It is the winter of 1945, seven months after the Nazi defeat, and Munich is in ruins. A killer is stalking the devastated city—one who has knowledge of human anatomy, enacts mysterious rituals with his prey, and seems to pick victims at random.

It falls upon U.S. Army investigator Mason Collins—former Chicago police detective, U.S. soldier, and prisoner-of-war—to hunt down the brutal killer. In a city where chaos reigns, Mason must rely on his wits and instincts. And before Mason knows it, the murderer has made him a target. Now it's a high-stakes duel, and to win it Mason must bring into deadly play all that he values—even his life.

"...this is going to be a must-read series for me." ~ *Lee Child, #1 New York Times bestselling author of the Jack Reacher novels*

❧

Haven of Vipers

Mason Collins risks everything to hunt down a gang of ruthless murderers in a case that will take him from a Hollywood-style nightclub and a speeding train, to the icy slopes of the Bavarian Alps. As both witnesses and evidence begin disappearing, it becomes obvious that someone on high is pulling strings to stifle the investigation—and that Mason must feel his way in the darkness if he is going to find out who in town has the most to gain—and the most to lose...

Haven of Vipers is the second in the Mason Collins crime-thriller series that Steve Berry, bestselling author of *The Patriot Threat* and *The Templar Legacy*, said: "Excitement melds with adventure as the tangled threads gradually unwind, revealing treachery coming from all directions. The whole thing is reminiscent of early-Robert Ludlum, and makes you clamor for more."

∽

Bones of the Innocent

Mason Collins grapples with a web of lies, secrets, and murder as he races against time to save the lives of abducted teenagers in a case as twisted as the streets of Tangier's medina. And as he digs deeper, he realizes everyone has a hidden agenda, including those who harbor a terrible secret. And just as Mason begins to unravel the mystery, the assassins have picked up his trail. Now, Mason must put his life on the line to find the girls and discover who's behind the heinous crimes before it's too late. If he lives that long…

Bones of the Innocent is the third in the Mason Collins series of historical crime thrillers that bestselling author Lee Child said, *"This is going to be a must-read series for me."*

∽

To Kill A Devil

When a shadowy organization fails to assassinate Mason Collins, they go after his colleagues, his friends, and the love of his life. Mason knows the only way to stop the killings is to cut off the head of the snake. Armed with only the leader's code name, Valerius, Mason will trek across Franco's Spain to war-torn Vienna to kill the man responsible. But targeting the most powerful crime boss in Vienna promises to be an impossible task, and Valerius has something special in store for Mason.

∽

A Standalone Historical Crime Thriller

Good Night, Sweet Daddy-O

1958 San Francisco

Struggling jazz musician, Frank Valentine, suffers a midnight beating, leaving his left hand paralyzed. Jobless, penniless, and desperate, Frank agrees to join his best friend, George, and three other buddies to distribute a gangster's heroin for quick money.

What he doesn't know is that George has more dangerous plans…

Inexperienced in the ways of crime, Frank quickly slips deeper and deeper into the dark vortex of San Francisco gangsters, junkies, and murderers for hire. To make things worse, Frank's newfound love, a mysterious, dark-haired beauty, is somehow connected to it all.

And when it becomes clear that a crime syndicate is bent on his destruction, Frank realizes that the easy road out of purgatory often leads to hell.

GET A FREE MASON COLLINS NOVELLA

Get a free copy of a Mason Collins introductory novella, *In Malevolent Hands,* when you sign up to join my Reader's Group. This novella is not available anywhere else.

You'll receive occasional newsletters from me with details on new releases, special offers, and other news relating to the Mason Collins series.

Go to http://johnaconnell.com/subscribe to receive you free novella!

ABOUT THE AUTHOR

John A. Connell writes spellbinding crime thrillers with a historical twist. In addition to his standalone, Good Night, Sweet Daddy-O, he writes the post-WW2 Mason Collins series, which follows Mason to some of the most dangerous and turbulent places in the post-World War Two world. The first, Madness in the Ruins, was a 2016 Barry Award finalist, and the series has garnered praise from such bestselling authors as Lee Child and Steve Berry. In a previous life, John worked as a cameraman on films such as *Jurassic* Park and *Thelma and Louise* and on TV shows including *NYPD Blue* and *The Practice*. Atlanta-born, John spends his time between the U.S. and France.

You can visit John online at: http://johnaconnell.com
or email him at: john@johnaconnell.com

 facebook.com/johnconnellauthor1
twitter.com/johnaconnell
 bookbub.com/authors/john-a-connell

ACKNOWLEDGMENTS

A historical novel is built upon the foundations of the work, passion and dedication of scholars, historians, archivists and librarians. I am indebted to them. In my attempt to compile a list of sources, books, articles, memoirs, archives, and websites, I realized just how many I had consulted, and too many provide an exhaustive list. However, I would like to acknowledge those sources to which I turned to time and again: Ian Sayer and Douglas Botting, *In The Ruins of the Reich* (1985) and *Nazi Gold* (1984); Wilford Byford-Jones, *Berlin Twilight* (1947); Edward N. Peterson, *The American Occupation of Germany: Retreat to Victory* (1977); Robert jay Lifton, *The Nazi Doctors: Medical Killing and the Psychology of Genocide* (1986); Giles MacDonogh, *After the Reich: From the Libertaion of Vienna to the Berlin Airlift* (1985); Vivian Spitz, *Doctors From Hell* (2005). And while I made every effort to adhere to historical facts and events, this is a work of fiction, and there are occasions where, for the sake of the story, or through mistakes that are solely my own, alert readers will inevitably discover errors or alterations.

～

I would not have the joy and privilege to write these acknowl-edgements if it weren't for my wife, Janine. It is she who rekin-dled the writer in me. She supported me without question, pushed me, inspired me, and tolerated my silences and absent-minded-ness as I "wrote" in my head. She slogged through many drafts, always offering encouragement and criticism whenever I needed them most. A most extraordinary woman.

AUTHOR'S NOTE: Most of the historical circumstances and locations in this story are as accurate as I could make them. The two Nazi doctors interviewed at Dachau were real people, as are several of the concentration camp doctors mentioned during the investigation. And as hard it is to imagine, let alone comprehend, the medical atrocities referred to in the story that were committed in the concentration camps are part of the historical record.

Made in the USA
Middletown, DE
08 June 2021

41527419R00253